# WHILE *the* WORLD *Is* STILL ASLEEP

# ALSO BY PETRA DURST-BENNING

## The Glassblower Trilogy

*The Glassblower*

*The American Lady*

*The Paradise of Glass*

# WHILE
### *the*
# WORLD
### *Is*
# STILL
# ASLEEP

*Petra Durst-Benning*

*Translated by Edwin Miles*

amazon crossing

Previously published as *Solang die Welt noch schläft* by Ullstein Buchverlag GmbH in Germany in 2012. Translated from German by Edwin Miles. First published in English by AmazonCrossing in 2016.

Published by AmazonCrossing, Seattle

www.apub.com

Amazon, the Amazon logo, and AmazonCrossing are trademarks of Amazon.com, Inc., or its affiliates.

ISBN-13 (hardcover): 9781503953338
ISBN-10 (hardcover): 1503953335
ISBN-13 (paperback): 9781503953321
ISBN-10 (paperback): 1503953327

Cover design by Shasti O'Leary-Soudant

Printed in the United States of America

*Vani,*
*To you our friend*
*and neighbor Cinderella*
*Cyclist, may you forever*
*Pedal on. Love, Vallorie & Steve*
*4.2018*

*Let me tell you what I think of bicycling. I think it has done more to emancipate women than anything else in the world . . . It gives [a] woman a feeling of freedom and self-reliance . . . The moment she takes her seat she knows she can't get into harm unless she gets off her bicycle . . .*

Susan B. Anthony, social reformer, 1896

# Chapter One

*Berlin, November 1891*
*Barnim Road Women's Prison*

Josephine looked around anxiously. Beds lined up side by side, thirty in all. Iron bars gleaming coldly in the light cast by the single bare bulb that dangled from the ceiling in the center of the room. The scene outside the barred window promised nothing better—a thin, dirty curtain was no more than a makeshift veil obstructing the view of a barren wasteland enclosed by a high wall.

Farther back in the prison dormitory, she could hear someone sobbing quietly. Jo turned and saw a haggard, red-haired young girl with the round belly typical of pregnancy. They had been admitted at the same time. A picture of misery, the girl lay curled and crying on a bunk. Josephine was tempted to console her, but then she changed her mind.

She had been awake for more than forty-eight hours. Her eyes burned and her head hurt. Her right shoulder was swollen and throbbing. Jo tentatively raised her arm a little, testing the joint. She could move her shoulder; at least nothing was broken.

She made her way hesitantly toward the bed marked "14," the one the prison guard had told her was hers. She pushed back the thin sheet that was supposed to serve as a blanket. The mattress was covered with stains, and when she lowered herself onto it, it sagged in the middle, slack from the bodies of the many girls who had cried themselves to sleep on it, night after night. It was so cold that Josephine's breath hung in the air in little clouds.

So this was where they were going to try to cure her of her "conceit" once and for all. Josephine fought back tears as she lay down on the bed and wrapped her arms around her legs in a futile attempt to stave off the cold. She closed her eyes and waited for merciful sleep to come, but what came instead were memories of the night before.

Early that evening, she had been undecided: Should she go out, or would she be better off staying home? The weather had been wretched all day, and the endless drizzle and wet autumn leaves had made the roads slick. The wind carried with it the first bite of winter—making for less than ideal conditions. Still, she had decided to go out. An error of judgment, as it turned out.

Despite the foul weather and the fact that it was well after midnight, several local people had witnessed the accident and ran out into the rain from their warm houses. Someone put a blanket over Josephine while others ogled her as they would some strange species in the Berlin zoo.

"What do we have here, then?"

"My, did you ever see such a thing?"

"Leave her! What's she doing around here?"

"The cops! Someone has to call the cops!"

Most of the people had been extremely hostile to her. But, in a thick Berlin accent, one old man said, "You're luckier than you know, girl. If you'd spent the whole night lying on this icy street, you'd likely have frozen to death." He wore pajamas and looked as if he'd jumped straight out of bed. Beside him stood an older woman with a bawling infant in her arms and a shocked expression on her face. She had plucked at Jo's coat with her sharp claws.

"Young lady, what's the likes of you up to at this time of night? And in that getup! That's not right at all." Her voice was shrill and full of reproach. It was she who bustled off to find a policeman. When the officer arrived, he fixed Jo with a suspicious eye and bombarded her with questions. "What's your name? What happened? Why are you dressed in men's clothes?"

All she had told him was her address. A horse and cart appeared, the horse's mane tangled with straw. Josephine was lifted up beside the coachman on his box seat, and the officer squeezed up beside them. She summoned the last of her strength to hold herself upright on the box and not fall over backward. Only then did she notice that the skin of her right hand was scraped all over. The knuckles of her left hand were caked with blood and muck from the street. Maybe she would die of blood poisoning. *Let it happen right now,* she had thought.

When they had reached her home, the officer pounded on the door with his fist. A moment later, a window on the second floor opened and her mother, Elsbeth Schmied, stuck her head out.

Josephine had been so afraid that she nearly threw up on the spot. She wanted to drop dead then and there. Instead, she let the policeman lead her into the parlor, where she stood with her head hanging low, her shoulder throbbing.

"My daughter had what? An accident? In those clothes? We won't have any of that in this house," her father had said. "We're honest people. I'm a farrier by trade, and I'll be hanged before I let such a creature set foot in my house." When her father finally looked at her, his eyes were filled with repugnance and contempt.

"This has to be some kind of mix-up. Our daughter does not go wandering around in the middle of the night," her mother had said harshly. Then she had pulled her robe more tightly around her chest, pressed her lips together into a thin line, and stared straight ahead.

3

Neither Josephine's father nor her mother had said a word directly to her.

"Don't go getting upset. The fact of the matter is that your daughter was involved in an accident out on Landsberger Allee," the policeman had said with some irritation. "And she's injured herself and very likely broken her shoulder. Don't you think you should send for a doctor?"

Josephine's mother glared at the officer. "If what you say is true, you can just take the little tramp away now!"

Josephine massaged her damaged shoulder as she lay on the prison bed. Now that she had stopped moving, it had begun to hurt even more.

The previous night her parents had not wanted to call a doctor. They would much rather have handed their daughter over to the officer on the spot, but he had given instructions that Josephine was to spend the rest of the night at home and then appear at the police station next to Görlitz train station at eleven in the morning the following day.

With heavy steps and a heavier heart, Jo had trudged into the laundry room. She did not immediately recognize herself when she looked in the shard of mirror on the wall. The grime and dried blood had transformed her otherwise striking face into an ugly mask. Her beautiful blond hair hung in dirty, matted locks. Josephine tried to contain her distress as she washed herself with cold water.

Later, in her room, she finally had broken into tears. It was all over! She had lied to her parents repeatedly. She had stolen. She had deceived. Because of her, Isabelle would get into serious trouble, and maybe even Clara, too. Isabelle, with her lust for life and short temper. And pretty, petite Clara. They had been through so much together over the years, and now she had betrayed them. And how was she ever supposed to pay for the damage she'd caused? She'd probably be in debt for the rest of her life. Or would her father have to settle her bill?

Tormented by a thousand questions, Josephine had lain in bed and waited for the night to end.

She had made her way to the police station the next morning, accompanied by her mother.

Josephine moaned quietly. Had that only been a few hours before? It felt like a lifetime ago.

"Don't even think about getting comfortable," one of the officers had said when she went to sit on the narrow wooden bench. "They make short work of young miscreants like you." Then he had personally escorted her and her mother to the local court on Park Street, where her trial was to take place that same day.

From that point on, Josephine had experienced everything as though through a fog. The judge had been pale and young and very busy. His desk was covered with towering stacks of files, and he had to push one aside to see her at all.

"The question in this case is whether or not one can speak of insufficient insight into her actions," he said after hearing the report from the officer. "If that were the case, an acquittal would certainly be conceivable . . ."

The officer frowned. "Your honor, the accused is no longer a girl of thirteen or fourteen; she will turn eighteen in a matter of months and be criminally liable for her actions. And according to her father—a respected farrier, incidentally—she was fully aware of the seriousness of her offense."

"Well," said the judge, turning to Josephine's mother. "Why hasn't the accused's father come in person to share his view of the matter?"

"My husband has to work," she replied in a brittle voice.

"And how is it possible that your daughter is able to leave the house in the evening without your noticing? Your daughter is still a minor, which means you bear a certain degree of supervisory responsibility."

"Don't talk to me about supervisory responsibility! She's always been a brat and a troublemaker! Our daughter never cared for rules. She has always put her own pleasure first," she added bitterly. "What is it they say? Pride goeth before the fall. After all that has happened, I declare that our daughter is dead to us."

Josephine had struggled desperately to come up with a suitable defense. Hadn't she labored day after day to the point of exhaustion to ease her father's workload? Hadn't she accepted any onerous task her mother had given her, in or out of the house? But she knew none of that counted anymore, that it had never counted. So she held her tongue.

The judge shifted another stack of files across his desk, then rose to his feet. As if at some secret cue, his secretary took out her pen to take down his judgment in writing.

"In accordance with the Penal Code of the German Empire, section fifty-six, paragraph one, and section fifty-seven, paragraphs one and two, and in consideration of the gravity of the offense, I hereby order that the accused be incarcerated forthwith in the Barnim Road Women's Prison. Given the young age of the prisoner and my unwillingness to deny her a certain potential for improvement, she is to be quartered in the newly created juvenile division. Daily work and lessons are to be undertaken. The period of incarceration is set at three and a half years."

He had looked sternly over his desk at Josephine as he spoke. "The Barnim Road Women's Prison is a great opportunity for young people like you who have slipped from the path of righteousness. I hope that during your stay there you will develop the spiritual maturity that is necessary to live an honorable life in peace and humility."

When two officers led Josephine away, her mother did not even turn her head.


They had taken her clothes from her and handed her a coarse woolen dress. She was only allowed to keep her underwear and her shoes. A guard then led her to the dormitory and told her that she was too late for the evening meal and that she had better get ready for bed.

Josephine was indifferent to all of it.

She heard footsteps approaching, then a voice behind her, rough as sandpaper: "Well, well. A newcomer. Bet she's still got her own underwear, too. Not the miserable scraps we have to wear."

A peculiar smell stung Josephine's nose. A mixture of bad food and sweat—it seemed that her fellow inmates had surrounded her bed, but Josephine kept her eyes fixed stubbornly on the wall. She didn't want to talk to anyone.

"What d'you think you're staring at?" said a second voice. Someone jabbed her in the back with a sharp fingertip, and she heard the laughter of several young women.

"What the hell is this?" Josephine spun around in a fury and sat up on the edge of the bed. She recoiled at the sight of the ragged figures in front of her. These were the people she was supposed to share her life with?

There were ten or twelve of them, girls and young women, some of whom looked like they were her age, some younger—still children. But their faces looked unnaturally wasted and hostile. Deep furrows had formed where the fresh bloom of youth should have been. All of them were unnaturally pale. One girl had a broad, red streak across her cheek, like a stroke from a whip. Another had a scabby chin and forehead, as if she had just gotten through some kind of pox. Their hair was unkempt, their hands dirty—some actually bloody—and their fingernails neglected. The girls reminded Jo of the hordes of alley kids all over the city who had thought it funny to pelt her with stones or spit on her. She and Isabelle had made off as fast as they could whenever they saw them. A shiver of fright ran through Jo. It was hard for her to believe that not one of these girls was older than eighteen.

"Number fourteen's my bed, so get up!" a tall, lean girl snarled at her and kicked her in the shins. The girl had deep-set gray eyes and no more than stubble on her head, as if her hair had been shorn to get rid of lice. Her eyelashes and eyebrows were pale, almost transparent. Josephine detected intelligence in her eyes, unlike the dull faces of the others, but they were ice-cold, too. The girl was not much older than Jo, but she looked thirty.

"But the guard said—" Josephine began.

"No one cares. *I'm* the one who decides what goes here. I'm Adele, and I say that this bed belongs to me," the girl said firmly. She gave a nod to two girls, who positioned themselves on either side of Josephine. But Josephine stood up of her own free will before they could take hold of her. The last thing she wanted was a fight.

"Then where am I supposed to sleep?" she asked.

"Do I look like I care?" Adele replied.

Josephine looked around the dormitory. She was tired. All she wanted was to lie down and close her eyes. She saw the red-haired girl cowering at the far end of the room. It appeared that several of the beds down there were free.

Josephine was halfway down the aisle when she realized that Adele was following her. Jo abruptly stopped and spun around. "What do you want now?"

The leader of the girls grinned and pushed past, blocking her path. "I'm not done with you. Give me your petticoat. I'm sure I can use it."

"You're out of your mind! I will do no such thing. If you want something from me, you'll have to come and get it." She planted her feet and stared at Adele.

Adele hesitated. After appraising her rival for a moment, she waved dismissively. "You're so big, your clothes wouldn't fit me anyway. Show me your other stuff!"

"What other stuff?"

"You must have brought all kinds of useful things. Soap, a comb, candy—show us what you've got!"

A strange excitement spread among the other girls. They exchanged looks and jabbed each other's elbows; one or two of them appeared to be holding their breath. They seemed to put great store in what was happening.

"You'd better do what Adele says," squeaked a small girl on the fringe of the group.

Josephine thought the matter over. This Adele seemed out for a fight. It would no doubt be wise to stand up to her. At least she would get some peace and quiet. With forced composure, Jo squared off in front of her challenger, causing Adele to retreat in surprise. She even looked a little frightened.

"I don't have anything. I didn't have time to pack the crown jewels this morning," Jo said, then pushed Adele aside. "Now leave me alone."

Adele furrowed her brow.

A murmur ran through the group of young women—rarely did anyone argue with Adele, and to defy her as Josephine just had was unheard of.

Jo sneered. She was not scared. Not only was she a head taller than Adele, she was also athletic and fit. Thanks to the many hours she had spent in the blacksmith's shop, she had broad shoulders, strong legs, and sinewy, muscular arms. Her training, too, had helped. She marched off, confident in the knowledge that she was physically superior to Adele and the others.

"Don't think you're getting off so lightly! You'll pay for that," Adele shouted halfheartedly behind her.

Josephine had just lain down on a new bed when she noticed that Adele and her entourage had turned their attention to the other newcomer.

"No, please don't take it. That hair clip belonged to my sister, who died. It's all I've still got of her," cried the girl. She was about fourteen and her mussed red hair made her look like some sort of wild creature. She let out a loud howl.

Jo closed her eyes.

"What else have you got?" one of the other girls asked.

"Nothing, I'm telling you." The redhead's voice sounded panicked.

"No such thing as nothing. Your undies. And your socks. Hand 'em over!"

Jo stood up, her exhaustion suddenly extinguished, and marched over to Adele and her gang.

There may have been plenty of things wrong with her, but being a coward wasn't one of them. She had resisted her tyrannical father's temper for years as he had tried to break her will. She had formed a hard shell as a result and wasn't about to let a beast like Adele get the upper hand on her first day. Adele could claim that her word was law until she was blue in the face, but Josephine would not let her attack the weak.

Josephine's eyes flashed with anger as she grabbed Adele by the arm and took the hair clip away from her. Without turning her eyes from her rival, she handed the bent piece of tin back to the red-haired girl.

"Leave her in peace, or you'll have to deal with me." Her voice was low and controlled, but all the firmer for that.

Adele's punch came without warning. Jo had no time to defend herself. The pain was so intense that she lost her breath for a moment. Then blows started raining down on her from all sides. Wailing, Josephine doubled over like a pocketknife and fell to the stone floor. A warm satisfaction spread among the other young women, who stepped back, murmuring and giggling.

The red-haired girl was beside her instantly. Her face was filled with fright and horror as she stroked Josephine's hair out of her face. "You're crazy. No one stands up to someone like that . . ." She whispered in Josephine's ear, fearfully keeping one eye on Adele.

"If you two aren't clear on who calls the shots around here, we can repeat this lesson anytime you like," Adele hissed, posturing victoriously.

Josephine groaned. One of the last punches had caught her in the middle of her ribcage and still hurt. With the last of her strength, she pushed past the red-haired girl. She caught Adele's left ankle just before Adele could pull it clear and sent her sprawling on the floor.

Jo pulled herself up and dropped down with all her weight onto Adele's chest. She pinned Adele's arms to the floor. Breathing hard, she glared down at Adele and said, "Before today, I would never have attacked someone weaker than me, not in my wildest dreams. But you've just shown me how it's done!" She pressed her right knee hard into Adele's chest until she cried out in pain. Jo smiled. "Don't like the taste of your own medicine? If you don't want any more of it, then leave the girl alone. And me, too!" Then she released Adele's arms and, with a final sniff of contempt, stood and turned away.

# Chapter Two

*The door of the barn creaks as the boy pulls it closed behind him. He is enveloped by darkness and the familiar odors of leather, hoof trimmings, and ashes. He listens, alert for the slightest sound, but no one and nothing is in sight on this sunny Sunday afternoon. Not even a mouse peeps out from under the bales of hay stacked in the rear of the barn. His parents are away visiting relatives, and he has driven off his annoying sister, Josephine. He is in the smithy where his father works every weekday from eight in the morning to eight in the evening, and he is thrilled to have it to himself. He can hardly believe that he's actually managed to steal the key! He will make sure he puts it back in its drawer before his parents return.*

*The boy grins, then bars the door. He knows he is forbidden to be in there alone. His mother, father, and sisters all know how much he loves his father's tools. They have told him countless times that the tools are dangerous. But the grown-ups have no idea. The sharp knives his father uses to trim the hooves, the large rasps for filing them smooth, the clinch cutter, and the nails—all kinds of exciting toys.*

*But today the boy does not even glance at the tools. Instead, he goes straight to the forge, where his father heats the horseshoes until the iron glows and they can be beaten on the anvil.*

*The boy loves fire. The red and gold flames, the heat, the crackle and snap—all of it so thrilling. Lighting a fire is also forbidden, of course. Or rather, FORBIDDEN—in all capital letters!*

*When you burn newspaper, the art is in keeping a single page alight as long as possible. This can be done in a number of ways. You can wad the paper up in a special way, or poke it around with a small stick and slowly break it up into small pieces while it burns. It is also fun to wrap horseshoe nails in the paper first, and thin hoof trimmings wrapped in newspaper burn really well. The boy is still undecided about exactly which method is the best, but he plans to conduct several experiments today to find out. In his own fireplace. In the center of the barn, on the stone floor.*

*He opens the drawer where his father keeps the boxes of matches. Forbidden. All forbidden.*

*"Felix? Felix, where are you? You rascal, where are you hiding?"*

*The boy's face tenses. Why does Josephine have to come looking for him just now?*

*All he needs is a few minutes to finish his tests for the day. He grabs a match and darts to the back door of the barn and bars that, too. All right. Now his dear sister can scream her head off!*

*He smiles.*

*He will sweep all the ashes together and open the door when he is done. "What's the matter?" he'll ask, meek as a lamb, and show Josephine his wooden horse. "I was just playing in the hay."*

*To reinforce the credibility of his excuse later on, he pulls out one of the bales of hay that is normally used to feed skittish horses as they are being shod. He pushes it into the center of the barn, where he has set up his fireplace on the cold stone slabs. He prefers to think of it as his laboratory. Mr. Günthner, his teacher, has said that there are scientists toiling away in laboratories all over the empire, all hoping to make new discoveries. He hopes to be among them. Filled with scientific fervor, the boy crouches down.*

*He burns a twisted up sheet of newspaper and counts to twenty before the last ember goes out. A sheet loaded up with nails will hold the heat—and therefore the embers—until a count of twenty-three. The other trials have yielded worse results.*

*This time, the boy sets fire to a new sheet of paper, then takes two long, thin sticks, one in each hand, and carefully pulls the paper apart until he has two burning pieces. Good! How many pieces will he be able to separate the burning sheet into? And how long will they burn?*

*As he always does when he is concentrating, he pushes his bottom lip up and over the upper one. Four pieces, five . . . How annoying. The small ones burn up very quickly. A flake of ash sails into his nose, tickling him, and he snorts. The small draft causes one of the bigger burning scraps to fly up. It comes to rest at the base of the hay bale.*

*The boy jumps back in fright. A shudder rocks his twelve-year-old body. Hay burns like tinder! Every child knows that! It isn't for nothing that his father always stacks the bales as far from the forge as he can, around the outer walls. While the boy is still searching for something to extinguish it, the burning scrap of paper wafts up again and flattens itself like gold leaf against the hay bale. A few glowing yellow tongues of flame lick at the hay. The smell is pleasant, but fear enters the boy's eyes.*

*Father's leather apron! The heavy leather will put the fire out! The boy runs and yanks the apron from the wall, together with its hook. But when he returns with his heavy load to the bale, he finds it burning brightly. Small black fragments leap through the air like fleas.*

*He hears hysterical screaming from the entrance. "Felix! What's going on in there? Open up, now!" Josephine. She just won't let go.*

*"I'll be there in a minute!" the boy calls back and begins beating frantically at the bale. Then he feels a wave of heat on his back. The other scraps of paper! With all his thrashing about, a couple of them have floated up and landed on the woodpile where he found the sticks. In the blink of an eye, the bone-dry wood is ablaze. The billowing dark-gray smoke obscures the boy's vision and disorients him. He lurches back, trying to gather his senses in the growing heat.*

*"Josephine . . . Help!" The boy beats desperately at the burning wood with the leather apron, but instead of extinguishing the fire, all he does is send the embers flying. Small fires merge into larger fires and the crackling of the burning hay grows louder. The doors have been blocked by the fire. Paralyzed with fear, the boy stares at the flaming inferno, in the heart of which is a solitary black place: his father's forge, stone clad in steel. If he manages to get in there, he can simply wait until the fire burns itself out. Half-blinded by smoke, the boy feels his way toward the forge. One step. No, not that way! He slaps at his sleeve, which has almost caught fire. Another step. There, he is almost there. The unbearable heat. Don't think about it. Almost . . . almost . . .*

*The boy feels his knees give way. A few feet from the shelter of the stones, he collapses to the floor . . .*

Josephine screamed and sat bolt upright in her bed. She looked around, perplexed. "Felix?"

"What was it? Bad dream?" someone beside her murmured.

Josephine blinked in confusion. The red-haired girl. Barnim Road Women's Prison.

Sweating and shaking, she sank back on her mattress. From farther back came the sound of snoring and someone moaning softly in her sleep, but otherwise the dormitory was silent. Beyond the barred windows, dawn was breaking. An owl or some other animal let out a shrill cry, reminding Jo of freedom and better days.

She had always been the first to wake in the morning. "While the world is still asleep . . ." Words she had said so many times! At that hour, the world was hers, and only hers. She was free. She had looked forward to every new day.

Now, though, she sought desperately to go back to sleep. But she could not push aside her memories of her younger brother.

In the first weeks after Felix's death, she had dreamed of him regularly. Strange, obscure dreams in which she sometimes saw the world through her own eyes, sometimes through his, as in the dream she had just woken from. The guilt had followed her into her sleep back then. But eventually, the dreams had grown less frequent and she became absorbed in her own life again.

***

Her brother had died in the spring of 1889, on a beautiful and unseasonably warm Sunday. More than two years ago now. After church, her father, known to all as Schmied-the-Smith, told Josephine that he and her mother wanted to pay his sister a visit. Josephine was to keep an eye on Felix at home. She had been furious. When she was Felix's age, no one had cared a jot about her. She would have liked to go visit her aunt, too!

She had watched listlessly while her little brother occupied himself with various activities. Then she had gone to visit her friend Clara, four houses down.

Clara was sick, and Josephine found her propped up among her lily-white embroidered sheets like a queen on her throne. She was surrounded by magazines, a glass of some deep-red juice, and a plate of pastries from the Ratsmann bakery. In the Berg family, being ill was always cause for celebration, like a birthday or christening. Ever since Clara had nearly died at the age of seven from an inflamed appendix, her mother, Sophie, would have liked nothing more than to keep her daughter packed in tissue paper. Josephine had always envied her a little. At home, it was always, *"Hurry up and get better, the work won't get done if you're lazing around in bed."*

They had looked through the magazines, and Clara had fallen in love with one dress in particular. Jo found it hard to believe that Clara and her mother would make a special trip all the way to Kurfürstendamm Boulevard to purchase it. The clothes that Josephine and her sisters wore—purchased at Reutter's Emporium, down on the corner—paled in comparison to Clara's stylish wardrobe.

When they'd grown bored with browsing through the magazines, Josephine suggested that they pay a visit to Frieda, an older neighbor who would surely offer them some lemonade and let them sit in her garden. Besides, a visit to Frieda was always interesting. The old widow lived a life they could only dream about. No tiresome rules or duties, no dull daily routine. Ever since her husband had died, Frieda did whatever she liked, and Josephine admired her tremendously for that.

But Clara shook her head. "I'm sick. Besides, Mother doesn't like my visiting Frieda so often. Just yesterday she said Frieda is the kind of woman who'll put ideas into your head before you can say *boo*."

Josephine had stayed on a little longer out of sympathy, but, enveloped by the intense smell of lavender and the bright floral wallpaper, she felt unable to last much longer. She stood up abruptly, crossed to the window, and threw it open.

Luisenstadt, always so bustling during the week, had looked utterly lifeless that day. Everything the residents of the district needed was within an easy walk: Just down from Clara's house, on the corner, was the large Reutter's Emporium. Then there were bakeries, butchers, grocery stores, Clara's father's pharmacy, and Schmied-the-Smith's forge. A few narrow apartment buildings were across the road from the pharmacy, and among those was a single, tiny, freestanding house where old Frieda lived. The lower end of the street was taken up entirely by Moritz Herrenhus's clothing factory, which extended almost as far as the park known as Schlesischer Busch. But the area had been going through a transformation of late: more and more skilled craftsmen were moving to the outskirts of the city where they could produce their goods more quickly and cheaply.

"Let 'em go," Schmied-the-Smith was often heard to say. "It may well be the end of the line for an old ropemaker's shop in the city, but horses will always need shoeing. I won't run out of work anytime soon."

Her father shod eight to ten horses every day, and it was often ten in the evening before Josephine was finished clearing and cleaning up the smithy. No one expected Felix to lend a hand. He was the little prince, after all. While she was no more than the maid. And he was the reason she had to miss out on visiting her aunt . . .

Work, work, work, from morning till night—that was all Josephine ever did! She had stared morosely out Clara's window and wished herself very far away.

Sophie Berg had appeared in Clara's room, interrupting Josephine's peevish thoughts. "There's smoke coming from your father's forge and on a Sunday at that—what do you think it could mean?" she had asked with a furrowed brow—

Josephine closed her eyes. She didn't want to remember. Not here, not now. But her thoughts would not stop. They rampaged through her head like wild horses.

The barn door had been latched shut from the inside. She could smell the stink of the fire and burning hoof trimmings as she shouted Felix's name. The little villain! How many times had her parents forbidden him from touching the matches? If they found out that he had been playing with fire again, they would blame her. She had hammered on the door with her right fist so hard that it hurt, her fury and fear growing with every passing second. "Open up!" Again, nothing happened. But she thought she heard a quiet laugh.

"Just wait!" Gathering her skirt, she had run into the toolshed in search of something large and heavy to break down the door. She grabbed the ax, ran back to the barn, and swung it with such force at the barn door that it fell out of her hands. The door did not open, but she managed to dislodge two of its boards with the force of the blow. Heat surged out through the gap, and the fire flared up a bright yellow, fueled by the fresh air.

Josephine's wrists burned and splinters drove into her flesh as she tore out the boards with her bare hands.

*Dear God, watch over my brother. He is just a child. He doesn't know what he's doing. Dear God, take what you want from me, but watch over my brother.*

She had prayed to God as she had never prayed in her life. But God was not there on that Sunday. The fire extinguished her prayers, as surely as it did Felix's life.

"Felix! Where are you?" Her voice sounded muffled, as if she were trying to speak through a heavy cloth rag. She squinted into the scorching sea of fire, and a stabbing pain throbbed in her ears as she groped her way forward into the inferno.

She was too late. Her brother had already perished in the flames.

# Chapter Three

Breakfast was a scant affair that took place under the eyes of two surly guards in a cold, gloomy hall. The narrow windows were positioned in the upper third of the walls, and little light found its way through them. *It's like eating in a basement,* thought Jo, as she sat down at one of the outer tables. Could it be that the rooms that made up the juvenile section of the prison were actually underground? When she'd been brought in, she had paid no attention to things like stairways, but now, after a single night, she felt as if she'd been buried alive inside a tomb. She wanted more than anything to stand up and leave.

She felt Adele's venomous glare on her as she chewed on a dry roll and sipped at the weak tea. The leader of the gang was whispering with the girls sitting around her and pointed repeatedly in Josephine's direction. Once, twice, their eyes met. Jo knew she had better be on guard.

"So? Why are you here?"

Reluctantly, Josephine turned to the redhead who had sat beside her. She didn't even know the girl's name, didn't know whether she was really pregnant or she just had a strange figure. And she didn't want to know.

"Theft," Josephine replied.

"Is that all . . . ?" asked the red-haired girl, evidently disappointed. "I was tricked!" she added, then launched into a drawn-out story in which three friends, an old couple, and money hidden under a mattress all played a role. The fact that the old couple lay dead in their narrow bed by the end of the story didn't seem to trouble the girl much. She repeated several times that she had had nothing to do with it.

As if Josephine cared! She chewed in silence, wishing she were able to close her ears as easily as she could close her eyes.

"And I got tricked the same way with this." The girl thumped her stomach with her right hand. "He said he'd be careful and that we'd both have fun. Fun my foot! But I suppose one good thing did come of it. If I wasn't knocked up, they'd have stuck me in the prison in Moabit. They only brought me here because the women's prison has a birthing ward." The redhead reached out her hand. "My name's Martha, by the way."

Josephine had no choice but to take the extended hand. It was moist, and a few breadcrumbs clung to it.

"Jo."

"At least your name isn't too long!" Martha laughed. "It sounds more like a man's name. But from what I know about you, it fits. It sounds really . . . tough."

For the first time since this nightmare had begun, a gentle smile appeared on Josephine's face. "Someone else once told me the same thing."

Martha, who obviously claimed Jo's smile as a personal success, beamed. "A girlfriend? Do you have one?"

Jo bit a chunk of the roll but said nothing. Did she have friends? God, yes, very good friends—the best anyone could imagine! She had been friends with Clara since she could walk and had known Isabelle since they were both small. But she and Isabelle had only really become close about a year and a half ago. And then there was Lilo down in the Black Forest.

"They won't want anything to do with me anymore," Jo said. "Not after I got caught stealing from Isabelle's father." Jo felt nauseous at the memory of his actions on the night in question. Instead of talking to her, he had immediately filed a complaint with the police.

"Oh," said Martha, but she did not look as taken aback as she sounded. "Friends!" She gestured dismissively. "They probably tricked you somehow and you didn't even notice. That's the second thing we have in common. The first is that we both got here yesterday."

Josephine looked at Martha with annoyance. What nonsense was she spouting? They had nothing—not a single thing!—in common.

Martha grasped Josephine's right hand and squeezed it. "I can be your friend, if you'd like."

Josephine jerked her hand free. "Just because I helped you out of a jam yesterday doesn't mean you have to stick to me like a burr! Let's get one thing straight: in the future, you look out for yourself. I do *not* feel like—"

A shrill bell sounded, cutting Josephine off.

***

Karlheinz Krotzmann had just passed through the gatehouse of the Barnim Road Women's Prison when he felt the old familiar rumbling in his stomach. His face contorted in pain as he surveyed the prison, which consisted of a U-shaped building housing several hundred inmates. The facility had been built a few years earlier by some notable architects, following a decision by the Royal Ministry of Justice. The left wing contained the apartments of the prison officers and the kitchens. The prison had its own boiler building and power plant that supplied the complex with power and light. Behind the main building were an orchard and a vegetable garden that were tended by the inmates. The architects had even added a prison chapel on the top floor.

Karlheinz Krotzmann sniffed. He would have bet that hardly anybody here had ever set foot in that house of the Lord. His discomfort increased with every step. Although the building was no more than twenty years old, everything looked dilapidated. The footpath that led to the main building was uneven and potholed; the walls were stained or covered in moss. The windows were grimy, the bars rusted . . .

*These people are like animals! They destroy everything, without the slightest hesitation about the damage they're doing,* Krotzmann thought. He was glad that the start of his classes did not coincide with the release of the inmates into the yard. The idea of breathing the same air as murderers and thieves any more than he had to made him uneasy.

He had almost reached the main block when he saw the caretaker coming around the corner pulling a handcart stacked with tools. The man lived in a small apartment on the premises and was busy with repairs from dawn till dusk. *What a life!* thought Krotzmann with a shudder, and he gave the caretaker a sympathetic nod. After a brief greeting, the man said, "I need a new helper. One of the younger ones for a change, I reckon. Maybe they're not as degenerate as the adults. Can you send me someone at the end of your class?"

Krotzmann nodded. He was responsible for assigning the young convicts to the laundry, the cleaning crews, and the kitchen.

"Didn't you have a skinny old woman helping you fix the chicken run fence last week? What happened to her?"

The caretaker snorted. "She tried to crack my skull with a hammer. I saw it coming at the last second. I managed to duck but just barely avoided it. They've thrown the old girl in solitary. Pity. I thought there was more good in her than that."

*Thought there was more good in her!* The man was an irredeemable fool if he believed that. The churning in Krotzmann's belly grew stronger. "I'll see what I can do," he said, then pushed open the heavy iron door of the main block. Its painful creak was the starting signal for the three hours of agony he endured every day in the newly built juvenile wing.

The juvenile wing was a waste of money, just like the chapel. It made no difference whether the younger whores and thieves were shut away separately for a few years or whether they were thrown in with the adult offenders from the start. *Maybe they're not as degenerate . . .* Ha! The mere thought of that Adele with her ice-cold eyes was enough to make him nauseous. To beat your own—drunken!—father to death from behind . . . One could only imagine what that took.

*What a disgrace,* thought Krotzmann, not for the first time, and felt his bile rise. An abysmal disgrace, that *he* of all people should be condemned by the Education Authority to teach behind the barred facade of the Barnim Road Women's Prison. Of course, the head of the authority had put it differently: "An attempt to lead wayward young members of society back onto the right path. An educational challenge requiring rigor and benevolence in equal measure." It was said that he, Karlheinz Krotzmann, could be entrusted with such a task. He was left with no other choice but to comply, in the hope that one or two years in the women's prison would help him achieve his ambition of higher office someday. For more than a year now, he had taken the trams halfway across the city, day after day, to this den of iniquity. And each day, his loathing of his pupils grew. It was revolting to even call them that . . .

Not that he hadn't started out with the best intentions! Because there were no lesson plans for this kind of "school," he had created his own. The lesson plans, which mainly focused on building his pupils' discipline and endurance rather than their intellect, consisted of multiplication tables, reading, writing, and memorization.

But he quickly became convinced that his cleverly conceived lesson plans were wasted on such ignorant, undisciplined rabble. A workhouse, in his opinion, would have been far more suitable for these lazy sluts than mental arithmetic or the poems of Goethe.

Krotzmann took a final deep breath, then pulled open the door of the so-called classroom, which was no more than just another gloomy, poorly ventilated room.

"Good morning, Mr. Krotzmann," thirty young women droned.

At least the morning greeting had been successful. But how they slumped in their chairs! One could identify their miserable characters simply by looking at their postures. There was no need to even look into their wicked eyes.

He spotted the two new arrivals instantly. A red-haired, scared-looking harlot. Either she'd been pushed around by the others, or she was a cunning little tramp. Beside her sat another young woman—

Krotzmann started. What was a girl like that doing here? She was tall and slender, with an even complexion and well-cared-for, curly hair. Unlike the others, she sat upright and radiated a natural elegance. Such a creature was clearly not a product of the gutter. Had things degenerated to the point that girls from decent households were no longer able to tell good from evil? What could her crime have been? Had she swindled some good-natured sucker? Robbed a poor mother? Perhaps killed someone? She was as good-looking as the actresses on the posters of the Berlin Schauspielhaus, which only served to stoke the fires of Krotzmann's malevolence.

He cracked his wooden cane impatiently against the lectern at the front of the room. He squinted as he looked out over his pupils.

"The sight of you all slouching there makes me sick! How many times do I have to explain the proper posture? Feet must be flat, with the entire sole flush with the floor! Thighs must rest straight and level on the surface of the seat! It's disgusting to you see sprawled out that way!" He took his cane and whacked a pupil in the first row across the back, causing a sharp clapping noise.

"And you! Keep your head up! The chin should never touch the chest!" Another swish of the cane, this time at the back of the first girl's neighbor. Neither of the girls so much as flinched. They could take it; he had to give them that. *But why do they prefer a stroke of the cane to following my instructions?* he wondered as he made his way to the back rows.

"Hurry up—feet parallel and flat on the floor! Thighs straight on the seat. Upper bodies may be inclined slightly forward, but woe betide anyone who leans against the edge of the table! And your shoulders! How many times do I have to repeat myself? Shoulders must be aligned with the edge of the table. The right shoulder no higher or lower than the left." He looked on grimly as the young women struggled to adopt his decreed posture. The slim newcomer seemed to be having particular difficulties. Looking closer, Krotzmann realized she had quite a broad, strong back. This evidence of physical strength angered him, although he could not have explained why. Instantly, he was standing beside her.

"You!" He brought his cane down on the table in front of her with a thwack. "Name!"

"Josephine Schmied," came the reply, soft but firm.

*Josephine.* He knew it. This was no Martha or Karla. What was she doing here? He glared at her.

"The deportment of your arms is unacceptable! This is a classroom, not some train station or wherever else you feel like loitering." His stick came down hard on her hand. His right eye twitched nervously when he saw the blood welling up from her knuckles. Bright-red blood. He withdrew the cane and felt a kind of pleasant relief. Two or three girls laughed, and he recognized Adele's voice among them. He cast a warning glare around the room, then turned back to the newcomer. "Your left forearm should rest entirely on top of the desk, and your right with the hand and wrist."

"I had an accident. My shoulder is injured. Unfortunately, I am not able to sit any other way," the young woman said and swept a lock of hair from her forehead.

Why would she not look at him? Did she imagine she was better than he was? Was she trying to flirt with him? The tension rose in him once again. "Do you believe for a minute I would accept such a ridiculous excuse?"

His cane came slashing down on her other hand. Once. Twice. The newcomer shook in a way that did not come entirely from the pain she must have felt, but from something else, something deeper. For a moment, he feared the young woman would leap from her chair and defend herself from his blows. But the moment passed and nothing happened. He exhaled. He looked down at her, his superiority established.

"I hope that will teach you not to answer back. And just so you know: There'll be no cozy potato peeling in the kitchen or ironing in the laundry for you. I'm assigning you to our caretaker. Let's see what your shoulder says to a bit of hard labor . . ."

*** 

Although it was shortly before midday, gas lamps were still burning in every house in Luisenstadt—it was one of those November days that seemed unwilling to brighten. Isabelle's lips were white with cold and her eyes were tearing up from the icy east wind. She pulled the collar of her coat closer around her neck.

"Where have you been? I've been twiddling my thumbs for ten minutes out here—next time I'll go by myself!" she said, when Clara finally emerged from the pharmacy.

"Stop complaining. I had a lot of trouble getting out at all!" Clara answered breathlessly as she straightened the strap on her bag. Inside it, in addition to a few medicine bottles, were a block of chocolate and some peppermint candy for Josephine. She had told her parents that she was going to deliver the medicine to several of their older, disabled customers. And before they could question her as to who and where, she was out the door.

The two young women strode quickly toward the tram stop and were just able to jump aboard before the tram rolled away.

"When I think of all the trouble I got into with my father because of Jo, I hardly feel like going on this little jaunt at all," said Isabelle as they crammed in beside the other passengers on a hard wooden bench. "She got me in serious hot water, and if my parents knew I was visiting her now, it would start all over again."

"Then why didn't you just stay home?" asked Clara. Her mother, too, would rake her over the coals if she knew where she was really going. But a year ago, when she had been lying in the hospital with a broken leg, Josephine had visited her every day. She couldn't turn her back on her friend now . . .

A shudder ran down Clara's spine. Josephine in the Barnim Road Women's Prison—the very thought made her cringe. That place was full of prostitutes, con artists, and other lowlifes. Josie didn't belong there, not her best friend for as long as she could remember!

"Besides," Clara said, "you're partly to blame for Josephine's being in prison in the first place. You were the one who was always filling her head with crazy ideas and all just because you were bored."

"That is . . . outrageous," Isabelle answered indignantly. "*I* certainly didn't make Josephine steal from my father. Just the opposite, in fact. I tried to stop her from going out that night. But all you could think about was your work. It made no difference to you what Jo was up to."

Clara looked away, clearly hurt. She'd accused herself of that very thing plenty of times—it was true that she hadn't tried hard enough to get through to Jo. Isabelle didn't have to rub it in.

"And that old neighbor, Frieda, the one Josephine liked so much—she could just as easily have said something to her," said Isabelle. "Frieda knew about Jo's obsession. She just chose not to do anything about it."

At the next station, they transferred to another tram. They had hardly sat down when Isabelle, keeping her voice low, picked up where she had left off. "Even if we had all used all our powers of persuasion, it wouldn't have made any difference—she was insatiable and completely immune to reason."

"Then why did you ever let it go so far? Opportunity makes the thief—that's what they say, right?" Clara said bitterly. "Besides, you certainly could have done more to stick up for Jo with your father. If you had, maybe he never would have reported her."

Isabelle let out a short, shrill laugh. "How do you know whether—or how much—I stuck up for Jo?! I . . ."

The girls continued bickering, throwing more recriminations at each other. When they arrived at the Landsberger Allee station—several tram changes and more than half an hour later—the mood between them was as chilly as the east wind.

"Friedrichshain Park looks so grim in winter," Isabelle murmured, glancing in the direction of the empty park, where a few stray dogs were the only sign of life. There was an unusual glimmer of trepidation in her eyes.

The girls began walking through the early winter wasteland toward the forbidding building with its many small windows. The prison exuded an aura of menace. Clara's steps grew heavier.

The man inside the small gatehouse looked up from his newspaper. His eyes narrowed to slits, and he looked the two young women up and down.

"What do you want?" A reek of decay escaped through the small window with each word. The man's mouth contained rotten black stumps where his teeth should have been.

The sight made Clara's skin crawl, but she forced herself to smile. "We would like to visit a friend—"

"This ain't a hotel. No visitors. Get lost."

"But . . ." Clara began. "How dare you speak to us like—"

Isabelle pushed her aside. "Please accept my apologies. My companion doesn't always choose her words wisely. We are from the . . . Committee for the Social Rehabilitation of Delinquent Girls. Our mothers sit on the committee's board of directors. They have sent us here to find out whether donated monies are being put to good use. Our visit is devoted solely to this end." She looked at Clara disdainfully, then took out her purse. With a sweet smile, she slipped a few marks across to the gatekeeper. "Your employer would certainly be grateful to you, were you to lend the efforts of such an indispensable committee your . . . unbureaucratic assistance. Which is to say, please let us in. The young woman with whom we would like to speak on behalf of the committee is named Josephine Schmied."

The gatekeeper's face contorted into an unpleasant grin. "Well, then, if that's how it is . . . though I'm going to have to convince my colleagues over at the main building of the importance of your committee. And one or two of the guards, too . . ." He held up the money suggestively.

"Get on with it, then. We're in a hurry."

\*\*\*

"Josephine Schmied!" The guard interrupted the lesson and looked from Krotzmann to the assembled class. Josephine hesitantly raised her hand.

"Come with me."

Josephine fled the room under the teacher's wrathful eye. What was this about? Was this the end of her ordeal? All of it just a misunderstanding? Had Moritz Herrenhus withdrawn his complaint? Josephine sighed quietly—what a pleasant thought.

The guard unlocked a small, narrow room where a table and a few chairs stood.

"Isabelle? Clara!" At the sight of the familiar faces, Josephine's heart skipped a beat. She threw her arms around Clara's neck. "You came . . ." Tears welled instantly in her eyes.

"Sit down, all three of you! Physical contact is forbidden," ordered the guard before leaving the room.

"What happened to your hands? You're bleeding!" cried Clara the moment she sat down.

Josephine hid her hands beneath the table. "That's from the accident . . ."

"But . . . an injury like that can get infected before you know it. You must have it treated right away." Clara looked from Jo to Isabelle, who sat beside Clara, looking aloof.

"It's not so bad," said Josephine. "I'm so happy you've come." She felt a lump rise in her throat and fought back her tears.

"It wasn't easy, take my word for it," Isabelle said. "My father's as angry as a bull. He couldn't talk about anything else at breakfast—you and the damage you've done. If he knew I was visiting you . . ."

Jo lowered her eyes. "I . . . I wish the earth would swallow me here and now when I think about what I did. I was so stupid . . ."

"Sadly, your epiphany is a little late," said Isabelle in a chilly tone.

"Isabelle didn't mean it like that," Clara rushed to say and shook her head brusquely at Isabelle. "How are you? Are they treating you well? When are they letting you out? Before Christmas? The man at the gate said they don't actually let anyone visit at all. We don't know if we'll be able to come again . . ."

Didn't her friends know that she'd been sentenced to three and a half years? "They've—" Jo began, then broke off. "We'll see," she said as breezily as she could. *Don't think about it. Don't talk about it.* Maybe then she would wake up from this nightmare. To change the subject, she said, "Clara, is it true that old Dr. Fritsche passed away? When I asked my mother to send for him after the accident, she told me he'd died. Strange that I didn't hear about it earlier."

"Does that surprise you? All you could think about was your own obsession," Isabelle replied. Clara jabbed her sharply in the ribs.

"Jo practically never gets sick, so it's hardly surprising. I, on the other hand, found out the very day . . ." Clara said, a tragicomic look on her face.

"He was a regular visitor to your place until the very end, wasn't he? Your mother would have just *loved* for you to marry old Fritsche. Then she would have had a doctor in the house for every little cough and cold you caught. Remember how we all used to joke around about that? Those were the days . . ." Isabelle looked at her two friends and smiled.

"Joke around? You two teased me mercilessly!" Clara replied in mock outrage.

The three young women laughed, and for a moment their old familiarity returned.

"Here. This is for you," said Clara and handed Josephine the block of chocolate.

*If Adele sees that* . . . thought Josephine. "Thank you. But I insist on sharing it with the two of you," she said firmly. Her hands ached as she set to work unwrapping it.

"Ever since Dr. Fritsche died, everyone's been coming to my father as a substitute," said Clara as she popped a square of chocolate into her mouth. "He's asked me to help him meet the extra demand by making the medicines, even if it means I have to stay up late in the laboratory every night."

Josephine looked fondly at her friend. "Don't go pretending you don't enjoy it. There's nothing you like more than stirring up some potion or other."

"Or crushing herbs with a mortar and pestle," Isabelle added.

Clara smiled. "You've caught me!"

As the banter flew back and forth, Josephine felt a pang of admiration for her friend. Ever since Clara first helped her father boil soap years before, it had been clear that she would someday go to work in his pharmacy. Her mother, however—who considered such work to be beneath her daughter's dignity—had sent her off to a home-economics school to prepare her for her future responsibilities as a housewife. Clara had nearly perished there from boredom. With a tenacity that nobody had seen in her before, she had finally managed to prevail against her mother's will. And now, she stood side by side in a fresh, white apron with her father in the pharmacy. Clever Clara had made her own dream come true, while she, Jo, had simply thrown her own dreams in the gutter.

Clara sighed. "But my father will be back to his old ways soon enough—being a know-it-all and hovering over my shoulder when I'm boiling soap or making liniment. A new doctor's coming by this evening as Fritsche's successor. It's taken so long to find anyone willing to take over his practice . . ."

None of them could think of anything else to say on the subject, and a silence settled over them. The illusion that they were just having a casual chat burst like a bubble, and all three of them suddenly felt self-conscious.

*I'm sorry,* Josephine wanted to say. She felt the words on her lips, but she kept them inside. "I'm sorry" was what you said when you stepped on someone's foot. In her case, it would never have been enough.

Isabelle cleared her throat. "We should probably be getting along. I . . . I still have to study my French vocabulary—Madame Blanche has set a test for tomorrow. Again! And there's an English test coming up, too. I'd like to know what the point of all these foreign languages is. I'm never going to get out of Berlin. Besides, we've been invited to a ball this evening, and we'll need time to get ready."

Josephine smiled. "Your hair is already perfect. Please don't tell me you're going to spend hours getting it done again."

Isabelle rolled her eyes. "It is my father's wish that I always look perfectly turned out."

"Has some marriage prospect turned up?" Jo asked, feigning interest. When would the guard come to fetch her? Did she have to go back to Krotzmann? A cold chill ran through her at the thought. Or would she have to go straight to the caretaker? If the caretaker was as repulsive as Krotzmann, then it was all over for her . . . Would she be able to work at all with her injured hands? That Krotzmann had better not try to strike her again.

"Me and marriage? Heaven forbid," said Isabelle. "I love my freedom far too much for that."

"So what became of that young Baron von Salzfeld, the one your mother thought so much of?" asked Clara. "She came into the pharmacy once and gushed about him as if wedding bells would soon be ringing."

"The one with the castle out in the country and the extensive estates east of Berlin and the *brilliant* connections to the Imperial Court? He was just the type my mother loves," said Isabelle derisively. "I, however, found him terribly dull, so I sent him fleeing, like all the others. I make a stupid remark or come up with an irritating mannerism—and they're gone! It's really very easy." She laughed. "Father is still trying to guess why the young gentleman beat such a hasty retreat. 'Dearest Father,' I told him, 'am I really supposed to marry some young peacock who can't even hold a candle to you?' I've always been able to calm him down that way." Isabelle looked very pleased with herself.

Clara raised her eyebrows in surprise. "But if it all really means so little to you . . . including all the ball gowns and jewelry and constant visits to the hairdresser . . . why don't you just tell your father you're not interested in getting married? Wouldn't that be better for everyone?"

"You don't know my father! He's got it into his head that through me—or rather, through the fine match I'll make one day—he'll climb into the highest social circles."

"But he's already there. He's been up there for ages," said Josephine. She was thinking of Isabelle's family's beautiful villa, which was stuffed full of valuable things. She had been wide-eyed when she had first seen it. She had never imagined that people lived like that, let alone that she would ever set foot in such a place.

Isabelle ran a hand through her mass of red curls. "Money is one thing. But there are many in the upper circles who still look at my father as a kind of tailor, an upstart *apron-maker*, someone who could never belong to the league of major industrialists like the Krupps or the Rothschilds. But that is exactly where he wants to be, and I am the means to that end."

Josephine frowned. "You sound so bitter . . . I always thought you enjoyed all those balls."

"You *thought* . . . For a change, you might have *asked* me just once how I felt about it." Isabelle looked from Jo to Clara. "How many times have I told you that these society balls are like an Arabian wedding market? And it's never occurred to you that I'm supposed to be bartered away to the highest bidder? You seem to think I live in some kind of paradise . . ."

The mockery in Isabelle's voice was impossible to ignore. Josephine, cut to the quick, looked down at her bloody hands. Had she really been such a bad friend? So selfish? She'd been so caught up in her own projects, her own thoughts. Only ever thinking of herself.

"Forgive me. I'm so sorry for everything . . ." she said, choking on her own tears.

Isabelle and Clara shifted uneasily on their hard chairs. Josephine cleared her throat.

"I don't want to seem rude, but . . . I've been assigned to the caretaker as his assistant, and he's probably waiting for me." Without a word of farewell, without any embrace, Josephine fled the room in tears.

\*\*\*

"So you're supposed to be my new helper . . ." The caretaker looked Josephine up and down. "You've got a broad back, at least. Well, we'll see. It's actually too late to start on any new tasks today, but if I send you away now, they'll stick you in the kitchen and I'll be back to square one." He turned to the guard who had brought Jo out to him in the yard. "You can go. Thank you."

"OK, let's get started." He grabbed hold of the handcart and told Josephine to follow him.

Although initially hesitant, Josephine trotted behind him. At first glance, he made a friendly impression. He was middle-aged with a shaved head. He reminded her of the coachmen who brought their horses into the smithy. They liked to talk big, but under their rough exteriors they usually had soft hearts.

The caretaker stopped at a shed behind the main building. "My name's Gerd Melchior." He held out his hand to shake Jo's. His handshake was firm and pleasant. "If you behave properly and work hard, we'll get along just fine. If not . . ." He left the sentence unfinished, but there was a threat in his tone.

"Josephine Schmied. But everyone calls me Jo."

"Fine with me," said Melchior. Inside the shed, he rummaged briefly on a shelf and pulled out an old paintbrush. He gestured with his chin toward a pile of boards that lay in the center of the shed on a kind of tarpaulin. "That's going to be the frame for a new compost heap. I don't want it to rot out after a year, so it needs to get a protective coat. I need you to paint every board with the *goudron*. And you'll do it carefully. No light spots, got it?"

"*Goudron?* Isn't that just plain old tar?" Josephine asked, screwing up her nose at the familiar, biting smell emanating from the paint pot.

The caretaker looked at her in surprise. "One and the same. But how d'you know anything about tar?"

Jo smiled. "My father shoes horses and I've always helped him. We paint rotten hooves with tar."

Melchior raised his eyebrows. "You're a smith's daughter? What are you doing in here?" But he immediately waved off his question. "I don't want to know. You children are all so foolish! Instead of using the chances you're given, you just get up to mischief. Now show me whether you can really work, or whether you're just one of those good-for-nothings we already have too many of."

\*\*\*

The dormitory had been quiet for a long time. From here and there came a soft snoring or someone groaning in her sleep. But as exhausted as Jo was—more so than ever before—she could not fall asleep. Her eyes stung from the fumes of the tar that she had spent three hours painting onto the long boards. Afterward, when she had asked a guard for permission to wash her blood-crusted, tar-spotted hands, she was told that inmates were only allowed to wash in the morning.

*"A lack of personal hygiene is behind many a malady,"* she suddenly heard in a voice from the past in her mind. Josephine sighed. Who had told her that? One of the doctors in the Black Forest, where she had spent some time because of her lungs? Or had it been Clara, with her pharmaceutical knowledge?

Before she could stop them, other voices joined in: *"All you could think about was your own obsession . . ." "You just get up to mischief." "Sadly, your epiphany is a little late . . ."* Clara's, Isabelle's, and Frieda's words fluttered in her mind like little bats; mixed up with them was Gerd Melchior talking about mischief.

*"Sadly, your epiphany is a little late."* Isabelle's tone had been so bitter.

Josephine rolled from one side to the other restlessly. Hindsight . . . Could she even claim that? Or would she do it all exactly the same way again? Wasn't everything that had happened a logical consequence of what had come before? Could it have happened any other way? Or was she oversimplifying when she thought about it like that?

As a wan moon shone through the close prison bars, Josephine's thoughts drifted into the past.

# Chapter Four

*Berlin, spring 1889*

"Tell her she'd better not cross my path at the funeral." Schmied-the-Smith reached for his coffee cup with trembling hands, then thought better of it and pulled a hip flask from his pocket. His wife opened her mouth to say something but changed her mind.

Josephine inhaled sharply, horrified. "Father, I—"

The smith's heavy fist thundered onto the table. Josephine jumped, as did her mother and her sisters.

"And tell her to keep her mouth shut. I don't want to hear another word come out of it." The icy coldness of his voice was worse than any shouting could have been.

Josephine looked to her sisters in despair. Like the rest of the family, the older Schmied girls were dressed in black, and both were holding umbrellas. The skies were weeping on this spring day. Gundel looked back at her blankly, but on Margaret's face Josephine saw open hostility. Neither said a word in her defense.

Elsbeth Schmied laid one hand on Josephine's shoulder and led her out of the kitchen. "Go to your room."

"But he was my brother—" She broke off in a fit of coughing.

"You should have thought of that when you went sneaking off to see that fancy pharmacist's girl. If you'd been looking after Felix like we told you to, our boy would still be alive!"

While Josephine's family accompanied Felix to his final resting place, Josephine ran over to Frieda's place. Pattering raindrops mixed with her tears and fell onto her carelessly bandaged hands. Beneath the strips of cloth, her flesh was inflamed and throbbing. The dressings should have been changed long ago. Dr. Fritsche himself had emphasized how important proper care and hygiene were for burns. And he had told Josephine's mother that something had to be done about her daughter's smoke poisoning. She needed to be inhaling menthol, eucalyptus oil, or a thin camphor solution. Elsbeth Schmied had nodded. But no one had yet paid a visit to Anton Berg to get the medicine.

"You're to blame, you're to blame—I can't bear to hear it one more time," Frieda said to her as she removed the dirty bandages from Josephine's hands. "Do you really think you're lord over life and death? What happened was God's will and *only* God's will. Yes, you should perhaps have listened to your parents and stayed with Felix. But that act of disobedience is the only thing you can blame yourself for. Your father could just as easily accuse himself of being careless with the key to the barn. Or of not locking the matches away. Your little brother was obsessed by fire. Everyone on this street knew that. Wherever he went, wherever he was, he was always pilfering matches. Something was bound to happen sooner or later. Once, I left my reading glasses and newspaper outside. And when I went to get them, there was Felix holding the glasses up to the sun, using them like a magnifying glass. The newspaper was already in flames! Because I love footbaths so much, I was lucky to have a bucket of water under the table. Who knows what would have happened otherwise."

"You never told me that," said Josephine, her voice low. She wrapped the old cardigan that Frieda had given her tighter around her body. A moment later, another fit of coughing racked her body.

"Child, you're going to cough to death!" Frieda handed her a cup of sweet herb tea. Then she began wrapping Josephine's hand in fresh white cotton gauze. "Your mother knew that Felix liked to play with fire. She clipped his ear every time she caught him, and that was that. Of course, she was deathly afraid that something worse would happen one day. But what was she supposed to do? Keep watch on a twelve-year-old rascal, day and night? Impossible." Frieda laid her calloused hand on Josephine's arm. "God's will is stronger than we mortals are. Besides, you did everything you could. You risked your own life trying to get Felix out of that barn alive. When the men from the fire department found you, you were unconscious in front of the barn. A minute, two minutes later and you would have been dead yourself."

Josephine shook her head. "No, I can't let myself off so easy. If only I'd . . ."

\*\*\*

The weeks passed. Josephine withdrew more and more into herself until, soon, there was nothing left of the sturdy, curious, and bold young woman she had once been. Pale, with sunken eyes, she dragged herself to school, where Clara, trying her best to console her friend, read her one Bible passage after another during the breaks. But Josephine's feelings of guilt carried more weight than the words of Matthew or John. After school, she continued to help her father at his forge. Schmied-the-Smith had begun the work of rebuilding his workshop the day after Felix's funeral. The people called him brave and clapped him on the shoulder. But they avoided Josephine's eye.

\*\*\*

It was rare for Frieda to visit one of her neighbors. *Now and then one has to make an exception,* thought Frieda, as she wrapped her "going-out" shawl around her shoulders on the evening of the first day of August 1889.

She made her way along the street, noticing the men and women in every yard as they battled through the last of their daily chores with worn-out faces and bent backs. She thanked her lucky stars again for her own beneficent fate. For fate had seen to it that, after the death of her husband, Robert, a toolmaker, she was finally able to live as she wanted. She could sleep late in the morning, then sit comfortably with her cat and the daily newspaper on the bench in front of her house. Or she could spend a whole day in bed with the books she indulged in from time to time. Other days, she spent hours learning the flute—music had always fascinated her—and she loved to paint and draw, too . . .

She wasted no worry on money. Thanks to the formidable sum her grumpy husband had stashed in the bank without her knowledge, she led a carefree life. The house and the large garden were hers, debt free. Of course, her neighbors were suspicious of her way of life. At first, they had all believed that she would sell the place or rent out the workshop. Or that she would marry the bachelor who had previously helped out in the workshop, and that he would continue to manage the business the way it had always been. But with the passing of time, they had grown accustomed to Frieda's eccentricities, and a few even discreetly dropped by for a glass of wine and good conversation from time to time. Schmied-the-Smith and his wife, however, were not among them, which left Frieda with no choice but to go and visit them.

"Josephine's coughing is growing worse. She probably breathed in too much smoke when she tried to rescue Felix. If you don't do something soon, you'll be carrying a second child to her grave," she said as she sat across the table from the smith and his wife. Josephine had been washing the dishes when Frieda arrived, and they had sent her out of the kitchen.

"Have you joined the ranks of doctors now? What do you care about Josephine's cough?" asked Schmied.

"Dr. Fritsche has no explanation for her coughing," said Elsbeth. "She's probably just doing it for show."

Frieda sighed. She had not imagined that the Schmieds' bitterness could be so deeply embedded. She turned to Elsbeth.

"Dr. Fritsche must have given you some sort of directive?"

"We're supposed to send her up to the North Sea or the Baltic. The clean sea air is said to be good for ailing lungs," Elsbeth Schmied said, rolling her eyes to show what she thought of the doctor's advice.

"Clean sea air! I slave away at the forge all day long and you don't see me in need of any sea air," said her husband derisively. "You want us to reward the little tramp with a long summer holiday while Felix is down with the worms?"

Frieda suddenly felt that she would not last another minute in that gloomy kitchen. She took a deep breath.

"I'd like to make a suggestion," she said, looking forcefully at the smith and his wife. "I have relatives down in the Black Forest, in a village called Schömberg, to be exact. My nephew works as the caretaker in a sanatorium there. It's a special hospital for people with lung diseases. They say the climate there is excellent. It could be just the thing for Josephine's cough. Joachim—that's my nephew—could arrange something for your daughter. A few weeks there, a small room, medical attention . . ."

"A sanatorium at the edge of the empire? Wonderful!" said the smith sarcastically. "And who'll help me in the workshop? Who'll pay for it? I'm not spending a cent on such an extravagance."

"Do you think I expect you to?" Frieda replied coldly. "If it helps the girl recover her health, I'm happy to pay whatever it costs. If you agree, Josephine could travel down there in mid-October. My nephew tells me that a room will be free then. And Oskar Reutter from the emporium on the corner will be going to Stuttgart on business at that time; he would be an ideal traveling companion for Josephine."

"Looks like you've put a lot of thought into this. But why wait? You might as well take the worthless thing with you right now. Then at least I won't have to look at her anymore. I can always find another helper."

None of the adults knew that Josephine was eavesdropping behind the door and heard every word with a stony face and a broken heart.

\*\*\*

The evening before she left, Josephine took the small, cheap suitcase Gundel had borrowed from her employer and stuffed her underwear, socks, and three dresses inside. Her hand already on the doorknob, she cast one last look around the room. Sadly, there was nothing that she wanted to take along. No book, no worn-out but beloved toy, not a single memento. She just wanted to be gone, gone from her father's hatred and her mother's coldness. Gone from the house, gone from the walls that seemed to accuse her day in and day out, gone from that gloomy place where even the air despised her.

When she went to the pharmacy to say good-bye to Clara, she was told by her friend's mother that Clara was busy.

The train departed very early in the morning and the journey proved uneventful. The steaming locomotive stopped only once, just before Nuremberg, on an open stretch of track. No one knew why. "Just a technical failure, I'm sure," said her traveling companion, Oskar Reutter, as he shared the food he'd brought for the journey with her. "The train is the greatest invention of our century. The railway network has been growing steadily, and soon, trains will be able to travel to the farthest corners of our empire. Distances that once seemed insurmountable are turning into nothing more than lines on a map. It is truly a blessing!"

Josephine could only agree as she—a girl who had never before left the Luisenstadt district—sat watching the many different landscapes pass by from the comfort of the train compartment. An unfamiliar sense of elation—of freedom and distance, of inspiration and boundlessness—came over her. She already felt as if she could breathe more easily.

Beyond Nuremberg, Oskar Reutter pointed out a large building to her. "Mr. Joseph Obermaier's telegraphic equipment factory. They're building the future there," he said enthusiastically. "We live in exciting times!"

They went their separate ways in Stuttgart once the emporium owner had ensured that Josephine was settled in the right train for the next leg of her journey.

Two hours later, Josephine arrived in Pforzheim. Mr. Reutter had explained to her that the railway had not penetrated beyond that point into the Black Forest region but that there were always people with wagons offering their services outside Pforzheim station. She would have to bargain hard, of course, but one of them would certainly be willing to drive her the final stretch to Schömberg.

In fact, the wagon drivers in the Black Forest seemed no different than the men who brought their horses to her father's forge, Josephine realized. Encouraged by this, she walked straight over to one of the younger drivers. She knew her way around such men, and despite some difficulties understanding their dialect, she quickly settled on an equitable price with the man.

With every mile they traveled, the Black Forest terrain grew hillier, the road rockier and more winding. Rarely could she see beyond the next curve, and steep slopes thickly forested with conifers loomed on all sides. The forests looked dark and downright somber. Was this gloom the reason this region was called the Black Forest? Once, they passed a mill, its enormous water wheel turned by a rushing stream. A few barefoot children were standing at the edge of the stream, poking the water with sticks as if they were looking for something. A short distance farther on, a resinous smoke suddenly filled the air. The two horses snorted and swung their heads from side to side with such force that they flung white spittle onto their sides. Fire! Josephine felt her stomach begin to knot and the old, familiar fear start to rise. She quickly pressed the sleeve of her jacket over her nose to escape the odor.

"A charcoal kiln," said her driver as he pointed to an enormous wooden dome covered in earth. "They make charcoal here for the glassblowers who work nearby. Goldsmiths and silversmiths use the charcoal, too, and several armorers get their supplies here." There was pride in the man's voice.

Soon, the forests thinned, and the road, still climbing, wound through more open country. Relieved to have escaped from the smell of the smoldering charcoal pile and the grim forests, Josephine closed her eyes.

"Wake up. We're here." The wagon driver stood beside her. He shook her roughly by the arm, then walked forward to tend to the horses.

For a moment, Josephine had no idea where she was. It had grown dark and streetlamps were burning. At the sight of the half-timbered houses, she remembered. Schömberg. The town in the Black Forest. The sanatorium. She had arrived.

While the driver set about retrieving her suitcase from the back of his wagon, Josephine looked at the large building in front of her. The words "Stag Guesthouse" stood out in large letters on a wooden sign attached directly beneath a gabled roof. Underneath hung a second sign made of metal that looked considerably younger than the first. "Schömberg Mountain-Air Sanatorium," Josephine read. So this was the sanatorium where she was to be cured of her cough. The place certainly looked inviting.

Josephine looked up the main street. The town was considerably larger than she had imagined. Numerous streets led off to the left and right, and Josephine spotted a church tower and several rooftops that obviously belonged to other large buildings. Could those be other sanatoria?

"Have a good rest, miss!" The driver tipped his hat then jumped back up to his seat.

Josephine watched the wagon roll away, then she picked up her case and walked up to her new quarters.

"This is your room!" The receptionist at the Schömberg Mountain-Air Sanatorium enthusiastically unlocked one of the doors in a row of ten or so rooms. "Mr. Roth, our caretaker—he's the one we received your registration from—said you would be quite satisfied with one of the smaller rooms."

Josephine stepped inside, her heart pounding. A smaller room? This was at least as big as her room at home! And much nicer and cozier, too. Beside a bed with pink-and-white checked linens was a table with a tablecloth of the same material and a chair; a large wardrobe and a washbasin occupied one wall. Everything was clean, tidy, and attractive.

"My own washbasin. I've never had such a luxury in my life," she said, her voice husky as she stroked her fingers almost reverently over the porcelain.

"A novelty for which we can only thank Hugo Römpler, the founder of the sanatorium. It is his belief that many diseases are, in fact, exacerbated by a lack of physical hygiene," the receptionist said, a note of pride in her voice. "Before this place was remodeled as a sanatorium, it was the Stag Guesthouse. The guests back then certainly did not have the luxury of a private washbasin, but Mr. Römpler saw the potential that the old Stag had to offer. He left the dining room and guest salon as they were." The woman pointed toward a door. "You'll find our library in there. We encourage our guests to choose whatever reading matter they might enjoy, because a cheerful spirit will hasten the healing process. The weather is still warm enough that you can even take a book and spend the day with it in our beautiful garden, if you like. Mr. Römpler brought in a gardener especially from Baden-Baden who transformed the old vegetable garden into a veritable oasis of calm, with benches for sitting and a pavilion. We even have a small lily pond! Isn't that marvelous? Look, Mr. Römpler had the garden lit in the evenings." The receptionist was clearly enjoying her presentation and pushed aside a checked curtain to show Josephine the view from the window.

"It really is quite lovely," said Josephine. For the first time in her life, she felt something like a joyful anticipation stir in her. A library. Reading books in the garden. And such a beautiful room . . .

She pointed to a long room directly below her window. "And what is that?"

"Our new extension. It houses the bath section. We have six tubs for hip baths, but we will only know tomorrow if they will be part of your convalescence here, after your medical examination." The receptionist frowned and looked at Josephine, then at the watch hanging on a chain around her neck, and she said, "My goodness, it's already so late! They'll be serving dinner in half an hour. But you still have time to freshen up a little before you come down for dinner."

"For dinner?" Josephine said with a squeaky voice. The pleasant feeling that had begun to spread inside her disappeared and gave way to a new and nervous rumbling in the region of her stomach that had nothing to do with hunger. The thought of meeting strangers with whom she was supposed to make conversation made her anxious.

"I'm not sure . . . I don't want to rush things . . . and I'm really not hungry."

"Don't worry. Everyone here is very nice and approachable." The receptionist laughed. "We are blessed with a particularly likeable group of guests at the moment. Although it's true that they're all older than you, our guests' afflictions and hope for recuperation are normally more than sufficient as a basis for conversation." She already had her hand on the doorknob when she stopped and turned to Josephine one last time.

"Oh, one thing I almost forgot . . . Here in the sanatorium, we use a special form of address. We don't go by Professor Suchandsuch or Director Soandso, let alone Countess of Whoknowswhere. Each of us thinks up a nice plain name for themselves, and otherwise we just use a friendly Sir or Madam. Though in your case, because you're still so terribly young, we'll go with Miss." A short pause followed. When Josephine said nothing, the receptionist spoke again. "What do they call you at home?"

With some trepidation, Josephine told the woman her name. *But that was on her registration form already, wasn't it?*

"And do you have any special nickname?"

"No. Well, my friend Clara sometimes calls me Josie."

"Josie." The receptionist let the name roll over her lips as if she were tasting wine. "Josie." She shook her head, then said firmly. "It doesn't suit you. It's much too sweet. We'll call you Jo."

"Jo?" Josephine let out a confused laugh. "But . . . isn't that a man's name?"

The woman flicked her hand dismissively. "Who cares? It's short and snappy and that can't hurt. My name's Roswitha, by the way." And even though she had already shaken hands with Josephine at the reception desk, she repeated the gesture now. "My dear Jo, welcome to Schömberg!"


Josephine could hear the clinking of cutlery and glasses from the hallway. The low buzz of voices was occasionally interrupted by laughter. Then she heard a hard, dry cough. Instantly, she felt a scratching in her own throat. She swallowed, a trick she had to subdue the urge to cough.

The aroma wafting from the dining room smelled delicious, like vegetable soup but also something sweet. Pancakes, perhaps? She was hungrier than she'd thought . . .

Summoning all her courage, Josephine entered the dining room. It was a square, wood-paneled room, its windows hung with the same pink-and-white checked curtains as those in her room. Most of the ten or twelve tables were already occupied. What now? Where was she supposed to—

Before she even had a chance to feel self-conscious, Roswitha was at her side.

"Ladies, gentlemen, allow me to introduce our new guest—Jo, from Berlin! She just arrived this evening."

Josephine gave the room a little curtsy and smiled timidly. Several guests raised their glasses in greeting, while others nodded pleasantly to her. One of the women didn't look up at all but went on writing incessantly in a small notebook.

"Your table is over here. You're sitting with Annabelle and Giuseppa."

A moment later, Josephine found herself sitting between two complete strangers, one of whom was the writer. A young girl with an apron set a bowl of soup on the table in front of her.

"Bon appétit! Nourishing meals are as important to recovery as the good air and medical attention," said the younger of the two women. "I'm Annabelle, and I've already been here for three weeks. You could say I'm an old hand by now!" A tired laugh brightened her haggard face for a moment. "If there's anything you want to know, just ask. Which room have they put you in?"

Before she knew it, Josephine had finished off the soup and was deep in conversation about the sanatorium, the Black Forest region, and Schömberg. Annabelle spoke with a strong Bavarian accent, so Josephine did not understand every word immediately. But it didn't matter. Only when she was back in her room did it occur to her that no one had talked about their diseases.

# Chapter Five

"Given your age and height, you could certainly stand to be a few pounds heavier and generally stronger, but it seems you don't have tuberculosis," said Dr. Homburger, one of the sanatorium doctors, after he had spent more than an hour auscultating, palpating, and interrogating Josephine. She had had to cough, hold her breath, and breathe again on command. She had had to run up and down the corridor until she was completely out of breath. Then the doctor had set his stethoscope on her chest and listened intently, his face set in a frown.

No one had ever examined her so thoroughly. Josephine was both impressed and intimidated.

"It's not whooping cough," said the doctor, making a note in Jo's file. "I could hear a light rattle but no threatening lung sounds. That gives me hope that your lungs have not been damaged. And you're not spitting blood. When did you say the coughing started?" Sharpened quill at the ready, he peered at Josephine.

"In the spring," she replied, looking back at the doctor, whose fine beard quivered slightly with every word. Dr. Homburger was extremely tall and thin with pale, almost transparent skin. He looked like the kind of person who spent most of his time in darkened rooms. Josephine thought he looked like he might have some kind of lung disease himself.

"That's a very long time. And the originating cause was a fire to which you were exposed. Did I understand that correctly?" He leafed through some documents and Josephine wondered where they had come from and whether they related to her.

She nodded. Before she knew it, she was shaken by a new coughing fit.

Dr. Homburger took his stethoscope and placed it against her back. "Strange," he murmured to himself once the coughing had subsided. He signaled to Josephine to follow him to a small, round table by the window. As he poured her a glass of water, he said, "We specialize here in the treatment of tuberculosis. I don't know what you know about the disease—what some people call *consumption* . . ."

Josephine shrugged. "In some quarters of Berlin, where people live very close together, an epidemic breaks out from time to time. At least, that's what I've heard. When that happens, the residents of the city's other neighborhoods are told to avoid going into the area. And if they *must* go there, they're told they should do so with a cloth over their faces and not shake hands with anyone who looks as if he might have consumption."

The doctor nodded. "In the past, tuberculosis was seen as a disease of artists or romantic souls, an image that still appeals to some of our guests." He laughed heartily. "But the fact of the matter is that consumption is mainly a curse of the poor these days. Until a few years ago, it was considered incurable. However, scientists now believe that recovery is possible, especially in places that are immune to the disease, meaning places where no case of consumption has ever been recorded. Schömberg, with its pure mountain air, was practically predestined to become a sanatorium village."

Josephine frowned. An immune place—how sterile that sounded. It seemed at odds with the lush greenery she could see outside the window.

"Tuberculosis continues to be highly contagious. The fact that you are *not* suffering from it means that the danger of infection represents an immediate and unnecessary risk for you, especially in light of your weakened condition. It would probably be for the best if I were to send you straight back home again . . ."

"Please don't!" Josephine looked at the doctor in horror. She had only just gotten used to the idea of spending some time in this strange and beautiful region. "How am I supposed to get well again if you send me away? No one can help me in Berlin. I've put all my hopes in this sanatorium. Please, I beg you!" When the doctor did not immediately reply, she went on, "I want to finally feel well again, to be free of the load crushing my chest so hard that I can barely breathe. I used to be strong, and I want to be strong again, but I don't have the slightest idea how to make that happen." She slumped in her seat, a picture of misery.

The doctor flicked through his paperwork again. When he looked up, he told her, "I see that your expenses have already been paid in advance for several weeks. Given that that is the case, perhaps we should do what we can."

Josephine nodded eagerly.

Dr. Homburger leaned back with a sigh. "All right then. We'll make an exception. But only if you stick to the most important rule of all."

Josephine nodded again. "What is it?"

"You must exercise the greatest of caution among our other patients. Tuberculosis is transferred by airborne droplets, meaning the liquid human beings spray into the air every time they sneeze or cough. So no hugging. Keep your distance at all times. Outside your room, you should keep a handkerchief over your nose and mouth at all times, and if someone should accidentally cough near you, turn and move away immediately."

Josephine nodded again; she was starting to feel like a nodding fool. If that was all there was to it . . .

"No resting on the balcony, and hip baths are out of the question. In both cases, our patients lie side by side," the doctor continued in a businesslike tone. "For your kind of cough, fresh air and light exercise are the best kinds of medicine. Take lots of walks! Around the village at first, and then, as you get your strength back, go out into the woods. With plenty of rest, a nourishing diet, and the Black Forest climate, we'll take care of your cough in no time. I will write out a plan for you, and I expect you to follow it to the letter. Have I made myself clear?"

Josephine cleared her throat. "I should take walks. To be honest . . . I've never just taken a walk. Not for exercise. Can you please tell me how that works?"

\*\*\*

In the following weeks, Josephine came to know something that she had never experienced before: leisure. And she came to know something else as well: herself.

The first time she set off for a walk, after a hearty breakfast, she felt rather strange. Walking around in the middle of the day, just like that! Doing nothing while everyone else was busy. She had retreated to her room after only half an hour. But on her next outing, her guilt lessened. There was so much to discover. Schömberg was a pretty place situated in a wild, natural landscape. It didn't matter that Josephine was a city child. She instinctively recognized the special character of the place and fell in love with it. She had no trouble walking—if her coughing became too harsh on a steep part of a track, she simply stopped and waited for it to pass. Apart from her cough, she was reasonably fit, which Josephine put down to her work in the smithy. As the days passed, she went out on longer and longer walks. Occasionally, she ran into one of the villagers or a woodsman cutting wood. If she happened to see one of the sanatorium guests, Josephine took another path. She did not want to stop and chat—not about God and the world, and certainly not about death.

As ordered by Dr. Homburger, she took long breaks between outings. She went to the library and read for hours—a new pastime for the girl who had practically never picked up a book at home. She was particularly taken by a novel by Gottfried Keller titled *Green Henry*. She felt she had found in young Henry a true kindred spirit. In the book, the young man is sent by his mother for an extended stay in the country, where events transpire that change the course of his life. During the more exciting passages, Josephine let the book sink into her lap and wondered whether she might follow a similar path. *Nonsense,* she would think, smiling. But now she finally understood the pleasure Frieda took in reading.

The reading also gave her a way to avoid getting pulled in to too many conversations. Dealing with the sick—and often incurable—guests was a burden for Josephine. She knew just how brutal and unkind death could be, and she wanted to keep her distance from it. So for the first time in her life, Josephine spent a great deal of time by herself, and she discovered in the process that she got along quite well on her own.

\*\*\*

It was December 31, 1889. The last decade of the century would begin in a few hours. All across the empire, people were taking time to reflect or look ahead. The newspapers were brimming with prognoses about a rosy future or bleak days ahead, depending on the mood of the writer and the position of the newspaper.

In the Schömberg sanatorium, too, a small New Year's Eve party was planned for that evening. While some of the guests decorated the dining room with paper roses and colorful streamers and the cook mixed a fruit punch, Josephine put on a coat, scarf, and cap and went out walking. A final stroll in the old year. But was she ready to look back on the past year? Perhaps up at the lookout in the forest. She always felt so lighthearted up there, and her thoughts practically flew up into the skies above.

Although it was only two thirty in the afternoon, the chill of dusk was already beginning to creep through the village. It had not yet snowed, but a thin layer of frost had settled over the whole region like icing. The snowless winter was a constant topic of conversation among the patients and employees of the sanatorium. According to Roswitha, there had been nothing like it in more than forty years.

Candles were burning in the windows of many houses, and Josephine wondered whether this was some special New Year's custom specific to the Black Forest. The smoke that spiraled from the chimneys and dissipated in the winter air smelled of pine needles.

Josephine stopped and gazed at one particularly stately house. No doubt a family was gathered peacefully inside . . . A gentle longing tugged at her. How was *her* family doing? Had Clara made the same pretty paper angels she had made the year before? And who was helping Frieda carry in the wood for her fire now that Josephine wasn't there to do it for her?

Hitching up her skirts, Josephine marched on toward the forest. She still had to stop occasionally on the steep slopes until her coughing subsided. Despite all her outings and the good Black Forest food and all the peace and quiet she enjoyed in Schömberg, her cough had not noticeably improved. Dr. Homburger now frowned in vague annoyance whenever he saw her, as if it were her fault that she had not yet recovered. But no one was more annoyed about it than Josephine herself.

She had just reached the first trees when she heard a crunching sound somewhere to her left. This was quickly followed by a swish and a grating crashing noise. Then a large shadow shot past so close that Josephine felt a rush of air as it passed.

A second later, the speeding shadow tumbled to the ground a few yards away.

Josephine gazed at the scene in shock: a young woman, her skirt disheveled, her face twisted in pain, lay bare-legged beside some kind of contraption made of wheels and metal rods.

"What in the world is that?"

But all she got in reply was a moan.

"Are you hurt? Can I help?" Josephine ran down to the young woman, who looked to be about Josephine's age, and tentatively reached out her hand. She had hair the color of wheat, which, now that she had lost her wool cap, fell in a tangle over her stunned face.

"It's all right," the girl groaned as she slowly pulled herself together and clambered to her feet. "It's not the first time I've fallen off. I just hope nothing's happened to the velocipede."

"The . . . what?"

"The velocipede. It belongs to Mr. Braun."

Josephine nodded, grateful for a piece of information that she could begin to understand.

"Mr. Braun is a businessman who comes here a few times a year. He doesn't just own the bicycle, he also owns the yellow house with the wrought-iron balcony, the last house on the street. You must have walked right past it. My father looks after the place when Mr. Braun's not here. I took the opportunity to borrow his velo," the girl explained as she pulled the strange machine up by one of its metal rods and scrutinized it thoroughly.

The thing that the girl had first called a velocipede and then a bicycle consisted of a curved, tubular-steel bar to which a seat was attached. It had two wheels, with the front wheel somewhat larger than the one at the back. Both wheels were considerably narrower than the wheels of a coach. They looked more like the wheels on the handcart of the milkman who plied his wares in Josephine's neighborhood back in Berlin. It looked very strange . . .

"The bicycle survived the crash just fine, and I'm not hurt. What about you?"

Josephine spread her arms out as if to say, *no harm done.*

The girl sighed with relief. "Thank God for that! If I'd crashed into you . . . But I couldn't have known that someone would be walking around here, and the bicycle doesn't have a brake, unfortunately. What are you doing out in the woods by yourself? You're staying at the sanatorium, aren't you? I've seen you marching through our village a few times now. I wanted to catch up and have a little chat, but you'd always disappeared by the time I got outside."

Josephine smiled and introduced herself.

"Jo? From Berlin? I thought so. You're the girl my great-aunt Frieda sent down here." The young woman tossed her hair, which just made it stand out even more wildly from her head. "I'm Lieselotte, but everyone just calls me Lilo."

Lilo's handshake was so hard that Josephine grimaced in pain.

"You're the daughter of Joachim Roth, our caretaker? I didn't even know he had any children. And Frieda never mentioned you, either . . ."

Lilo snorted in disgust. "Terrific. Just goes to show what they think of me. My father doesn't surprise me—he doesn't want me coming into contact with the sanatorium's sick guests." Lilo grabbed her bicycle and began pushing it down the hill. "And he doesn't know anything about this—so don't breathe a word of it!"

Josephine had to hurry to keep up with her. "I'm no snitch. But hold on a second. What *is* that thing? I've never seen anything like it. And what were you doing with it before you fell off? You were faster than lightning!"

Lilo stopped abruptly. "Are you kidding me? You come from Berlin, right? There must be tons of bicycles there. I just read in the newspaper about some women who were supposedly riding velocipedes in your city park. It seems the other people in the park pelted them with stones, and the man who wrote the article talked about a 'scandal for the female sex.' You didn't hear about that?"

"No, really, not a word. I . . . We don't read any newspapers at home. It's the first time I've seen such a . . . velo."

Lilo frowned, still skeptical. Then, in a more forgiving tone, she presented her vehicle. "This is a velocipede, also known as a pedal bicycle. You sit here on this saddle, then put one foot on each side, on these pedals. With your hands, you hold onto the handlebars, which you use to steer in whatever direction you want to ride. Pressing on the pedals sets the bicycle rolling. I believe it's faster than a horse. And *awfully* expensive, too," said Lilo, her eyes glowing with pride.

Josephine shook her head in disbelief. "But it's so narrow! Don't you fall over as soon as you're on the saddle?"

Lilo grinned. "Well, it takes a bit of skill and practice, of course. You have to keep both feet on the ground until you're ready to pedal, and then you have to get going very quickly. Come on, I'll show you!" She turned the contraption onto a level path that led into the forest.

Josephine watched in fascination as the strange girl lifted her skirt and stuffed as much material as possible beneath her rear end, which did not look very becoming at all . . .

Then the caretaker's daughter swung both feet up onto the pedals and began to turn them. With a labored and not very elegant motion, the bicycle started to move, and Josephine realized why Lilo had gone to such trouble with her skirt. She did not want to imagine what would happen if the material caught between the spokes of the wheel. The bicycle's wheels turned faster and faster, and before Josephine knew it, Lilo was out of sight around a curve.

She set off after her at a trot, but Lilo had already turned and was pedaling back. She was grinning from ear to ear, her blond hair billowing in the slipstream. She laughed and called out to Josephine, "Get out of the way, or I'll run into you after all!"

Lilo pedaled back and forth along the path another three or four times while Josephine watched, her heart pounding with excitement.

She wanted to try it herself. She *had* to try it herself! But when she asked Lilo if she could, the other girl shook her head.

"It isn't that easy. Riding a velo takes practice. Besides, I've never let anyone else try it, because it doesn't belong to me. What if something happened?"

"Nothing's going to happen. I'll be careful," Josephine replied. The longer she looked at the shining velocipede, the greater her desire to sit on its saddle grew.

"But I hardly even know you. You're probably one of those chatty girls who can't keep a secret. Then there'll be hell to pay. For me."

Josephine looked Lilo in the eye. "I swear by God above that I won't breathe a single word to a soul about this, ever, anywhere."

Lilo hesitated for a moment, then said, "All right. But tomorrow, not now. I have to get home soon. Let's meet again here tomorrow morning. And if you utter so much as a single traitorous word . . . !" She climbed back onto the bicycle, then rode off down the hillside without turning back.

Josephine lay awake for a long time that New Year's Eve. But it was not thoughts of the year before or the one ahead that kept her from falling asleep. And it was not her cough, nor her homesickness, that disturbed her rest. It was the thought of sitting on that bicycle the next day.


"Hold both hands tight on the handlebars. *Tight,* I said. And stop shaking like that. Now put your left foot on the left pedal."

Josephine laughed nervously as she followed Lilo's instructions. Her skirt was crushed into a wad beneath her, but despite the many layers of cloth, she felt the hardness of the saddle between her legs.

"I don't know . . ." She looked at Lilo in embarrassment. "Is it decent . . . sitting on this thing with my legs apart?"

Lilo laughed. "Do you want to try it sidesaddle? Like the fine ladies on their fine nags? I've tried it. It doesn't work. Either you do it like this or you don't do it at all." The firmness in her voice drove the last scraps of doubt out of Josephine's mind. She tensed the muscles in her thighs to get a better grip on the saddle. But as she did so, those same muscles began to tremble and—

"Look, no one's here to see us," Lilo practically shouted. "Focus on the path ahead of you, then go."

Josephine nodded uncertainly. The forest path that Lilo had used the day before to demonstrate the bicycle looked a lot narrower today. It had rained overnight, a cold rain that had frozen into a thin layer of ice in the higher parts of the forest. Josephine had slipped and almost fallen several times on her way here. Perhaps the conditions were not suitable for riding?

"As soon as you swing your foot up onto the right pedal, you have to start pushing. Go on!"

Josephine ordered her right foot to rise from the ground. Nothing happened.

"There's no need to be afraid. I'll be running alongside, holding you, so nothing can happen."

"I . . . don't know. I'm sitting so high. I'm going to fall over as soon as I lift my foot . . ." There was no way that petite Lilo would be able to hold her up.

"You won't fall over. I showed you how it works," said Lilo with touch of impatience.

Josephine nodded miserably. "I know, I know. But I don't trust myself." While her left foot rested on the pedal, her right remained on the ground as if it had put down roots.

"Then get off and let me ride. I don't get this opportunity often, either. I won't get to ride anymore once Mr. Braun comes back to Schömberg." Lilo was already reaching for the handlebars.

Josephine chewed her bottom lip. If she didn't trust herself now . . . she might never get another chance.

"Just a little ways, straight ahead, OK?" said Josephine, looking beseechingly at her new friend.

Lilo grinned. "Do you think I'd let you ride down the mountain on your first try? And riding around a corner is also an art. You won't master that the first time, either. Just go as far as that cluster of three trees up ahead, then stop pushing the pedals."

That didn't sound too difficult. Josephine took a deep breath, lifted her right foot, and set it on the right pedal. Now she had to be quick. *"Push, push, and don't stop pushing,"* Lilo had told her.

The bicycle started to wobble forward. With every turn of the wheels, the movement became more fluid.

"I think I can . . . do it!" Josephine laughed, moving her legs in vigorous rhythm.

"That's good. But hold the handlebars straight. You're all over the path!" Lilo ordered as she ran along beside Josephine.

"So what? That's why the path is there!" Josephine shouted. Then she let out a cry of joy. Elation filled her heart, her head, her entire body. "This is amazing! Lilo, I feel like I've grown wings."

"Crazy, isn't it? Now stop pushing on the pedals and you'll slow down," said Lilo.

"Slow down? What for?" Instead of following Lilo's instructions, Josephine pedaled harder and harder. She wanted to fly. She wanted to see the trees zooming past as if she were inside a train.

"Don't! Stop!" With the hand she'd been using to stabilize Josephine, Lilo now tugged at the handlebars. For a moment, Josephine almost lost her balance, but then she found her rhythm again.

"In a minute, just a bit farther . . ."

The last thing she wanted was to stop. She wanted to ride! To feel the slipstream, the icy prickling of the air against her cheeks, her hair lifted by the wind.

"Stop now, you silly fool! After the next curve the path starts to go downhill. It's much too danger—"

Before Josephine knew it, she was already in the bend in the path. The track, which had been going more or less straight through the trees just a moment earlier, now wound down to the village in a series of steep curves. *Oh my Lord, what now?*

From one second to the next, Josephine started gaining speed, and it was only with a huge effort that she managed to scrape around the first three or four curves. Handlebars left, right, farther right, left. Her feet were off the pedals and scraping desperately over the crusted surface, but they found no grip, and she slipped and slithered on. She was leaning far forward over the handlebars. She would soon go headfirst over the handlebars and . . .

"Lilo! Help!"

"Into the forest! Steer left! You have to turn the velo uphill!" Lilo's voice was shrill and frightened—and very far away.

Uphill? Left, right, left . . . Everything was going so fast, faster than Josephine could think. She saw trees everywhere and no way through. With a jerk, Josephine yanked the handlebars to the left. The front wheel slammed into a fir tree and she was flung over the handlebars and onto the forest floor, her cheek scraping the hard bark of the tree as she fell.

"Jo? Josephine?"

Someone was shaking her right arm. Searing flames shot through her skin. Groaning, she opened her eyes.

"Have you broken anything? Can you move your arms? And your legs?" Lilo bent down over Josephine's curled body, her eyes wide with dread.

Josephine moved her right foot first, gingerly, then her left. Her shoes were ruined, that much was clear. She had the metallic taste of blood on her tongue. All her limbs, especially her right arm, hurt. Her joints ached and her lower back felt like it might break in two, but otherwise . . .

Groaning, she pulled herself up until she could lean against the tree that had so brazenly stood in her path moments earlier. She looked at Lilo, eyes shining.

"Can I have another go?"

The bicycle was intact, aside from a scratch on the front of the frame that Lilo said she could hide with some paint from her father's workshop.

Josephine, who had so often struggled with God above, said a silent prayer of thanks that she had been so lucky.

Lilo was furious. She complained bitterly the whole way home, as she pushed the bicycle, and Josephine, dejected, hobbled along beside her. How could anyone be so senseless? Hadn't Lilo said loudly and clearly that Jo should ride more slowly? She had gone to all the trouble of giving Jo a riding lesson, and that was how Jo had repaid her?

The businessman's house, from which Lilo had "borrowed" the bicycle, was already in sight when Lilo suddenly stopped. She took a deep breath and grinned mischievously at Josephine.

"But it was fun, right?"

Back at the sanatorium, Josephine sneaked up to her room. She examined her shoes gloomily. They were positively shredded from her attempts to slow down. Thank God she had a second pair with her.

Next, she carefully washed her blood-smeared face. Her right shoulder still throbbed, the pain growing by the minute. What if she really had broken it?

"I slipped on some ice," she said to Sister Agatha, who immediately bent and twisted the arm in every direction and pronounced it to be nothing more than a sprain. Painful, certainly, but not as bad as a broken bone. An ointment bandage with comfrey would take care of the worst of the pain.

"Well, don't you know how to start off the new decade," said the nurse, at which Josephine burst out laughing. Sister Agatha could only shake her head in incomprehension.

The two young women met up again at Mr. Braun's house at the edge of the village the very next day.

"Can you even ride with your arm like that?" Lilo asked, pointing at the sling wrapped around Josephine's right arm.

Jo slipped her arm out of the sling. "I'm just wearing it to please Sister Agatha. It's fine," she said, suppressing a squeal of pain.

"I must be insane, letting you back on the velo after your last escapade," said Lilo, unlocking the shed in which the bicycle was stored. "But I'm telling you, from now on, we practice on level ground! I know a street where hardly anyone ever goes. It used to connect the village with a house in the hills, but the house has been empty for years. It's quite a ways out of town, but the road is perfect for riding."

Josephine didn't care, as long as she got to ride the bicycle again. As she pushed the heavy machine along the uneven country lane flanked by thick hedges, she thought about how wonderful the handlebars felt in her hands. So soft and round and heavy all at once.

"If you see a coach or someone out for a walk, put the velo down and we'll hide behind the hedge," said Lilo, who kept a constant lookout all around.

"Why don't you just ask Mr. Braun if you can borrow it now and then when he's away? I mean, it's just sitting there. Maybe he'll give you permission," said Josephine. Lilo's secretiveness made her so nervous that she cast a glance behind them every few steps as if the devil himself were breathing down their necks. But the harvested fields lay fallow and lonely in every direction, disturbed only occasionally by a crow flying up and cawing as the girls passed by.

Lilo looked at her in horror. "Are you mad? I'm a girl, in case you hadn't noticed."

"So what? What—"

"I told you what the newspaper said about women who ride bicycles. They're only meant for men and boys, not for us, *the weaker sex*." Her last words were heavily laced with sarcasm. "Mr. Braun would never, ever entrust his valuable vehicle to a girl. And what do you think would happen if I went pedaling through the village with my skirt all bundled up? They'd run me out of town."

Josephine laughed, certain that Lilo was exaggerating.

The lane they were following was icy and bumpy, and Josephine had to focus on steering the bicycle between the largest potholes. After walking along in silence for a while, Josephine said, "Where can you actually buy a machine like this? And how much would one cost? And when was it invented?" These questions—among many others—had been going through her head all night.

"How am I supposed to know all that?" Lilo replied. "Actually, I thought someone from the big city would know more about those kinds of things."

"I think you have the wrong impression of what life in the city is like," said Josephine, frowning. "Our neighborhood isn't all that different from a village. We've got a baker and a butcher and a general store where we can buy shoelaces. And I almost never leave." Then she changed the subject. "But how is it possible for you to just disappear like this for a few hours a day? Don't you have homework to do? Or chores? When I'm at home, there's always so much that needs to be done that I hardly have any time for myself. I really only have the visits to your great-aunt Frieda—I won't let anything keep me away from those."

Instead of answering Josephine's question, Lilo asked her to tell her more about the great-aunt she had only ever heard stories about.

Josephine obligingly described Frieda's garden, her many books, and her interest in God and the world. "Frieda has a new hobby every month. When I left to come here, she'd just taken up wood carving," she said.

"Interested in God and the world. That sounds nice," said Lilo. "My father has no particular interest in the world or in me. The only thing he cares about is his work. That's why I can do—or not do—whatever I like." She snapped a bare twig from a bush and broke it into little pieces. "When my mother was still alive, things were different. My father was the caretaker at the Stag before it was converted into a sanatorium, and it kept him very busy. But in the evenings, once the work was done, he was always there for Mother and me. He carved wooden horses for me and built a stall for them. He played hide-and-seek and blind man's bluff with me. And on my birthdays, he set up the barn so that my friends and I could jump down from the hay bales." Lilo smiled.

A shudder ran through Josephine at the mention of the word *barn*. She said, "Your mother died? I'm sorry."

Lilo nodded. "Four years ago. A cow kicked her in the stomach. The kick must have injured an internal organ. The doctor couldn't tell us exactly what it was, but Mother completely lost her appetite. She used to go about holding her stomach and complaining about the pain. She tried to keep up with her work, milking the cows and feeding the goats and sheep and so on. But one day we found her lying unconscious in the goat pen. She died six months later. The last weeks were terrible. She couldn't even get out of bed." Lilo took a deep breath. It seemed to Jo that it was still difficult for Lilo to talk about it. Shoulders sagging, she stopped walking.

Josephine laid her painful right arm around Lilo's shoulders. She knew only too well how Lilo felt.

"After the funeral, Father sold the herd and said that from then on, he would make his living only as a caretaker. So in addition to looking after the sanatorium, he took on the caretaking duties for some of the summer residents, like Mr. Braun. If he lost one job, he always had the other, and that was important because he wanted to look after me as well as he could." Lilo paused again and drew breath. "It all sounds very caring, doesn't it?"

"But it isn't?"

"You know, I look like my mother. My father says that when he looks at me, he sees her again as a young woman. And I don't think he can stand that. So he goes and buries himself in his work, all so he doesn't have to be anywhere near me." Lilo shrugged. "I don't think he even noticed that I finished school in the fall. All my school friends already have an apprenticeship or a job. Two of them are already engaged. But God alone knows what's to become of me."

Josephine laughed. "I know just what you mean. I don't have the slightest idea what to expect when I go home. My mother's probably found a maid's position for me. She and my father can hardly wait to be rid of me." Even as she spoke, she realized the old pain had faded just a little. Things simply were what they were. She had to accept that some things wouldn't change.

As though reading her mind, Lilo said, "What can you do? Life is what it is. And nothing's ever gotten better just by complaining about it. I'll start looking for a job after Epiphany. There's a new sanatorium opening in Schömberg. For the upper classes, they say. I'm sure they'll be able to use workers there. Who knows? Maybe I'll even become a nurse." Lilo's voice had returned to its usual cheerfulness.

Josephine looked at her new friend with admiration. "A nurse! That's quite a plan . . ."

"Don't you have plans? If not, you've only got yourself to blame," said Lilo. "For now though, I mostly do whatever I feel like. And you know what that is right now?" She hardly waited for Josephine to shake her head before she said, "Bicycle riding, as often as I can!" With a laugh, she took the handlebars from Josephine and pushed the machine onto the street.

The street was ideal for riding. Dead straight, it ran through the hilly landscape, the winter-weary fields and meadows.

Lilo, of course, wanted to ride first. Josephine watched as she flew down the road, growing smaller as the distance grew between them. She could not get over that it was possible to go so fast without sitting astride a horse. Or inside a train, itself a wonder of the modern age. Josephine furrowed her brow. Even if she saw it a thousand times with her own eyes, she somehow still could not believe it.

Josephine's second time on the bicycle went much more smoothly. As she set her second foot fearlessly on the pedal she even enjoyed the sensation of losing touch with the ground.

"Don't go getting up to any more tricks!" Lilo shouted after her as she started to roll away. Lilo had told her to ride only as far as an old linden tree with a bench around its base, then slow down and turn back, and Josephine had nodded obediently. The tree wasn't even visible from where they were, so she would get to ride a decent distance.

Press down on the left, then down on the right and left again—with every turn of the wheels, Josephine felt more secure. The air swept by, cool and refreshing on her cheeks. A few locks of hair came loose from her braid, fluttering in the wind like silken bands.

Winter was so quiet out here. So different from the city. She was alone, alone in an ocean of silence. And she could fly! Could fly away from everything. The faster she rode, the colder the wind against her face, the colder her hands, and the clearer her thoughts.

Her little brother was dead. Nothing and no one on this earth would ever bring him back to life. But she was alive! She had legs that could drive the pedals hard and hands that could hold tightly to the handlebars. Felix would never get to experience this sensation. Didn't she owe it to him to keep breathing, to keep living, for herself, as well as for him? Didn't she owe it to him to do all the things that he no longer could?

Life lay ahead of her like this road. A little bumpy and stony, but full of promise and excitement. Maybe she would even have plans of her own, like Lilo.

The muscles in Josephine's thighs burned as she turned the pedals more and more quickly. She was free! She could ride away from all the sadness in her life.

Josephine squinted hard against the wind and tears ran down her face, cleansing her of all her sins. A roaring began in her ears and her lungs burned, but she did not cough, did not feel even the slightest need to clear her throat.

Who had she been wanting to chastise all this time? God, perhaps, for letting her survive? Shouldn't she be thanking him instead? After all, the fire had almost engulfed her as well. But she had escaped.

Faster, faster, fly away! The linden with the bench was already in sight when the iron clamp that had been crushing Josephine's chest for so long finally gave way. With a wail of redemption and release, Josephine cried, "I'm still alive!"

\*\*\*

Her coughing abated. Her body and her spirit healed. When she looked at her face in the mirror above the washbasin, she was amazed at how much it had changed. Her cheeks were a rosy pink—the locals called them "apple cheeks." Her skin had developed a healthy glow, and her hair, which shone like gold straw, was a hand longer than when she had arrived. Now she could style it into a lovely, long braid. Her lips were full and as red as if she was wearing lipstick. Her body had changed, too. Thanks to all the good food at the sanatorium, she had gained weight, which had developed into beautiful, feminine curves that Jo had never before seen on herself. In the sanatorium, she had finally come to know her own body for the first time. When she had first arrived, she had known only that she had two legs for walking, two arms for working, and a strong back. Now, she discovered that her skin had taken on a mother-of-pearl sheen. And that her nipples were pink, and they crinkled when she touched them. She was young. And she was pretty.

*\*\*\**

On April 4, 1890, Josephine was declared to be cured, and she was discharged from the sanatorium.

Sister Agatha, Roswitha, and some of the patients gathered in front of the Stag to wave good-bye to her. With eyes both smiling and weeping, Josephine gave them small gifts that she had bought in the village. Lilo was not there. "I hate good-byes," she had said.

A few hours later, Josephine was sitting on a train, heading toward Berlin, watching the treetops of the Black Forest diminish in the distance. What a wonderful time she had had in Schömberg! How well, how deeply, she had come to know the unique landscape and its clean air.

Josephine thought of Lilo and smiled. They had promised to write to each other at least once a month. And Lilo wanted to visit her in Berlin, perhaps as soon as that summer.

# Chapter Six

In lieu of a greeting, her mother had stayed at the sink and said, "Let's get one thing straight. As of this minute, your life of indolence is over. Now that you're no longer in school, you'll help your father in the smithy. After all that's happened, this is the least we can expect from you."

Josephine set her suitcase on the floor and looked at her mother in dismay. "But I thought you would find a job for me, just as you did for Margaret and Gundel." She wanted to earn money. Her *own* money.

"A position for the little miss?" her mother snorted. "Maybe in some fine household where you can lie in a warm bed until seven every morning and finish work at seven every day—is that what you were thinking? Haven't you had enough of being idle?" Without another word, her mother picked up a basket of laundry and disappeared into the backyard.

*What a welcome,* thought Josephine as she unpacked her case. Her mother had not asked her a single question about the trip or about her health. Angry and disappointed, Jo took the Black Forest ham that Joachim Roth had given her to bring to Frieda, and she left the house.

She rang the bell at the Berg family's house first. The door flew open a few seconds later.

"Josie! Finally! I've been waiting for you all morning," Clara cried. "Oh, I missed you so much! Berlin was so miserably dull without you." They fell into each other's arms before Josephine even made it inside.

"You look wonderful, really revived. Your skin is downright glowing. And your hair, too. Watch out, or I'll get jealous! The sanatorium seems to have done you a great deal of good." Clara stroked Josephine's cheek and hair in admiration. "Dear Josie . . ."

A pleasant feeling surfaced in Josephine at that moment. It was good to be home after all. "Let's go visit Frieda, then I won't have to tell everything twice," she said and hooked Clara's arm in hers.

"What is Schömberg like?"

"How did you fare down there?"

"Did you make any friends? With Lieselotte? How wonderful!"

"How did they cure your cough?"

Frieda and Clara peppered her with a thousand questions, and Josephine happily answered all of them as they sat in Frieda's kitchen and tried the ham Josephine had brought back.

Old Frieda was particularly impressed that Lieselotte and Josephine had been riding a man's bicycle.

"I would have been up for an adventure like that myself, in my younger years," she said. "These days, I have to content myself with other hobbies." She gestured toward a pile of colorful cards on the table.

Reading cards . . . Josephine smiled at Frieda's new passion. How long would this one last? Then, brazenly, she said, "How do you know you're too old to ride a bicycle if you've never tried? You could buy a bicycle, then—"

"You'd love that, wouldn't you?" Frieda broke in, laughing. "Riding a bicycle is *your* dream, not mine."

Josephine looked at her aging friend. "How did you know that? It really is my greatest dream to one day have a bicycle of my own."

"What a crazy notion . . . but that's what I like about you, my child. Dreams are as important as the air we breathe, I always say. When I was younger, there was no room for dreams. So I grant myself a few *smaller* ones now." She fell silent for a moment. "But you're still young, and the world is yours. And do you know what's even better than dreaming?" Frieda's eyes sparkled mischievously.

Josephine looked at her curiously.

"Making your dreams come true. That, of course, takes some doing . . ."

"But that's just what I was planning to do," said Josephine. "I wanted to put aside every penny I could earn as a maid and save until I had enough for my own bicycle. But my mother's just announced that I have to work in the smithy, and I won't get a penny for it, that much is certain."

"Maid! Smithy boy!" Frieda sighed. "I tried so hard to convince your mother to send you to a secondary school for girls, so you could keep studying."

A secondary school for girls? *That wouldn't help much,* Josephine thought, but she said nothing.

"I think you'd be better off dropping this whole bicycle-riding business," said Clara, who had followed the conversation in silence up to that point. "It's really very dangerous. We constantly have gentlemen coming into the pharmacy asking for ointment and bandages because they've fallen off their boneshakers and opened up their knees or their noses. The Beiersdorf company must be rich off the money we make selling their bandages."

"You make it sound like Berlin's streets are teeming with bicycles. I haven't seen a single one," said Josephine.

"It's becoming more and more popular," Clara replied. "My mother thinks riding bicycles is terribly chic. Would you believe that she actually wants my father to buy one for us?"

"Well? Is he going to?" asked Josephine, sensing an opportunity. Riding bicycles in Berlin was suddenly *chic*?

"My father? Never! For one thing, he says a bicycle is horribly expensive. Second, you have to drive a long way to even be *able* to buy one. And third, he doesn't have time for such a hobby. Besides, hobbies are only for rich people with time on their hands, like Moritz Herrenhus, who owns the clothing factory. *He* has a bicycle."

"Moritz Herrenhus? The father of Isabelle, the girl with the red hair?" Josephine's eyes widened.

Clara nodded. "That's the one. Strange, I haven't thought about Isabelle for ages . . . I don't even know whether she still lives at home. They may have shipped her off to some genteel boarding school by now, perhaps even overseas?"

Isabelle Herrenhus was a year older than they were. Many years earlier, when they were all little and Moritz Herrenhus's factory was still new, she was always out with the other children in the street. They had played hide-and-seek, hopscotch, and tag. Often, they had teased pale, red-haired Isabelle. "Witch girl!" they cried at her. And, "Show us your broom!" And they had laughed whenever they succeeded in making the girl cry. Eventually, a high white wall appeared around the family's villa. And Isabelle disappeared. No one missed her much, and the children's games simply went on without her.

"After church this morning I saw Moritz Herrenhus riding in Schlesischer Busch. He cycles the way other rich men play hockey or tennis. The way they show off with their boneshakers, it's positively embarrassing," said Clara.

Boneshaker. It was the second time Clara had used the word. Josephine would have to mention it in her next letter to Lilo!

She sighed yearningly.

"Oh, you can't imagine the feeling of freedom it gives you! The speed . . . It's like you're flying. And it's not that dangerous. I simply must find a way to ride one again."

"Are you mad? Don't you know what the papers are saying about women who ride bicycles? They're all talking about how they're corrupting the morals of the female sex."

"Lilo told me about that, but I didn't want to believe it . . ." said Josephine.

"One needn't put too much store in everything they write in the newspapers," said Frieda. "The young women in question, if you ask me, were not particularly smart when they decided to ride through the Tiergarten. If they had ventured out into the open countryside, they could have had their fun and no one would have taken any notice."

Clara frowned, but Josephine nodded enthusiastically. "Exactly! Lilo was always careful to ensure that the coast was clear."

Frieda laughed. "I'm liking that girl more and more. I hope they're able to visit this year. I've invited her and her father so many times, but nothing has ever come of it."

"Isabelle's father . . ." said Josephine slowly. "Do you think he'd let me have a look at his bicycle?"

"Josie, you can't just walk up to his villa and knock on the door, not for something like that," Clara said, appalled at the thought.

"And why not?" Josephine said, lifting her chin.

"Because . . . because . . ." Clara looked to Frieda, but Frieda said, "It's worth a try. Why don't you two just go by and see if Isabelle is home? She might be happy to see you again after all these years."

"We'll do it!" said Josephine, then cleared her throat. "And there's one more thing . . . From now on, could you call me Jo?"

# Chapter Seven

Josephine paused as she was about to ring the bell. Wasn't it a bit rude to show up at Isabelle's house after all these years? And with such an unusual request?

"Let's just go," said Clara and plucked at Josephine's sleeve.

But Josephine was already ringing the bell, and a moment later came the melodic sound of bells from inside.

The heavy, carved door opened, and an attractive young woman stood before them, wearing a daffodil-yellow dress with matching gloves and hat. Could that possibly be Isabelle?

"Oh, I thought . . ." the young woman began, then hesitated. "Who are you?"

"We . . . uh . . . My name's Josephine and this is Clara," said Jo, her voice suddenly husky. "Do you remember us? From before? We played together when we were kids . . ."

Isabelle narrowed her eyes and looked at Josephine. "Of course I do! Weren't you part of the mob that was always teasing me about my red hair?"

"Actually . . . I don't remember that," Jo stammered. "Your hair is gorgeous!" she added, and she meant it. She had never seen such elaborately styled hair before. With her glittering combs and artfully set curls, she was a match for any bride . . . and a thought occurred to Josephine. "You . . . are so beautiful. You're not getting married, are you?"

Isabelle laughed in confusion. "Nonsense! What makes you think that?" She smoothed an invisible wrinkle from her silken dress and then said, "But I do have a date. When the bell rang, I thought you were my gentleman caller." She didn't sound particularly happy.

"A date?" asked Clara, who had stayed in the background until then. "I'd love to have one of those, but my mother thinks I'm still too young. And besides, no one's ever been interested in me." She frowned. "We didn't want to disturb you. Come on, Jo."

"No, please, stay!" said Isabelle quickly. "The gentleman who's supposed to pick me up is exceptionally wealthy and not bad looking. But honestly, he's as dull as dishwater. My father thinks the world of him, but I would much rather spend the afternoon with you." Her eyes flashed adventurously, and she clapped her hands. "So, why are you here?"

"This way. We have to go to the shed at the far end of the grounds," said Isabelle, striding across the white-gravel yard without the slightest consideration for her yellow shoes. She seemed to find nothing strange in Josephine's request.

"But . . . what if the young man wants to collect you and you're not there? You'll get in trouble," said Clara warily.

Josephine gave her a dark look. The last thing she wanted was for Isabelle to change her mind.

But Isabelle just laughed. "I'll tell my parents the truth, plain and simple. Namely that two old friends paid me a visit and I was so caught up in our lively conversation that I lost track of the time. So, here we are. This is where my father keeps his latest toy." She turned the handle on the shed door, and it swung open with a high-pitched shriek. In the center of the room, lit by sunlight coming through the windows, stood her father's bicycle, shimmering silver and smelling of rubber and lubricating oil.

Her eyes wide and shining, Josephine stepped toward it. She ran her hands reverently over the handlebars, the tubes that connected the two wheels, and the saddle, as if she wanted to absorb through her fingers its every curve and angle and memorize them forever.

"It's beautiful. Much sleeker and lighter than Lilo's bicycle." Josephine crouched and inspected the vehicle. "On Lilo's velocipede, the front wheel is bigger than the back wheel. And it didn't have a chain like this; it had pedals up front. How does this bicycle work, I wonder . . . ?"

"And just who is this Lilo? Does she also live on our street? I can't remember her at all," said Isabelle. "But I know someone else who's interested in bicycles. One of my schoolmates, Irene, rides one. Her last little outing wasn't very well received, to be sure—" Isabelle broke off as a heavy shadow darkened the doorway.

"Can someone please explain to me what is going on here?"

"Father . . ."

"Isabelle! Haven't I told you that my bicycle is off-limits? What are you doing here? Graf von Kyrill is waiting for you in front of the house with his four-in-hand carriage," he snapped.

But before Isabelle—who had turned chalk white—could reply, Josephine said, "Pardon me, but it is not Isabelle's fault. I had begged her to show me your bicycle for so long that in the end she simply had no choice. It is beautiful . . . Thank you for allowing me to look at it." She reached out her hand to Moritz Herrenhus and was amazed to see him actually accept her gesture. He eyed her soberly.

"I know you! You're Schmied-the-Smith's daughter, aren't you?"

Josephine nodded without taking her eyes off his.

"That's a good one! The smith's daughter is interested in my bicycle!" he said and laughed, instantly mollified. It seemed that Graf von Kyrill was forgotten, at least for the moment.

Josephine and Clara exchanged a look.

"What do you mean?" asked Isabelle.

Her father made a sweeping gesture with his hand, taking in the entire storage shed around them.

"Do you see any hay or straw in here? Or stable boys? Any expensive tack or dubbin or horse balsam? No. And why don't you see these things? Because they aren't needed for a bicycle. A bicycle is considerably easier to look after than a horse, and for that reason also cheaper in the long run. I'm telling you, in a few years we won't be seeing any horses on the streets anymore, and in their place will be bicycles. Getting around on horseback will be a thing of the past. Bicycles are the future. Your father will soon be able to close his smithy . . ."

"The bicycle replacing the horse? Never," Josephine blurted. "They're much too expensive. Only rich people like you can afford them."

"For now. But that will change, take my word for it. Once the demand is there, the supply will increase. And the bicycle makers will adjust their prices downward. Besides, it's not as though everyone can afford a horse, either." He crossed his arms and said, "But how is it that a young woman like you has such a deep interest in a novelty like this?"

Josephine shrugged. "I . . . In the Black Forest, where I went to convalesce recently, there was also a bicycle. The pedals were on the front wheel and it looked much different from this one. I was very taken by it. And when I discovered that you were also the proud owner of such a marvel, I simply *had* to see it." She ran her hand reverently over the handlebars once more.

Isabelle's father nodded benevolently. "You have rightly recognized that this is, in fact, a particularly advanced model." He dropped into a crouch, just as Josephine had done earlier, and gestured toward it.

"This bicycle is what they call a Rover, the latest and best bicycle available on the market. It's driven by the rear wheel. The pedals are connected to the rear wheel by the chain, as you can see here. This allows riders to choose the gear ratio that suits them best, which you never used to be able to do."

"Gear ratio . . . What does that mean, exactly?"

Moritz Herrenhus smiled. "Until now, bicycles have had a very large front wheel to which the pedals were attached directly. The size of the front wheel determined the distance traveled for each turn of the pedals. With the Rover, the size of the drive wheel no longer makes any difference, which is why the front and rear wheels are the same size. Instead, the two cogs—here at the pedals and here at the rear wheel—determine how far each rotation of the pedals propels you forward. Depending on their size, a rider can increase or decrease the distance per revolution. We can thank the Englishman Harry Lawson for this invention. With the support of his friend, an industrialist by the name of J. K. Starley, he created the first so-called 'safety bicycle.' This one is called the Rover Safety because it is far safer than any high-wheel bicycles, which are highly prone to accidents."

Moritz Herrenhus pulled off his jacket. Then he put his cuff links aside, rolled up his sleeves, and said, "I'll give you a little demonstration, if you like." He pushed the bicycle out of the shed and rode several laps around the yard.

Josephine watched, enraptured. This bicycle was so fast, so nimble! The crunching of the rubber tires on the gravel sounded like the most beautiful music. Her toes began to tingle, and a restlessness spread through her entire body. She would have given anything to be able to ride a lap on the bicycle herself.

With a final turn, Isabelle's father pulled up in front of the trio of girls. His fine vest was stretched tight across his back, his sleeves were crumpled, and his calf's-leather shoes were covered in dust, but he didn't seem bothered in the slightest. With a gesture more appropriate to a young man than to a reputable businessman, he swept a lock of hair out of his face and said, "Pretty impressive, eh?"

Isabelle pressed her lips together and held her tongue.

"Your Rover is so maneuverable," said Josephine. *Rover Safety.* The name tasted sweeter in her mouth than caramel. "You're an excellent cycler," she added, when she saw Mr. Herrenhus's expectant face.

"You rode a bicycle? You must be mad," Clara whispered to Josephine. Then, aloud and with a trace of reproach, she said, "I think it looks awfully dangerous."

Moritz Herrenhus dismounted stiffly just as the honey-colored sun was disappearing behind the white walls surrounding the yard. All of a sudden, the air felt cooler.

"Dangerous? Well, it depends. Cycling—once you've mastered it—is actually quite harmless. It only becomes dangerous on a busy street. Just yesterday, I was nearly run down by a carriage, and I was as far to the right as I could possibly be. The driver seemed to find fun in forcing me off the road. The carriage drivers are at loggerheads with the cyclers, that's a fact. They claim that their horses shy at the sight of us. Admittedly, some cyclers ride down the middle of the street, and some endanger themselves and others with daredevil stunts. Just the other day, I encountered a young man in the Tiergarten who wanted to make a race of it. When I didn't go for it, he decided to show me that he could let go of the handlebars as he rode and promptly took a header. But you can't throw all wheelmen into one pot just because of people like that."

Josephine hung on every word. If the carriage drivers were complaining, then riding bicycles was far more widespread in Berlin than she had thought!

Suddenly, a shrill whistle sounded, scaring up some birds in a blooming forsythia bush and making Clara jump, too.

Josephine looked toward the factory. Everything had been so quiet, but now she heard the groaning of machines and the clang of iron on iron. Gray smoke began rising from one of the chimneys.

Moritz Herrenhus cast a glance at his gold pocket watch. "The Sunday afternoon shift," he said.

Ignoring the din, Isabelle spoke up. "If a bicycle caused our horses to shy while Mother and I were sitting inside our coach, you wouldn't like it, either. Maybe bicycles should simply be banned from the streets?"

"Rubbish!" Moritz Herrenhus practically shouted, turning on his daughter. "I'm delighted that cycling is once again permitted in Berlin. It was prohibited as recently as 1858. Even today, one has to follow countless rules, many of which I consider to be ridiculous. And you have to have a license." Not without a touch of pride, he withdrew a small piece of paper from his breast pocket and opened it.

"Velocipede License for Mr. Moritz Herrenhus," Josephine read from the right-hand side of the license. On the left stood the date of issue and the name of the local authority that had issued it.

Josephine swallowed. Angry coachmen, cycling licenses—riding a bicycle in the city seemed considerably more complicated here than in the sparsely populated Black Forest.

The businessman was about to push his machine back into the shed when Josephine summoned up all her courage and said, "May I . . . be permitted a brief turn as well?" Her own courage almost made her dizzy.

"You? Ride my bicycle?" For a moment, Moritz Herrenhus seemed at a loss for words. Isabelle and Clara could only look on, aghast.

"It's late," Clara finally managed to whisper. "And it's getting cold. Come, let's go home."

Ignoring her friend, Josephine quickly continued, "I was allowed to do it in the Black Forest. Don't worry, I won't damage it."

"Cycling is no sport for young women," said Moritz Herrenhus sternly.

"Oh, Father, there you're mistaken," said Isabelle in a tone sweeter than sugar. "My friend Irene rides a bicycle. She borrows it from her brother."

"Irene Neumann? The daughter of Gottlieb Neumann, owner of the Elektronische Werke Berlin?"

Isabelle nodded. "Irene told me about it just this afternoon. She says it's good to break with convention now and then."

The businessman scowled. "Break with convention? I can't imagine Gottlieb would be pleased about that. The man's as stiff as if he swallowed a walking stick."

The girls suppressed a giggle. Adults rarely spoke like that around them.

"Well, I doubt that Gottlieb Neumann knows everything his daughter gets up to," said Isabelle. "Irene probably borrows Adrian's bicycle *secretly*. So she's not exactly flaunting convention." She gave her father a challenging look. "But if *you* were to allow Josephine to try your bicycle *officially*, that would truly be progressive!"

Moritz Herrenhus eyed his daughter suspiciously. Then he squared his shoulders and blustered, "My sentiments exactly! It is *my* bicycle, and *I* decide who may or may not ride it. I don't care a jot if the rest of the world likes it or not. Come on, I'll help you mount up." And he held his hand out to Josephine.

In the golden light of the setting sun, Josephine swung one leg over the bar of the Rover Safety, then she bundled her skirt—already mended in several places—and pushed it along with her petticoat beneath her rump.

Clara let out a gasp at the sight of Josephine's stockinged legs. She stepped forward and began frantically arranging Josephine's skirt back over her legs.

"One has to be very careful not to let the material catch in the spokes," Josephine said, pushing the skirt back up a little higher. She looked at Moritz Herrenhus and shrugged apologetically.

But Isabelle's father just laughed. "It's no sport for a young woman, as I said. But no one will see you here." Then he nodded to Josephine. "Now show us what you learned down in the Black Forest. I'll brace you as you ride." He took a step toward the bicycle, but before he could even reach out to support her, she pedaled away without him.

"I don't believe it." Moritz Herrenhus could only look on in astonishment as Josephine confidently steered his bicycle around the yard.

"The girl rides like a man! The strength, the physical control . . ."

"But what if she falls and breaks something?" murmured Clara, wringing her hands helplessly.

"Can't you see that your friend can ride like the devil? Or better!" said Isabelle, who was also watching in disbelief. "She's not about to fall."

Josephine grinned from ear to ear. It was so good to be back on a bicycle!

"Excellent, Josephine. Phenomenal! If you lean a little farther forward, you'll find it even easier to keep your balance. Yes, just like that." Moritz Herrenhus clapped appreciatively. Turning to Isabelle, he said, "Your friend is a real natural talent."

As Josephine rode past the small group again, Isabelle stepped directly in her path. With an abrupt hop, Josephine jumped off the bicycle, the front wheel spraying small gravel stones.

"What the . . . ?" her father snapped at his daughter. "A bicycle has no brake. Josephine almost crashed because of you."

"Sorry," said Isabelle indifferently. "But now that she's had her turn, how would you like to let me try it? I may not be a *natural talent*"—she pronounced the words as if they were an insult—"but with a little help and some practice, I'm sure I'll get it."

***

That day marked the beginning of a friendship, one that each of the girls—not to mention the people around them—saw very differently.

Isabelle's mother found it rather disconcerting that her daughter was now associating with two "street girls," as she put it. But because Moritz Herrenhus tolerated Isabelle's friendship with the pharmacist's and the smith's daughters, she could not really say much against it. As long as Isabelle did not neglect her numerous other duties—her secondary-school studies, her dance and ballet lessons, and her language and etiquette classes—she was quite welcome to ride a few laps in the yard with the bicycle, he said. Besides, he enjoyed demonstrating his Rover to the young women and keeping them up to date about the world of cycling.

Isabelle was happy to have found in Josephine and Clara two uncomplicated friends with whom she did not feel the constant need to strive upward, as she did with all her schoolmates—who were all the daughters of diplomats, or from aristocratic circles, or whose fathers were from the officer classes or captains of industry. Compared to any of them, her father was a little fish among sharks, and they all made sure she knew it. All that aside, Isabelle had also developed a desire to outshine Josephine on the bicycle. Cycling was a lot of fun for her, as well.

For Clara, who attended and loathed the home-economics school, riding bicycles made no sense at all. She was frankly afraid of the machine and quite satisfied to simply watch the others ride. Her mother, however, was overjoyed at Clara's newfound friendship with the wealthy factory owner's daughter. She dreamed of Clara finding her way into the upper circles of Berlin society and someday finding herself an affluent husband there. She did not know that the girls met to ride Mr. Herrenhus's bicycle. If she had, she would probably have fainted from fear for Clara's health.

Josephine was simply happy. She had not dared to hope that her dream of riding a bicycle in Berlin would come true so quickly. Although Herrenhus's backyard hardly compared to the wide-open roads of the Black Forest, it was better than nothing. She did not tell her parents anything of what she did in the evenings when she was done with her work, as they would have put an end to it immediately.

Only Frieda was allowed to know. Josephine went on and on to her about Moritz Herrenhus's generosity and his knowledge of bicycles and cycling sports. She would never have found out otherwise that cycling schools—and even dedicated cycling paths—existed.

***

Several weeks after riding Moritz Herrenhus's bicycle for the first time, Josephine made her way along Görlitzer Strasse toward Frieda's house. Although the sun still shone from a brilliant blue sky, most of the street already lay in shadow. A balmy breeze whirled scraps of paper through the air, which smelled of machine oil and sweet, rotting trash. Josephine nodded to the neighbor digging weeds out of her tiny vegetable garden in an attempt to give the beans and kohlrabi half a chance of ripening in the scant summer sunlight filtering down between the houses. Young girls with swinging skirts and ruffled hairbands strolled arm in arm toward Schlesischer Busch Park while the young men still stood at the entrances to their homes and brushed the day's dirt from their shoes. A few whistled at Josephine as she passed, which she ignored with a smile. It was summer.

Frieda, too, was out in her garden, although she was not digging up a vegetable garden. She was digging a grave.

"It flew into my kitchen window, the silly thing," she said and gestured with her chin toward a blackbird lying dead on an old handkerchief, its claws outstretched. Sweat glistened on the old woman's forehead, and her face was flushed with exertion.

Josephine kneeled beside her, took the trowel, and dug deeper. The earth was dry and crumbly, the going tough. When the little grave was big enough, she laid the handkerchief and bird together inside, then shoveled the excavated earth back over the top. She marked a cross in the earth with the tip of her forefinger.

For a moment, Frieda stayed on her knees in silent prayer. Then she climbed to her feet with some difficulty before Josephine could help her up.

"I was beginning to think you'd forgotten all about me, what with all your bicycle riding." A warm embrace followed, then the old woman pulled a letter from the pocket of her apron. "Lieselotte is coming next week. Isn't that wonderful?"

"She wrote to me, too," said Josephine. "I can hardly wait to see her again. She'll be amazed when I show her Moritz Herrenhus's Rover! Oh, I'm so infinitely grateful to him for letting me ride it, even if it's only in his yard. He keeps telling us that there'll be hell to pay if he ever catches us out on Berlin's streets." She was smiling as she followed Frieda to her table in the garden, although her thoughts were already moving on to the Herrenhus villa.

"*Infinitely grateful?* I'm sure the great Moritz Herrenhus likes that. He loves being adored, that man, and if it's a young, pretty girl like you doing the adoring . . ." Frieda set a plate of gooseberries on the table.

Josephine glared at Frieda. "Isabelle's father is a gentleman. Those hours on the bicycle mean the world to me. I'd have gone crazy in the smithy by now if it weren't for that. It's always so dark and dusty in there. Do you have any idea how dreary it is? One old plug after another, from morning to night, the same routine. Holding the hooves, front right, front left, back right, back left. Then there's the monotonous banging of iron on the anvil, and the shushing sounds you have to make to calm the horses—sometimes I fear I'll go mad! And the pain in your back and your arms after the fourth or fifth horse . . ."

"Why don't you look for a job that you actually enjoy?" Frieda asked, as if it were the most obvious thing in the world.

Josephine lifted her hands in resignation. "I can't just leave my parents in the lurch."

88

"Can't you? Are you just going to let your father bark orders at you for the rest of your life? Let him slap you around like some idiot apprentice? You're young and you're smart. Do you really want to spend the rest of your days holding onto horses' hooves and sweeping up their shit?"

How did Frieda know her father slapped her? Josephine shrugged. "As long as I can still ride the bicycle . . ."

"And what about your dream of owning your own bicycle one day?"

"The tips I get from the coachmen will never add up to enough for such an extravagance. But the cyclers will eventually win out over the horses—at least that's what Moritz Herrenhus says. And then bicycles will become much more affordable. Can you believe there are already cycling schools? And Mr. Herrenhus says the demand is huge. Gentlemen practice their riding in large halls away from the wind and the weather. A cycling instructor watches over everything, and there are assistants to help, as well. He didn't say anything about women practicing there. But regardless, bicycles seem to be getting more and more popular."

"Quite frankly, dear, I don't care," said Frieda. "But what I do care about is you. And the fact that you are doing nothing with your life."

Josephine popped a gooseberry into her mouth and frowned. "You're being far too pessimistic. Some unimagined opportunity might be looming just around the corner," she added, but only for Frieda's benefit. She herself did not believe any such thing.

Frieda reached across the table and took Josephine's hand in hers. "Even if riding a bicycle means a great deal to you, you must listen to me: don't let yourself be blinded! All that glitters is not gold, they say, and it's true. Moritz Herrenhus might well talk up how progressive he is to you young things, but he rules his clothing factory like an old general. The seamstresses aren't allowed to make so much as a peep while they work, and woe betide them if he catches any of them actually chatting. They're only permitted to go to the ladies' room twice a day, and as far as I can tell they have no meal break at all. It's hot inside that factory and hard to breathe with all the fluff flying around, but they're forbidden to open the windows. Herrenhus is apparently afraid someone might smuggle out a piece of his valuable cloth! Tell me now, how progressive is that?" Frieda gazed piercingly at her.

Josephine said nothing. As far as she was concerned, the workers were better off staying inside their factory. She was terrified that one of them might look out and see her on the bicycle in Isabelle's garden. What if one of them snitched to her father? She could kiss the cycling good-bye.

"And you can well imagine that none of them would dare complain about the working conditions or suggest any improvements!"

Josephine sniffed. "Have the neighbors been crying on your shoulder again? Do you think my 'working conditions' are any better? I'd be happy to work for a gentleman like Moritz Herrenhus. At least I'd get a wage for all my toil. Oh, you have no idea!" She stood up then and left without saying good-bye.

The last thing she needed was to waste her precious free time listening to speeches from Frieda. Herrenhus had opened up a new world for her. If Frieda didn't understand that, there was nothing she could do about it.

# Chapter Eight

When Lilo arrived a week later, Josephine greeted her with tears in her eyes. It was so good to see her friend again. Much to Frieda's annoyance, Jo spirited Lilo away on her very first evening in Berlin to visit Isabelle. Clara met them there, and they all became fast friends. Shortly after they arrived, Isabelle pushed the Rover out of the shed to show it off to their guest. After Lilo had duly admired it, she pulled a newspaper out of her bag and showed them a full-page article about bicycle riding. Both Josephine and Isabelle wanted to snatch the paper away from her, but Lilo wasn't about to give it up.

Relishing the moment, she opened the newspaper and read aloud to the spellbound girls. The article described a form of artistic cycling performed in teams, then went on to cover road racing, track cycling in velodromes, and other variations on the sport. Lilo looked up. "Now here it is! It says here that several military officers are planning to ride from Vienna to Berlin. But it's not just a ride. They'll be racing an Austrian military officer on horseback." Lilo's eyes sparkled as she looked at the girls gathered around her. "The headline reads, 'Who Will Ride the Three Hundred and Sixty Miles First? Horse or Wheelman?'"

"Three hundred and sixty miles on a bicycle? That's almost to the moon and back!" Josephine exclaimed.

Lilo nodded. "They still haven't set the start date. It seems they haven't collected enough money for it yet. But if it actually takes place, I'd give anything to be at the finish line."

"I'd come, too," said Josephine, spontaneously reaching out her hand to Lilo.

Isabelle extended her hand in agreement, too, but Clara held back. She was still skeptical about bicycles, and she was perfectly content to go about her life without participating in follies like long-distance cycling races.

"What makes you so sure the horse won't win?" she said sullenly.

Lilo glanced at her, then rolled her eyes in adulation. "Long-distance cycling is the absolute top, the real art. I'm determined to try it myself someday."

"As if a woman could ever do such a thing," Josephine sniffed.

"Why not?" Lilo retorted. "We just have to fight for it!" She looked intently at the others. "We have to show people that women can ride bicycles just as well as men. But people will never change their minds if we continue to ride in secret."

"And in the meantime, we're supposed to let them throw stones and spit at us?" said Isabelle. "That's exactly what happened to my friend Irene when she went riding through the Tiergarten last spring. She's only ridden in secret ever since." She straightened up. "But I've got some good news for you! I've managed to persuade my father to take us all to the new cycling track in eastern Berlin for my birthday next week. It'll be wonderful! Of course, a few *very important* businessmen will be coming with us, and no doubt they'll be bringing their eligible sons along—Papa would never do anything like that without ulterior motives." She sighed extravagantly. "But I know how to fend them off."

"Why do you want to fend the fellows off?" Lilo asked, looking at Isabelle with a frown. "I wouldn't have any objections to a dashing cyclist."

The others laughed.

"If that's all it was . . ." said Isabelle, when they had calmed down again. "The young men my father considers to be suitable candidates for marriage are almost certainly *not* cyclers. They're the kind who wear top hats and balance reading glasses on their noses so they can study their companies' balance books more closely."

"If that's what they're like, you can keep them then," said Lilo.


The bicycle was glossy and black and smelled vaguely of fresh chain oil. Like the Rover Safety, it had a saddle, handlebars with two handgrips, and two identical wheels. It wasn't as high as the Rover, nor did it look as stable, but there was something far more *agile* about it. It was beautiful.

Like a circus director extolling the next act, Moritz Herrenhus presented the bicycle to his daughter.

"It's your birthday present!"

Isabelle's expression managed to combine speechlessness, rapture, and fascination.

"A bicycle . . . for me?"

"Or should I have bought you a sewing machine? I'm a modern man, so you shall have a modern gift from me. And the bicycle is as modern as anything, especially this one. The tires are the latest invention—they are filled with air instead of being solid rubber. Thanks to them, you'll sit more comfortably than in a rocking chair. There can't be more than a dozen bicycles like this one in all Berlin, if that!" He puffed out his chest like a preening peacock. "I told the salesman, for my daughter, only the best is good enough." Looking for additional kudos, he turned to his dumbstruck audience, which consisted of Josephine, Clara, and Lilo.

The machine gleamed like black silk beneath the summer sun. Josephine swallowed. She had never seen anything so beautiful. Her desire to inspect the bicycle more closely was so strong that her hands were practically shaking. The tires were not the only innovation, she soon realized. This model was designed without the top tube that the Rover had. Instead, the stabilizing tube ran in a kind of V between the front and rear wheels. Josephine immediately understood the benefit of this new type of construction: because they could mount the saddle without lifting their leg over the top bar, women in skirts could easily ride the bicycle as well. The wheels were also covered with a kind of wire mesh, which reduced the danger of catching one's skirt in the spokes.

This bicycle had been built for a woman.

Isabelle sat on the saddle with unaccustomed ease and without doing anything to secure her lace-trimmed skirt. She squealed with delight as she rode her first lap around the yard. Clara and Lilo applauded.

"In a white dress on a shining steed, Isabelle . . . you're as pretty as a princess!" Clara called.

"A princess? Our Isabelle has been one of those for a long time," said Isabelle's mother, Jeanette, who had just joined them. She was wearing an elegant, dusty-blue outfit with a matching hat that made her look quite intrepid. "I must say, I still find this new hobby a little eccentric," she said to her husband. "But if things are really as you say, and men from the finest circles are indulging, then . . . I'm sure our princess will strike up some very interesting friendships. She might even find her prince."

Josephine said nothing. *"Our princess," "men from the finest circles," "her prince"*—Mrs. Herrenhus could spout such nonsense! Cycling was about the wind in your face and the feeling that you could ride away from all the cares of the world, just as Isabelle was doing at that moment on her very own bicycle.

Deep down, Josephine felt a craving that she had never experienced before. Something at once covetous and passionate. Envy. She wanted a bicycle like that, too.

Finally, Isabelle stopped and dismounted. "Thank you, Father. It's wonderful," she said and pressed a kiss to his cheek.

Moritz Herrenhus patted his daughter's shoulder patronizingly. Then he clapped his hands once and said, "Now it's time for your birthday party. We'll take your friends along with us. They should enjoy a treat once in a while, too!"

The trip in the four-in-hand carriage, which had been specially rented for the day and had enough space for eight to ride, took half an hour and led eastward through the sun-drenched city. The streets were full of pedestrians. Everyone seemed to be out strolling in Berlin's parks and gardens. Children knocked steel hoops along in front of them with sticks and set paper boats afloat in the Spree, while their fathers smoked pipes or strolled arm in arm in with their wives along the shore. Street vendors had set up their stands on the busiest corners and were doing a brisk trade in red fruit jelly, lemonade, and pastries. Spend a penny here, another there, and very soon you felt like a real gentleman or fine lady. Tomorrow they would all go back to their factories, the drone of the machines in their ears, the fumes from the motors in their noses. But today, Sunday, was a day to celebrate life.

Josephine also spotted a few cyclers. Gentlemen defying the heat in their elegant suits, with top hats on their heads and silk scarves around their necks. Once, Jo believed she had spotted a woman on a bicycle, but on second glance it became clear that the cycler was wearing pants.

Feeling miserable, Josephine turned away from all the hustle and bustle. The high spirits of the others only made her own dark mood worse.

"The bicycle cost two hundred and fifty marks," she heard Moritz Herrenhus say. "So you can see how much you're worth to us!"

"Oh, Papa, you're the best."

"So much money," Clara sighed.

Moritz Herrenhus looked over at Clara. "Isabelle will let you ride it, I'm sure. I have to justify spending two hundred and fifty marks somehow!" He laughed at his own joke.

Clara let out a small, self-conscious cough. "Maybe . . . you could lend me your bicycle? The new shape finally lets women ride with some decorum. Then Isabelle and I could practice artistic cycling together. We could decorate the bicycles with flowers and colorful ribbons."

"That would certainly be *très chic!*" said Jeanette Herrenhus. "I've heard that some theaters in Berlin are already including artistic cycling in their stage shows. I gather they are very impressive performances."

Colored ribbons on bicycles? Isabelle and Josephine looked at one another for a moment, and a smile united them.

"You are so lucky to be here in the city. New things only make it to my village years later. You probably had gas lamps when we were still making sparks with flint," said Lilo, putting on a tragicomic face.

Most of the girls laughed.

But Jo was angry. As if Clara's babbling wasn't enough, now Lilo was doing it, too. She wanted to tell her friend that her homeland was hardly a backwater. After all, she had seen her very first velocipede in Schömberg! But it was like her throat was blocked. If Moritz Herrenhus mentioned how expensive the bicycle was one more time, she thought she would scream. She shook her head like an impatient horse. What was wrong with her? Why couldn't she be happy for Isabelle? Or grateful to her friend's father? It was actually very decent of him to invite them all along on this jaunt. *You envy her!* whispered a nasty little gnome inside her head. And Josephine could not deny it.

Josephine was relieved when they reached their destination. She couldn't have put up with Isabelle's giggling a minute longer. She pushed the door open without waiting for the coachman. But then she stopped and looked around, perplexed. Where was Berlin's latest attraction?

The way Moritz Herrenhus had described it, Josephine had expected a huge hall with polished floorboards. Or an enormous, empty warehouse, or perhaps an auditorium with high windows and a high ceiling. But the cycle track was an open-air affair surrounded by nothing more than a low fence. Gesticulating broadly, Moritz Herrenhus paid for his little group, announcing loudly as he did so that this excursion was a birthday present for his daughter. But apart from the cashier, a portly woman with her gray hair tied in a bun, no one paid any attention to him—the spectators were far too busy cheering on their favorite cyclers, who were already speeding around the sandy oval on their bicycles.

"Go, Willy, go!"

"Faster, Joseph, faster!"

"Keep it up, Karl-Heinz!"

The visitors were all well-dressed, many of them outfitted in high-quality suits, and Josephine even saw one gentleman in a tailcoat and top hat. There were also several women present, all of whom were at least as nicely turned out as Jeanette Herrenhus. And though she found the gentlemen somewhat intimidating, Josephine soon found herself infected by their relaxed, lively mood. She had just turned to watch the racers on the track when Isabelle approached her.

"Father has invited a few business friends, so I have to be a good girl and go say hello to them. But he'd like to offer you, Clara, and Lilo a glass of sparkling wine—that will be nice, won't it? See the grandstand there, where my parents are standing? They've got sausages and fish sandwiches there, what they call a cycler's snack—I've never eaten such a thing in my life!" Isabelle laughed. "This is just my kind of birthday party! I can hardly wait to tell Irene and the others about it tomorrow. They'll be green with envy! But I have to go and greet our guests, or Father will be cross with me again."

Instead of following Isabelle up to the covered grandstand, Jo stayed down below, beside the oval track. She was captivated by the men on their bicycles, who were completing each lap faster than the one before. Almost all of them were riding a Rover Safety. Unlike the sartorially minded guests, the wheelmen wore short pants, shirts, and tight vests over the top of them. On their feet, they wore close-fitting boots that covered their ankles. Bending low over the handlebars, with their arms bent almost at right angles and tucked in close to their bodies, they reached incredible speeds. Jo blinked. She would never have thought of riding in such a bent-over fashion herself.

"So, have you already sniffed out one of these racetrack heroes?" Lilo asked, laying a friendly arm across her shoulders. "One thing I'll give you Berliners—you all have some really remarkable experiences."

Josephine laughed. "The men don't interest me a bit, but the way they ride is amazing. They're so fast!"

"But is it just because of the way they're bent over? Unlike us, the men don't have to deal with big puffy skirts. And those outfits they're wearing couldn't weigh more than ten pounds. Our dresses weigh can twice as much, and then some," said Lilo quietly.

"You're right," Josephine sighed fervently. "I suppose we should probably be happy that we get to ride bicycles at all."

They watched the riders in silence for a while. *Some of them are certainly attractive,* thought Josephine. One tall blond fellow in particular had caught her eye. He and his bicycle seemed almost fused into one being, and he took the curves with more grace than any of the others. She watched him intently as he flew past on every lap, but he seemed not to notice her at all.

Lilo leaned close to her and whispered in her ear. "Can I tell you a secret? Lately, I haven't just been borrowing Mr. Braun's bicycle. I've also been borrowing an old pair of gardening pants of his that he keeps in the shed for when he's working out in the garden."

For a moment, Josephine thought she must have misheard her friend. But when she turned to look at Lilo, she realized she had heard exactly right.

Lilo's eyes sparkled. "It's a completely different experience, riding like that. What's even better is that if I put on a hat and wrap a scarf around my neck to hide my chin, no one even recognizes me. Just the other day, I passed my teacher out on the road when I was dressed like that—you know I'm doing an apprenticeship as a nurse's assistant in the new sanatorium—and when I saw Dr. Jacob, I nearly had a heart attack! But he greeted me like I was just a patient."

An apprenticeship as a nurse's assistant. Cycling in disguise. A trip to Berlin to visit her great-aunt Frieda—Lilo certainly led an exciting life. "One thing I have to give *you* . . ." said Jo. "You've got some spunk. What I wouldn't give to be able to go cycling through a forest again. Or along an open road toward the horizon . . . I'll never forget that feeling of freedom."

"Then why don't you do it?" Lilo replied, a hint of challenge in her voice. "I'd die of boredom if all I could do was ride in a circle. It doesn't matter if it's on a racetrack like this or in Isabelle's father's yard. And oh, that artistic cycling that Clara keeps going on about!" She made a face as if she'd tasted something sour. "In any case, I've got a new plan. The next time Mr. Braun goes away, I'm going to ride from Schömberg to Pforzheim in my own clothes. We'll see what people have to say about it."

"You're *what*?" said Josephine, loud enough that she drew puzzled looks from the people nearby. Even one of the riders on the track who was riding by just then looked over at her. As he did, he swung dangerously close to the rider on his right, and the front wheels of their two bicycles touched. A moment later, the young man slammed into the fence. It was the blond man whom Josephine had been admiring.

Josephine threw both hands over her mouth. "My goodness, are you all right?" she said. Leaning over the fence, she suddenly found herself gazing into a pair of gray-green eyes more enchanting than anything she had ever seen before. A strange and not unpleasant feeling ran through her. She blinked and reached out to help the young man up, but he ignored her hand and got to his feet on his own. He brushed the dust from his clothes and gave Josephine an unfriendly look.

"Why don't you take your gossiping elsewhere? We're engaged in some serious sport here, in case you hadn't noticed."

"But . . ." Josephine tried desperately to find an appropriate reply, but the young man with the beautiful eyes climbed onto his bicycle and rode away without a backward glance.

# Chapter Nine

The accident happened a week later.

It was a sweltering, sticky summer evening. Clouds swelled over the western part of the city, the sun long since vanished behind them. Occasional lightning cut through the sky overhead, and the outside walls of the houses almost shimmered in the heat. Not a single leaf moved, and in the silence before the storm, the machines inside the factory halls seemed to drone even more loudly than usual. The storm would break very soon.

Isabelle and Josephine stood a little more than arm's length apart in the yard of the Herrenhus villa. Each held a broom in the air, the brush ends crossed in the space between them while Clara and Lilo ducked and rode through this makeshift gate on the bicycles. Isabelle had told the others she thought it would improve their sense of balance. Of course, she had been the first to try it, and she passed through it with flying colors. The girls had already tried riding in the stooped position of the racers, but they did not like it.

"This isn't so hard," Clara whooped as she steered Moritz Herrenhus's bicycle through the narrow gap—wobbly but with success.

"Then let's make it harder," Lilo said and let go of the handlebars. "*This* will definitely help your balance!" With her head high, she rode with no hands across the yard.

"My new bicycle! Watch out!" Isabelle shouted after her.

Josephine lowered her broom with relief. The new exercise certainly didn't need an honor guard. Normally, she would have wanted to match Lilo's feat immediately. But she was tired, her clothes were clinging uncomfortably to her body, and her arms ached from the long hours in her father's workshop. It had been oppressively hot all day, and more than once she had felt as though she was glowing with heat—much like the horseshoes her father held in the fire. The horses had all been skittish, constantly flicking their heads to fend off the flies. A brown gelding had thumped her in the side, and her ribs still hurt.

She'd had enough for today. *One more glass of lemonade, then I'll go home,* she thought. Just then, she heard Clara shouting from behind.

"I can do that, too! Look at me, look at me!"

Clara had actually succeeded in letting go of the handlebars. Although her friend's hands hovered only a few inches above them, Josephine would not have credited Clara with so much pluck. But the handlebars suddenly swerved to the left, and before Clara could grab them, the front wheel turned, the bicycle came to an abrupt stop, and Clara was thrown headfirst over the handlebars. She lay in the dusty gravel, whimpering, her right leg strangely twisted.

Josephine ran to her friend. "Are you hurt? Clara, what's the matter? Say something!" They registered Clara's grazed, bloody knees and the small stones, dirt, and threads that clung to them. Blood was running down her right calf.

"My leg. It hurts so much . . ."

While Lilo held Clara's head, Josephine tore frantically at Clara's skirt, which had gotten caught in the spokes of the front wheel. She finally pulled it free with a loud rip. Carefully, she tried to stretch Clara's twisted leg straight, but Clara shrieked with pain at the first touch. Josephine let it go.

"I think her leg's broken," said Lilo softly. "I've seen something like this before, with a cow. The poor creature. We had to—"

"That's enough," Isabelle broke in harshly.

They crouched and looked at their friend helplessly as she lay crying on the gravel. Just then, the heavens opened, and fat, penny-sized raindrops began pelting down on them.

It was Isabelle who recovered from the shock first. She looked frantically from Clara to the others.

"We have to get her away from here. And the bicycles have to go back in the shed right away. If my parents find out how Clara hurt herself, they'll never let me ride again."

Josephine looked at Isabelle in disbelief. "How can you think of yourself at a time like this? We need to fetch a doctor, immediately."

Lilo shook her head. "A doctor couldn't help her. Clara has to get to hospital. A break like this needs to be splinted. She might even need an operation," she said, at which Clara wailed even louder.

"Not so loud," she hissed, glancing up at the house with a fearful expression. "I'll get help, I promise! But the bicycles have to go back in the shed first. Then we'll carry Clara out to the sidewalk and say she broke her leg out there."

\*\*\*

"It was the skirt!" Josephine looked firmly at Isabelle and Lilo. "If it hadn't got caught in the spokes, Clara wouldn't have fallen."

"If only we'd given her my bicycle, then Clara wouldn't have fallen so idiotically and we could keep on riding," Isabelle grumbled.

Jo glowered at her friend.

They had just visited Clara, whose leg really was broken, in the Deaconess Hospital. A day had passed since the accident. Lilo had taken Clara some fruit from Frieda's garden, and Isabelle brought her newspapers and candy that they all shared. But after a few minutes a stern-looking nurse had bustled in and driven the girls out, informing them that the patient needed rest. They had eventually found themselves sitting together in the backyard at the Herrenhus villa, tired and listless from the August heat.

"Maybe she hit a hole and her skirt only got caught in the spokes when she actually fell," said Lilo, poking the white gravel with a stick.

"There aren't any holes. Look around," said Isabelle sharply.

Lilo nodded despondently. "I wish I hadn't shown her I could ride with no hands . . ."

"She didn't have to try to copy you. She knows full well that she isn't the best cycler," Isabelle replied.

It wasn't the first time they had been through this.

Moritz Herrenhus had seen right through their fabricated story—that Clara had broken her leg falling on the sidewalk—and called them silly, careless ninnies. Then he'd stated loudly that, in his opinion, women were far better suited to sitting at a sewing machine than atop a bicycle. He'd gone on to ban them from riding either of the bicycles until further notice.

Josephine looked longingly toward the shed where the bicycles stood. She doubted that Isabelle's father would ever allow them to ride again.

"If Clara's skirt really caused her to crash, then it's all the more reason to ride in pants," said Lilo, looking defiantly at the others. "Why won't you give it a try?"

"Because it's a downright horrible thought! And completely unfeminine, to boot." Isabelle shuddered. "I'd never put on anything so uncomfortable or so tight." She placed her hands protectively on her skirt with its yellow-white flowers, as if she thought someone might try to rip it from her body.

"When I think of the greasy pants my father wears, ugh! I honestly can't imagine putting on anything like that," Josephine added. "Besides, it hardly matters since we're not allowed to cycle now."

"Who cares?" Lilo rolled her eyes. "You think you're all so progressive here in the city. But what would you say if I told you that in France, it's actually the fashion for women cyclers to wear a kind of divided skirt when they ride?" Josephine and Isabelle looked intrigued, so Lilo went on. "Last spring, a group of women stayed in our sanatorium as guests. One of them had brought a bicycle along with her. When she rode it through Schömberg, the people just stood there and gaped!" Lilo giggled. "And she was wearing just such a divided skirt. After a few days, I worked up my courage and asked her about her unusual outfit. She said that where she came from in Paris it wasn't unusual at all. You could even buy them in the shops, ready-made. She called it a *costume rationnel*."

"A sensible outfit," Isabelle said, translating, and she chewed her bottom lip. She abruptly stood up and started gathering the material of her skirt together in the middle. "If one were to pleat the material here and, let's say, sew it up with a few stitches below the knee, would that turn it into a *costume rationnel*?"

Lilo shrugged. "That's about what it looked like."

Holding the material of her skirt in the middle with her right hand, Isabelle lifted her right leg as if climbing onto a bicycle. "That's definitely much easier!"

"Altering a skirt to make it as comfortable as pants for riding but so it still looks like a skirt . . . It's not a bad idea," Josephine murmured to herself. She looked up. "My skirt is old, and I won't be able to wear it much longer anyway. If you like, we could try it out on mine, just as a test. Isabelle, we just need a needle and thread . . ."

\*

Josephine sat there in her underskirt as the other two quarreled about how high the inner seam should go.

"Just above the ankle, no more than that. Any higher would be indecent," Isabelle said.

"No point stopping halfway," said Lilo, and Josephine agreed. With more or less even stitches, they sewed the cloth up the middle to just above the knee, creating two "legs."

"How can you go around in a rag like this! There's as much here that needs to be patched as stitched. If only Clara were here," Isabelle muttered as she sewed. Like Lilo and Josephine, she was not exactly a talented seamstress.

Time to try it on. Accompanied by the laughter of the others, Josephine pulled on her newly divided skirt.

"Well . . . from a distance, it still looks like a skirt," said Isabelle. "How does it feel?"

"Quite good," said Jo. "But I can't judge whether it's really any more practical than a normal skirt without getting on a bicycle."

"You know that my father prohibited us from doing that," said Isabelle, but after some hesitation she went into the shed to get her father's Rover. She warned Jo to stay out of sight behind the shed, then she let her take the handlebars.

"So?" asked Isabelle and Lilo simultaneously when Josephine was firmly mounted on the seat.

"Getting on is easy enough . . ."

"But?"

Josephine pointed at the back wheel. "Look. The material can still catch in the spokes back here."

"The Frenchwoman's looked different, too," said Lilo, her head tipped to one side and a critical expression on her face. "The material was sort of gathered around the hem at the bottom of each leg, like with linen underwear, you know? Like some kind of . . . knickerbockers."

"You want us to cycle in underwear now?" Isabelle asked, her eyes wide.

Josephine could hardly suppress a grin. "Who knows? Maybe they'll be all the rage one day, and your father will be making them in his factory." She looked down at herself. As misshapen as her skirt looked, she could still get away with wearing it in the smithy. So she took a deep breath and said, "It doesn't matter now anyway. Let's really turn these into knickerbockers!"

This time, she wielded the needle herself, careful not to make the "legs" of the skirt too tight. When she was finished, she pulled the garment back on and turned around to show her friends how it fit. "How do I look?"

"I don't know," said Lilo. "The *costume rationnel* was more elegant, somehow."

"Plain ridiculous is how it looks!" Isabelle cried. "Jo, absolutely not. You're never going to—"

"Aren't I?" Jo said, laughing, then swung herself onto the Rover again. She looked down critically at her legs. Instead of coming dangerously close to the spokes, her skirt now hugged her legs but without restricting them. Her ankles and a small section of her lower legs were visible, but her knees were covered. What more could she want?

"How does it feel?" Lilo asked.

Jo looked at her and smiled. "What was it you said? A completely different riding experience!" And she rode off around the yard without giving a second thought to her skirt.

***

On the following Saturday, Lilo returned to the Black Forest. Frieda was tired, so Josephine and Isabelle accompanied their friend to the train station.

"Your turn to visit me next," said Lilo, giving both of them a farewell hug.

Josephine watched the train rumble out of the station in a cloud of stinking fumes. Her turn next—if only that were true. She wondered if she would ever see her friend again.

"And then there were two," she said to Isabelle, sighing deeply, as they left the station.

"Don't start crying or I will, too!" Isabelle crooked her elbow around Josephine's and they headed down the busy street arm in arm.

When they were nearly home, Josephine stopped abruptly and said, "Enough moping. I've got an idea."

Isabelle immediately pricked up her ears. "What is it?"

Josephine closed her eyes for a moment and reveled in the images—both enticing and frightening—in her mind: *long streets, broad boulevards, the forests of Grunewald* . . . How many hours in the smithy, how many nights in her bed had she dreamed of it. She was ready to make those images a reality. She took a deep breath and exclaimed, "Let's cycle through the city!"

"On bicycles?" Isabelle's eyes widened, at once horrified and fascinated. "But that's . . . Oh, you'll really get us in trouble. How could we possibly do it?" She sounded breathless and thrilled.

Jo smiled. She could always count on Isabelle to be part of an adventure.

"We'll have to take some precautions, of course, but . . . we'll go tomorrow morning, while the world is still asleep!"


The next morning, it was raining, and the air smelled of wet cobblestones. Jo ran down the street in the dawn light, her father's old flat cap pulled low over her eyes, her shoulders hunched forward. On the one hand, the weather was ideal for what she had in mind, as Berlin's residents would certainly not leave their houses unnecessarily on a rainy Sunday morning. On the other hand, the streets would be covered in a slick coating of wet grime and horse manure, which would turn their outing into a slippery one.

Isabelle was already waiting at her gate for Josephine. The two bicycles were leaning against the wall beside her. When they caught sight of each other, they broke into laughter—like Jo, Isabelle was wearing her father's pants, jacket, and cap. One red lock of hair peeped out from beneath the cap, and Isabelle hurriedly tucked it out of sight.

"I've brought something else," said Jo, as she produced a small piece of coal from her jacket pocket. Before Isabelle could say anything, Josephine drew a thin moustache on her friend's face, then a black line on her own top lip.

"Now we look like a real pair of fellows, eh?" she said with a grin and threw the piece of coal in the gutter.

"You're absolutely mad, do you know that? Where are we riding to, by the way?" Isabelle asked, laughing quietly as she pushed the bicycles in the direction of Schlesischer Busch. As they'd hoped, the streets were completely deserted.

"I thought we'd ride out toward Friedrichshain. No one will be out at this hour," said Jo, getting onto the bicycle. Her heart was pounding in her chest. She hated to think what would happen if they were caught . . .

"You want to ride through the park in Friedrichshain? Through the fields and trees? That sounds boring." Isabelle shook her head. "I want to ride down the same grand boulevard our emperor uses. Let's ride over to Unter den Linden. You and me, on bicycles, through the Brandenburg Gate. If we're going to risk our necks, we might as well make it worthwhile."

Although Jo held the handlebars tightly and concentrated on riding straight, the Rover's narrow, solid-rubber tires did not grip the slick cobblestones well. After a few minutes, she was so tense that she could hardly breathe. Isabelle, riding next to her, kept her eyes on the road ahead. Both were thinking the same thing: *What if the front wheel slips and I have an accident? And so soon after Clara broke her leg? Moritz Herrenhus would bite our heads off!*

As they cycled past the Deaconess Hospital, Josephine's thoughts turned to Clara, who was no doubt still sleeping peacefully behind one of the many windows up there—*if the bulky plaster cast around her leg allows her to get any rest, that is.* Poor Clara. Josephine hoped that neither she nor Isabelle would soon be joining their friend in there.

They turned left onto a street that began to climb steeply but was also drier. Jo's legs shook with the exertion, and she had her mouth open to get more air into her lungs. Isabelle, riding on Josephine's left, seemed to be faring no better. Her face was almost scarlet with the effort, but, like Jo, she was gritting her teeth and pedaling on.

After a few more minutes, the burning sensation in Josephine's legs faded. Her muscles grew accustomed to the unfamiliar work, and they found their rhythm. Jo found herself riding more quickly. The gray tenements flew past like storm clouds, and the air brushed their cheeks like a cool veil, a delicious sensation. Inside Josephine, choirs of angels were positively singing. She was close to taking one hand off the handlebars to pinch herself. Was this all a beautiful dream? Could it possibly be real? She was not riding through the Black Forest; she was riding through her own sleeping city. A sigh that was more a sob escaped her throat. And then she laughed. She laughed loud and pure and long, something she did only rarely. *My God, how wonderful this is . . .*

Soon, they saw the Fischerbrücke ahead of them, and beside the wide bridge a few boats bobbed in the water. A flock of seagulls flew up, squawking at the wheeled newcomers. As they drew alongside an inn, with a sign over the entrance that read "Berliner Kindl Brewery," the door opened and a young man wearing a filthy apron hurled a bucket of water onto the street directly in front of Josephine. Instinctively, she jerked her handlebars to the left, just in time to avoid a collision with the man. Her sudden maneuver almost caused her to run into Isabelle, however, and her friend let out a curse.

"Got a bit of a shock, did we? Keep your legs up round here, y' fancy snobs!" the guy shouted after them.

To Josephine's horror, Isabelle stopped and turned around. "Are you blind? Fancy snobs, my foot. You wouldn't know a girl from a hole in the ground!"

The man from the inn lowered his bucket, his face suddenly transformed into a dumbfounded question mark. "Well, I'll be! Yous ain't laddies; you're ladies!"

"And damn fine ones, too!" Isabelle called, quickly remounting and pedaling off. Jo, who had stopped a little way ahead, did the same. Encouraged by Isabelle's cockiness, she called back, "Have a nice day!" as she rode away.

They were giggling so much they could hardly ride straight. "Think we'll end up in the newspaper, like Irene and her friend Jule when they rode through the Tiergarten?" Isabelle asked.

"Probably best if we don't, OK? So what now? Do we cycle across the Spree, or follow the left bank?"

"Let's stay left," Isabelle said.

As they looked at each other, each saw the sparkle in the other's eyes.

They had just reached the broad boulevard of Unter den Linden when Josephine felt the first warm rays from the rising sun on her back. A pleasant warmth spread through her body. As she rode along beneath the canopy of linden boughs, she was overcome with happiness. When they crossed the broad expanse of Pariser Platz and cycled beneath the Brandenburg Gate, the sunlight lit the way ahead in gold.

They arrived home a good two hours later, and just in time, because the streets were starting to fill with the first pedestrians and churchgoers. Josephine held both bicycles while Isabelle ran to the yard to check that the coast was clear. Then they quietly stowed the bicycles back in the shed.

The two girls shared a conspiratorial look. It had been a success! The breeze had mussed their hair despite their caps, their cheeks practically glowed, and their eyes shone like polished precious stones.

"That was the best thing I've ever done in my life," said Isabelle, and she pressed a kiss to Josephine's cheek.

Jo, not used to such displays of affection, swallowed and blushed.

They decided right then that they'd do it again as soon as they possibly could, and, with a final embrace, they parted ways.

# Chapter Ten

Autumn passed with the usual workaday tedium. Clara was finally able to leave the hospital. After the forced rest and weeks in a cast, her right leg was thinner than her left, but the break had healed completely. At home, a pleasant surprise awaited her. "Father and I have been thinking about you a great deal in the last few weeks. You know we only want the best for you," said her mother. "And we've decided that a year at the home-economics school is enough for you to manage your future husband's household efficiently. But until that time comes, you will help your father in the pharmacy, just as you have always wanted. Your father will get the extra help he needs, and I can keep an eye on you."

Clara gazed wide-eyed at her mother. This was the last thing she had expected. It had taken a broken leg to create a miracle.

Isabelle, too, was very busy. Through circuitous connections, Moritz Herrenhus had managed to secure an invitation to the Imperial Court. The evening was entitled "A Rose Ball for Chivalrous Young Men and Blossoming Beauties," and he planned to attend with his family. Even for a factory owner of good standing like Moritz Herrenhus, such an invitation was unusual, and his excitement was correspondingly great.

"You will meet the very best young men there and have all sorts of entertainment," Isabelle's mother exulted to her daughter.

"And if you don't find a suitable marriage candidate at this ball, you'll be sorry. I've had just about enough of your airs and graces," her father threatened, tarnishing Isabelle's enthusiasm in an instant. In the evenings before the ball, she had to spend hours with an aging countess who reeked of mothballs and who was supposed to instruct her and her mother in the most important rules of etiquette for a visit to the Imperial Court. She also had to choose a suitable gift. But the most important challenge of all was finding the perfect ball gown. Isabelle knew that, in this matter, all resistance was futile, so she simply conceded defeat and let herself be primped for the occasion. While an eager dressmaker meticulously took her measurements, she dreamed of the green, tree-lined boulevards that she and Jo had cycled along.

The Rose Ball ended like every other ball: Isabelle danced and flirted and successfully fended off her potential suitors. And her father's mood did not improve in the slightest.


In Schmied-the-Smith's workshop, there was less work than in previous years. There were a number of reasons for this: Some of his customers had deserted to the competition. The drivers of the post coach and the local cabs weren't exactly sensitive souls, but Schmied-the-Smith's surly attitude had become too much even for them. And several private individuals had either sold their horses or taken them to the butcher. Why go to all the trouble of taking care of a horse if one could get from Point A to Point B more cheaply and comfortably by tram or cab? And then there were all the cyclists . . .

"Oskar Reutter has taken up riding one of them boneshakers, too! That's why he sold that pretty team of his. With customers like him, I might as well close up shop tomorrow," the smith grumbled, when he saw the emporium owner cycle past the smithy one day. He glared at the businessman as he pedaled slowly by.

Jo waved to her former traveling companion. "I think it's good that a man like Oskar Reutter has found a passion for cycling," she said, knowing full well that she was only provoking her father by talking that way. "If you ask me, we could use more cyclists on the road. They liven up the streets, don't you think?"

She saw his hand coming and grabbed hold of his wrist before the blow landed.

"Don't you ever hit me again," she said, quietly but firmly. She was quaking on the inside, but she forced herself to look her father in the eye. "Felix is dead! And it doesn't matter how horribly you treat me, you can't change that. I will never, ever forgive myself for not staying home with him. I made a mistake. But his death was God's will, not mine! If you want to spend the rest of your days blaming me, I can't do anything about it. But if I'm supposed to go on working for you, I ask that you at least treat me decently."

Her father had listened to her outburst in silence.

"Decently! Give me the hammer," he growled and turned away.

"You'd think you'd have learned something about humility, given the things you've done. Instead, you talk back to your father with an arrogance that would make God blush. But I'll tell you this, God's punishment will come," said Josephine's mother that evening, as she scrubbed an iron pot with a coarse brush. She was shaking with anger as she glared at her daughter.

Josephine returned her mother's look, unmoved.

"I will take God's punishment when it's due. But I will no longer accept Father striking me for nothing—for nothing!—or humiliating me in front of customers. If it happens again, then you can look for another dullard to work herself to death for you for free. I'll walk out on the spot!" Without another word, Josephine left the kitchen.

\*\*\*

As 1890 came to a close and the New Year began, Clara started working in the pharmacy. When the weather began to warm up in the spring, Josephine asked Clara whether she would like to go out riding with Isabelle on one of their early morning outings. But Clara shook her head. She had more important things to do. Like thinking about the best combination of scents for soap, for example. She didn't understand her friends' ongoing obsession with such lunacy as cycling.

\*\*\*

The summer of 1891 was a carefree, happy time. Josephine and Isabelle met at the gate to the Herrenhus villa in the early morning as often as they could. Now, when they saw each other in men's clothes in the pallid predawn light, they no longer giggled or teased each other. Their fathers' fusty old pants and jackets gave them the freedom to ride through the city incognito. They eventually began hiding the clothes where they would always be handy, behind a pile of junk in the same shed as the bicycles. If Isabelle had been to a social event the night before and was too tired to go out riding so early in the morning, she always left the gate ajar so that Josephine could get into the shed alone.

Jo had become so attached to Moritz Herrenhus's Rover that she now almost considered the bicycle to be her own. Her sense of ownership was only reinforced by the fact that Herrenhus was too busy to ride the bicycle himself.

In the early days, she had only cared about the act of cycling itself. Now, though, she often found herself crouched beside the Rover for a few minutes, trying to work out the mechanics behind the machine.

The drive mechanism struck her as an engineering marvel, and she was captivated by the ingenious steering mechanism that started at the handlebars and ended down below at the head of the forks. Who had invented such a thing?

When she asked Isabelle whether the factory that made the Rover had supplied them with some sort of description along with the bicycle, Isabelle told her, "It actually came with quite a thick booklet, with descriptions of all the parts and a lot more. The text is all in English, though. And Father keeps it in his office with all his other paperwork, so I can't get my hands on it, if that's your question."

Josephine frowned. "Do you have any idea where else I could find a book or some sort of brochure about bicycles?"

"If there's anything about cycling in print, you're most likely to find it at the big bookstore on Alexanderplatz."

Josephine had not so much as opened a book since her time in the Black Forest, and she had never been inside a bookstore in her life. But she was now determined to visit the one on Alexanderplatz as soon as she could get there. Cycling was a wonderful thing. But there was more to it than just riding, and that had begun to interest her just as much.

*** 

"It's so ugly here. Everything's just different shades of gray," said Isabelle as they rode through the Stralau district one morning. It was July, and the day promised to be hot. It had not rained for almost two weeks, and the ground and air were parched and dusty. "Not a bit of green anywhere. And there aren't any shops, or even a workshop. And there's all these grim-looking characters loitering about. If you ask me, it's spooky."

"Those people aren't loitering about. They *live* here. And they have to work very hard to get by," said Josephine, with unaccustomed passion. She had a tremendous respect for working-class people. She pointed with her chin toward the multistory tenements where factory workers lived in cramped quarters. With dour faces and hunched shoulders, they were making their way to the factories, casting the girls on their boneshakers hostile glances as they passed.

"Whatever," Isabelle replied. She was pedaling hard, and it was clear she wanted to get out of this bleak neighborhood as quickly as she could. "What if we have a breakdown here? They look so unfriendly they'd probably stone us."

"First, the bicycles are so well made that we haven't *had* any breakdowns yet. And if a screw were to come loose, you wouldn't need to worry. I've brought tools along. I can take care of any minor repairs myself," said Jo with confidence, although she desperately hoped that her father would not notice the missing tools—and that they would be the right ones in an emergency.

"Since you're part of the working class, I'm not surprised you like these places," said Isabelle, who was evidently in a quarrelsome mood. "But don't expect me to get my hands dirty. I'd much rather cycle past the fancy houses in the elegant parts of town. The streets are much cleaner and in better condition. We wouldn't have to worry about ripped-out cobblestones or the ruts left by the heavy wagons. Then I could show you where the rich people live."

*I couldn't care less about that,* thought Josephine, but she said instead, in a conciliatory tone, "Let's take a detour through the zoo."

Isabelle's expression brightened instantly. While most of the city still slumbered, the wildlife behind the walls of Berlin's famous zoo was already wide awake. The shrill cries of birds, trumpeting of elephants, and animal noises that Josephine could not ascribe to any particular beast pierced the morning air. The place smelled of hay and adventure.

"Let's see if there's a hole in the fence somewhere. If there is, we can sneak inside and pay the elephants a visit."

Josephine sighed. It was not the first time Isabelle had come up with an idea for a daring escapade. Sometimes, riding wasn't enough for her. For Jo, though, such skylarking was pointless. She would much rather use the little time they had for cycling.

"It's amazing how free it makes you feel, isn't it? It's like you don't have a care in the world," Isabelle said as they approached the zoo, and there was a kind of awe in her voice.

Jo nodded. She knew exactly how her friend felt as the world flew past.

They did, in fact, find a hole in the fence of the Zoological Garden. Isabelle, who was a little shorter than Josephine, slipped through first and did a little joyful dance on the other side. When Josephine tried to follow her, she caught herself on a broken wire and ended up with a bloody arm and elbow. She waved it off as little more than a scratch, but they decided to postpone their visit to the elephants.

By the time they reached the Herrenhus house, the open wound was throbbing and prickling uncomfortably.

"Hurry," said Jo. "I want to get home quickly and clean my arm."

Isabelle was about to push open the gate when it was pulled open suddenly from inside. Her father stood before them in a checked vest that he'd had specially made for cycling. He glared at the two young women.

"Just as I thought!" Although he began quietly he grew louder, and Josephine could hear the anger in his voice.

"Father . . ." The last drop of blood drained from Isabelle's face.

He took a deep breath. "Just this once, I decide to treat myself to a well-earned ride on my Rover, and what do I find when I open the shed? Yawning emptiness and a pile of women's clothes! I thought my eyes were deceiving me. Didn't I *expressly* forbid you from riding the bicycles? And out on the street at that! As if that's not enough, you decide to dress up in this . . . ridiculous way! That is the absolute height of impudence," he ranted. Windows opened along the street, and a few curious faces appeared in them. Herrenhus grabbed the girls by the arm and dragged them inside the gate.

"I want an explanation. On the spot!" he snarled as soon as the gate was closed.

But apart from a whimper, Isabelle could say nothing.

Jo's bleeding arm was forgotten, and with the courage of desperation, she cleared her throat. "It's . . . not what you think. Isabelle and I, we . . ." Her mouth was so dry that her tongue felt glued to the roof of her mouth. *Oh, dear Lord, please find me an excuse!*

"Isabelle told me that you're celebrating an important birthday at the start of August. And I suddenly had an idea for a very special surprise." The words began pouring from her mouth. She sensed Isabelle's horrified eyes on her, but she didn't stop. "Your daughter and I have been rehearsing a little . . . play. About two wheelmen. It seemed appropriate since you are so taken by cycling. We've been practicing in secret, not here in the yard where you would see everything. We wanted to surprise you and your guests, didn't we, Isabelle?"

Isabelle stood wide-eyed in amazement. But she nodded hurriedly. "I thought Josephine's idea was wonderful," she said with a slight tremble in her voice. "Because you do so much for me, and I'm so infinitely grateful to you for all of it."

The angry furrows in Moritz Herrenhus's forehead deepened. He did not look satisfied with their explanation.

"I'm also very grateful," Jo added. A little moisture was gradually returning to her mouth, and the words came more easily. "Now you've caught us in the act . . ."

"And our surprise is no longer a surprise," Isabelle added, and promptly burst into tears.

Josephine felt a lump form in her throat, and tears started flowing down her own cheeks. Their morning rides were over. It was all over . . .

"I ought to tan your hides. But if things really are as you say, then you didn't mean any harm. Still . . . that has to be the stupidest idea I've heard in a long time. Isabelle!" he growled at his daughter. "How could you even think that I would let you dress up in front of my guests in this . . . costume?" He gestured toward her outfit as he spoke.

"You wouldn't? It was meant to be funny," said Isabelle in a quiet voice.

"If your friend wants to dress up as a clown, I would certainly find it amusing. And it would no doubt be wonderfully entertaining for our guests. But your mother would bite my head off. She likes things to be stylish, you know that." He actually sounded a little disappointed. Then he clapped his hands. "Enough of this monkeying around. Let's get the bicycles back in the shed. And don't let me ever catch you out here again! Isabelle, I want you decently dressed and in the salon in ten minutes. I'd like a word with you about yesterday evening. You disappointed me yet again . . ."

Isabelle and Josephine exchanged a relieved look. They'd gotten away with it! Then Isabelle trudged away behind her father, her head down.

"You wanted to break into the zoo? That's how you injured your arm? And then Moritz Herrenhus caught you?!" Clara stopped in the middle of applying ointment to Jo's elbow and looked at her friend in disbelief.

Jo nodded unhappily.

"You're even crazier than I thought." Clara slammed the ointment pot angrily onto the round table in front of her window. "And here I am mixing up a healing ointment for you!" With her lips pressed together tightly, she wiped her hands on a white cloth. "You can treat your own wounds in the future."

"Oh, don't be like this," Jo pleaded. She rolled the sleeve of her blouse carefully over her injured elbow. "All our fun with the bicycles is over and done. At least for now. I could scream when I think about it."

"Fun! Is that all that matters to you? With all the *fun* you're having, have you forgotten how to tell the difference between right and wrong?" Clara began counting off Jo's sins on her fingers. "You lie to your parents. You 'borrow' Moritz Herrenhus's bicycle. You dress up as a man. You ride a bicycle through the city, which is clearly something for men! And then you break into the zoo! If you ask me, it's outrageous!"

Jo could not remember Clara ever being so angry at her. "I know that what I'm doing isn't right. But I'm not doing anyone any harm. Moritz Herrenhus's bicycle was standing around, unridden, for months. How were we supposed to know he'd suddenly get it into his head to go for a ride?" She took Clara's hands and squeezed them. "Please try to understand. The moment I sit on a bicycle, all the anger and strain of my life at home simply vanishes. And the feeling of freedom . . . All these years, my life has been limited to our little street. Thanks to the bicycle, the world has suddenly become limitless."

Her eyes swept across Clara's desk, which was piled with heavy books: *Handbook of Modern Pharmacology*, *Toxic Diseases of the Skin and Their Treatment*, and several more—Clara seemed to be taking her work in the pharmacy very seriously indeed. Just a few weeks earlier, Josephine would have teased her friend, but now she could understand her hunger for knowledge. She thought of her visit to the bookstore that Isabelle had recommended. She had found one book in there about competitive cycling. It was almost two hundred pages, packed with illustrations and exciting information—she would have given anything to be able to walk out with it. The bookseller had proudly explained to her that an academic publishing house in Munich had just released it, and he asked if she wanted to buy it for her father. Jo had simply nodded and asked about the price. Afterward, she had crept out of the store like a beaten dog. She had never considered how much books cost. She would have to save her tips for a very long time to be able to afford it . . .

"Limitless freedom! Don't make me laugh. Your freedom disappears the moment the sun rises and the city wakes up," Clara said, jolting Jo out of her thoughts. Clara pressed the pot of ointment and a rolled bandage into her hand.

"I'm worried about you. Really. When I see the dark rings under your eyes, it scares me. But it's no wonder, considering how little sleep you've had in the last few weeks, on top of all your hard work in the smithy. Sooner or later, you'll be so exhausted you won't be able to concentrate properly, and you'll have a serious accident. Maybe at work, maybe on the bicycle. What then? Frankly, I'm relieved that you can't go out riding again."

"I feel better than I ever have before," Jo answered defiantly. "And as far as the smithy is concerned, I may not be there much longer. I have plans of my own . . ."

Clara raised her eyebrows. "Oh yes?"

Josephine nodded toward the stack of books. "You're not the only one with a hankering to learn."

# Chapter Eleven

The following evening, Josephine headed out the door as soon as she'd finished work and went in search of Oskar Reutter, who was just closing up his emporium. She helped him carry in the baskets of small items that stood in rows on the sidewalk in front of the store, then took a look around inside. She pointed to the shelves in the back that held various small appliances and gadgets—cameras, alarm clocks, kitchen helpers, and the like.

"Who repairs all these things?" she asked.

"Why? Do you have something that needs to be repaired? I can't remember your parents ever coming in here."

Jo laughed. "No, it's that . . . I'm interested in how mechanical things work myself."

"Mechanical things." Oskar Reutter frowned. But if he found her statement curious, he did not let on. "Well, if something on a grandfather clock or some other clock breaks, you'd normally take it to a mechanic. For the more complicated timepieces, it's a little different. In that case, you'd be better off going to a good watchmaker." The emporium owner stepped over to a shelf and took down a black, boxlike device. "To repair a transformer like this would require an electrician.

And if you're talking about optical equipment, then you'd want to speak to someone skilled in precision mechanics."

Josephine swallowed. "It all sounds so complicated! I thought there'd be one man for everything . . ."

"Once upon a time that was probably true. You took whatever was broken to a metalworker or a carpenter. He took his hammer, file, or anvil to it and fixed it for you. But things have gotten more specialized since then . . ." He indicated to her to follow him into his office. Once inside, he sat down at a small table on which stood a plate with several slices of bread and liverwurst. He offered the second chair to Josephine.

"My wife made this for me, because I have to do the books later. Help yourself. If I remember right, you quite liked the sandwiches I had on the train on the way to Stuttgart."

Josephine, whose stomach had started growling the moment she saw the bread, did not need to be asked twice. The liverwurst was spread thickly on the bread, not the way it was at home, with the merest scrape. After the first bite, she said, "You have one of the new bicycles, don't you? Are you happy with it?"

When Oskar Reutter had finished singing the praises of his bicycle, Josephine said, "And do you happen to know if there are people who repair bicycles?"

Oskar Reutter laughed. "Can you read minds? Two weeks ago I had an accident and the front fork broke. My beautiful boneshaker has been lying in the stable ever since. The metalworker I went to refused to weld the fork back together because he was afraid it wouldn't be stable enough. And it will be quite some time before the manufacturer can send a replacement." He opened a bottle of beer with a loud pop and held it out toward Josephine. "Would you like some?"

Josephine shook her head. Her mind was spinning so fast that she had to make an effort to keep her thoughts organized. So there was nobody who specialized in repairing bicycles . . .

"May I ask you something else?" she asked as she took another slice of bread.

"Of course."

"How does one become a mechanic? Or an electrician?"

"A very good question. There are special professional apprenticeships these days. They take at least two years but more often three or four years to complete. Usually it's the big factories who train such specialists to meet their own requirements, but there are also small workshops where master tradesmen train young men as apprentices."

"Young men? So you've never heard of a . . . girl becoming an apprentice?"

"Ah, so that's what you're getting at! I'm a bit slow on the uptake this evening," Oskar Reutter replied, laughing. "So you plan to abandon your father and finally do something for yourself?" When he saw the shocked look on her face, he threw his hands up defensively. "Don't worry, this stays between us. Do you really think I'd run to Schmied-the-Smith first thing tomorrow morning and tell him about our little conversation?"

Josephine gave a sigh of relief and leaned back in her chair. *Would it be all right to take another slice of bread?* she wondered.

"Your idea isn't a bad one, my girl. And I dare say you'd do a good job of it. Quite frankly, though, I don't think any girl is likely to find her way into such a profession. But the moment I hear of anyone in the mechanical trades who is prepared to take on a young woman as an apprentice, I'll let you know. And when you're ready, I'll be your first customer."

\*\*\*

"I must be jinxed. I'll have knocked on every door in Feuerland soon, and I have nothing to show for it," said Josephine to Frieda two weeks later. They were sitting at the old kitchen table in Frieda's garden, protected from the midsummer sun by the heavy foliage of the walnut tree. The table was covered with tubes of paint, brushes, old cloths, and a container of turpentine. In front of Frieda, there was an easel with a blank canvas. Painting was her latest passion.

"I've tried at least ten different factories, from an iron foundry to a huge engineering works. Every one turned me away."

"Feuerland?" Frieda mumbled, holding a paintbrush between her teeth and looking quizzically at her palette.

"That's the industrial area behind the Spandau Ship Canal. I know it from our cycling trips," said Josephine impatiently. "You should have seen the reactions I got when I asked about apprenticeships! 'Women have no technical understanding whatsoever. It's simply not in their blood,' one man declared. 'Women aren't intelligent enough for such work,' said the next, and he looked at me like I was mad. Another one explained that women have no 'spatial awareness,' which makes a technical profession impossible for them. Yet another said that all they needed was for 'harpies' like us to take over the workbenches." She threw her hands up in despair. "They think we're all fools. Not one—not one!—was willing to take a chance on me. The fact that I've been slaving away in my father's workshop for years counted for nothing." Jo slumped in her chair like a bellows drained of all its air. After what Oskar Reutter had told her, she had known that her search for an apprenticeship would not be easy. But she had not thought that it would be impossible.

Frieda dabbed some yellow paint on her canvas and scrutinized the effect for a moment before putting the brush aside.

"Good things take time! So now you've been to ten factories, fine. You may have to visit twenty or thirty to find a master prepared to take you on as a toolmaker."

"Mechanic," said Josephine. "That's the person who puts machines together or takes them apart and fixes them. A toolmaker makes tools."

Her old friend waved off the distinction. "Makes no difference. The important thing is that you don't give up too soon!" She pointed to the extension built onto her house, which used to house her husband's workshop. "You can have a look in there. Perhaps you'll find a tool or two you can practice with."

Josephine smiled affectionately at Frieda. "That's very kind of you. But I don't just want to tinker about. I want to really *learn* something. I—" She broke off and sighed. "It makes no sense. Women are just second-class human beings, whether we want to learn something useful or join a cycling club."

Frieda looked up abruptly from her palette. "Cycling club? So has Herrenhus allowed you and Isabelle to start cycling again?"

"No. That's why I went out to Schönefeld last week. There's a cycling association out there with its own training track, and they even hold small race meetings. At least, that's what it said on the poster I saw at Görlitzer station. I thought that if I became a member, I might have another way to cycle." She paused and frowned. "Frieda, it was horrible! There were lots of handsome, athletic men cycling around on terribly expensive bicycles, laughing and joking, drinking beer, and having the time of their lives."

"What's so horrible about that? That sounds very pleasant."

"I know! But the problem is that they don't accept women in their club!"

Frieda laughed. "What did you expect? That they'd welcome you with open arms? Offer you their bicycles and cheer you on? Men prefer to be with other men, whether it's in the workshop or in a bicycle club."

"You know what I'd love to do?" Without waiting for Frieda to answer, she continued, "I'd love to start my own women's cycling club! Find some empty hall or bare patch of land where we women can cycle without being attacked for it. And without someone like Moritz Herrenhus telling us yes or no."

"Then do it," said Frieda.

***

"Father's rekindled his interest in cycling," said Isabelle as she took a sip of lemonade. "He goes out for a ride almost every morning. I wish he'd invite me to go with him!" she added. "I wonder why he even bothered giving me a women's bicycle if I'm only allowed to ride it around in the yard. Sometimes I think he didn't buy it for *me* at all, but really he just wanted to use such a flashy gift and the outing to the cycling track as a way to show off to his business friends."

It was the start of August, Isabelle's summer vacation had just begun, and the young women were sitting in the Herrenhus garden in the light of the setting sun, enjoying a glass of lemonade. Clara had wanted to join them, but she had not appeared yet. She was probably still at the pharmacy. Again. Isabelle's parents had gone out and, for once, had not insisted that Isabelle accompany them, leaving the girls in peace.

Josephine nibbled at her bottom lip. The thought of father and daughter taking a congenial bicycle ride through the city did not please her at all. She would have much rather gone out cycling with her friend *herself.* But after the incident with her father a month earlier, Isabelle said she no longer trusted herself to secretly "borrow" the bicycles. Josephine had begun to feel that she was slowly going mad without the cyclist's wind in her face.

"If we could only go away in the summer the way my school friends do! But no, Father is 'indispensable' at the factory right now. He's instructed Mother to organize as many picnics and coffee get-togethers as she can over the next few weeks—and to invite all the eligible men in the city! Yesterday we had a visit from a Baron von Salzfeld. Most of the time he sat there as silent as pillar of salt. I get a headache just thinking about our conversation. Besides, he had bad breath," said Isabelle, continuing her tirade. "If we could go cycling now and then,

I'd at least have a little distraction from the agony. I swear, suffocation couldn't be any worse than this!"

"I've had an idea for how we can cycle without getting harassed," Josephine suddenly said. "Let's set up a cycling club just for women!"

She told Isabelle about her visit to the cycling club in Schönefeld, and when she was finished Isabelle said, "A cycling club for women . . . that's not a bad idea. I can't believe we're the only young women cycling in secret. There must be lots of us. We wouldn't lack for members, that's for sure."

Josephine's eyes shone as Isabelle went on, "We'd finally be able to cycle in peace. But what about the cost? We'd have to rent an empty hall somewhere. Or better yet, buy one. Rent, maintenance—it would take loads of money. My father certainly gives me a generous allowance, but that would never come close to covering the costs. And I don't imagine other young women are much better off. No, perhaps it's not such a good idea after all."

A despondent silence settled over them, the only sound the hum of hundreds of wasps in the wild grapevines covering the wall of the house. After a while, Josephine could no longer stand the oppressive silence.

"I've got another idea to add a little spice to the school holidays. What would you say to getting the bicycles out after midnight? Your father will be sound asleep and would never miss his Rover."

"You want to ride at midnight, in the pitch darkness?" Isabelle looked at her with incomprehension.

"Summer nights aren't as dark as in winter. We've got a full moon at the moment and the skies are clear." Jo swept a lock of hair from her forehead. "Think about the advantages: if Berlin is asleep, we can ride for much longer than we ever could in the morning. We could finally explore the Spree out to the east! Or visit the southern part of the city."

"I don't know . . . What if we were to run into a bunch of drunken nighthawks? Or cross paths with one of the gentlemen my parents have introduced me to? Or have a breakdown in the middle of the night?"

"Oh, come on, you're not normally such a fraidycat. I think a nighttime cycle out to Wannsee lake could be great fun," said Jo, challenging her friend. "Or have you been deceiving me all this time?"

Isabelle snorted. "I know full well that you're just talking like that to bait me. But you're right. Life is too tedious to let even one adventure slip away. Let's go out tonight!" She held out her hand to Josephine, who grinned and shook on the deal. But as Jo tried to take back her hand, Isabelle held it tightly. Her eyes flashed roguishly, and she said, "But just so one thing's clear. If we're going out to Wannsee lake in the dark of night, then we're going to take a swim there, too!"

Isabelle claimed that any respectable dinner or dance would be long over by one in the morning, so that would be a good time to take off. Because Josephine had no alarm clock, and because she was afraid she'd fall asleep, she didn't so much as close her eyes that evening. When the church clock struck midnight, she was sitting in her room, fully dressed, waiting for the next hour to pass. Her escape route was the same as always—she would simply creep quietly downstairs as if she had to visit the bathroom, then disappear out the back door. Still, when she finally set off, her heart was beating harder than usual.

The night was bright and clear, the moon high in the sky as Jo waited impatiently at the entrance to the Herrenhus villa. To Jo's relief, Isabelle appeared a moment later, pushing the two bicycles in her direction. She seemed in high spirits and not nearly as timid as Jo felt herself. Instead of a chatty greeting, they simply exchanged a quick look. They were about to leave the yard when Josephine stopped. "Do you smell that? It smells like your mother's perfume. Are you sure no one followed you?"

Isabelle laughed softly. "You idiot. You're smelling the white moonflowers that grow around the pavilion in the garden. They only give off their sweet perfume at night."

"Ah," said Jo meekly. Then she held Isabelle's arm tightly. "Are you sure you know how to get there?"

Her friend nodded. "We ride past the Tiergarten, then, like it or not, we have to go through Charlottenburg. From there, it's not far to Wannsee lake. Now come on, before *I* chicken out, too!"

The streetlights in Luisenstadt had all been extinguished hours before, giving the city a spooky feeling. It was all incredibly captivating. Josephine felt as though they were cycling along unknown roads. Her initial anxiety dissolved with the first push of her foot on the pedal, and her senses grew sharper than ever. She loved the sensation of the air flowing past like someone stroking her naked arms. The silhouettes of the houses, standing out in a clear, deep black against the lighter sky, looked as if they had been drawn with a sharp quill. The scent of moonflowers filled the air.

As they approached the center of Berlin, they crossed paths with pedestrians and carriages—more than either of them had anticipated. But the night owls were too busy with their own affairs to pay much attention to who they would assume were two young men on bicycles. Josephine soon realized that riding at night was infinitely better than doing so in the early morning.

"See up there on the left, halfway up the hill? That's the Reichsgarten restaurant. Father has taken Mother and me there to eat a few times," said Isabelle when they had crossed from Charlottenburg into Pichelsberg. "I'd say we're about ten minutes from Wannsee lake."

"That's good. My legs are starting to get heavy," Jo replied. She took one hand off the handlebars to wipe the sweat from her brow.

"Same. We're out of practice," Isabelle puffed.

At the shore of the lake, Isabelle dropped her bicycle in the grass and pulled off her scratchy, sweat-soaked woolen clothes. Dressed only in her bodice and underwear, she tiptoed into the water.

"I can hardly wait to cool off. What's keeping you?" she called back to Jo over her shoulder.

But instead of following Isabelle into the water, Jo remained motionless on the shore. In a voice heavy with feeling, she said, "How the lake shimmers in the moonlight! I've never seen anything so lovely . . ."

"Now don't go getting all emotional," Isabelle said as she dipped her hands in the water and sprayed water in Josephine's direction.

Jo squealed in shock, but a moment later she returned the favor. Carefree and laughing, they splashed in the water like two children.

A little while later, they sank back exhausted in the damp grass. Night insects buzzed around them, frogs could be heard croaking in the high reeds, and a water bird cried shrilly in the distance.

Isabelle ran her hand through the bristly grass. "I feel like I've washed up on a lonely island in the middle of the ocean. Or in some exotic jungle. Where all my worries have fallen to the wayside. If only we could lie here forever."

"You and your *worries*!" said Jo teasingly. She swept her hands wide, taking in the lake and all the space around them. "This moment—it belongs to us and us alone. I don't think there are many young women who are able to enjoy something like this."

Isabelle propped herself up on one elbow to look at Jo. "Beautiful moments . . . They're as fleeting as a whiff of perfume. But what if that isn't enough for me? What if I want more from life? The thought of being bored to death from dawn till dusk as Baroness von Salzfeld is unbearable. Sometimes, when I think of Clara and her enthusiasm for making pills, I envy her. I'd like to have a job, too. I want to do something useful."

Jo nodded. She understood exactly how her friend felt. "Clara tells me that women are going to start being admitted to various faculties at the university in the next few years. She wants to find out if she can study pharmacology." It was strange. Of all people, it was Clara—to whom no one had ever really given much credit—who was making one dream after another come true.

"Women at the university?" Isabelle snorted. "She might have to wait a long time. Just think what you went through when you were looking for someone to take you on as an apprentice. Do you really think the professors at the university are about to let women just waltz into their hallowed halls?"

"Oh, blast it, why is life so unfair!" Jo pounded her fist on the ground beside her. "Why can't we just do—or not do—whatever we like, whether that's going to university or becoming a mechanic? Or riding a bicycle whenever we feel like it?"

Isabelle grinned. "I'd much rather marry for love, or not at all. And I want—"

"To choose for myself whether I wear a skirt or a pair of pants," said Jo, finishing her friend's thought with one of her own.

They burst out laughing.

Jo sighed longingly. "Will such possibilities ever be open to women?"

For a moment the only sound was the chirping of the crickets. Finally, Isabelle answered, "Perhaps . . . when the new century arrives."

"Do you think it will only take nine years?" Jo could not suppress the skepticism in her voice. "The wind that's blowing so hot in our faces will have to shift a great deal to blow away all the dusty, old views about us."

"There may just be such a wind one day," Isabelle said boldly.

"It would have to be a turn-of-the-century wind," said Jo drily and got to her feet. It was time for them to be heading back home.

They were already sitting on their bicycles when Josephine paused and looked thoughtfully at her friend.

"A turn-of-the-century wind—I like that!"

\*\*\*

Josephine experienced their nighttime cycling expeditions in a kind of rapture. When she rode through the silent streets silvered by moonlight—especially when she went out without Isabelle—Jo felt herself ennobled, courageous, even majestic. Again and again, she gave thanks to God that Moritz Herrenhus never locked the gate to his property at night. Jo pursued her passion like a drinker who can never quench his thirst for alcohol. In the fall, she went cycling practically every night, forgetting the long, hard workday she endured in her father's workshop. Forgetting that she was actually tired, that her back ached and her arms were sore. Forgetting that her head still buzzed from the blows of her father's hammer, that her eyes still burned from the forge's fumes. Some evenings, she did not even have enough time to eat. But as soon as she was riding through the city's leafy, sparsely lit boulevards, she forgot the growling of her hungry stomach, and goose bumps prickled the skin on her back. The knowledge that the winter cold would soon bring these rides to an end sent Jo into a panic—she had to take advantage of every conceivable opportunity.

*** 

Come October, the birds began to wing their way south. All along the Spree, the fog lay like a feather blanket over the streets, and the cold east wind tore ruthlessly at the trees until they dropped their mantle of leaves in exhaustion. The fall, which had descended upon the countryside weeks earlier, now engulfed the city as well.

Jo's eyes watered and she had to blink to be able to see anything at all. Despite her single-minded concentration, the bicycle's front wheel slipped constantly on the cobblestones, which were slick from the rain and fallen leaves. It took all her effort to avoid a fall.

"You're not thinking about going out tonight, are you?" Isabelle had asked, horrified at the very idea, when they had run into each other on the street earlier that evening. Isabelle had been on her way home from school, and Jo had been shoveling coal from the street through a hatch that opened into the basement of their building.

"I certainly am," Jo had grumbled back. She needed something to look forward to, especially since she had suffered another rebuff that very morning, this time by a metalware factory where she had gone to inquire about an apprenticeship. She had been to more than two dozen places now.

Isabelle had shaken her head and stated flatly that as far as she was concerned the riding season was well and truly over.

*We'll see,* Jo had thought, but she kept her opinion to herself.

As she rode through the grim and threatening streets that night, she wondered if her friend had not perhaps been right. The wind grew stronger at every corner, and jagged chestnut leaves whirled through the air, slapping her in the face and making her flinch.

*I'll just go a little farther down Landsberger Allee, then I'll turn back,* Jo thought. Her warm, comfortable bed was suddenly very tempting.

A moment later, she heard a low crack high in the canopy of branches of the trees lining the street, and a branch crashed onto the street right in front of her.

When she came to, she felt a burning pain in her right shoulder that grew so intense it took her breath away. Where was she? What had happened? She blinked.

"She's opened her eyes! There, officer, see for yourself!"

"What luck, the girl's come to."

"I told you she was alive, didn't I?"

"Hey, you, girl!"

Jo groaned in pain as someone shook her roughly by the arm.

"Wake up! Hey!"

She blinked again and found herself looking into the faces of a handful of strangers.

"Where . . . what . . ." She ran her tongue over her lips and tasted something metallic. Blood. A cold shudder ran through her. She tried to look down at her body. Her pants, her coat, everything was soaking wet and dirty.

"You've had a fall. Looks as if you cycled over this branch here, and the fork on your bicycle broke," said a man in uniform. "You're lucky you didn't break your neck! The people who live here found you and called for me."

A policeman. Jo closed her eyes in despair. She saw in an instant the impossible position she had put herself in. She was lying on a rain-soaked street in the middle of the night, wearing men's clothes, far from home, and her shoulder was probably broken. But one thing was far worse: the fork on the bicycle was broken, too.

She had destroyed Moritz Herrenhus's Rover.

# Chapter Twelve

*Berlin, November 1891*
*Barnim Road Women's Prison*

Jo pulled the smelly blanket farther over her head. How was she ever supposed to repay the debt for the damage to the bicycle? Or would Herrenhus demand the money from her parents? What a terrifying notion! But only one of many.

"Do something with your life!" Frieda had always told her. Her aging friend had put so much stock in her . . .

Jo's empty gaze focused on the heavy iron bars set over the window. She had bitterly disappointed every person who had ever meant anything to her. And instead of doing something with her life, here she was, behind bars.

\*\*\*

Moritz Herrenhus glanced nervously at his gold pocket watch. Five past one. They had agreed to meet at one. What did this delay mean? Gottlieb Neumann was known for being punctual. The owner of

Elektronische Werke Berlin, or EWB as it was commonly known, a major company in the field of electrical equipment, had a reputation for precision. By arriving late, was Neumann trying to tell him that *he*, Neumann, was the one who set the tenor of their dealings, regardless of the currently poor state of his business? Or had the man reconsidered and decided not to show up at all? Had he found another solution to the acute problem afflicting him? But what solution could there be? As far as Moritz Herrenhus knew, no bank was willing to extend the important industrialist any more loans—his existing obligations were already excessive. True, the spirit of entrepreneurship was everywhere. But when Neumann had snapped up yet another of his competitors without first securing the necessary financing, a buzz spread through the Berlin business establishment. While some called it farsightedness and others called it sheer madness, they all agreed that electrical engineering would be the preeminent industry in the years ahead.

Moritz Herrenhus had settled on the foyer of Berlin's Central Hotel as their meeting point, but he wondered why he hadn't chosen a restaurant instead. Then he could have eaten a little something while he waited. He loathed waiting. It was trying enough that he should have to have this conversation at all. And who did he have to thank for this displeasure? At the thought of his daughter, Isabelle, a soft growl escaped his throat.

They had been on the lookout for a husband for her for more than a year. He had paid exorbitant hairdressing bills and bought dozens of evening gowns, along with jewelry, shoes, accessories, and courtesy gifts. "Go the whole hog or don't go at all" was his motto. He didn't want to regret making too little effort someday. Isabelle's own efforts, however, left a lot to be desired. She had preferred to go gallivanting around town with her criminal friend, Josephine, rather than take the business of getting married seriously. How could that girl have dared to take his bicycle as if it were her own! Well, at least she had received her just desserts. He could have settled the matter privately with

Schmied-the-Smith—he had had to pay for the damage to the bicycle of course—but with Josephine Schmied behind bars, she would no longer be able to distract Isabelle from what really mattered. That thought, at least, gave Herrenhus a measure of satisfaction.

If Isabelle had been ugly or lacking in charm, he could have accepted the fact that there was still no sign of a marriage proposal on the horizon. But even with her unruly red hair, Isabelle was always one of the prettiest young women present at any social event they attended. She was consistently the center of attention of a cluster of young gentlemen, always earned admiring looks and compliments, and received invitations to even more parties. Isabelle laughed and flirted with the young men and rarely sat out a dance. His wife, at one time the grande dame of the Berlin ballet, enjoyed herself immensely at such parties. If it were up to the two of them, Isabelle could go on playing her games for years. But he was fed up with it. He wanted results.

It wasn't that he felt any pressing need to see his daughter actually tie the knot or to bounce a grandchild on his knee—heaven forbid. Or even that he wanted to find someone to provide for his only child. He had more money than he knew what to do with. As a young man, he had not even dared to dream that it might be possible to put together the kind of fortune he'd amassed simply by making aprons and long underwear. But money was one thing—and social status quite another. More than anything, he wanted to hear Herrenhus mentioned in the same breath as the names Krupp, Rothschild, and Neumann. And because money was not the means to that end, his only option was to make the best possible match for his daughter.

Moritz Herrenhus's eyes flicked to the large grandfather clock beside the reception desk. Half past one. He was losing patience. With forced calm, Herrenhus asked one of the hotel pages to bring him a cup of coffee. His relief was great when he finally saw Gottlieb Neumann hurrying toward the entrance shortly before two.

"There was a fire on Friedrichstrasse. No carriages could get through. I had to cover the last stretch on foot," said Neumann instead of a greeting. Despite being almost an hour late, he offered no apology—it was unbelievable! Three attendants immediately appeared to relieve the magnate of his top hat and coat. Herrenhus couldn't help but note that only *one* of the attendants had made such an effort for him. Airily, he said, "Alas, there are some things we cannot control, but others we can." He waited for his counterpart to take his seat before adding, "As I understand it, your EWB has run into some . . . pecuniary difficulties with the takeover of Mayer's Engineering?" He stirred his coffee pleasantly as he spoke.

The corners of Gottlieb Neumann's mouth twitched almost imperceptibly. "I see you're not a man to beat around the bush," he replied gruffly. "Then neither will I! It boils down to this: I need money, and you have it. And it appears that you're prepared to invest it in EWB. The question is whether *I* want to . . . pay your price."

Moritz Herrenhus offered a slight smile as he said, "Who's talking about a *price* here? I'd much sooner talk about a gain for you and your family!" He took a sip of lukewarm coffee before continuing, "I've heard that your son completed his economic studies summa cum laude. I'm sure you can hardly wait for him to come to work for you and carry on the family tradition. And then start a family of his own to carry your name on to the next generation . . ."

The industrial magnate frowned, then said in a scornful tone, "So that's the way the wind is blowing, eh? I might have guessed. Your daughter and my son."

Moritz Herrenhus raised his eyebrows. "Why not? Whoever ends up with Isabelle should consider himself a lucky man."

"Just as you would consider yourself lucky, finally being able to ascend into certain circles as a result of our children's union?" The taunting tone in Neumann's voice was unmistakable, but Moritz Herrenhus was not bothered by it.

"And if that were so?" He gestured casually with one hand.

"But . . ." Confronted by Moritz Herrenhus's frankness, Gottlieb Neumann's carefully controlled facade began to crumble. "Adrian is a clever young man—astute, perceptive. At the merest hint that I was trying to influence him in this matter, he would be onto me!"

"Then why not play your hand openly? Tell Adrian how things really are. Anyone can overspeculate, and I'm sure your astute son will understand that." Moritz Herrenhus grinned. "For my part, I would be more than willing to put whatever sum you like at your disposal as an interest-free loan for the next five years—on one condition: your son and my daughter become engaged within the next twelve months, and they be married within two years." He leaned across the table, his eyes shining with both arrogance and audacity. "The only question now is, how much influence can you exert on your son? Or is your influence on him just as negligible as on your current financial situation?"

*****

The Christmas party of the Berlin Factory-Owners Union, better known as the BFU, a consortium of businesspeople in the manufacturing industries, took up the entire seventh floor of the Berlin Hotel.

A large raffle had been set up directly behind the entrance, opposite the cloakroom. The prizes had been donated by the guests themselves, and the proceeds from the ticket sales were to go to a charitable cause. Two long tables creaked ominously under the weight of the various items stacked on top of them: silver-plated cutlery in elegant boxes lay beside piles of lily-white sheets, saucepans beside top hats, mother-of-pearl buttons beside thimbles. Someone had pinned numerous aprons and dark skirts on the wall behind the tables. The attractive ticket sellers were already surrounded by guests. *Do all these men and women really want to win a Herrenhus apron?* Isabelle wondered as she waited with her parents for the cloakroom attendants to take their coats.

She was in good spirits as she wandered through the festively decorated room arm in arm with her father. The place smelled of fir trees, roast turkey, and baked apples. The gala dinner had been set up in the main hall, and an adjoining hall had been reserved for dancing and music. At the moment, all there was to hear from inside was a few off-key notes from violins—the musicians were tuning their instruments. Several trays with wine and French champagne had been set up in alcoves on either side of the main hall, and Isabelle accepted a glass of bubbly from the first one she passed. She intended to milk every drop of enjoyment from the evening. As for her father's plans . . . She simply smiled. She had managed to fend off his potential suitors so far.

"Tonight is a very special evening, my dears!" Raising his glass, Moritz Herrenhus made a private toast to Isabelle and her mother, then set his glass down. "Let's see where they've put us."

They had just taken their places at one of the long tables when an older gentleman in a tailcoat approached them, stiff-legged and wearing a dour expression. Isabelle narrowed her eyes. Wasn't that the father of her classmate Irene? She had seen the man several times at school, and she knew that Gottlieb Neumann was one of the institute's patrons. Isabelle's fine mood fell at the thought that her fellow pupil, with her arrogant, affected behavior, was also there.

"My dear Gottlieb! How nice to see you here." Her father practically leaped from his chair and shook the newcomer's hand enthusiastically.

Isabelle started. *Gottlieb?* Since when was her father on such intimate terms with the magnate?

Only then did she see that the older gentleman had a younger man in tow. He was tall and slim without being gawky, and she guessed he was in his early or midtwenties. He had deep-blue eyes and golden hair, like a hero from an old legend. Isabelle could not remember ever seeing such hair on a man. Because the young man—in contrast to most of those present—wore no beard, Isabelle was able to observe, inconspicuously, his attractive, full lips, although on second glance they seemed slightly pinched. He looked irritated, as if peeved at something beyond his control. Isabelle grinned inwardly. She knew that mood only too well. That wasn't Irene's brother, though . . . or was it? *If he is, then the dear Lord distributed the looks in the family in a most unjust way,* she thought, smiling. The young man was certainly handsome.

"Adrian has just returned from his studies in Munich. He only came home to Berlin on a few rare occasions during that time, and the city is practically foreign to him now. He has not yet had a chance to refresh his old friendships. If your daughter would do Adrian the honor of being his companion for the evening, I would be very grateful," said Gottlieb Neumann, a smile frozen on his face. "Perhaps a hot chocolate to kick off the evening?" He glanced with displeasure at Isabelle's champagne glass, then nodded toward the café down a corridor from the main hall.

"The honor would be all Isabelle's, wouldn't it, my dear?" Moritz Herrenhus said.

Somewhat distracted, it took a moment for Isabelle to realize that the men were talking about her.

"Now don't act shy, my girl. Go spend a pleasant evening with Adrian Neumann."

***

"Hot chocolate or coffee?" Adrian asked brusquely as soon as they were seated in the café. The waitresses looked bored. They would be much busier later in the evening, but for the time being, Isabelle and Adrian were the only guests, occupying one of the small tables decorated with candles.

"Coffee," answered Isabelle without enthusiasm. From the corridor came the smell of roast meat. Her stomach growled quietly. No doubt they were already serving the soup in the main hall. She hoped to return to her place at the table soon.

After Adrian had placed their order with one of the waitresses and the coffee arrived, he leaned across the table to Isabelle. His blue eyes shot tiny, angry arrows at her as he hissed, "Don't think for a minute that this was my idea. Just because your father has money to burn and my father, coincidentally, needs it, don't imagine I have even the slightest interest in you. I am doing this out of loyalty to my family and for no other reason. But when I think of what they expect of me . . ." He gestured in disgust. "It makes me sick. I should have stayed in Munich."

Isabelle felt as if she'd been struck by lightning. What nonsense was this guy babbling? It was . . . She'd never heard anyone be so rude!

"Why are you taking such a horrible tone with me? As if *I* want to be sitting here drinking coffee with you. It was *your father's* idea for me to play nursemaid, not mine. I'd much rather be chewing on a turkey leg now." In her agitation, she swept a red curl that had worked loose from her elaborate hairdo out of her face. Then she grabbed her pearl-studded handbag and stood up. When her father found out about this crude young man's impertinence, he'd see why she didn't want to spend another minute with him. And even if he didn't see it, what difference did that make to her?

She looked down at Adrian. His own wrath seemed to have dissipated somewhat after her display of righteous fury, and he was now looking more unsettled than angry.

"But there's one thing you have to explain to me—what was that you said about my father's money?"

"Are you kidding?" Adrian Neumann asked then, frowning.

"Not at all," Isabelle replied sharply. His ingenuous face just made her angrier. "What's that all about?" she barked.

"But I thought . . ."

"You thought what?" said Isabelle, exasperated. If she hurried, she might still arrive in time for the main course.

"I thought you knew."

Isabelle rolled her eyes. "Look, the last thing I need now is to guess at riddles."

Adrian leaned back in his chair. In the most nonchalant tone he could muster, he said, "It's quite simple. Our fathers have decided that we are to marry. Just like sealing a business deal. If you and I walk down the aisle in the next two years, your father will help my father out of his dire financial straits." He sounded as if he were talking about the weather.

Isabelle slumped back onto her chair like someone had knocked the wind out of her. "Say that again . . ."

Isabelle listened to Adrian without moving a muscle. She would never have thought her father capable of selling her off like one of the products his factory churned out. *"Tonight is a very special evening"*—his words echoed loudly in her ears. It was only with effort that she fought back the tears lurking just beneath her eyelids. She took a sip of the lukewarm coffee in a daze. It tasted like a rotten lemon.

"Now don't go looking like I've done anything to you," said Adrian. "I don't feel any better about this than you do. Seriously. But my father desperately needs the money, or he would never have asked me to . . . do something like this. I have no idea what to do."

"Are you mad? Have you taken leave of your senses?" Isabelle glared at him wide-eyed. "I'm supposed to marry you just so that your father can get his hands on my father's money? I *don't want* to get married! Not to you, not to anybody else. And my father knows that. He has sold me out . . . and sold me!" Droplets of spittle landed on the table in front of her and she wiped them away in an unladylike gesture with the sleeve of her ruby-red silk evening dress.

"Marriage is quite far down on my own list," Adrian murmured. "I have so many other plans. And a very special dream right at the top . . ." His face assumed a faraway look, and for a moment Isabelle considered asking Adrian about his dream. But then she caught herself. What Adrian thought or did made no difference to her. She wanted freedom and adventure, and instead she was sitting in a trap, like a goldfish in a glass of water.

As a gloomy silence settled over them, Isabelle sunk into her grim vision of the future, Adrian into his.

Did her mother know about her father's plan? Did she endorse it? She was still shocked by the news that her father had been scheming behind her back. At the same time, an unbridled fury was welling inside her. If her father thought he could sell her like a harem bride, he was going to be sorely disappointed. She would defend herself. The only question was how.

"What if we . . ." she pursed her lips, musing. She hated it when her thoughts came galloping through her head like wild horses and she couldn't rein them in.

Adrian, who had ordered a glass of schnapps by then, threw back the drink in a single swig. The glass clacked as he set it down on the table. "Yes?"

"What if we turn our fathers' weapons back on them?" Isabelle's chest was rising and falling as if she had been riding her bicycle too fast. She was so excited she could hardly breathe. A moment before, she had felt nothing but despair, but now she was suddenly confident that she had found a way out of the mess they were both in. She grasped Adrian's right hand, which was cold from the schnapps glass, and said, "We could act as though we accept their plan. Admittedly, we would have to go out with each other a few times, but in Berlin one is more or less forced to cross paths from time to time." She made a disparaging gesture. "And we would have to pretend that we didn't dislike each other. They won't expect any more than that, anyway. At some point, we'll also have to plan our . . . *engagement*"—as she uttered the word, her face twisted as if she'd bitten her tongue—"to make it all look genuine so that *my* father is ready to help *your* father out of the bind he's in. But if we play our roles well, it doesn't have to go as far as a wedding, does it? We can string them along, and in the meantime we can each lead our lives as we like."

Adrian nodded, evidently considering the idea. "You mean we stall our fathers as long as we can, then just before the big day you suddenly lose your nerve or I come down with the measles. Or something else happens that stops us going through with it. Do you really think we could pull it off?" Skepticism was fighting a pitched battle with his desire to run with Isabelle's idea, a battle that showed on his face.

Isabelle smiled. "I'll have a nervous breakdown on the church threshold if I must."

Adrian's full lips widened into a grin. "If your performance just now is anything to judge by, I believe you'd actually do it! It's certainly worth a shot. But we'll have to arrange our next rendezvous here and now. The banks are breathing down my father's neck, and he'll be overjoyed if I go back to him with some positive news."

Isabelle shrugged. Whatever! All she cared about was putting one over on *her* father. "Just tell me when and where."

"I've heard from my sister, Irene, that you're not averse to bicycling. How would you like to go to my cycling club together at the start of the new year? I only rarely had a chance to go cycling while I was in Munich, and I can hardly wait to get back on two wheels. You could watch while I train. Then it wouldn't be a complete waste of time, at least."

He looked at time spent with her as wasted? Isabelle was about to get angry at his choice of words, but then the pleasure she felt at conning her father won out.

"So I look on admiringly while you cycle around?" she said mockingly. "That would be just the sort of thing a good little future wife would do. Perfect for what we have in mind."

Half an hour later, they left the café arm in arm. Adrian Neumann led Isabelle to one of the bubbly bars and ordered a bottle of their finest French champagne.

"To our deal!"

Isabelle smiled at him. "To us!"

# Chapter Thirteen

Tea and pastries? Or canapés and a glass of wine from the red goblets? Sophie Berg had spent the entire day puzzling over such questions. After all, it wasn't every day that they had a doctor pay them a visit. And this doctor would be the successor to Dr. Fritsche, God rest his soul.

"We have to establish a good relationship with the new doctor. We want his patients to buy their medicine from *us*, don't we?" her husband, Anton, had cautioned her that morning. Typical of him. All he ever thought about was his pharmacy. Then he had added, "We should be thankful that they managed to find anyone at all prepared to take over the old practice. The people here in the district need a real doctor. That's not something I can replace in the long run."

*Most importantly,* thought Sophie Berg as she admired her elegantly laid table, *Anton is a pharmacist, not a doctor, and that won't do for Clara in the long term.* Clara was so delicate, so fragile . . . Sophie hated the fact that her daughter came in contact with sick people every day in the pharmacy. What if Clara came down with some terrible disease? She would not entrust her daughter to Anton's medicine in such a case. Nothing could replace trained medical assistance. This was the real reason Sophie Berg felt a need to establish a good relationship with the new doctor.

She was probably correct in deciding on tea and pastries. It was quite likely that the doctor belonged to the ever-growing group of teetotalers in Berlin who were against the consumption of alcohol in any form. Some of those men and women had gone so far as to picket the pharmacy for selling rubbing alcohol. The nerve! Sophie Berg, who was not opposed to an occasional glass of spirits, had watched them from upstairs, shaking her head.

For the umpteenth time, she looked toward the grandfather clock that they had acquired, along with the house and pharmacy, from Anton's parents. Sophie hated the huge, ugly piece of furniture, but she had to admit that it had not once broken down in all the years they'd had it. Three in the afternoon. Anton was planning to close the pharmacy at six that evening, and Dr. Fritsche's successor had accepted their invitation for six-thirty. Sophie smoothed an invisible wrinkle from her gray outfit. Was it right for the occasion? Or should she put on her dark-blue, marine-style dress? And shouldn't she at least put out a carafe of Advocaat? What did Clara think?

"Clara? Clara!"

***

When the doorbell rang at six-thirty, Clara leaped frantically to her feet to welcome their guest. Finally!

Her mother had called her up from the pharmacy countless times that day to debate this or that question about the evening ahead. More important to Sophie than a shop full of customers was the question of which tablecloth looked prettier, the Plauen lace or her own hand-stitched one. With every interruption, Clara, too, had grown more anxious. Now, she only hoped that Fritsche's successor would not stay too long. And that he wouldn't regale them with hour-long monologues about his service in the Franco-German War. She was tired and her legs hurt from standing all day. Besides, she still had something important to do. She glanced eagerly at the paperwork that had come in the mail earlier and was now lying on the sideboard: the statutes of the University of Jena, the rules for admission, and additional information that might perhaps be important for her . . .

Clara forced herself to smile and opened the door. The University of Jena was instantly forgotten.

*"You?"*

"They wanted to offer me the chief physician's post in the Deaconess Hospital, but then I saw the announcement in the newspaper. 'Successor Sought!'" Gerhard Gropius looked over the top of his teacup first at Clara's parents, then at Clara herself. For a brief moment, their eyes met. A burning sensation shot through her and she quickly lowered her eyes. Oh, how well she remembered those brown eyes . . .

"Chief physician?" Sophie Berg gasped in admiration. "You would give up such a career for our district?"

Gerhard Gropius smiled ingratiatingly at his hostess. His lips were as full and perfectly formed as Clara remembered them.

"I admit that it was not an easy decision to make."

Gropius was to take over from Dr. Fritsche? Clara's thoughts whirled like leaves in an autumn wind.

Anton Berg looked thoughtful. "As a tenured doctor in a hospital, you could organize your free time as you liked. As a local doctor with your own practice, your patients will determine the hours you work." He laughed. "The people around here were always fetching old Fritsche out of bed in the middle of the night. My own dear wife did just that more than once, didn't you, Sophie?"

Clara gave her father a stony glance. Did he have to say that?

"Only for the well-being of our daughter," said her mother waspishly. When she turned back to their guest, her tone was once again as sweet as sugar. "I'm sure Dr. Gropius has the greatest compassion for that."

The young doctor reached across the table, took Sophie Berg's hand, and squeezed it. "A mother's true heart beats with concern for the ones she loves. Especially when it comes to such a charming young lady as your daughter." He smiled at Clara, who nearly fainted.


It had happened the previous summer. After her fall from the bicycle, she had been taken to the Deaconess Hospital. Her broken leg had been examined, then set in a plaster cast. She did not tell anyone that the accident involved a bicycle. She could live without all the accusations that particular revelation would involve. Even her mother still believed that she had suffered the break on the way to Isabelle's house.

Initially the pain had been intolerable. The doctors ordered absolute bed rest, then only light exercise for the next four weeks. After a week, she was bored half to death. So one mild, sweet-smelling summer evening after her parents had left she climbed out of bed and ventured out toward the hospital's green courtyard. She did not make it as far as the garden, though, for at the end of the long, narrow corridor she discovered the hospital library. Curious, she peeked inside and saw the extensive book-lined shelves. The room was empty. First her eyes, then her fingers, wandered avidly across the spines of the books. *The Relationship of Sensory and Motoric Perception to the Cerebral Surface in Human Beings, On the Convalescence of the Retina*, and *On the Causes of Pigment Migration in the Retina: Some Observations on Photographing the Fundus Oculis*—the hospital's library seemed to specialize in works devoted to ophthalmology. But wait, what was that? *Textbook of Human Anatomy.* Clara began leafing through the six-hundred-page tome, which was embellished with many colorful woodcuts. The book was heavy and bulky, but the illustrations of the human heart, liver, and lungs were extraordinarily enlightening.

Even today, she did not know how it happened. From one moment to the next, her plastered leg gave way. She fell over backward, the book fell to the floor with a loud crack, and she blacked out.

When she had come to, she did not immediately know where she was. Her leg . . . the library. She had fallen again, this time without a bicycle. She hoped she would be able to make it back to her room, though her injured leg had begun to hurt again. She was clumsily trying to get back to her feet when a man appeared in the doorway.

"Oh my, what have you done to yourself?"

Embarrassed, Clara had looked up to see a man with a slim face with full lips and brown eyes, the irises shining silver at their edges. He wore a white shirt beneath a white coat decorated with an emblem that showed him to be an assistant doctor. He looked to be in his midtwenties.

She tried frantically to come up with an explanation as he felt her pulse. His hand was warm and soft and comforting. Then he ran his right hand down over the cast. Despite the plaster, Clara felt a gentle prickling in her leg.

"Everything seems to be in order. Now tell me, young lady, what in the world are you doing in here?"

"I . . . was feeling a little bored and I thought . . . The doctor who's been treating me said I had to get some light exercise."

The doctor looked aghast. "My colleague had in mind light exercise while sitting in bed, not strolling around the hospital corridors alone with your leg wrapped in plaster! Too much movement for a delicate female body is never a good thing."

Clara looked down sheepishly. "I'm sorry." She was mortified.

The man tilted her head up and looked earnestly into her eyes. "And well you should be. The thought of a pretty young woman like you having to walk with a limp for the rest of her life because of such carelessness is unbearable to me." Then, with an endearing smile, he reached out his hand to her. "I actually came in here because I wanted to use the peace and quiet of the library to research an interesting case, but that can wait until tomorrow. After all, I can't allow you to be bored. So I will accompany you back to your room, arrange a cool glass of lemonade for us, and, if you will allow me, keep you company for a while." With a smile that made Clara's heart melt, he added, "My name is Gerhard Gropius."

"Clara Berg," she breathed back, enraptured. What a handsome, charming man! Would this count as a kind of rendezvous? Isabelle and Josephine would be floored when she told them about it.

They were just leaving the library when she remembered the book that had fallen from her hand. She pointed at the floor and said, "Would you be so kind as to pick up that book? I'm afraid I was quite clumsy with it earlier."

*"Textbook of Human Anatomy?"* Gerhard Gropius looked at her in astonishment.

"It's very exciting, isn't it? What do you think? Could I perhaps borrow it for a day or two?" She reached out for the book.

But the doctor clutched it to his chest. With a frown and an irate look in his eyes, he said, "Miss Clara, please. That is not proper reading matter for a young lady, as God is my witness. The illustrations alone! Crucial for a doctor, to be sure, but for a young woman . . . You'd give yourself a shock!"

Shortly after that, she walked down the corridor silently on the arm of the doctor. He had left as soon as they reached her room, making some flimsy excuse to go. There was no more talk of sharing a lemonade. For the rest of the evening she was afflicted by the pain in her leg, but even worse was the feeling that she had—somehow, inexplicably—let this attractive man down. He had been so courteous and kind, then suddenly, he'd grown cool and aloof, almost hostile. What had she done wrong? Frustrated and confused, she had finally fallen asleep.

Gerhard Gropius . . . She dreamed of him not only that night but many others. For weeks afterward, she was consumed by his beautiful eyes and full lips. But she had not seen him in the hospital again. She told herself over and over that it was not meant to be. But it was poor consolation.

And now . . . earlier, at the door, she had nearly had a stroke. Her heart had begun hammering so hard she could feel the pulsing in her throat. *I think I'm going to faint,* she thought, but didn't. What kind of impression would that have made? She could tell that he had recognized her, too. A soft sigh escaped her.

"The weeks since Dr. Fritsche's death have been hard. The people have been coming directly to me for medical advice. Had my daughter not been there to help . . ." Anton Berg shrugged. "I don't know how I would have managed the workload."

Her father's words pulled Clara out of her thoughts. "You're exaggerating, Father," she said fondly. Though she felt flattered by his words, she tried frantically to think of some observation to divert the attention away from herself.

"I can well understand that your customers would have enjoyed having your lovely daughter pack their medicine or hold the door open for them. With so much charm and grace on hand at the pharmacy, I can imagine that more than one gentleman calls by every day to purchase cough drops or snuff, am I right?" The young doctor smiled at Clara, causing her to redden immediately. So he thought she was charming?

"Dear Miss Clara, if you promise to serve me in person, then I shall drop by your pharmacy first thing tomorrow morning."

She would see him again tomorrow! "Gladly," she said quietly and stroked her hands over her slightly creased skirt. Blast it, why had she stayed in the pharmacy until the last minute instead of spending a little time on her appearance? She nibbled covertly at her bottom lip to give it a little more color.

"Well, now that you are the new doctor here, you and Clara will no doubt bump into each other quite a bit." Sophie Berg was all smiles, as if she were personally responsible for that circumstance. "More tea? Or cookies?" She held out the highly polished silver bowl toward the young man.

"My dear Mrs. Berg, you are a most gracious hostess." He took a cinnamon cookie from the bowl and bit into it with a boyish appetite.

Clara looked jealously at her mother. Did she have to monopolize Dr. Gropius like that?

"The homemaker's virtues are indispensable for a lady," added Sophie Berg. "Which is why we sent our Clara to the best home-economics school in Berlin for a year."

"Where I practically died of boredom," Clara added with a laugh. "But the horror finally came to an end, thank God. I can bake cookies and serve tea perfectly well without those kinds of lessons." Smiling, she reached across the table for the teapot and refilled Gerhard Gropius's cup with a skillful flourish. "I hope that's all right?"

Sophie Berg opened her mouth as if to say something, then changed her mind.

Anton Berg cleared his throat. "Pardon me if what I said a moment ago gave you the wrong impression," he said, turning to his guest. "You mustn't think that we compel our daughter to do simple assistant work or cleaning in the pharmacy. We would never demand that of our child. I've been teaching Clara something of the profession—and with quite a bit of success, if I do say so myself. Clara's healing ointments are even better than my own."

"Father . . ." Clara lowered her eyes, abashed. First her mother brought up the home-economics school, and now her father chimed in. Why did they feel such a need to extol her merits to Gerhard Gropius? Of course, she wanted him to like her as well. But not in such an obvious way! She was beginning to get an idea of how Isabelle must feel at the balls her father dragged her to.

With her head still bowed, she looked over at Gerhard Gropius, and their eyes met. Had it been so warm there in the salon the whole time? Clara felt hot suddenly, almost feverish, as if a cold was on the way.

"The truth is the truth, Clara," said her father, patting her hand. Then he turned back to Gerhard Gropius. "Honestly, I didn't initially believe that a young woman could demonstrate a talent for the pharmacist's profession. But my daughter has proven me wrong." He spoke with clear pride in his voice. "I can even imagine that Clara will be among the first young women to be accepted into a course of study in the biological-pharmaceutical faculty of the University of Jena. In any case, the masters there are currently discussing such a possibility. Should they decide to accept women, I will wholeheartedly support Clara in her wish to attend."

"Your daughter wants to study at the university?" Gropius abruptly set down his half-eaten cookie on a plate. His tone suggested that he might as well have asked, "Your daughter wants to fly to the moon?"

Clara giggled in embarrassment but immediately collected herself. "Well . . . it's true—" she began. But before she could explain any more, her mother cut her off.

"Pipe dreams!" said Sophie Berg, narrowing her eyes at her husband. "Anton, please. The way you talk, you're bound to give our guest a false impression. You'll have Dr. Gropius thinking our daughter is one of those bluestockings who is so wedded to her studies that she can't so much as knit a sock."

"Why must we spend all this time talking about me?" asked Clara bitterly. "I would be far more interested in finding out what plans Dr. Gropius has for his practice."

But instead of following up on Clara's objection, the young doctor turned to her mother.

"My dear Mrs. Berg, I would never think of comparing your charming daughter Clara to one of those addled furies! It is shameful the way some young women abuse the trends of our day to pursue their own ends, but your daughter is certainly not one of them. I find it wonderful when a young woman is ready to assist her parents, as Miss Clara does in the pharmacy. But I also believe that too much hustling and bustling is not appropriate, and I would therefore like to make a suggestion." He smiled slightly, then turned to Clara. "I would like to invite you for a cup of coffee, if I may. On my way here, I passed a very pretty little café at the end of the street. Perhaps I will be able to distract you a little from all your work."

# Chapter Fourteen

In the past, she had had to make sure that she got enough to eat so that she had the strength and stamina to ride the bicycle. These days, she had to make sure she got enough to eat just to avoid losing too much weight. This was what was going through Josephine's mind as she stuffed the dry, slightly blackened roll into her skirt pocket. Slices of black bread, coarse rolls, a little bland marmalade, and chamomile tea—that was the extent of prison breakfast every day. Even today, Christmas Eve. But the baker had made one exception: either he was in love or he thought the special day needed a little something extra, because he'd burned everything he'd baked. Still, Jo reached greedily into the bread basket in the middle of the table one more time. *No doubt Mother has baked the round gingerbread cookies she makes every year,* thought Jo wistfully. Everyone at her table was trying to hoard as much food as they could. Not that having the food on your plate or in your pocket meant it was safe. Most of the girls were quick to hand over whatever rations they had to Adele or one of her entourage. Even Josephine had occasionally been left with no choice but to give up her food; avoiding a fight was usually worth a piece of bread. But today was different; today her stomach was growling far too loudly. She fixed Adele with a glare that said, *Don't even think about trying to take anything from me today!*

"I feel sick. If I eat one more bite of this black stuff, I'm going to throw up," whispered Martha, who sat beside Josephine. "Do you want this?"

Just a few weeks earlier, Josephine would have rejected the nibbled roll in disgust. Today, she added it to the one already in her pocket.

"So now you're pinching the food from Martha's mouth, too?" Adele hissed at her from across the table. "She's got to eat for two. The decent thing would be for you to give her something and not the other way around."

Josephine did not respond. Talking at the table was forbidden, and the guards were not to be trifled with. If someone was caught, punishment was swift, and the talker would have to help with incinerating the garbage, cleaning the latrines, or scrubbing the greasy pans in addition to her regular work. Adele was the only one who put herself above the ban on speaking and got away with it. Adele with her cold eyes . . . Sometimes Josephine had the feeling that even the guards were afraid of her. But Josephine was not. For her, Adele was more of a troublesome pest. What was Adele trying to prove with her endless harassment? It was always about not missing out, in any way. Snatching the choicest scrap of food. Getting the best place. Which was why Josephine did not understand Adele's remark about Martha. No doubt she was just saying it to annoy Jo. What nonsense! Wouldn't they be better off sticking together? As if life behind bars wasn't hard enough already!

Silent night, holy night—as if.

*If only Gerd Melchior were here and I could spend a few hours with him in the workshop,* Josephine thought. But the caretaker had gone to stay with his son for a few days, a circumstance that only added to Jo's bad mood. The time passed much more quickly when she was working with Melchior. Sometimes she was even able to forget where she was.

The chief guard of the juvenile wing, a powerfully built, middle-aged woman, appeared at the door of the refectory. The low whispering stopped instantly.

"Some of you have received Christmas mail. I shall call the names in alphabetical order, and you will step forward one at a time in an orderly fashion!"

Josephine felt her heart beat faster. Mail! Was there a letter for her? Perhaps from her parents?

Four names were called, and then Jo heard her own. She walked to the front of the room on shaking legs. The guard handed her two letters. Neither one was from her parents. One was from Clara, the other from Frieda. Josephine pressed the two envelopes to her chest. A message from Frieda. It was the first time her old friend had written to her. During Isabelle's and Clara's visit, Josephine had asked Clara to tell Frieda how truly sorry she was and that she felt completely miserable at the thought of having let down Frieda and everybody else.

Whether Clara had ever fulfilled her request she did not know. Perhaps the letter would say something about that. Carefully, as if she were handling the finest lace, Jo ran her forefinger over the glued side of the envelope. Would she dare to open at least Clara's letter?

"There will be no reading now!" The guard's voice shot across the room like an arrow. "Off to your lessons! Do not think that idleness will be tolerated just because it is Christmas Eve."

That night, Josephine retreated to her bunk and pulled the two letters from her skirt pocket. They were warm and crumpled. Clara's letter gave off a hint of lavender and lemon. When Jo slit open the envelope with her fingernail, the noise sounded loud in her ears.

*Dear Josephine,*

*Four weeks have passed since our visit and I feel terribly guilty that I haven't been back to visit you since. But there is so much to do in the pharmacy every single day! The cold season has always been hard on the people, and they're buying piles of cough syrup, menthol drops, and creams for rubbing on their chests. I'm having trouble keeping up with the demand.*

Josephine smiled. She could picture Clara in her clean white apron, stirring an ointment, a blissful expression on her face.

*I haven't seen Isabelle since then, either. She is off in her own world, as usual. I think her father is probably after her to finally "make a good catch." Just imagine, sometimes she even gets mentioned in the newspaper! It says things like, "clothing manufacturer Moritz Herrenhus honored this or that social event with his presence, accompanied by his charming wife and his daughter Isabelle." She was even in a photograph once and looked very elegant, too. Oh, what wouldn't I give to be able to attend such an event, just once!*

*But I don't want to complain, dear Jo, and I also have some exciting news: Do you remember how I went on and on to you about an interesting doctor I met when I was in the hospital with my broken leg? Dear Jo, hold on to your hat! The very same doctor, Gerhard Gropius, is old Fritsche's replacement!*

Josephine closed her eyes. She could hear Clara's voice in her mind and picture her cheeks, rosy with excitement, before her. She would have done anything to be drinking a cup of tea and chatting with her now. She read on with a heavy heart:

*Dr. Gropius is a fine person and the patients love him. The waiting room in his practice is already overflowing from morning till night. But that's no surprise, for he has a wonderful way with people. He takes his time with them and listens to their problems. Just like his predecessor, he sends his patients to us, which of course makes Father very happy. Sometimes, the doctor himself comes by. My dearest Jo, you can't imagine how my heart beats when he appears! I can hardly get a word out in his presence. I'm so excited I can't think straight, and I know I must come across as a silly goose.*

*Gerhard, however, always has plenty to say, about his studies or his time in the hospital. Oh, he is simply wonderful . . .*

*Best of all, though, is this: last week, Gerhard invited me to join him for coffee and a slice of poppy-seed cake at the Ratsmann bakery. I was so jumpy I could hardly swallow a bite! I eat like a sparrow, he said. He thinks that all the work I do must make me tired and that I need to get outside more. So he wants to go walking with me in the spring. Perhaps he's right and I really do work too much? I've decided to put aside my evening reading— medical books mostly—for now, just to be on the safe side.*

*Oh, Josephine, I can hardly believe my luck. That such a clever and good-looking gentleman would court me, of all people. I'm knitting him a scarf for Christmas to keep him toasty and warm during his house calls. I realize it's a bit meager, but Mother believes it will be a nice gesture that Herr Doktor—that's what she calls*

*Gerhard—will certainly appreciate. I think she can already hear wedding bells ringing! If I'm perfectly honest, the idea would please me as well. Oh, Jo, I'm so happy . . .*

Jo lowered the sheets of paper into her lap. Dear Clara, how I'd like to be with you now! I'd listen to you rave about how in love you are for hours . . . A sob escaped her throat.

Adele looked up. "You're not going to start bawling over some letter, are you?"

Jo cast her a cold look, then folded Clara's letter neatly and put it away.

Frieda's letter consisted of a single sheet of paper, but it was covered on both sides in Frieda's small handwriting. It smelled not of lavender and lemon but of cleaning powder and the sauerkraut vat she had in her basement.

*My dear child,*

*I wish you a merry Christmas from afar. Unfortunately, I am not able to come to visit you, because my legs are again making it hard for me to get around. The new doctor says it's gout. I say it's age. And there we have our first difference, but I forgive him because he has such a pretty face.*

*Alas, there is something that hurts much more than the pain in my legs: the thought that you are locked away in that women's prison like some prostitute! I will never forgive myself that it has come to this. I should have looked after you better! While I was frittering away my time with all sorts of nonsense, I was neglecting the greatest and most important task of my life, that of accompanying you on your path to adulthood. I should*

*have been standing beside you, ready to help not only
with clever words but with action . . . That would have
been a far more sensible use of my time. I should have
fought for you to find a better job than working in your
father's smithy. I should have taken you in with me. You
and I, under one roof, that would have been a fine thing.
Instead, I let you run headlong to your downfall.*

The angular letters in black ink blurred before Jo's eyes. She blinked
several times before she could read on.

*Dear girl, I promise you this: I will be there for you
when you have done your time. I won't forsake you ever
again. I swear it, so help me God. For now, I have no
other choice but to wish you all the best for Christmas in
this letter.*

Frieda, dear Frieda . . . Jo pressed the letter to her cheek as if doing
so could bring her closer to her old friend. She felt drained by loneliness
and grief. She pulled her knees up to her chest, wrapped her arms
around them, and laid her head in the nest they formed. She made
no effort to fight the rising wave of tears. Salty drops gathered at the
corners of her mouth as she cried softly to herself.

# Chapter Fifteen

Riding the city trams—in unheated cars full of coughing and sniffling commuters—from one end of Berlin to the other to get to Adrian's cycling club was no treat. But Isabelle, all wrapped up in her new fur coat, put up with it gladly. The silver-gray polar fox coat was a Christmas present from her father. When he had handed it to her, he said, "As the future Mrs. Neumann, you'll need to dress the part." The future Mrs. Neumann! She hadn't ever believed that their ruse would work as well as it seemed to be working. But from the moment her father believed that she and Adrian were planning a future together, he had left her in peace. No more going from one ball to the next, only to be subjected to an interrogation the next morning about all the eligible young men who had been there. She could once again do whatever she liked! True, she had to meet Adrian from time to time to keep up the charade, but that was a small price, and one she was happy to pay.

Isabelle looked boldly at her "future fiancé," and Adrian gave her a reserved smile. They disembarked in Berlin-Halensee.

So this was the First Berlin Cycling Club. Her eyes widened as she looked around. The grounds were so vast that, had she not known better, she might have believed she was visiting an elegant horse track.

"Our cycling track," said Adrian, with a sweeping gesture toward the huge oval velodrome before them. "Built with the latest technology in sport cycling. One lap is precisely three hundred and thirty-three point three yards, no more and no less. This has proven to be the most optimal distance across numerous studies and tests. The angle of the curves has been carefully calculated taking into account centrifugal force and other criteria. The surface material creates minimal friction, so that the only resistance we face is that of the air. Speed, size, average weight of the riders, tangential forces . . . The engineers took every conceivable factor into consideration to build the best possible racetrack. And they have done it!"

Isabelle nodded as if she had understood every word of his rather technical presentation. "For my birthday two years ago, my father took me to a bicycle track somewhere out in the east of Berlin. They had a sausage stand and sparkling wine, but this looks so much more professional."

Adrian laughed. "I know that place. I've ridden there a few times, but that place draws more show-offs than serious riders." He pointed toward a narrow extension built along the long side of the oval. "Just up ahead is where we store our bicycles. We change right next to it, so it's all very practical. There's also a shower and towel room, so you can make yourself presentable before accepting your trophy after a race. My father insisted on the shower room. He's one of the club's founding members. And I must say, it was an excellent idea." Adrian laughed. "The open grandstand over there holds five hundred and fifty spectators. But during the big races in the summer, there'll be twice that many up there—it's a big draw!" He spoke with genuine pride.

"And what are those small covered areas beside the grandstand?" Isabelle asked.

"On the left is the judge's rostrum, and on the right is the music pavilion—something else my father argued for. He couldn't imagine a cycle race without a proper marching band to set the rhythm." Adrian's tone was ironic.

Isabelle furrowed her brow. Gottlieb Neumann had funded a shower room, a music pavilion, and very probably many other modern amenities—wasn't it all a bit . . . much? She began to understand how the businessman had gotten himself into financial hot water.

"Let's go in. You can warm up with a cup of coffee in the clubroom while I ride a few laps," said Adrian, holding his arm out gallantly. "Irene may come by later. She likes to watch us cycle."

Isabelle mentally rolled her eyes. She would have been quite content without the company of Adrian's sister.

Inside, Adrian was met with a chorus of greetings from his club mates. Everyone seemed overjoyed to see him back in Berlin. No one took any notice of Isabelle; they were all too busy bringing Adrian up to date on all the latest news. The men were so absorbed that it was a good five minutes before the first one turned to Isabelle and said, as if she had magically just appeared, "Who do we have here?"

"Allow me to introduce Isabelle Herrenhus, my future fiancée!" Adrian said, giving her a small wink.

One after the other, they reached out to shake hands with Isabelle, but they were soon back to swapping stories about their favorite topic: cycling.

*"Fiancée" doesn't seem to carry much weight in this particular circle,* thought Isabelle, as she headed to the counter to order a cup of coffee from a young woman in an apron who was polishing glasses. She then took a seat on one of the leather-upholstered chairs set out around the lustrous wooden tables. *It's like an upscale tavern,* she thought. The main thing that distinguished it as a clubhouse was the piles of newspapers, books, and journals strewn about on the tables, all dedicated to one topic: the sport of cycling, in all its manifestations. The walls, too, were decorated with posters, illustrations, and photographs of men—always men—on bicycles. Beside those hung several advertising posters, all

framed behind glass. The Rais Bicycle Factory in Mannheim prided itself on its annual production of nine thousand upscale men's and women's bicycles. The German Rubbergoods Factory advertised its touring and racing tires. A firm from Magdeburg called their bicycle a Panther, describing it as light, first-class, and built with flawless workmanship. Every poster was elaborately designed with curlicues and more reminiscent of a work of art than an advertisement. Did these companies also help finance the cycling club? If so, Isabelle conjectured that was probably how the cyclers could afford such plush surroundings.

"I'm just going out for a few laps," said Adrian, who had changed and now stood before her in a close-fitting tricot and pants that revealed almost every muscle in his powerful legs. He wore soft leather shoes that came up only to his ankles. *The ideal getup for cycling,* Isabelle thought with admiration. And no one gives two hoots about how tight the clothes are! She thought about how she and Josephine secretly donned men's clothes just to escape the heavy—and, in the case of cycling, dangerous—skirts . . . The world was truly an unjust place.

"You'll have the best view of me from here," said Adrian, pointing to a table in front of the large window that separated the clubrooms from the track.

"Or me," said another man, also dressed in cycling attire.

"Perhaps the young lady wants to watch a real professional at work?" said a third. "Then she should keep her eye on me!" The men laughed and thumped each other good-naturedly as they strolled off together.

As Isabelle watched them walk away, she suddenly felt overwhelmingly lost and alone. The last time *she* had felt such camaraderie had been a year and a half earlier, when she had spent the summer riding bicycles in her yard with Josephine, Clara, and Lilo. They had laughed loud and long, teased each other, egged each other on, and consoled each other when a certain technique didn't work as they imagined it should have. Those had been wonderful hours. The idyll had only started to crack when Clara broke her leg.

After stretching their arms and legs, the men climbed onto their bicycles. Isabelle watched as they completed lap after lap. She waved to Adrian a few times, but he took no notice of her at all. Bored, she picked up one of the magazines on the table: *Cycling Today and Tomorrow*. She opened it to a random page and was immediately confronted by the title of an article that went on for several pages. Beneath the title was a large photograph of a handsome man who looked to be around twenty years old. He was holding a bicycle in the air in his two hands, and he wore such a cheeky expression that Isabelle smiled to herself. Her curiosity piqued, she began to read the article.

### Leonard Feininger: Hero of Road and Mountain

**If we were ever to single out one man as the world's greatest wheelman of the open road, it would have to be Leonard Feininger. The scion of a winemaking family in beautiful Rhineland-Palatinate, Leon—as he is known to his friends and family—is one of bicycling's pioneers, a man who continually draws the attention of the public to our burgeoning sport with his many spectacular feats. One cannot imagine any better advertisement for bicycling than Feininger's heroic deeds!**

Isabelle raised her eyebrows. The journalist certainly didn't lack for enthusiasm when it came to his subject.

In addition to cycling over the mountains from Austria to Italy, Leon Feininger had completed a long-distance tour from Vienna to Berlin—just the previous summer, in fact. Hadn't Lilo mentioned that trip? At the time, the endeavor had still only been in the planning stages, but now she saw that the three-hundred-and-sixty-mile trip had actually taken place. Did her father know that? Did he even care anymore? As Isabelle read on, she discovered that Feininger had suffered a strained tendon in his left leg, but he had not let it stop him from cycling. Because of this complication, he had fallen short of setting a new time record, wrote the journalist, who was evidently a little let down. Feininger had taken just over thirty hours to cover the distance.

From Vienna to Berlin in thirty hours, on a bicycle! Isabelle was impressed. But if the real-life Leon Feininger was as courageous, resolute, and confident as he looked in the picture, she would not have put it past him. Her thirst for adventure roared inside her, like a lion locked in a cage far too small to contain it. She'd give almost anything to be able to experience such adventures for herself. At least once . . .

A moment later, her attention was drawn back to the track. An old man stationed at the edge of the track was shouting something at one or another of the cyclers as they rode past. Isabelle could not understand what he was saying through the window, but she assumed he must be some kind of trainer giving his charges helpful tips.

A wave of discontent, as sudden and unexpected as a summer cloudburst, washed over her. These elegant cycling clubrooms, a trainer, the sporty gear the wheelmen wore, daring journeys from Vienna to Berlin—did men have any idea how good they had it? Isabelle suddenly realized just how much she missed cycling. Why hadn't she kept it up? Why hadn't she stood up to her father and persuaded him to allow her to ride her own bicycle again? But she had simply bowed to his will. So much for her thirst for adventure . . .

"It's all terribly unfair, isn't it?" a familiar voice said beside her.

Isabelle turned around. "Ah. Irene." *And now this, her,* Isabelle thought.

"I really don't know why I keep coming here," Irene said, sitting down opposite her. "I always go home more frustrated than when I arrive." She nodded toward the racetrack.

"Humph. We women ought to have such opportunities for ourselves," Isabelle agreed. "When I think of all the hard work Josephine and I put into teaching ourselves to ride a bicycle . . . how we worked to figure out the best technique for climbing a hill. And how to get down again in one piece. The safest way to take a curve. All of it."

Irene narrowed her eyes. "Josephine. Wasn't she the one who pinched your father's bicycle and had an accident with it? I read about it in the newspaper."

Isabelle nodded. "None of it would have happened if we hadn't been damned to this miserable secrecy. If Josephine and I had been able to ride bicycles openly, like any man, Jo would never have gotten into such a bind. My father is to blame for all of it. It makes me sick just to think about it."

"My father tolerates my cycling, but only when we are at our country house in Potsdam. At least no one can see me out in the country, he says," Irene said. "I'm curious to find out what he'll say when he discovers his future daughter-in-law is also one of these vixens on wheels." The sarcasm in Irene's tone was unmistakable.

Isabelle turned away. Although Adrian had sworn that he hadn't told a single soul about their agreement, she had the feeling that Irene could see right through her. And she didn't like the feeling.

"Riding bicycles is only one of many things that Adrian and I have in common," she said in her most sugary voice.

Irene raised her eyebrows knowingly, but she said nothing. Perhaps her father had forbidden her from talking about it?

They sat and watched the men in silence for a while. *If Josephine ever sees how extravagant this place is, her eyes will pop out of her head,* thought Isabelle. She knew opening a bicycle club just for women had been Jo's dream. One of many that had gone down the drain.

After a few minutes, Isabelle abruptly turned to Adrian's sister and said, "You know what I'd love to do?"

# Chapter Sixteen

Adrian would be her way in. He would be the one to convince the other members of the First Berlin Cycling Club that its premises should welcome a women's cycling club. With this common goal, Isabelle and Irene put their mutual resentment temporarily on ice. They prepared a robust list of arguments in its favor. Isabelle was even prepared—if it came to it and Adrian refused to help—to sacrifice the secret agreement she and Adrian shared. Now that the idea had taken shape in her mind, she had no intention of backing down from her cycling club plan.

Irene felt that the most compelling argument was that establishing a women's club would not cost the men—including her own father—a single penny, in stark contrast to the men's club. Because the women would do all of it themselves, and could happily live without leather club chairs and shower rooms with gilded faucets.

When the two of them finally met with Adrian one evening at the cycling club to convince him of the merits of their plan, they were ready for anything. Anything except being welcomed with open arms.

"A small cycling club for women? That's a great idea. I should have come up with it myself. I've been of the opinion for some time now that bicycles should be made accessible to a much wider range of social strata. A women's club is a good start. But we should take the factory workers into consideration, too. Imagine what a blessing bicycles would be for workers who spend practically all their waking hours in some airless factory. Or think about the servant girls who spend their days scrubbing floors on their knees. They could all enjoy some outdoor activity after work. Or cycling out into the country. Bicycles could change society!" Adrian said with evident excitement.

Isabelle and Irene had trouble suppressing their laughter. Factory workers on bicycles? Servants cycling out to Wannsee lake after work? Adrian's ideas were even crazier than their own.

Adrian met with them again a week later. "It wasn't easy convincing our board and the club's founding members that Berlin's first women's cycling club should be formed here. Most of them simply don't believe that the fairer sex is suited to the sport. However"—he grinned mischievously—"using all my persuasive power and charm, I managed to win their assent. Father was a great help, I must say. He is extremely supportive of me at the moment." He looked intently at Isabelle as he said this.

Isabelle nodded grimly. She had no trouble believing *that*. Her father—highly satisfied with the progress of her relationship with Adrian—had already transferred an initial sum to Gottlieb Neumann to help him out of the worst of his difficulties. Adrian's old man was certainly indebted to his son.

"We're actually going to get our own room?"

Adrian nodded. "Not only that. You're allowed to use our track, but only when none of the men are on it. It's the best outcome you could have hoped for—now it's up to you to make something of it to silence all the naysayers."

The room they had been granted was small indeed—it had previously served as a storeroom for bicycle parts and tools—but Isabelle and Irene thought there could be no lovelier room on earth.

The following day Isabelle marched into Oskar Reutter's emporium and emerged laden with cleaning supplies, paint, sandpaper, and a roll of strong fabric for curtains. She had bought so much that Reutter instructed one of his apprentices to help her carry her purchases home. "Not home," said Isabelle. "It all has to go to Berlin's first cycling club for women!"

The young women spent the following weeks setting up. Neither Isabelle nor Irene had ever held a paintbrush, let alone a washcloth. But thanks to Irene's old friend Jule—the one with whom Irene had caused such a stir riding through the Tiergarten—the work pushed ahead. Jule's parents ran a large furniture-making outfit, and Jule and her brothers had grown up in the workshops and picked up a few useful skills.

Every afternoon, when school let out, Isabelle and Irene went straight to their new clubroom to paint, hammer, measure curtains, and cut cushion covers. Isabelle still considered Irene to be snobby and arrogant, but she had to admit that she had extraordinary stamina and strength and did not shy away from hard work. And Irene, who had been quite happy to call the Herrenhus family social climbers in the past, discovered that Isabelle was not at all afraid to get her hands dirty.

Jule, who worked in her parents' company, usually only arrived in the evening. Then she praised, chided, tinkered, and improved upon what had been done. She could only manage a tired smile when she saw the pleasure Isabelle and Irene took in their work—she herself had known for a long time how satisfying it was to work with one's own hands.

The male club members watched the women's activities with amusement and a touch of condescension. "So how's the dollhouse coming along?" they heard more than once. "Where are you going to put the sewing machines?" one young man asked, earning a chorus of laughter from the others. One afternoon the young women discovered that some of the men had hung up an advertising poster from Singer, the American sewing-machine maker. No one believed that the women would maintain a long-term interest in cycling or show any talent for the sport.

Meanwhile, Isabelle and Irene kept a lookout for future members. Nothing would be worse than a club with no members! Jule was the first to sign on. She brought two other young women with her; both owned their own bicycles, but because of the hostile attitudes to women cyclers, they did not dare ride on Berlin's streets. Then one of Isabelle's and Irene's fellow students inquired about joining. She was the daughter of a French diplomat and had recently gone cycling in Paris, where women could ride with significantly more freedom.

Sweating and tired from the unaccustomed physical labor, Isabelle and Irene sat on their newly upholstered chairs at their freshly planed table and mulled over the statutes of their new club: Who should they admit? Who should they reject? What were the club's objectives, and what rights would membership bestow? What obligations would it involve? Everything had to be administered at least as professionally as the men's club. They both agreed that they should give priority to members from the upper classes. Ownership of a bicycle was a second basic requirement. And they both felt that it would be crucial to find a fitting name for the club. After long discussion, they agreed on Isabelle's suggestion, which was both straightforward and fitting: First Berlin Cycling Club for Women.

Finally, on a radiantly beautiful Sunday in the summer of 1892, they were ready. The First Berlin Cycling Club for Women opened its doors with a grand opening celebration.

\*\*\*

Clara cast a final glance in the mirror and felt very satisfied with what she saw. The violet skirt and lighter blouse formed a flattering ensemble and went nicely with her small rosewood-colored hat. The fresh outfit lent a bit of color to her normally pale complexion, and her lips looked rosier than they normally did. It was Gerhard who had encouraged her to switch from the forlorn pale gray and dark blue that her mother always chose for her to more colorful clothes.

Clara took a step back and studied herself from a greater distance. Could the fact that her face shone like a thousand suns have something to do with the color? Wasn't Gerhard's proposal of marriage the night before the reason for her permanent smile and flushed cheeks?

Clara sighed deeply. Her whole life long, she would never forget that moment . . .

Gerhard had kneeled on the ground before her, taken her by the hand, and looked deep into her eyes. She had felt like one of the heroines in the French novels she and her mother read so avidly.

"Will you be my wife?" Gerhard's voice did not waver, and he did not seem to doubt her answer for a moment.

Her *Yes* had been not much more than a breath, but she had been so excited that that was all she could utter.

It was enough to satisfy Gerhard. They had embraced, a little stiffly, before going to her parents to announce the good news. Sophie Berg began to laugh and cry at the same time, and Anton Berg couldn't stop clapping his future son-in-law on the shoulder. "Now that's something to celebrate! I'm inviting you both to the finest restaurant in Luisenstadt, tomorrow evening," he said. Amid all the revelry, Clara seemed almost forgotten. It was only when she gently mentioned that she and Gerhard already had an invitation for the following day that the others took notice of her again.

"The inauguration of a bicycle club?" Her mother's expression made it clear how she felt about such a thing.

Clara was about to explain that it wasn't just *any* club—it was the first *women's* club in Berlin—but she didn't get that far because Gerhard took her hand and said, "If it is Clara's wish . . ." Oh, how her heart swelled! Finally, what mattered to *her* counted for something, and Gerhard was standing up for that.

"Besides, it can't hurt to mix with Berlin's high society," he added. "Wheelmen are prone to falling off their bicycles. They may scrape open a knee or go so far as to break a leg. I might be able to turn Mr. Herrenhus and his family into patients. God knows I've inherited more than enough poor devils from Dr. Fritsche." He laughed endearingly, as if to ask forgiveness for what he had just said.

Oh, how she loved his laugh!

Mixing with high society? Clara's mother had nodded approvingly. Of course he and Clara must go to the opening celebration. And the invitation had come from Isabelle Herrenhus—whose engagement to Adrian Neumann, son of the industrial magnate, had been the subject of much speculation, which hinted at the social circles involved in the club.

Clara smiled. Ha! Isabelle would be stunned to find out that wedding bells would soon be ringing for Clara, too. Blissfully happy, she blew a kiss to her image in the mirror. The future Mrs. Gropius looked lovely this evening. She snatched her embroidered handbag and ran down the stairs.

Gerhard was waiting for her.

"This place doesn't look as if it's just opened today. Are you sure we're in the right spot?" asked Gerhard, pointing up to the entrance, beyond which an oval cycling track could be seen. "First Berlin Cycling Club for Women. Even the sign has some patina."

"The address appears to be right." Clara looked uncertainly at the invitation she had received from Isabelle. From inside came the sounds of a trombone band mixed with laughter and scraps of conversation. "Let's go in and see." She held out the invitation to a young attendant, and he let them enter.

"Good day to you sir, madam!"

Gerhard Gropius nodded condescendingly, then whispered to Clara, "Banners, flowers, a brass band—seems a rather fancy affair." He smoothed his jacket with a quick tug, then scanned the place thoroughly. "I imagine this place draws a rather wealthy crowd—I'm even more surprised than before that you received an invitation."

Clara smiled. So she had actually managed to impress Gerhard for once! Still, if she were honest, she had not imagined Isabelle's cycling club would look like *this*. The club looked so fine—so elegant. And the men and women were all so well dressed. It was nothing like the dusty and rudimentary bicycle track they had visited with Isabelle's father. The merry atmosphere only added to the effect . . . Clara felt the cheerfulness rubbing off on her as she walked around.

Everywhere she looked, young women were pushing shiny bicycles along, flanked by their proud fathers and beautifully dressed mothers. Some were even accompanied by an admirer. A few children cavorted in their Sunday best—younger siblings, envious of their older sisters.

"Come on, then. We want to see you ride!" The voice belonged to an elegant, middle-aged woman whose purple outfit and hat the size of a wagon wheel would not have been out of place at a fashionable horse track.

"Yeah, sis, show us what you can do!" shouted the little boy standing beside the woman.

A moment later, a blond girl swung onto the saddle of her women's bicycle and pedaled off to do a lap around the track, cheered on by her family.

Gerhard Gropius frowned in consternation. "Did you see that?"

Clara nodded. She was having trouble comprehending what she was seeing: young women indulging their passion for cycling in public.

What a change from all the secrecy involved when she, Isabelle, and Josephine had been cycling around the Herrenhus family's yard. Could she even still ride one? Or had she completely forgotten how? She suddenly felt an intense desire to grab a bicycle and cycle a lap herself. She giggled a little at the thought, which earned her a sideways glance from Gerhard.

"Look, there's Isabelle!" She had already released Gerhard's arm and was winding her way through the crowd toward her friend, waving as she went. Isabelle stood with another young woman at the entrance to a long building, shaking hands with arriving guests. At the sight of Clara, she left her post and came toward her, her arms flung wide.

"Welcome!" she cried. "Welcome to the First Berlin Cycling Club for Women." She embraced Clara effusively. "How wonderful that you came. And in such charming company . . ."

Clara did not overlook the coquettish glance that Isabelle cast Gerhard. She immediately felt a pang of jealousy. She was well aware of the effect Gerhard had on the female gender, starting with her own mother and the elderly receptionist in his practice. They were over the moon about the young doctor. And now Isabelle, to boot.

"Allow me to introduce Dr. Gerhard Gropius. My fiancé!" The pride in her voice was unmistakable. She was beaming as she turned to her beloved and reached out possessively to take his arm. But Gerhard took a step backward just at that moment, and Clara's hand caught only emptiness.

"Did I hear that right? This is a *women's* club?" Gerhard looked from one woman to the other in what looked like confusion.

Isabelle smiled broadly. "My dear Dr. Gropius, that is exactly what it is. Irene Neumann and I have managed to do what no one thought we could—we have founded a club where women can enjoy the sport of cycling unmolested." She nodded to Irene, who stood a few steps away, welcoming new arrivals.

"If only Josephine could be here . . . She would be overjoyed to be part of this day," Clara sighed as a small group of athletically dressed men pedaled past. A moment later, two women cycled up behind the men, laughing and chattering as they went. Clara and Isabelle exchanged a surreptitious glance. And for a moment, the old bond of friendship that had united them that summer returned.

"What you've managed here is truly marvelous," said Clara quietly, wishing that she had contributed in some small way to the venture.

"But . . . riding bicycles is positively harmful for women! From a sports-medicine perspective, there is nothing worse than sitting on one of these machines. How many broken bones have I seen at the hospital that could be attributed directly to a bicycle? Furthermore, this kind of sport puts the internal organs at risk, leads to numerous ailments of the heart, and causes spinal deformation and hunching of the back within a very short time. Quite aside from the . . . sexual effects. Clara!" Gerhard snapped, with such intensity that she jumped. "What were you thinking, dragging me here? I hope that you yourself have not taken part in such an unfeminine diversion?" His voice, normally so soft, had become strident, almost shrill.

"No! Yes . . . I . . ." Clara looked hopelessly from her fiancé to Isabelle. She had never seen Gerhard so upset.

"Please compose yourself, Mr. Gropius," said Isabelle with a half-amused, half-agonized smile. "I am not unaware of the reservations of some doctors when it comes to riding bicycles, but I can assure you that there is nothing to them. Since I began cycling, I feel better than I ever—"

"What you *feel* and what modern medical research says are two very different things!" Gerhard Gropius broke in harshly. He looked with disgust at a woman who was cycling past just then. "Your statement reveals no more than the depth of your ignorance about the consequences of what you are doing, and increases the culpability of your parents and your own fiancé if they do not put a stop to it. Where is your family? Do your parents know what you are doing?"

"Gerhard," said Clara, with a note of warning. "Moritz Herrenhus gave Isabelle her bicycle himself. I see nothing objectionable in Isabelle and her friends cycling around the track here. It's a hobby, an enjoyable pastime, nothing more. I . . ." but when she saw his expression, she thought better of continuing.

"A fine pastime indeed!" Gerhard spat. "One that violates every female moral. One in which sexual stimulation is paramount! Unless I am mistaken, one *sits* on the saddle of a bicycle? I don't even care to imagine what . . . *feelings* are thus quickened. Disgusting is all I can say." He took Clara roughly by the arm. "I will not allow you to watch such goings-on. Some have been corrupted merely by looking on. We're leaving!"

Clara was tired when she got home. To the annoyance of her mother, who wanted to hear all about her day, she went straight to her room. She sat at her desk and took out notepaper and ink. She did not write letters to Josephine often because she was usually too tired after work, but she had thought of her friend many times that day.

*Dear Josephine,* she wrote, then lowered her quill again. What a long, dramatic day it had been. Where to begin? And where to stop?

After their hurried departure from Isabelle's party, she had trotted after Gerhard like a whipped puppy, confused and anxious. She wanted to talk it all through with him in peace and quiet, but she had not been able to find a good way to start. Still stone-faced, Gerhard had taken her to an elegant café on the banks of the Spree, where his mood soon improved. They had eaten ice cream and talked about what it must be like to live in Italy. Gerhard had raised the topic of their honeymoon.

"What would you say to a trip to the land of *la dolce vita?*" he had asked Clara. And although she was having trouble keeping a cool head in the hot June sunshine, she reminded him of the burden of debt he had taken on when he took over the practice.

---

"Perhaps we should postpone our honeymoon by a few years?" she suggested.

"As long as we don't postpone our wedding!" Gerhard had replied, laughing, then added that her parents would most likely be more than happy to help their only daughter a little, financially speaking, in such a matter.

Clara was not so certain about that. The mere idea of knowing that she was in another country would send her mother into a fit of anxiety.

She sighed. Her mother would soon have no more to say over her actions. Thank God.

Could she tell that to Josephine in a letter? She resolutely dipped her quill into the ink bottle, only to set it aside again a moment later. Nonsense! She could not write to Jo about finally being free of her mother, or being free of anything.

And she was no longer sure what to write about Isabelle's cycling club. Wouldn't that just increase Jo's longing for freedom? Or just make her more aware of what she was missing behind bars? Wouldn't she just be deeply hurting her friend with such news? That was the last thing she wanted to do.

Besides . . . Clara chewed pensively on the end of her quill. There was no way she could report on Gerhard's behavior at the opening celebration. Jo would not understand that his outburst had sprung from his concern for her welfare. In retrospect, Clara wondered how she could ever have even considered taking him there! If she were honest, she had wanted to show off a little with her friendship with Isabelle. Well, that had certainly misfired.

Perhaps she should simply focus on the things that really mattered . . .

*Ever since Gerhard asked me to marry him, I've been the happiest woman in the world! Our wedding will take place in the fall, and after that we'll move into the small apartment above the practice. Gerhard has already checked with Mr. Jablonsky, the owner, to ensure that it will be all right. Once the practice is flourishing and Gerhard has paid off all the debts, he has promised me a bigger house.*

*Dearest Josephine, though my happiness is now within reach, I can scarcely believe that I will soon be the mistress of my own household. Then I will finally be able to do what I like, and how I like, without Mother constantly interfering or Father always knowing better . . .*

***

Josephine lowered the letter. Clara and her doctor. It was so impossibly strange that her friend was going to get married that she hardly felt anything at all. Hadn't Clara wanted to study pharmacology? That would probably no longer be possible once she was a married woman. Or perhaps she no longer wanted to study now that she would soon be a doctor's wife. So many questions and no answers. And there had been a time when she thought she knew Clara inside out.

"You look like you've seen a ghost," said Martha as she made her bed.

Jo, whose bed was already freshly straightened, sighed. "I wish I had." She held up the letter. "It's from my best friend. She tells me that she's getting married. It makes me feel strange, like I hardly know her anymore. Sometimes I lie here and try to imagine Clara and Frieda's voices, and I can't do it. It feels like the people I used to know are fading away, and it frightens me! It's like all I have left in my ears is the monotonous beating of my father's hammer. But I'm forgetting the faces of everyone I knew."

Josephine looked out thoughtfully through the barred window. What did the summer feel like out there? Was it as wild and reckless as the one before, when she and Isabelle had turned night to day?

Josephine closed her eyes and desperately called up the way she had felt while riding her bicycle. Along tree-lined boulevards, the scent of elderberries in her nose, the sun bright, and small insects peppering her face. She achieved this kind of mental escapism more effectively some days than others. Today was one of her better days, and in her mind's eye, in addition to the boulevards, Josephine conjured up Frieda's garden with its sprawling walnut tree.

She had received another letter from Frieda the week before. She had written that the elderberry bush that grew against the house was full of aphids, and that a pair of storks had built their nest on the church tower two streets away. The young birds were already trying out their wings for the first time, taking short test flights. Frieda loved to watch them through a pair of old field glasses. It was, she wrote, a picture-book summer.

Summer in Frieda's garden . . . Jo sighed wistfully. Summer there meant buttermilk, cooled in a bucket of water. And freshly plucked raspberries in small bowls. The yellow roses would be blooming on the grave of Frieda's old cat. Had Frieda planted anything at the spot where the bird that had flown against her window was buried?

As she usually did, her friend had included a few newspaper clips with her letter. These included articles about events in the wider world and things that she thought might interest Josephine. One half-page article was about an American woman named Mary French Sheldon, who had set off the year before on an expedition to East Africa. Her aim was mainly to research the living conditions of women and children there. *As if anyone would take any notice!* Jo thought as she read. African women probably led lives that were as hard as those of their German or English or French counterparts. Another clipping was about an American cycler, Fanny Bullock Workman, who was traveling the world on a bicycle with her husband. According to the article, Mrs. Workman was planning to map the routes she had followed and publish a guidebook for future bicycle travelers. What was Frieda trying to suggest with these articles? That she, too, might one day be capable of such heroic acts? Josephine wasn't sure.

The loud clang of a bell dragged her back to the present. It was time for her to head off to work. Her heart felt instantly lighter. While Adele and the others grumbled on their way to the laundry or kitchen, Josephine made her way happily out to the workshop.

Gerd Melchior was already at his workbench, peering into the inner workings of a sewing machine. Without looking up, he said, "This is the second time it's broken in three weeks. Probably the women in the laundry being careless again."

Josephine looked over the caretaker's shoulder. She had developed a keen interest in finding out what caused a machine to malfunction. Often, it took her only a few moments, for she had discovered that it was always the same parts that caused the problem: a worn cog, a misaligned axle, a broken connector. Sometimes a machine did not run smoothly simply because it had not been lubricated well enough. If the problem was not immediately recognizable, she could sink her teeth into the challenge for hours. *Like a terrier into someone's calf,* she thought and smiled. But that was not necessary with the sewing machine. Josephine pointed confidently to a spot inside the Singer.

"The teeth are worn down on the little cog up there, top left. The women in the laundry can't help that. The cog has to be filed to get the teeth to mesh properly," she said.

Melchior nodded. Then he pushed his chair back with a loud squeak. He narrowed his eyes at Josephine as if weighing her up and said, "Think you're up to it?"

Josephine smiled from ear to ear. She went to a rack where a dozen files stood and selected one of the finest. Then she went to work.

Of all the tasks the caretaker assigned to her, she loved the metalwork the most. All of the shaping and grinding, turning and drilling called for a good eye, a steady hand, and dexterity. Melchior had made it clear more than once that Jo possessed all of those qualities. She had come to learn which hammer or file was right for a particular job, and the correct way to hold it. She had developed a feel for how tightly she could tighten something in a vice without damaging it. The block plane felt as comfortable in her hand as a file. And she had recently begun working with Melchior's latest acquisition, a lathe! He seemed to trust her more than she trusted herself and gave her a free hand. Melchior explained techniques, guided her hand, praised and criticized her work. Sometimes, he even deliberately let her make mistakes. Like the time she was supposed to file a triangular piece of sheet steel that Melchior needed to replace part of another tool. After a few minutes, she realized that the coarse file she'd chosen was completely unsuitable for the job. Melchior had simply laughed. "There's a right file for every job. This here's the one you need," he said, handing her a different tool. Josephine absorbed his guidance, making his knowledge her own. Every word, every lesson, was permanently engraved in her memory. The hours she spent at the caretaker's side did more than make everyday life at Barnim Road Women's Prison bearable. They gave it meaning.

"How'd you get interested in mechanical things?" Melchior asked her one day.

She had been on the verge of saying *from riding bicycles*, but instead she merely mumbled something about her father's workshop.

In all her time in prison, she had not told a soul about her cycling. Oh, she'd been tempted often enough. To wax on at length about the long rides she'd done, in an attempt to experience them vicariously a second time . . . but she always had stopped herself, afraid that she would lose control, start crying, and be unable to stop. But not a day passed that she did not think about riding a bicycle again. At night, in particular, as she lay in bed amid the snoring and whimpering of the other young women, she fled the stifling, cramped dormitory in her mind and recalled each of her routes, trying to picture every curve, every bump in the road, every building. The bicycle was her anchor, her window to freedom.

And yet, despite all the hours she had spent on Moritz Herrenhus's bicycle, it had somehow remained a stranger to her.

With a mixture of melancholy and anger, Josephine remembered how hard she had tried to understand the bicycle's technical refinements. What did the bearings inside the headset look like? And what did the little rings inside the hub of the rear wheel do? What if one of them went missing? Isabelle had not shown the slightest interest in the way they worked, and they had never been able to get their hands on the manual. Now, Jo tried to remember the individual parts of a bicycle and apply her newfound knowledge to those memories.

She had once asked Melchior if he owned a bicycle, hoping that they could have examined it together . . . but Melchior had replied, "Do I look like Croesus?"

Although Josephine was quite certain that Melchior would have understood her passion for cycling, she still said nothing to him about it.

"You do a fine job, for a woman," said the caretaker when she was done refinishing the teeth of the little cog. "When you get out of here, you could go to work in Ludwig Loewe's sewing-machine factory. They could use someone as skilled as you, I'm sure of it. Especially now that the economy's on the upswing. The public wants to buy, buy, buy! And the factories are hell bent on producing more, more, more. When I think of my youth . . . Hard times, they were. Not many of us had work, and them that did worked for a pittance." The caretaker made a dismissive motion with his hand. "You young people today, you've got all the chances in the world. But what do you do? You throw them to the wind and end up in this ugly place."

Jo laughed. "Sometimes you sound just like my old neighbor, Frieda. Frieda thinks the world is full of opportunities, and it's just up to us to grab them by the scruff of the neck." She grew thoughtful. "I'd like to believe it, but it's not that easy. I wore my feet off trying to find an apprenticeship as a mechanic. I walked from factory to factory, from workshop to forge, and all I got for it was looks of incomprehension and ridicule. 'A woman who wants to learn a technical trade? How did you get that bee in your bonnet!'" She shook her head sadly. *How ironic that I had to go to prison to learn what I never could as a free woman,* she thought.

Melchior sighed. "I'm sure there's a lot of bosses cut from old cloth. But the times are changing, girl, believe me."

"Frieda always said that, too." Josephine heaved a sad sigh. Of all the people from her old life, she missed her warmhearted neighbor the most.

"Sounds to me like your Frieda's a clever woman. And she's a widow, you said? Maybe I should go pay her a visit," said Melchior with a grin. He laid his arm across Jo's shoulders in a comradely gesture. "Well, maybe I'd better wait until you're out of here. Then I can check in on you, as well. I don't want to see you head off down the wrong path, not a second time!" He did his best to adopt an earnest tone.

"That won't happen," said Jo, and she meant it. She took a dust rag and wiped it over the newly repaired sewing machine. "I've messed up so much in my life, enough to last me to the end of the world. Being able to work with you and learn how to fix things means everything to me." She turned to the caretaker with a look of both affection and gratitude. "If I have to run from pillar to post to find the right job, I'll do it. I don't care if it takes a lifetime. That's my plan, and nothing, not a thing in this world, will stop me."

But she did not tell Melchior about the other plans she was hatching.

# Chapter Seventeen

*Berlin, March 1895*

Three years, three months. One thousand one hundred and eighty-six days. And as many nights. An eternity. Three springs, three summers, three autumns, four winters. Springtime was always the worst, when a slight, warm breeze blew in through the bars. When the delicate green of new leaves appeared as if by magic on the branches of the linden trees. When the sky looked as if someone had scrubbed it clean. When the scent of blooming flowers made the air sweeter than three cubes of sugar in a cup of tea . . . that was when Josephine wanted to get out of the prison so much that she felt like howling. Winters were not much better, with the poorly heated rooms, the reek of mold and unwashed bodies. She hungered for her warm room and the feather blanket on her bed, for the hot pea soup her mother had always cooked on Saturdays.

Martha had left much earlier, as had many others. New ones had come and gone. Josephine had formed no close friendships with anyone, which meant that she at least avoided the pain of saying good-bye whenever another of the young women was released. A prison was not a place to look for common ground.

Josephine still shared common ground with Lilo, with whom she exchanged occasional letters. And with Clara, when she recalled the days they had spent together as children.

Clara was a doctor's wife now. Her old friend had only been in sporadic touch since getting married. Josephine's stomach tightened when she thought of Clara. What would their reunion be like? And Isabelle . . . Jo hardly dared to think about her. She had not heard anything from her for three years. It seemed that all the bridges that had bound them to each other had collapsed long ago.

People come and go. Was that the great truth behind everything? Josephine was despondent as she straightened the thin blanket on her bed for the last time. Who would cry herself to sleep there that evening?

Her eyes swept through the dormitory one last time. Pale March sunshine fell through the barred window. The room was gloomy and seemed somehow depleted. Nightmares, fear, and loneliness had spoiled the air long before Josephine arrived. Even after three years, she still found it hard to breathe in there. *But why don't I feel happy to be putting this wretched place behind me?* Jo asked herself silently. She actually felt a pang of jealousy that someone else would be taking her place.

She and the caretaker had said their good-byes the previous evening. But there was one consolation: Melchior had promised to visit her at Frieda's house no later than that summer. "I'll want to see what's become of my apprentice!" he'd said and stroked her shoulder clumsily.

Gerd Melchior was her savior. Without him, she would have gone mad, and it was only thanks to him that she was leaving prison with her spirit and soul intact.

Physically, three and a half years of bad food, poor hygiene, and a lack of fresh air had taken their toll. The dress that Jo had been wearing when she arrived and which was returned to her that morning in the prison's administration building hung on her body like a sack. Her skin was pale and scaly, her hair dull. She looked like a haggard woman of thirty. Like someone leaving prison. Like someone that life had dealt a bad hand. Or someone who had dealt her own life a bad hand? Is that what people would think when they saw her?

*I'll spoil you like a sparrow that's fallen from its nest too soon,* Frieda had written in one of her letters.

Josephine smiled at the recollection as she went to the door. Tonight she would sleep in a decent bed with a decent blanket over her.

On her way to the main entrance, she spotted the shadow of a woman waving at her from the other end of the yard. Adele. She had been moved across to the adult wing a year earlier, and they had only ever seen each other in the yard or in the dining hall since then. In there for life . . . The word alone was enough to frighten Josephine. Perhaps it frightened Adele, too, since her wave seemed surprising and sad. Josephine gave a tentative wave back.

In the office, she had to sign a few papers. Then she was given enough money to cover a single tram journey plus a tiny bit extra, along with a note with the address of a place to contact as she began her search for work, a company in Feuerland that made shoes. Josephine vaguely recalled walking past it when she'd been looking for an apprenticeship. The proprietor took on former female prisoners as workers, the guard explained as she handed Josephine the note. And that was not all. There was even a dormitory above the factory where the women who worked below could rent a bed.

"A fine and charitable gentleman!" said the woman. "He does what he can so depraved women like you can find their way back to a life of decency."

Josephine took the note, tied her shawl around her shoulders, and left without another word.

Forget the shoes. She didn't need a contact address. Frieda was waiting for her.

*

As Josephine stood waiting for the tram with the March sun upon her face, she thought of Frieda's most recent letter, which was neatly folded in her shoulder bag along with her other possessions.

*I have masterful plans for you,* Frieda had written. *Masterful*—she had even underlined the word. *A strange word to use,* thought Josephine, not for the first time, as she climbed aboard the tram. She had been wondering what Frieda had in store for her ever since she received the letter three weeks before. Why the secrecy? Had she managed to find a place willing to take her on as an apprentice mechanic? The idea should have pleased Josephine, but once again, the elation she thought she should feel did not come. The fact was she already had her apprenticeship behind her, and she had been taught by the best master craftsman for miles around. And Frieda knew that. Did her plans have something to do with riding a bicycle? Had she found a way for Jo to cycle, legally and in daylight? Jo's heart skipped a beat at the thought, but she did not get her hopes up too high. In all the letters she had penned to Frieda, she had not written a single word about cycling. It would have hurt too much to do so. How could the old woman possibly know that her desire to ride a bicycle was stronger than ever?

Jo had pleaded for a few more hints in her last letter. But she had received no answer. Frieda probably wanted to tell her about her *masterful plans* in person so she could see Josephine's face light up. Jo felt an excited rumble in her stomach. To distract herself, she looked out the window at the passing city, which was bathed in the most beautiful sunlight. Everything looked so different . . .

New buildings had sprung up everywhere, and the city seemed to have grown beneath the surface as well. Entire streets had been opened up like a gutted fish. Sand lay in huge piles by the side of the road, and enormous pipes were being lowered into the ground by countless workers. She saw only a few bicycles amid the chaos. And where were they supposed to go anyway, with all those sewage works under way? Though there were few bicycles, many people were out and about on foot, coming and going from the numerous department stores, fashion boutiques, hardware shops, and other stores besides. Josephine was amazed at how much Berlin had changed in the past three years. To all appearances it was not a change for the worse, which was a comforting thought. Would that be true of her own life as well? Jo finally felt a tiny seed of anticipation sprout inside her. Berlin awaited her. A whole new life awaited her.

The garden gate stood ajar, the shutters open. At first glance, Frieda's house looked unchanged.

"Frieda? Are you out in the garden?" Instead of knocking, Josephine walked around the outside of the house, her heart pounding. In this glorious weather, her old friend was probably out tending to the first tender lamb's lettuce leaves. Frieda always made a great celebration of that. Along with the salad that she dressed with white-wine vinegar and oil, she always put out a few quail eggs and ham, which she consumed with wine that shimmered in her glass.

Jo's stomach rumbled again, this time with hunger, even though it was not yet midday. Her first meal in freedom . . . It didn't have to be quail eggs. A roll would do just fine.

But the garden was empty and untouched. The vegetable garden was covered with fir tree twigs, and there were no bright green lamb's lettuce leaves to be seen.

"Frieda?" Jo crossed the few steps to the door, but no one stirred in the house when she knocked. She waited for a moment, a frown crossing her face, then approached one of the windows. The parlor inside was dark. Frieda was probably out shopping. After all, she was expecting Josephine that day. No doubt Frieda wanted to delight her with a special meal, even though it wasn't necessary . . . In any case, her old friend wouldn't be away long.

Jo deposited her bag in the small shed where Frieda stored her garden tools, then she went back out to the street.

Reutter's Emporium, the ropemaker's shop, and the pharmacy were all as she remembered them. With timid steps, she walked slowly down the street. Deep down, she felt the need to call out—to scream—"I'm back!" at the top of her lungs. But at the same time, she would have liked nothing more than to make herself invisible. What would her old neighbors think when they saw her? Would they turn away from the girl who'd been in prison? She was relieved that no one was walking toward her along the narrow pavement.

From a distance, Jo heard the monotonous clang of her father's hammer, and a lump instantly formed in her throat. She stopped outside the building. The large gate that opened into the barn and smithy stood wide open. A skinny kid was doing his best to calm a horse down while her father held a horseshoe in the fire. Another horse tied by the barn door lifted its tail and sedately dumped a pile of manure onto the floor of the barn. The lump in Jo's throat hardened at the old familiar smell.

It was not sentimentality that had led her there. Not even homesickness, she told herself, as she watched her parents' house from a safe distance. It was that she could not get around having a certain discussion with her parents. If her father had paid for the damage she had done to Herrenhus's bicycle, she wanted to pay him back. Of course, that would not happen instantly. But she'd arrange to repay him in monthly installments as soon as she found work. She didn't want to owe her parents a single penny. That was all she wanted to tell him. After that, she would leave.

The door to the house opened and a young girl came out with a basket of laundry under her arm. Josephine's mother followed a few steps behind. She looked exactly as she had three years earlier. The two of them began to hang the laundry in the yard. The young girl said something and Jo's mother laughed. It sounded foreign and painful in Josephine's ear. She never knew that her mother could laugh so melodically.

She would wait in Frieda's garden, sit on the bench, enjoy the sunshine. She could always visit her parents in the next few days.

Jo had just turned away when her mother glanced in her direction. Then she bustled toward the barn as if to make sure her husband had not seen his daughter. She said something to the young girl, who went into the house.


"What do you want here? If you think you're coming back to stay, think again. You're not welcome here."

No warm greeting. No embrace. A cold, sharp pain tore a hole in Josephine's soul.

Her mouth was dry as she said, "I only wanted to find out how you are."

"We're doing just fine. As you can see." Her mother swept her hand in an arc, as if to include the smithy and the house. "The ropemaker's niece helps me in the house, and her brother helps your father in the workshop. Their parents both died of influenza the winter before last. The ropemaker took them in, and we've found work for them to do. So another family's children are helping us run the house, though we raised three of our own . . ." The accusation in her chilly voice rang loud and clear.

Josephine took a deep breath. "I wanted to talk about the damage to the bicycle—"

"Your father paid that off long ago!" her mother snapped. "We won't have anyone speak ill of us. Your being in prison was bad enough. That was plenty of gossip for everyone. It took three months' earnings to pay off your debt. Not that you'd care."

"If you say it's so, then it must be true." Jo straightened her shoulders and looked the woman she called her mother in the eye. "I will repay the money. You have my word."

"As if your word means anything."

Josephine was already walking away when her mother called after her. "It would be for the best if you didn't show your face around here again. We're getting along quite well without you. The sight of you would only upset your father unnecessarily."

With a heavy heart, Josephine walked away, her mother's gaze boring wrathfully into her back.

She was still some distance away when she recognized Clara in Frieda's garden. Her friend was holding a watering can and gently sprinkling water onto a container of seedlings. Her chestnut hair shone brightly in the spring light.

"Clara!"

"Josephine!"

The two young women threw their arms around each other.

"I missed you so much . . ."

"And I you." Jo closed her eyes and nestled her cheek against Clara's shoulder. The unaccustomed proximity of her friend moved her almost to tears. She swallowed heavily.

"I live just two houses down now!" said Clara when they finally separated. She pointed to the building where an old couple had lived before. "The Wittgensteins passed away just after Gerhard and I married. My parents bought the place from their heirs. The apartment above the practice was really very small. Wonderful, isn't it?"

Josephine looked from the house to Clara and nodded. *Where's Frieda?* she wanted to ask, but Clara was already speaking again.

"Of course, I knew from Frieda that you'd be coming today, but my heart nearly stopped when I saw you just now from the window. I ran down here, but you were already gone. I don't have much time just now. Gerhard needs my help in the practice, and he doesn't like it if I'm gone too long. And I have to go to the pharmacy later to pick up some medications that Gerhard needs. But I absolutely had to be the first to come and greet you!"

Somewhat overwhelmed by Clara's effusiveness, Josephine just nodded. She looked at her friend in admiration. "You look so lovely."

Clara's rust-brown dress fitted as if it had been tailored to her body, and her hair was pinned up in a high and elegant knot. It gave an extra vulnerability to the finely chiseled lines of her face. Her skin was winter-pale but as clear as a baby's.

Clara laughed. "Marriage becomes me." Then she screwed up her face. "But don't expect me to return the compliment. Your hair's in desperate need of a vinegar rinse. It's as flat as straw! And your skin is chapped all over. I'll bring you a cream from the pharmacy tomorrow."

Josephine laughed drily, as she retrieved her bag from the small shed. "I know. I look terrible. But a few weeks of Frieda's care will work wonders, you'll see. Where is she?" She looked inquiringly toward the house.

"Frieda . . ." The smile vanished from her face. "I wanted to let you know, but . . ." As she spoke, she drew Josephine to a bench next to the house. She sat down and gestured for Josephine to sit beside her.

But Jo stayed on her feet, fighting with all her might against a rising panic. "What is it? Is she sick? Is she in the hospital? What are you keeping from me?" She felt like taking Clara by the shoulders and shaking her. Her chest heaved as if she had been running.

"Frieda passed away," said Clara. Her voice was flat, and she looked at the ground as she said it. "She died the week before last, with no warning whatsoever. She spat blood. A lot of blood. It was like something inside her burst, a vein or an ulcer or something. It was horrible. Gerhard was up all night with her. He tried everything he could, believe me . . ."

Josephine felt like she was drowning.

"I'm so very sorry. I was going to write to you. I had the paper and a pen in my hand. But I couldn't find the words. Oh, Josephine . . ." Clara wanted to take Josephine's arm, but Jo pulled away, then slumped impotently onto the bench.

Josephine took in everything around her with extreme clarity. The soft twittering of the blackbirds building a nest. Clara, sitting silently beside her. The gray cat, mewling around their legs . . . Every detail would be burned into her memory forever.

"Frieda wrote to me just a few weeks ago. I've got her letter here," Jo whispered. "She had plans . . ." *Masterful plans.*

She looked around, distraught. What would become of this place? Who would harvest Frieda's lamb's lettuce? Who would look after her cat?

"Frieda and her plans. She was really a very special old lady." Clara smiled sadly. As if she could read Josephine's thoughts, she said, "I've been feeding her cat ever since she died and taking care of the garden as well as I can. I can't bear the thought that everything that was important to her might fall apart." She managed a small shrug.

*I'd have done the same,* Josephine wanted to say, but no words came out. Sadness washed through her like a poison, forcing its way into every pore and making it impossible for her to think straight. *Why can't I cry?* she wondered and blinked.

"Frieda talked about you all the time. She could hardly wait to see you again. She'd already set up a room for you weeks ago. It's upstairs. She showed it to me. She was so proud of it. I haven't got the slightest idea what's to become of all this." Clara's eyes filled with tears.

They sat together for a moment in silence, each mourning the old woman. Then Clara laid her hand gingerly on Josephine's arm.

"I'd love to invite you to stay with us, but . . ." She stopped and bit her lip. "Our life is dictated by our sick patients and their needs.

Gerhard is often called out in the night and sometimes on weekends as well. A guest would have trouble getting used to our rhythm."

"Don't worry. I've got an address," Josephine replied with forced lightness. As if to underscore her statement, she took the note with the address in Feuerland out of her bag. She had crumpled it up on the way there, not imagining that she would ever need it. "Where is Frieda now?"

"She was laid to rest in the churchyard near Belle-Alliance Square. Everyone on the street went to the funeral. Her grave is beneath a big chestnut tree, right out on the edge. It's easy to find."

Josephine stood up with the tired motions of an old woman. "I'll be going now, then. I'm sure we'll see each other again," she said without really believing it. What was left for her here? Frieda was dead, her parents didn't want anything to do with her, Clara and her husband were busy. And Isabelle had forgotten her long ago.

Josephine already had her bag on her shoulder when she asked, "How is Isabelle, by the way?"

Clara opened her mouth to reply but then seemed to change her mind. "Isabelle," she finally said. "We've lost touch. She always has so much to do and is constantly racing off to one place or another, so it was terribly difficult to stay in contact with her. And when it comes down to it, we move in different social circles anyway. I read something about her and her fiancé in the paper occasionally, but that's all."

"She isn't married yet?" Jo asked, her voice scratchy.

Clara shook her head. "That would certainly have been mentioned in the paper. They write about everything else she does. Parties that Isabelle attends, painting exhibitions she 'graces with her presence.' The Herrenhus family has become *très à la mode*." Clara's voice had taken on a sarcastic undertone. "The newspaper also has stories about the cycling club Isabelle founded! A cycling club for women, can you imagine that?" She made a disapproving face.

"Isabelle did *what*? When? Where?" Josephine dropped her bag. She had to hear more.

Clara waved it off. "She set it up together with her old schoolmate Irene about three years ago. And you know she couldn't stand Irene— remember how Isabelle was always sniping about how arrogant she was? But now that she's engaged to Irene's brother, the shoe's on the other foot. Moving in better circles always meant a great deal to Isabelle. I guess she's decided she can put up with a bit of arrogance after all."

Josephine heard the arch tone in Clara's voice very clearly. She couldn't care less which parties Isabelle visited and with whom. She did, however, want to hear more about the cycling club.

"Her club . . . Do you know where it is?"

So Isabelle had established a cycling club for women . . . That had always been *her* dream! She could remember exactly when she told Frieda about her idea. The old woman had replied, "Then do it!" as if it were the most obvious thing in the world.

A little sullenly, Clara told her where the club was located. "I must say, it's very nice inside. But if you ask me, I find the whole idea a little childish. Riding bicycles was really just a youthful lark. But we're adults now. You'd think Isabelle would be more sensible. Gerhard says it's scandalous that grown women would sit on the saddle of a bicycle. If you heard him speak about it, you'd feel quite ill! It turns out riding a bicycle is quite dangerous. If I'd known that back then, I would never have dared to climb aboard one. And Gerhard knows. He's a good doctor, after all. The best there is, if you ask me. Gerhard says . . ."

Without another word, Josephine picked up her bag and walked away.

Frieda Koslowski. Born March 1830. Died March 1895. She was sixty-five years old. Why couldn't she have lived longer?

Sadly, Josephine brushed yellow pollen from the unadorned wooden cross. It felt strange that nobody had ever addressed Frieda as Mrs. Koslowski. She always had been just Frieda. Frieda who drank red wine instead of beer and who read the newspaper every day. Frieda, on whose kitchen wall hung no calendar of devout sayings but a map of the world. And who kept Meyer's *World Atlas* on the table beneath it. Frieda, who tended to her hobbies the way others tended to their homing pigeons. Frieda, who named her cat Mousie.

In summer, she always had a glass of buttermilk for the children who lived on the street. She kept the bottle cool in a bucket of water that stood underneath her garden table. In winter, she made caramels, and anyone who stopped by her house was allowed to sample the delicious treats. She was there for Jo when she needed to cry her eyes out and there to celebrate with her when that was called for. Nothing like Jo's parents, whose staid and sober lives left no room for such "follies." Frieda loved follies. And she loved the people behind them.

Suddenly, it was all too much for Josephine. She sank onto the cold earth beside Frieda's grave.

She had not wept when her brother died. She had wanted to die, to be as dead as Felix, certainly. But she had not shed a single tear. There had been many times when it would have been reasonable to weep—at the thought of the damage she had done to the Rover, during the most difficult times in prison—but she didn't let anyone see her cry.

Now her eyes burned. Her throat tightened like a cord was wrapped around it, and the muscles in her back grew cramped and painful. One teardrop rolled from the corner of her eye, then another. It was a strange and not unpleasant feeling. More and more tears trickled down and gathered at the corners of her mouth. Salty, almost resinous. A wave of feeling washed over her, and, for the first time in her adult life, she gave free rein to her tears.

\*

Josephine could not have said how long she sat there. The sun receded behind a thin layer of clouds; the ground beneath her was cold, last year's grass brittle and hard. But Josephine was so exhausted from crying that she could not imagine ever standing up again.

Her old life was over. With Frieda's death, the last bridge to her past had collapsed.

She stroked the cross with one strangely calm hand.

Now she would never find out what plans Frieda had had in mind for her.

But as her hand lay on the rough-planed wood, she felt a new power begin to flow inside her.

Thinking about all she had lost was pointless. She was free! She had paid for her actions, and she would pay off her financial debt as well. She was a twenty-one-year-old woman who had been given a second chance. A second life. A *new* life. One in which everything was possible. She would have to forge her own plans instead of relying on others' plans for her. She did not have to acquiesce to anything. She herself would set the course.

Of course, it would be more difficult now that Frieda was gone. She would have to take the job in the shoe factory and sleep there as well. She would have to pay for her accommodation, and she had no doubt that the factory owner charged handsomely for his "charity"!

But it would only be a temporary measure. Nothing and nobody would stop her from fulfilling her dreams. She would simply have to do it without Frieda's help. But she still had Frieda's blessing! Her old friend had always believed in her. Now it was up to her, Josephine, to prove herself worthy of that belief.

Jo stood.

"I'm still alive!" she murmured to herself, but her voice was steady. When, and where, had she said that before?

# Chapter Eighteen

When all her tears had dried, Josephine set off toward Feuerland. Jo didn't have enough money for a second tram journey, but the air was still pleasantly mild and the long walk would do her good. She eagerly breathed in the various aromas of the city. The smoke rising from a chimney. The smell of frying sausages, roasted almonds, and smoked fish emanating from the roadside stands. The brackish odor of the Spree slapping weed-green at its dirty banks. The musty reek rising from poorly laid drains. Berlin. Her city. Her old home, her new home.

Josephine discovered with pleasure that, thanks to her cycle tours of the city, she still had a very good sense of Berlin's layout, despite the building work going on all around. She took a shortcut here, a particularly lovely detour there, and occasionally simply followed the tram route on foot. She estimated she would reach the shoe factory in about two hours and be able to move into her new lodgings before evening. With a little luck she would start her new job the next day— and start earning some money of her own.

As she walked, she began to see cyclists everywhere. Young men in tight cycling pants. Older gentlemen holding the handlebars with one hand and their top hat with the other. Men quickly weaving among the horses and carriages. And others who seemed to have all the time in the world pedaling along sedately. Josephine was amazed. Before she had gone to prison, cyclists had been something special. But now they were simply part of the traffic on the streets, along with the trams, carriages, handcarts, and pedestrians. How was that possible? Only rich men like Moritz Herrenhus had been able to afford a bicycle before. Had they become more affordable in just three years? If that were the case, she might be able to buy a bicycle of her own in the foreseeable future. Her own bicycle . . . It was her greatest dream. The thought alone was enough to energize her, and she walked faster. The only thing that dampened her enthusiasm was the fact that every cycler she saw was a man.

In her mind's eye, she suddenly saw herself as a younger woman wearing her father's clothes and riding through Berlin. Ever watchful, always taking care not to be recognized. Had nothing improved in that regard? Were women still harassed the way they had been in the past?

Arriving at Pariser Platz, Josephine was so hungry that she decided to spend the last of her money at a sausage stand. She was about to take her first delicious bite when a poster hanging from a tree caught her eye. It showed a smiling young woman in a skirt and billowing blouse riding a bicycle. A white scarf swept out behind her in the slipstream. Beneath the stylized illustration was an inscription:

### THE FIRST BERLIN CYCLING CLUB FOR WOMEN
### INVITES ALL RESIDENTS OF BERLIN
### TO THE
### GREAT TRACK RACE FOR WOMEN

Beneath that, in smaller letters, was information about the date and venue. The race would take place in just under two weeks.

Josephine felt her skin prickle and the hair on her arms rise. The cycling club for women really existed! And it was advertising a race. Unbelievable.

That had to be the club that Clara had mentioned to her earlier, the one that Isabelle had founded. How stunning that Josephine should see this poster, here, now . . . She shook her head. What a stroke of fate.

Her hunger was forgotten, and she stuffed the bread and sausage heedlessly into her bag. Then she looked around. No one was looking at her, so she untied the poster from the tree, folded it up, and put it in her bag, too.

"Bed number seven is still free," said the gaunt clerk at the Strähle Shoe Sole Factory. "We provide bedding, if required. Rental is fifty pfennigs a month. If you want to have it washed, it's another fifty pfennigs. The wash service is not provided more than once a month, however. Do you require bedding?"

Jo nodded, and the woman made a note on her blotter.

Josephine looked around with a feeling of dread. The dormitory, situated beneath the factory roof, was barely distinguishable from the one she had just left at the prison. It even smelled like the one in Barnim Road. Of unwashed bodies. Of mold. Of badly dried laundry, resignation, and weariness.

Jo sat on the bed, testing it. The mattress was so thin and worn that she could feel the boards underneath. Out of the frying pan into the fire—no saying was more fitting. Jo smiled involuntarily, and the clerk looked at her with skepticism.

"This is our common kitchen," said the woman, leading her into a second room that was considerably smaller than the first. "Who uses it and when is something the tenants sort out for themselves. The monthly charge to use it is one mark, which includes the cost of the wood for the oven. You have to bring in water yourself from the yard. Like the fee for the bedding and laundry, the charge for the kitchen will be deducted from your wages."

An ancient, soot-blackened stove dominated the center of the room. Next to it was a sink, also antiquated; it was chipped but more or less clean. The wall on the other side of the stove was taken up by a wooden cupboard divided into many small compartments. Each compartment was covered by a wire grille, which reminded Josephine of a chicken coop. She let out a quiet sigh.

With her fingers held as if she was about to pick up something unpleasant, the clerk indicated the cupboard. "The compartments are numbered. There is one for each bed. Our tenants can use the compartments to store food. It is absolutely forbidden to keep food in the dormitory! Anyone caught doing so can pack her bag on the spot."

Josephine frowned. "But the compartments are so small. You couldn't even fit a loaf of bread in there. And there's no padlock that I can see. It's practically an invitation to a thief." A decent piece of sausage or a jar of marmalade wouldn't last long in there if it weren't locked up.

"This is not the Grand Hotel," the clerk replied sharply. "If you can't live with it, you can leave anytime. There are more than enough young women who would be thankful to have such a secure and clean place to sleep. And you'll have to look long and hard to find as good a position as you'll have in Mr. Strähle's factory."

Jo raised both hands in a placating gesture, then listened to a litany of additional rules and prohibitions.


Josephine was scheduled to work the late shift, from midday to ten in the evening. She had planned to pay a visit to the cycling club for women as soon as possible, but now she would have to wait until Saturday, which was half an eternity away! At least she would be earning money, she told herself by way of consolation.

The clerk handed her over to a supervisor, who led her to a table covered with a long row of punch machines. Her job was to take precut leather soles from a box and punch small holes all the way around the edges. It was crucial to maintain an even distance between the holes, as this was the seam to which the upper portion of the shoe would later be sewn.

The work was dull and arduous. The punching machine was a cumbersome device that did not operate smoothly. When Josephine asked the supervisor whether she could lubricate it with a little oil, she was told no. The oil might stain the leather. The only solution was to use more force.

Although Jo was used to hard work, her wrists began to hurt after the first hour, and boredom set in. Again and again, her eyes blurred and she lost focus.

The factory was basically clean and well-lit, and it wasn't particularly loud, but there was a sharp, almost biting smell in the air that came from a huge pile of skins that lay up front. Several women were busy dipping the skins into some dark, foul-smelling liquid and then hanging them on long iron bars to dry. Other women then took the dry leather down and cut it into different sizes with small, curved knives. Wooden blocks in various shapes and sizes served as templates. *Even that step could easily be accomplished with punching machines,* thought Jo, but it didn't look like the Strähle Shoe Sole Factory was that advanced.

Josephine guessed there were at least a hundred women working there. At her bench alone there were ten other women performing the same task. She would have loved to strike up a conversation with them. The most pressing question concerned her wages. The clerk had not mentioned a word about that.

"What are you doing staring into space? Concentrate on your work!" came a sharp voice behind her. "Can't you see that the spacing between your holes is uneven?"

Jo murmured an apology and turned her gaze down to her work.

The supervisor had only just left when Jo's neighbor, a young woman who appeared to be the same age as Jo, whispered, "If that happens again, they'll dock the damage from your wages, and those are already miserable enough. So watch out!"

"How much do we actually get paid, then?" Jo had not even finished her sentence when the supervisor reappeared at her side.

"Talking is strictly forbidden! It distracts from the work. You're new here, so I'll turn my head this time. But starting tomorrow, it will cost you five pfennigs every time I catch you talking. Have I made myself clear?" The woman waited for Jo's nod, then looked sternly at all the other women and stalked away.

Jo glanced grumpily at her departing figure before placing a new sole beneath the punch. One thing was clear: she would not stay there any longer than absolutely necessary! She would keep her eye out for a new job starting first thing tomorrow.

# Chapter Nineteen

Instead of sleeping late the next morning, Jo was awoken by the chattering of her cotenants getting ready for the early shift. After a sparse breakfast of tea and a dry roll—everything in the kitchen compartments really *was* fair game for the pilferers—she went into the washroom. The water she drew into a dented, galvanized bucket with a piston pump was so icy that it hurt Jo's back and wrists, which were already sore from the hard bed and the long hours on the punching machine. But to Jo, cleanliness mattered. She had never once missed her daily wash in prison. On the third day, the piece of soap she had bought for ten pfennigs disappeared. Everybody denied stealing it, of course. She had no money to buy new soap because her first wages would only be paid the Saturday after next. Purchasing a new dress would also have to wait, so she sewed up the only dress she had, taking it in so that it fit her again. Recalling Clara's words, she asked a woman in the kitchen for some vinegar and used it to rinse her hair after she had washed it. The vinegar returned at least a little of the original shine, and one of the women offered to trim her split ends. Jo felt a great deal better about herself after that.

In her clean dress, with her hair freshly cut and washed, Josephine set out every morning to look for a better job. She had to be back in the Strähle factory by half past eleven if she wanted to eat something before starting work at twelve. Luckily, she did not have to walk far. The factories were lined up one right beside the other in Feuerland. Factories had shot up everywhere since she last rode through the area and now filled every gap. Sometimes, she hardly recognized the old streets. The air was still infused with soot, and carriages piled high with every imaginable product occupied the wide streets. New rails were being placed along the streets as well. *Is Feuerland going to get its own station?* Jo wondered. But she did not have much time to spare for such thoughts, and the answer did not particularly interest her.

She got the same answer everywhere she went. No. There was no job for her as a mechanic. The factories were geared toward skilled men who carried out all the necessary repairs and maintenance. The looks of mistrust, rejection, and condescension she got from gatekeepers, overseers, and factory owners themselves were all too familiar. But Josephine was far from giving up hope. Let those men hang on to their old prejudices. All she needed was *one* person willing to take a chance on her. Just *one* willing to cross that line and employ a woman as a mechanic. Someone like Gerd Melchior. It might take knocking on hundreds of factory doors, but she would eventually find the kind of employer she was looking for.

After a long Saturday afternoon stroll through the city and a visit to Frieda's grave, Jo finally found herself at the entrance to the First Berlin Cycling Club. A smaller sign indicated that the clubrooms also housed the women's bicycle club. She was in the right place. Jo stepped through the entrance, her heart pounding. The first thing she saw was the broad oval of the racetrack. Three young men were riding laps despite the light drizzle. Jo watched them with envy. Hunched over the handlebars, their legs tucked in close to the frame, they flew past so quickly that she could hardly believe her eyes. She would never have believed that a bicycle could move so quickly. The bicycles themselves looked lighter and sleeker than the ones Josephine remembered. And they were so quiet! Apart from a soft hum there was no noise at all as the young men rode by. She discovered the reason when she studied the surface of the track, which was as smooth as a finely planed piece of wood.

Every time the cyclists flashed past, her own longing to ride increased. The wind in her face. The feeling of being able to fly like a bird. The freedom of taking her feet off the ground and not falling over. She was nearly desperate to experience it all again for herself. It wouldn't have taken much for her to pull one of the young men off his bicycle and swing into the saddle herself.

She stood and watched them for a good half an hour before finally dragging herself away from the strip that separated the racetrack from the spectator area. Her hair was curling in the moist air, and her cheeks were red from the cold. She followed the sign that pointed the way to the clubrooms. If anyone asked her what she was doing here, she had decided that she would mention Isabelle's name. But no one even took any notice of her when she stepped inside.

In the clubroom, she found a kind of bar decorated with trophies and posters all pertaining to the sport of cycling. It was warm and smelled of freshly brewed coffee and hot soup. A young woman was running madly back and forth behind the counter, seemingly attempting to do ten things at once. A dozen men sat at several tables, talking excitedly, drinking beer, and leafing through cycling magazines. This was meant to be a *clubroom*? To Josephine, it looked more like a restaurant or tavern! A large poster on the wall caught her eye. It was an advertisement for sports clothing that featured "Anwander's Sports Salon" and "First-Class Specialist for Cycling Outfits and Equipment" in large letters. Beneath that came a list of the products the sports store carried: "English sweaters, distinctive French caps, finest Bavarian loden sports jackets, stockings in silk and wool, bicycle clips, specialist outfits for tourists and serious wheelmen." She was amazed to discover how many different kinds of clothing now existed for cyclists. Apparently it was no longer enough to have a pair of pants, a jacket, and a decent pair of shoes. Judging by the elegant appearance of the men at the tables, shops like Anwander's Sports Salon did a brisk trade.

One of the men looked up then and asked her in a rather cool voice, "Have you lost your way, young lady?" Several pairs of eyes turned and looked at her.

"I'm looking for the Cycling Club for Women," Jo murmured.

"Their ladyships are in the back room. And that, as the name suggests, is in the back." The man jabbed his thumb toward the door. Jo heard laughter behind her as she hurried out to the corridor.

The first door on her right displayed a small, brass plaque that read "Changing Room 1." Right next door was "Changing Room 2." Then came a "Storeroom," "Washroom 1," and "Washroom 2." Jo looked around in confusion. Where was the women's clubroom?

"Girl, are you planning to put down roots? Ever since Edith got sick, nothing around here works. I've been waiting for my beer for half an hour and I'm nearly dying of thirst!" snapped a young man who had just emerged from one of the washrooms. He was tall, blond, and extremely good-looking; it seemed as though he was used to people jumping to attention when he gave an order. He was dressed in the smartest, sleekest cycling clothes Josephine had ever seen.

She nonetheless lifted her chin and said, "I'm sorry to hear you are thirsty, but I don't know any Edith and I am not a bargirl. I'm looking for the women's cycling club." As she spoke, she was puzzling over when and where she had seen this man before. Then it came to her: he'd been riding around the racetrack that Moritz Herrenhus had once invited her to. It felt like an eternity ago! If she recognized him again now, then he had obviously made quite an impression on her then . . .

His expression changed instantly, becoming more open, almost friendly. "*You* want to join the women's club?" Under his appraising eye, Jo suddenly felt terribly ill at ease in her old dress and her unadorned hair. She had thought that clothes wouldn't matter as much in a cycling club. It was all about the sport, wasn't it? But the sight of the well-dressed men in the bar had already disabused her of that notion. This seemed to be a place where the upper classes congregated.

"Do you have anything against that?" she nearly hissed, her eyes flashing. She was not about to be intimidated by a jerk like this! Even if her knees were quivering.

The man grinned and raised his hands defensively. "Not at all. On the contrary, I find it outstanding that young women of your . . . station are finding their way into the sport, too." He smiled and pointed to a door at the end of the corridor. "The women's clubroom is back there."

Jo stalked away without replying. "Young women of your . . . station"—*what was that supposed to mean?* Josephine wondered as she turned the handle to the door of the women's clubroom.

\*\*\*

"So are we serving sparkling wine *and* French champagne on Saturday, or just one or the other?" Chloé, the wife of one of the racing cyclists, looked inquiringly at those assembled around the table. She had a cup of coffee and an untouched piece of cake in front of her.

"We could serve the sparkling wine *before* the race and the champagne *afterward*," replied Melissa, the daughter of a pharmaceutical entrepreneur. Like Chloé, she was relatively new to the club and the upcoming race was the first major event she was helping to organize.

"Sparkling wine, French champagne, that's all well and good! But shouldn't we be moving on to the things that really matter?" asked Irene. She pushed her empty coffee cup away as if to say, *Enough gossiping!* "For example, our press coverage. God knows it would help if the reporters who cover the event aren't as scathing as the last time. How can we get some positive, sympathetic press?" She looked intently around the table at the twenty women of various ages who were assembled there.

All she got in reply was a helpless silence.

Isabelle had nothing to suggest, either. One journalist had described them as "hellcats on wheels" after the fall races, while another had called it an "embarrassing spectacle" and compared the meet to a circus show. Her father had been furious. Any more reports like that and he would ban her outright from taking part in any more such frivolous affairs. A future Neumann should not make herself an object of ridicule. "What about Irene?" Isabelle had shot back, but he had simply ignored her. As usual! She sullenly stirred sugar into her cup of coffee.

Isabelle's mood had been at a low ebb for weeks. The club that she had founded with such enthusiasm was getting on her nerves. New cliques had begun to form, each trying to hijack the club for its own ends. Isabelle sometimes felt as though she and Irene were the only true cyclists there.

In addition to her disappointment with the club, there was a more general dissatisfaction with her life. Where was the vaunted freedom that she had thought awaited her after her "engagement" to Adrian?

The first months had been pleasant enough. Her parents had left her in peace for a while once she and Adrian had announced publicly that they were a couple, and she had been able to do whatever she liked—including setting up her cycling club.

But things had changed. After almost three years of being engaged and two postponements of her wedding day—once she had really been sick, and the second time, Adrian's father had had to resolve a crisis involving striking workers—her father was putting enormous pressure on her. He wanted the bond to the magnate's family sealed once and for all.

Adrian, too, was feeling increasingly uneasy about their arrangement. He wanted to follow his own path, free of the constant presence of his fiancée. They often found themselves debating how they could explain a final split to their parents, but they had not yet settled on a mutually acceptable approach. Like Isabelle, Adrian feared the wrath of their fathers.

"And then we have to decide whether we're going to do match races on top of the main race. We all know the spectators love head-to-head racing. But aren't we overloading the program if we do that?" It was once again Irene who lobbed the question into the room.

Luise Karrer, one of the oldest—and most dedicated—cyclists, answered. "Considering the importance of sympathetic press coverage, I think it would make sense to offer the audience something spectacular like the match races. Besides, I'm looking forward to trouncing Isabelle."

Isabelle and a few others laughed. Her sporting rivalry with Luise was well-known.

"I'd love to thrash you as well. But at the end of the show, all the newspapers will write is that we crazy she-devils battled it out in completely unfeminine duels," said Isabelle with a sigh. "Perhaps we'd better just get used to the idea that we'll never be able to please everyone." A casual dismissive gesture accompanied her words, earning murmurs of agreement from one side and sneers from the other.

"We have to fight for the rights of women or we'll always be subservient to men!" said Gertrude, a thin teacher with a dyspeptic look on her face, garnering even more peevish looks in reply.

"But I don't feel subservient at all," said a smoky voice. "Perhaps we ought to use the race day to showcase our sport in the best possible light?" Fadi Nandou, a beautiful Persian woman, was a member of the Berlin Theater and one of the leading lights of her profession. Her admirers followed her as far as the entrance to the cycling club, and large floral arrangements were always being left at the bar for the beautiful actress. No one was sure how she had found her way to the club, as Fadi was only rarely seen on a bicycle, but Isabelle assumed that the actress boasted often outside the club of her involvement in the sport. That, too, counted as a motive for riding a bicycle.

"We have to be able to offer the people something. Bread and circuses, as the ancient Romans used to say, right? *I* could offer our spectators something . . ." Fadi's almond-brown eyes scanned the others with determination. She was so accustomed to getting her way that she refuted the possibility of any objections at the very start.

Long peeved at the actress's vain posturing, Isabelle said in a mocking tone, "And how do you propose that would work? Should we dress up as Romeo and Juliet and perform a play on bicycles?"

"More attractive clothes would certainly not be unwarranted," Fadi replied. "These new bloomers are a catastrophe. And a sure way to put off admirers!" She screwed up her pretty face in disgust.

Isabelle abruptly stood up, her chest rising and falling as she vented her pent-up frustration. "I have had it up to here with these eternal discussions! What are we all doing here? We drink coffee and talk about sparkling wine and French champagne as if we were organizing a ball! We fret about clothes and the press! But there's one thing we never talk about—cycling!—when that's the only thing that really matters."

"Exactly," came a strange but also familiar voice behind her.

All heads turned to the door.

*"Josephine?"*

For a brief moment, Isabelle felt as if she'd been struck by lightning. Josephine looked so different. So grown up, far older than her years. The last two years—or was it three?—must have been very hard for her. A life behind bars, while she, Isabelle, had danced from one ball to the next. And had barely given a thought to her old friend . . .

Isabelle felt a surge of guilt wash over her. She went to the door, unsure that her shaking legs would carry her.

"You're back?" she asked, so quietly that only Jo heard her.

Josephine nodded. "I've been back for a week. Clara told me about your club. I came as soon as I could."

The smell of cheap curd soap and old wool stung Isabelle's nose as she embraced Josephine stiffly. Then she turned back to the gathering.

"I'd like to introduce my old friend Josephine!" she said, her voice artificially cheerful. She cleared her throat to get rid of the lump that had formed there. "Jo was already riding a bicycle when most of us didn't even know how to spell the word . . ." She laughed, and it sounded even more contrived.

Instead of the bright reaction she had expected, she found herself looking into a sea of skeptical faces; some looked downright hostile.

"*That* is a friend of yours?" Irene asked, raising her eyebrows. "And here I was thinking one of your factory workers had wandered in by mistake."

"Irene!" Isabelle rebuked her angrily.

But Josephine smiled. "You're absolutely right, madam. At the moment, it's true, I really am working in a factory." She shrugged indifferently, as if to say, *Think what you like!* Isabelle could only admire Josephine's self-confidence. "But I'll soon have a job as a mechanic. Technical work is my specialty. And I would very much like to be a member of your club."

"That won't be any problem. We're happy to welcome any new member," Isabelle said quickly. Supporting her old friend was the very least she could do.

"No problem, dearest Isabelle?" said Irene icily. "We are most certainly *not* happy to welcome any new member. Our statutes specify that we only accept members from the upper echelons of society. We also require that each member have her own bicycle. Your . . . *friend* doesn't look as if she would fulfill either of those requirements."

"I'm surprised at you, Isabelle, since you helped write our bylaws in the first place," said Melissa. "We can't just accept anyone who happens to wander in!"

"I agree," said Chloé. "We're 'a club for ladies only,' are we not? Today it's this . . . person, and tomorrow my cook will come waltzing in here, wanting to join."

A chorus of shrill laughter rang out all around, and Isabelle could see from Josephine's expression that her self-confidence was beginning to waver.

"Now settle down, all of you," said Luise Karrer. "This young woman is Isabelle's guest, and we ought to treat her as such with all due courtesy. We can discuss this at a later date, although I must say I find all your airs completely over the top. Shouldn't we at least listen to why this young woman—whom we so far only know by her first name—wants to become a member here?"

"As if anyone cares," snorted Irene, and she began leafing through a cycling magazine.

Isabelle cast Luise a look of gratitude. Then she asked Josephine to take a seat at the table. She hoped that Jo would not say the wrong thing.

"My name is Josephine Schmied. Riding bicycles is my greatest passion. Unfortunately, I have not been able to do it for the last three years because I was doing my apprenticeship to become a mechanic."

*An apprenticeship to become a mechanic?* Isabelle raised her eyebrows. A nice way to describe her time behind bars.

"But several years ago, I even rode an old-style bicycle in the Black Forest. I can only say those are dangerous contraptions."

A few of the women nodded in agreement, and here and there an unfriendly expression turned to one of interest.

"You're from the Black Forest? Isn't that a terribly primitive region?" asked Fadi.

Josephine laughed. "Not at all. The people down there are very open to advancements of all kinds, technological or otherwise. My friend Lilo, for example, works as a nurse in an exclusive sanatorium that uses the most modern treatment methods to help cure people suffering from lung disease."

Isabelle was astonished. She had not thought that Josephine would be able to handle herself so skillfully. Not a word about the Barnim

Road Women's Prison. Instead, vague insinuations about her origins—did she come from the Black Forest or not? And an apprenticeship as a mechanic. Was there any truth in that?

"Josephine is quite well-traveled and has seen and experienced a great deal." Isabelle could not stop herself from commenting.

"An apprenticeship as a mechanic? How could a young woman ever manage something like that?" Luise asked.

"It's thanks to my passion for bicycles, madam," Jo replied with a smile. "I wanted to do more than just ride one. I wanted to know what every cog and bearing was responsible for, how the diameter of the front wheel related to the distance traveled, how to adjust a pedal to optimize its performance . . ."

Luise nodded appreciatively. "Most of us lack that sort of knowledge, I'm sad to say. I'm certainly able to ride quickly, but a breakdown is a real predicament!"

"I'd be happy to show you a few of the most useful tricks, if you like, madam."

"I don't know . . ." Luise looked around uncertainly. "It would certainly be interesting, especially because the men here make such a fuss about explaining anything technical."

Isabelle noted Irene's grim expression with satisfaction. It was clear that she was unhappy that Josephine was making up so much ground so fast.

Suddenly, Isabelle realized that Josephine's presence in the club could shift its focus in a very promising direction. Josephine would be another member for whom the main attraction was the cycling. She wouldn't spend hours yapping about the merits of sparkling wine versus French champagne, and she would ally herself with Isabelle rather than Irene or Fadi. Her mere presence would be enough to tick Irene off. She had to think hard and fast about how to circumvent the stupid club statutes for Josephine.

Isabelle took Josephine's hand and said, "You don't have to speak so formally to Luise. We're all on casual terms here. It's something we picked up from the men. It's so much easier to speak informally in sport, don't you think?"

Josephine smiled and nodded.

"That's it!" Irene looked up from her magazine. "Let's get one thing straight. As far as that woman is concerned, I am still Miss Neumann. She can call me madam till the cows come home. And the only way she will ever be a member of this club is over my dead body."

# Chapter Twenty

The following Saturday, Josephine received her first wages. Once the cost of lodging, bedding, and kitchen use had been taken out, she was paid fifteen marks for a week and a half of sore wrists, sore feet, and crushing boredom.

Josephine didn't know whether to laugh or cry. She would never be able to realize her dream on such a paltry wage. She decided to intensify her search for a new job in the week ahead. If necessary, she would even sacrifice her regular visit to Frieda's grave.

With the money in her pocket, she set off on the long trek back to Luisenstadt. When she passed by Reutter's Emporium, she toyed with the idea of going inside and inquiring about a job with Oskar Reutter directly. Perhaps his product range had expanded and now included more technical equipment? Perhaps he could use his own mechanic? But what if he said no because he already had a good man on the job? Or because he didn't want anything to do with her now? Being rejected by the genial old gentleman would be more than Josephine could bear. She hurried past the emporium, her eyes fixed stubbornly straight ahead.

When she got to her parents' smithy, she went directly into the kitchen, where her mother was cutting yeast cake to have with the midday coffee. Jo felt a momentary pang at the familiar sight of the dry cake, which scratched the back of your palate and could only be washed down with large mouthfuls of coffee. She took a deep breath, then put five one-mark coins on the table.

"As promised, I will pay off my debts. But don't worry; I won't be coming here with five marks every Saturday. I just wanted to show you that I'm true to my word. I'll come back when I have put together fifty marks."

Her mother looked at the money and nodded, evidently surprised.

Josephine cleared her throat. She could afford neither vanity nor the luxury of being overly sensitive, so she took a deep breath and said, "There's something else . . . Would it be all right if I took a few of my old clothes? I'm sure you have no use for them."

"Your old clothes? But . . ."

Josephine waited for her mother to come up with some nonsensical reply intended only to wound her. But her mother paused, then gestured toward the stairs. "Go and get what you need. Everything's right where it always was. But hurry! If your father catches you taking anything from his house . . ." She let the sentence trail off unfinished.

Not ten minutes later, Josephine walked out of her parents' house, a heavy cloth bag slung over her shoulder and her heart lighter than it had been on her way there. The underwear, dresses, skirts, and blouses she had taken from her old cupboard were not exactly the latest fashion, but at least they would give her something half decent to change into.

She spent the rest of the day at the large table in the common kitchen, ironing her crumpled clothes with a borrowed iron. Then she carefully selected a dark-blue skirt and a pretty yellow blouse for the following day. She hoped that no one would mistake her for a barmaid in that outfit. Satisfied with her handiwork, she treated herself to an evening stroll and dreamed of the next day.

***

Isabelle looked at the clock for the umpteenth time. Twenty minutes until the start. She had just used the ladies' room, but she felt like she had to go again. Her excitement had reached fever pitch now that the race was about to begin, though she did everything she could not to let it show. She nervously swept aside a curl that had worked its way loose from her tightly pinned-up hair.

It was a cool Sunday in April, and she felt chilled by the light breeze sweeping across the racetrack. She knew that she would warm up plenty over the course of the ten-lap race. Still, she eyed with some envy the warm jackets that most of the arriving guests were wearing. Almost everyone was rushing to get to the best places around the track. Only a few drifted toward the stands where sparkling wine *and* French champagne were being served.

Isabelle was deeply absorbed in her own thoughts as she pushed her bicycle across the competitors' area. She had trained hard, and she felt healthy and strong. But would it be enough to win? She went through the starting lineup in her head yet again.

Luise Karrer was the strongest of her rivals. She was a fast starter and just as quick around the track. And she was consistently fair. Disruptive tactics, like deliberately riding into another cyclist's path, were not a concern with Luise.

But Chloé was a different matter altogether. She would not hesitate to make unsporting use of her elbows to clear a path to the front.

Then there was Irene—

"Child, don't you think you should drink something?"

Isabelle was startled when her mother appeared, holding a glass of apple juice. The acidic smell of it was enough to turn Isabelle's stomach. "No, thank you," she said.

"Leave her alone. Let her concentrate," said her father, pushing his wife away. Then he planted himself in front of her and continued,

"Remember to pedal hard at the start. You shouldn't spend the race trying to catch up like last time."

Isabelle gritted her teeth. She hated the way her father preached at her before every race!

"And make sure your future sister-in-law doesn't pass you on the inside on the first curve. She took you completely by surprise last fall . . ." Moritz Herrenhus frowned. "I don't want to see Irene Neumann at the top of the podium. This time, I want you up there."

"Then perhaps you should ride in my place?" Isabelle replied peevishly, but all she got for it was a jab in the ribs from her mother.

She felt some relief when she saw Adrian making his way over to them. As a racer himself, he knew how those long minutes leading up to the start felt. Unlike her father, he would not do his best to get on her nerves. She glanced back at the clock. Still fifteen minutes to go . . . The wait seemed forever!

After a kiss on the cheek and a few words of encouragement, Adrian said, "I saw your old friend standing in line out front. You know, the one who was here just the other day. Have you accepted her as a member yet?"

"Old friend? New member? Who do you mean?" Moritz Herrenhus said.

Isabelle rolled her eyes. This discussion was the last thing she needed just then. On the other hand, it was unavoidable if Josephine were to start spending time there. As much as she dreaded the confrontation with her father, she was equally determined to put it behind her. Josephine might otherwise find herself in a very uncomfortable situation . . . and not only Josephine. So why not here and now? Even if it went terribly, she could always escape to the starting line a few minutes early.

"Josephine came to visit me here at the club last week. She's back in the city after all these years, and she has expressed interest in becoming a member," she said in as neutral a tone as possible.

"Josephine?" her parents replied simultaneously.

"Josephine Schmied? The daughter of Schmied-the-Smith?" Moritz Herrenhus clarified, his brow furrowed.

"But that's the young woman who—" her mother began.

"Adrian is very much in favor of the idea of accepting a few workers into the club, aren't you, sweetheart?" Isabelle broke in. She batted her eyelids coquettishly at her fiancé, a gesture he noted with a slight frown.

"But Josephine was the one with Father's—" her mother began again.

"Oh, Mother, we don't need to bore Adrian with our old family history, do we?" said Isabelle, cutting her off a second time. She smiled to take the edge off her rudeness. "Josephine would like to become a member of the First Berlin Cycling Club for Women, and that's all there is to it. You know how much she used to love cycling." She raised her eyebrows significantly, then quickly continued before anyone could say a word. "Unfortunately, Adrian's sister is balking at letting her join. Irene is polishing up her social superiority like an expensive pair of shoes. Adrian sees the matter very differently, don't you, dear?" But again, without waiting for an answer, she carried on, "And you, dear Papa, do, too, I'm sure! Don't you consider your workers to be human beings? When I was younger, you encouraged me to have fun with the girls in the neighborhood, remember? You even joined us sometimes."

It was a rare thing to see confusion and uncertainty on Moritz Herrenhus's face, but Isabelle grinned inwardly at the sight of it. "I'm sure you remember—when you so willingly let Josephine borrow your bicycle," she added in a voice thick with significance. Then she touched Adrian lightly on the arm. "Dear, would you be so kind as to push my bicycle to the starting line? I'll be along in a minute."

When Adrian had left, Isabelle whispered harshly to her parents, "Not a word about Josephine's past! If my fiancé finds out that there are people with a criminal background living in our neighborhood and that I'm still in touch with them, I doubt he'll care to be seen with me."

She took a moment to savor the shock on her parents' faces, then trotted away triumphantly. She had no need to fear that they might spread any scandalous gossip—that much was clear.

***

"Did you see that? A bare calf . . ." A middle-aged woman was pointing an accusing finger toward the track, where the racers who were about to compete in the main event were gathering.

"And you can even see that one's knee!" said a second woman, who was somewhat younger than the first. Both women laughed hysterically. Their cheeks were red and their eyes shone with anticipation as they stood on tiptoes and craned their necks to get the best possible view of the spectacle.

*Factory workers like me, no doubt,* Josephine thought. At least, that's what she assumed from their frilly skirts' cheap material, their chapped hands, and their pale skin that obviously only rarely saw the light of day.

The crowd that had assembled along the fence for the main race was a motley lot composed of factory workers like the two women, as well as middle- and upper-class types—lawyers, doctors, professors, clerks, and businesspeople—in correspondingly fancy outfits. A few tradesmen were there with their wives, who were turned out in their Sunday best and not looking especially at ease, and a few simple maids and young men as well. Society's elite had gathered in a separate, roofed spectator area that had been reserved for them.

Josephine would never have believed that so many people would want to see a women's cycling race. When she had arrived at the club an hour before the official starting time, the two women selling tickets had already started dismantling their stand.

"It's closed. We're full," one of them had said tersely. But when Jo had mentioned Isabelle's name—

Josephine jumped when she heard a hiss beside her.

"The underskirt! Look at her underskirt! Lily-white and so finely starched it looks like it belongs to a wedding dress. Oh, I'd love one like that . . ." The woman sighed deeply.

"A lady plans to ride a bicycle in that?" said the other, in an envious tone.

"I wouldn't exactly call them *ladies*. I've got a few other words in mind for harpies like that," said a man who had just pushed his way forward through the crowd. He had a scruffy beard and wore the kind of cap favored by errand boys. He dug one elbow roughly into Josephine's side to get her to make room for him. But Jo stood her ground—*don't try that on me, you bastard,* her stance implied. He shot an unfriendly glance her way, then passed two liverwurst rolls back through the crowd to the two women. The spicy smell reminded Josephine that she hadn't had a bite to eat since her meager breakfast. She had had to choose between lunch and the price of entry since her slim budget would not allow both. She clenched her teeth and ignored the growling of her stomach.

The older of the two women bit into her roll so clumsily that part of the liverwurst immediately fell out the side. Swearing, she bent down to pick it up, but the man said, "Leave it! Soon as the first of them lands in the mud, I'll go and buy you another."

"If a second one takes a header, do I get another roll, too?" asked the younger woman, and all three laughed hysterically.

Josephine turned away in disgust. These people were just here for the spectacle! The well-being of the cyclists meant as little to them as the race itself. What they wanted to see was naked skin and hair-raising accidents.

The crack of the starter's gun roused Josephine from her dour thoughts. Instantly, a dozen women on the opposite straight began to move. All wore elegantly designed but practical cycling outfits comprised of tight-fitting tops and loosely cut bloomers that did not restrict their movements. One or two were wearing hats, but most had braided their hair and pinned up the braids to stop them from flapping in their faces as they rode.

Jo's eyes followed the field of riders with fascination. After just half a lap, Isabelle and a second woman had pulled away from the others. Cheered on by the crowd, Isabelle leaned even lower over the handlebars, and her bicycle seemed to fly even more quickly along the track. And how sharply she took the curves! How must it feel to ride on such a fast track? The hunger in Jo's belly grew stronger, but it was not a hunger for food. It was so all-consuming that she could not hold out against it for long. She abruptly turned away from the race and wandered back out of the crowd. A group of young men stood close to the entryway to the track. They were all were dressed in cycling outfits, so Jo assumed they were members of the men's club. They evidently had no interest in the race going on out on the track, because instead of watching, they appeared to be in the middle of a heated discussion. Josephine edged closer to the group as inconspicuously as she could.

"I'm not backing down—if you're not able to average fifteen miles per hour in a road race, you've got no business even competing!" one of the young men said adamantly.

"Fifteen? Strong words. How many races are you basing that on? Are you taking into account all the races that take place in England, France, and Germany in a year?" asked another of the men.

Josephine started. Wasn't that the blond fellow who'd taken her for a servant girl the first time she'd visited?

Although she'd done her utmost to appear confident that time at the club, she'd been shaking like a leaf. Everything was so new and strange, and when Isabelle's clubmate Irene had attacked her verbally like that . . . she had almost gotten up and run out. But hadn't she vowed to never again let herself be intimidated? Not by anything, not by anyone. And definitely not by blond men, although she had to admit that this one had a special radiance.

She was trying to inch a little closer when he looked over at her. For a brief moment, their eyes met. Josephine suddenly flushed, as if caught red-handed in some mischief. The man grinned broadly. Jo quickly averted her gaze and pretended to be looking for something in her bag. The young man returned his attention to the men's discussion.

"Fifteen miles per hour? That's ancient history," said one of the men loftily. "I was clocking nearly twenty in Land's End last autumn."

"With two pacesetters, boyo! You never would have done it without 'em," the blond replied, patting the showboat teasingly on the shoulder.

The men laughed, and the one who'd been bragging fell into an insulted silence.

Josephine did her best to follow their discussion from where she stood leaning against an ash tree a short distance away. She did not understand every word, but she was well aware that speed records were being tossed around like leaves in an autumn wind. As they debated the question of who was the fastest, where and under what conditions, the conversation turned to the criteria for measuring the speed of races.

Even if Jo had been standing directly beside the men, she would have understood no more than half of what they were saying. Was winning really all that mattered? Why didn't anyone talk about the sheer pleasure of cycling?

After the race, Isabelle received the congratulations of her friends and competitors alike with the grace of a queen, while Moritz Herrenhus stood beside her, puffed up with pride. Second place went to Irene, the same Irene who had been so scathing to Jo just days earlier. She stood with her own family just a few steps away from Isabelle. Members of one of the families occasionally wandered across to the other group to exchange a few words. They all seemed to know each other well.

Isabelle's father had hardly changed. *Perhaps the lines of his chin are a touch more aggressive,* thought Jo, standing some distance away. She wondered why she had never before noticed the unpleasant way he sized up the people around him with his eyes. His wife looked just as she always had—beautiful, bored, and somehow irrelevant—as she stood there swinging a champagne glass in the air. *Damn it all,* thought Jo. It had simply never occurred to her that she would run into Isabelle's parents here. If there was one thing she could live without right now, it was an encounter with the man who had put her behind bars.

Josephine had already turned to go when someone called her name. Isabelle came up to her, quite out of breath, pushing her bicycle. "Are you leaving already? Out of the question! You must meet some friends of mine! And you're coming to my victory party, too." She had already hooked her arm in Josephine's. "Don't worry. My parents won't say a word," she whispered, not letting down her victory smile for a second. Arriving back at her circle of friends, she pushed Josephine forward.

"I'd like you all to meet Josephine Schmied, an exceptionally experienced cyclist! She would very much like to join our club. Mother, Father—you and Jo are already acquainted."

Moritz Herrenhus nodded icily, and his wife did not move a muscle. The others in the group murmured a brief greeting.

Isabelle took a step toward the second group, still gathered around Irene, and tugged briefly at the sleeve of a young man.

"And this is Adrian Neumann, my fiancé."

"*This* is your fiancé?" The words escaped Josephine before she could stop herself. She took a step back as if someone had struck her in the belly.

The blond young man reached out his right hand toward her and said, "Delighted to meet you. Isabelle has told me a lot about you."

Josephine could not reply. Her hand trembled, and after a fleeting handshake, she jerked it back as if she'd received an electric shock.

*Why him?*

Isabelle frowned, then said, "Would you like to take a turn on my bicycle? You could ride it over to the storage room for me." She held her Rover out for Jo to take.

Josephine shook her head, mumbling that she wasn't properly dressed.

Isabelle frowned a second time, then pushed her bicycle into Adrian's hands. "If you would be so kind . . . We're all heading off to the party. Cycling makes you terribly hungry, don't you think?" she said to the group gathered around her. "And that one glass of champagne certainly hasn't taken the edge off my thirst, either." Laughing and joking, the group made their way into the club restaurant. Josephine trotted along behind them.

Confident that his daughter would win, Moritz Herrenhus had reserved the entire club restaurant. The family's guests, friends, and business partners sat down to enjoy a victory dinner at eight tables covered with white damask tablecloths and laid with fine silver.

Josephine had been directed to a seat at a table close to the door. When Moritz Herrenhus was finished with his obligatory speech and before the soup was served, she and the other guests at the table introduced themselves. On Josephine's right sat a journalist who worked for one of Berlin's largest daily newspapers and was apparently one of the few newspapermen actually well disposed toward women's cycling. In his view, female cyclists presented a particularly graceful sight, and if it were up to him, far more women would take up the sport. He ventured as much in a loud voice, and his comments earned a poisonous look from his stick-thin wife sitting beside him. Their daughter, who had taken part in the race but was one of the last to cross the finish line, hunched morosely between her parents. Opposite Josephine sat Moritz Herrenhus's dentist and his wife, as well as an engineer who had some convoluted connection to Herrenhus's factory. At the far end of the

table sat one of the young cyclists whose conversation Josephine had
eavesdropped on earlier. He was a friend of Adrian's, but Josephine was
not sure what he did for a living. Perhaps he was a professional son, in
the same way that Isabelle was a professional daughter?

When it was her turn, she introduced herself simply as Isabelle's
friend. Her voice shook slightly, but she was spared any need to give
more details because they began to serve the soup just then.

For some time, the only sound was the soft clattering of spoons
and bowls, but the other guests gradually struck up conversations
around her. Jo listened mostly in silence. What was she supposed to
say? She could contribute nothing to a discussion about the purchase
of a new country house close to Potsdam, nor could she add anything
to a conversation about the challenges of employing a new chauffeur.
And never in her life had she adopted such a whining tone of voice as
that of the journalist's daughter as she tried to convince her father that
he simply *must* buy her a new bicycle. The soup bowls were just being
taken away when the journalist finally caved. "For God's sake, then we'll
buy you a new bicycle!"

The young woman looked at the others around the table
triumphantly.

"Admittedly, the women's race today was a real public drawcard. But
it's only the sprints and long-distance races that catch the imagination
of the wider public," said the young cyclist at the end of the table,
waving his fork wildly in the air as if to underscore his statement.

"I'm with you on that," said the journalist. "But isn't it also worrying
that a certain, what? . . . gigantism? . . . is taking over the sport? When
I think of the long-distance races, well, it's unbelievable, to think about
the amount of sheer donkeywork involved."

"But where's the problem with that?" the engineer replied. "Human
beings have always tried to test their boundaries. And technological
advancements help a man do just that. And thank God! Where would
civilization be if we didn't constantly strive to get ahead? Without a

certain—let's call it peaceful megalomania—the Eiffel Tower would never have been built. Without faith in technology, there would be no passenger steamers carrying us to New York in days instead of weeks or months. Without the pioneering spirit of progress and technology, we might all still be sitting in trees and eating leaves!"

"We certainly do have good grounds to be grateful for progress. Without it, we wouldn't be enjoying this delicious roast veal," said Josephine, which drew a laugh from the other guests at the table. Happy to have made at least one small contribution to the conversation, Josephine turned her attention back to her dinner. She had never eaten anything so delicious in her life. She enthusiastically helped herself to a third thick slice from the serving platter.

"I must say, I'm not used to seeing a young woman with such an appetite," said the cyclist, raising his eyebrows at her. "Most of them pick at their food like sparrows, afraid for their waistlines." As he spoke, his eyes wandered suggestively over Josephine's body.

She gave him a frosty smile. "I don't have an appetite. It's called hunger. You'd know what it was yourself if you hadn't yet eaten anything today."

The guests laughed again, assuming Josephine's words were meant in jest.

*If you only knew,* she thought. Although she had just plonked another potato dumpling on her plate, her throat suddenly clenched and her hunger dissipated. Though she did her best to come across as plucky and not let herself be intimidated by all the talk of wealth, this was not her world. More than the width of a table separated her from these people, she thought. Without waiting for the "Dessert Surprise," she put her napkin beside her plate and murmured a farewell.

***

The tool room at the club was stuffy and smelled of rubber, talcum powder, oil, and dirty old rags. Adrian rummaged through the tool cupboard with both hands, looking for the right tools to dismantle the front fork of his bicycle. Surrounded by various wrenches, pliers, the pots of bearing grease . . . his mood was improving by the second. He was in his element!

A little while later, he carried his toolbox out to the covered area in front of the bicycle garage, where he had already set up his machine. He pulled off his jacket and threw it over the railing, spread an old blanket on the ground to protect his pants, and set to work. But his good spirits suddenly vanished.

Why couldn't he love Isabelle?

He began digging roughly through his tools. Damn it, if he was going to be plagued by such thoughts now, he might as well have stayed at the party. Both Isabelle's parents and his own had greeted his sudden departure with indignantly raised eyebrows. No doubt he'd be subjected to another lecture afterward. A lecture, as if he were a fourteen-year-old boy! *But who cares?* he thought defiantly. For the time being, he just wanted to enjoy some peace.

He was fed up with all of it. The same old prattling from the same old prattlers. He'd needed a little fresh air in his lungs, so he had ridden a few laps of the now empty track alone. He felt better after that and decided to spend the rest of his Sunday afternoon fixing up his bicycle. He had received a parcel from a specialized equipment firm the day before, and inside it was the new front fork he had been craving for so long. The manufacturer's catalog had called it "a technological wonder"—and he could hardly wait to see for himself whether it lived up to that grandiose claim.

Adrian set the adjustable wrench on the top of the fork to loosen the counter-tensioned nuts that held the fork in place.

Isabelle was a great girl. She was attractive—assuming you liked redheads. She had style, intelligence, and a dry sense of humor. She was sharp, too, and extremely popular in the circles in which she moved. And she was a good match, socially speaking, to boot. On top of all that, she was pleasantly uncomplicated—a characteristic that he had never expected to find in such a spoiled young woman. So why on earth couldn't he love her? It would have made everything so much easier! He and Isabelle would have long been married by now and his father would finally leave him in peace. Instead, he'd been brooding for ages about how to extricate himself from the whole mess.

The contracts that Moritz Herrenhus had presented to his father—which involved enormous sums—were full of legal twists. Isabelle's father could demand the return of large portions with the wag of a finger if he and Isabelle . . .

"Stop! What are you doing?" a woman's voice called out behind him. Adrian turned around and saw Isabelle's friend standing behind him. "You'll never be able to loosen the bottom nut with an adjustable wrench! You need a cone wrench, or you run the risk of damaging the fork itself—" The young woman abruptly fell silent and looked at him aghast. "Excuse me, I didn't mean to speak so out of turn, but the women in the club said it was all very informal here . . ." She kneeled beside him and pushed her blue skirt under her knees without a fuss. Then she dug around in the toolbox he had assembled. With practiced ease, she set a flat wrench on the lower nut. Then she eased the fork downward and out of its mount and set it aside, catching the ball bearings that dropped out after it skillfully in her other hand.

Adrian could only look on, astounded. All thoughts of Isabelle and the fateful situation he was in had vanished.

The young woman smiled and pressed the bearings into his hand. "So . . . what do we do now?"

"Now we put the new one on," said Adrian and laughed.

For the next few minutes, he obediently handed Josephine the tools she asked for, while she focused on reassembling his bicycle. First, using the bearing grease, she positioned the little balls correctly and slid the new fork into place. Then she assessed and adjusted the tightness of the bearings. Finally, she counter-tensioned the nuts again to stop them from loosening. "Done!"

Adrian was amazed. She was so focused when she worked! And so sure of herself! It would have taken him at least twice as long to attach the new fork.

"Where did you learn all that?" he asked.

Josephine shrugged. "I had three years of lessons from one of the best mechanics in Berlin."

"*You?* A woman?"

"Anything wrong with that?" she asked, looking at him intently, her eyes sparkling.

Adrian raised his hands defensively. "Not at all! But you'd have to admit that this kind of knowledge is pretty unusual for a woman. What did your parents have to say about your taking up this profession?" *Hadn't Isabelle said something about Josephine working in a factory?*

"My parents?" Josephine rubbed pensively at her right earlobe. "My father is a smith, and he was firmly convinced I'd slave away beside him at the forge my whole life. Without pay, mind you. He could never accept that I had other interests. I'm a great disappointment to them, so there's been a wedge between us for years." She looked at Adrian defiantly. "Now I live my own life, with rules I've set for myself. And I don't care what anyone else thinks about it." Then she took a rag and began to polish Adrian's bicycle.

"And then?" he asked, somewhat breathless. Why didn't she put down the stupid rag and keep talking?

"What then?"

"Well . . ." He waved his right hand helplessly in the air. He had so many questions going through his mind simultaneously that he didn't know which one to ask first.

"I find it admirable that you've freed yourself so completely from the pressures of your family," he said stiffly. *I'd love to do that myself,* he added to himself.

Josephine dropped her right hand to her knee. Her eyes darkened slightly, and she looked thoughtful. "I didn't go looking for it. Life is just the way it is. There's no reason to admire me for anything."

Adrian looked at Isabelle's friend. There was nothing affected about her words, nothing contrived, nothing forced, as he was so used to hearing from the young women in his world. As he had heard so often from Isabelle herself, who loved to be the center of attention. And from his sister, Irene, who was constantly trying to impress everyone with her cleverness.

As Jo returned to polishing the bicycle, she began speaking again. "It would be foolish to keep crying about the past and things that shouldn't have turned out the way they did. Instead, I'm trying to turn my plans into reality. But first, I have to find a good job as a mechanic. Right now, I'm working in a shoe-sole factory, which is far from pleasant." She screwed up her face at the thought.

"I can imagine," he said and smiled. "If I can be of any help . . ." *"It would be foolish to keep crying about the past and things that shouldn't have turned out the way they did."* Josephine's words had hit the nail on the head. In his life, too, there were so many things that shouldn't have turned out as they had . . .

"Thank you, but I can do it on my own," Josephine said, waving off his offer. "As soon as I've got a decent job and I'm earning good money, I'm going to buy a bicycle. Then I'll be able to ride whenever I feel like it." Josephine stopped polishing and put the rag aside. "You've got a lovely bicycle here. The new fork has a rather peculiar profile. I assume it will make the bicycle more immune to bumps." She ran her hand over the new part with interest.

Adrian looked first at Josephine, then at his bicycle. "Have you learned the text in the catalog by heart?"

"What do you mean? It's obvious what it's for."

He held out his bicycle to her. "If that's the case, then I'd be happy to have you put the new fork through its paces. Go on, ride a lap!"

Josephine shook her head. "That's awfully nice of you, but no, thank you. I've sworn to myself never again to sit on a bicycle that doesn't belong to me."

Adrian narrowed his eyes, confused. This conversation was getting more and more bizarre. "Why, if I may ask? I thought riding a bicycle was your greatest passion?"

"That's true. Even so, it's one of the rules I've set for myself in my new life."

"But . . . aren't you making your life unnecessarily difficult like that? I mean, earlier you turned down Isabelle's offer to ride, and now mine, too." Josephine grew more mysterious—and more intriguing—with every word she uttered.

"Following your own set of rules . . . I'd love to do that," he murmured to himself, hardly aware that he was speaking aloud. So he was startled when Josephine said, "Then why don't you?"

Adrian laughed dejectedly. Then he told her about how he was the only son in his family—the heir!—who was supposed to lead his father's empire in the future. "Elektronische Werke Berlin is growing all the time. Berlin and the whole region are flourishing. Industry needs more and more power, more and more electricity, and we're leading the market."

"But?" Josephine asked. And in that one word, Adrian heard more understanding, more perception than he had ever heard from anyone in his life.

"But it isn't what I want!" he suddenly burst out. "Cycling is my great passion, too. At least, I look at a bicycle differently than the men and women in there do." He waved his hand vaguely toward the clubhouse. "If you ask me, it's far too brilliant an invention to be merely a toy for the rich or a sport machine for people who want to prove themselves physically." He snorted disparagingly.

"Go on," said Josephine.

"I see it like this. Two things have to happen. First, people need to understand that a bicycle is the best, cheapest, and simplest means of transport in the world. And second—" He paused uncertainly, but when he saw how mesmerized Jo appeared to be, how she hung on his every word, he went on. "Second, we have to find a way to produce bicycles more cheaply. They need to be within reach of the common people." He spontaneously reached out and took hold of Josephine's hand. "Picture the freedom that the bicycle would bring to workers slaving away all day long in loud, stinking factories! Or to maids wearing out their fingers scrubbing sheets on a washboard. Haven't those hardworking people truly earned the right to go enjoy the fresh air after a hard day's work?" Adrian breathed in deeply. Then he looked in surprise at her hand, which he still held in his. What was he doing? Here he was, sitting hand in hand with this young woman, a total stranger, telling her things he had only ever told those closest to him. He felt himself reddening, and he let go of her hand.

"But Adrian!" Josephine said. It was the first time she had called him by name. "How can you even say such things? If everyone could ride a bicycle, it would completely spoil all your clubmates' fun!"

It took him a moment to realize that she was being sarcastic.

Then they both laughed and meant it.

"You forgot about women," said Josephine, when they had settled down again. She leaned closer to him and said, "Bicycles would not only be good for factory workers but also for housewives lugging bread, butter, and flour home from the grocer in heavy baskets. It would be so much easier to carry it all on a bicycle!"

Adrian nodded vehemently. He looked into her radiant eyes and knew that they reflected the gleam in his own. "I've already thought about that. We'd have to build a very robust bicycle, with large baskets on either side to transport things in. A kind of steel mule."

They laughed again.

Adrian felt better than he had in a very long time.

"I think you have wonderful ideas," said Josephine, her voice filled with admiration. "Why don't you just go to your father and tell him about them? As a businessman, he would have to see the opportunities in what you've just been talking about. He could support and guide you as you got started." Her face had taken on a dreamy expression, but there was something very determined in it, as well. Adrian could hardly get enough of it. Just as he couldn't get enough of her words . . .

"Maybe you'll start manufacturing those cheap bicycles yourself? I'll be your first customer, that's a promise!" Josephine smiled and held out her right hand, and Adrian shook it firmly, as if they had just struck a deal.

It was after four when they parted. No doubt they would bump into each other again at the club, said Adrian, obviously convinced that nothing would stand in the way of Josephine's becoming a member.

Josephine's heart was aflutter as she marched briskly back toward Feuerland. Her conversation with Adrian had churned her up inside. What a man he was! To have such vision! And the way he thought about the lives of other people. What would make the son of an important industrialist even *begin* to think about factory workers and maids? Josephine promised herself she would ask him that the next time they met.

The bicycle as a means of transport for everyone . . . How revolutionary! Her own plans seemed trivial and inane by comparison. But perhaps one had to be as wealthy and carefree as Adrian to be able to have such high-flying ideas. All of *her* experience had shown her only that life was an eternal struggle and that one had to take it by the horns every day, like a belligerent steer. Pride would bring you crashing down fast—that, too, was something she'd learned from experience.

What a day! The women's race. The encounter with Isabelle's parents. Adrian . . .

It was strange. He had not uttered a single word about Isabelle. Now that she thought about it, why hadn't he been inside with her and her guests? What could that mean?

She had been out all day, but she did not feel the least bit tired. The thought of the unwelcoming dormitory and the grim common kitchen suddenly seemed unbearable. What was she supposed to do there? Lie down and sleep? Impossible. Listen to the others fighting? Intolerable.

She could return to the dormitory just before bedtime, she decided. At the moment, she had to find someone to talk to about all her swirling emotions. And she knew exactly who that would be. Paying Clara a visit would mean killing two birds with one stone: Jo could tell Clara all about her exciting day, and she could admire Clara's new home in the process.

She turned around with a spring in her step.

After a good hour's march, she arrived, worn out, thirsty, and with aching feet at Clara's door. *A cup of tea and a baked treat would be just the thing,* she thought as she pressed the doorbell. After waiting a minute, she pressed it again. Nothing. Josephine frowned and looked up at the windows. There was a light burning up there, so why was no one answering? After another minute of shifting her weight from one foot to the other, she walked away, disappointed.

\*\*\*

Clara watched sadly as her friend walked away down the street. For a moment, she had almost given in, run down the stairs, and flung open the door. But it was better this way. If Gerhard came home and found a visitor—and Josephine, of all people!—it would only make him angrier.

Clara tugged the white bedroom curtains straight, then she sat on the edge of the bed with her shoulders slumped. Everything had been fine that morning. She and Gerhard had enjoyed their breakfast and speculated about when the first patient would call to disturb the Sunday peace. Then Gerhard had seen Isabelle's invitation to the cycle race on the console table. Was she planning to go? Secretly? Without him? Without his consent? Despite knowing that he deeply disapproved of such . . . filth?

She had laughed and taken the invitation out of his hand, intending to throw it away. *Why didn't I already get rid of it?* she wondered. It had been a simple oversight. Gerhard was right when he said that she was too forgetful.

With the thumb and forefinger of her left hand, she rubbed her right wrist, now blue from where he had grabbed her so tightly that she had cried out. He had snatched the invitation out of her hand, torn it into a thousand tiny pieces, and thrown them on the floor. And then . . . Clara closed her eyes. It was best not to think about it. She was sure he was sorry.

"So you see what I think of this nonsense!" he had practically spat at her. He had left the house without another word and had not yet returned.

Where was he? Would he be hungry when he came home? Or had he gone somewhere to eat without her? Uncertain whether she ought to cook something special for him, Clara went over to their medicine cabinet to fetch a cooling ointment for her wrist.

The compartment above the household medications caught her eye. Almost tenderly, she ran her fingers over the pile of books she had stuffed in there.

*Handbook of Modern Pharmacology, Toxic Diseases of the Skin and Their Treatment, Sepsis*—it had been a long time since she had so much as glanced inside one of those books.

She rubbed the ointment into her damaged wrist. Then she dabbed a little on the red area on her right cheek as well.

# Chapter Twenty-One

In early May, two things happened that turned Josephine's life upside down from one day to the next.

One day, when she had finished her shift, weary in mind and body, she was on her way to the dormitory when the clerk stopped her and handed her two letters. One was from Isabelle, gleefully telling her that the other members had approved Josephine's membership into the club. Though she was unsure how it had happened—she still didn't own her own bicycle, and she was still just a simple factory worker—Jo let out such a jubilant cry that it made the clerk jump. She wanted to visit the club as soon as she possibly could!

At the sight of the second letter, however, Josephine felt a shudder all the way down to her bones. It was extremely official looking. Langbein and Kompagnon, Public Notary, Dieffenbach Strasse 11. Josephine knew the address, if not the name of the notary. It was a stately, cream-colored building on the edge of Luisenstadt. She opened the stiff envelope with jittery fingers. As the clerk stretched her neck toward her, Jo turned brusquely and marched away.

She sat down on the first landing on the stairs, just outside the dormitory. As she read the letter, her eyes grew larger and larger. What in the world did it all mean?

\*\*\*

The notary peered at Josephine over the gold rim of his glasses and frowned. "To be absolutely frank, young lady, I cannot make heads or tails of the following passage in the will. But listen for yourself. *'My dear Josephine, you have always been the daughter I never had. I will probably never be able to forgive myself for leaving you on your own when you most needed me. Dear child, I can only hope that your unfortunate experiences have not broken you but have instead made you stronger than you already were.'*"

Frieda's nephew, Joachim Roth, cast Josephine a sideways glance.

Josephine looked straight ahead. It was the reading of Frieda's will that had brought her to this gloomy lawyer's office.

"Of all the places to meet again," Lilo's father had said by way of greeting, but he had not expressed any pleasure at the sight of her. His answers to Josephine's questions about Lilo's health and well-being had been curt. After that, they sat silently in the wood-paneled anteroom until the notary called them in.

"*'I don't know whether I can make amends for my failures. But I have one great and heartfelt wish upon my death, and I am in the fortunate position of being able to fulfill it—'*" The notary paused briefly. He leafed through the pages of the will, the first few of which had covered the terms of Joachim and Lieselotte Roth's inheritance. Josephine had been astonished to hear the sums Frieda had left to her Black Forest relatives. Did she really have so much money in the bank? Her old friend had always lived so modestly and had taken pleasure in the simplest things.

"*'In my last letter, I wrote enthusiastically about the great plans I had for you. Unfortunately, it seems my time is running out too soon, and I won't be there to support you. Now it is up to you alone to create a change in your life. I hope, however, that you will allow me to help you.'"* The notary raised his eyebrows meaningfully. Jo couldn't care less what he thought. She smiled sadly. With every word, she heard Frieda's loving voice. What had Frieda planned for her?

The notary soon answered her question.

*"'To you, my dear Josephine, I leave my house and the attached workshop. I know that both will be in the best possible hands with you. I am being very selfish, but in this case, my selfishness has a good side; now you can finally realize your dreams.'"*

"An unknown woman is inheriting my aunt's house?" Joachim Roth erupted. "That . . . that . . . *that* was her greatest wish? That's nonsense! Can the law even allow such a thing?" He leaned across the notary's desk.

The notary recoiled. "I have checked everything most thoroughly," he said, raising both hands in a gesture of apology.

"But . . . the old woman was clearly not in her right mind when she wrote that!"

It was so disrespectful of Lilo's father to talk about his aunt like that. Josephine frowned. "I . . . I'm sorry," she said weakly. Nothing else came to mind.

Her own house! Frieda's house. Though stunned and overjoyed, she also felt uneasy about inheriting such a treasure. How could she possibly be entitled to such a thing? Shouldn't she turn it down? Tell Joachim Roth that he could have it? Or that Lilo could?

"Excuse me, Mr. Roth, but I must contradict you there. Your aunt was very much in her right mind when she wrote this testament, because she did so here in my office, and there were two people present who are able to bear witness to precisely that fact. We cannot influence—nor would we want to—the content and choice of her words. It is, after all, the final will of a human being."

"But . . ."

"I understand your anger. Still, I can only advise you to accept the deceased's will. Keep in mind the substantial sums you and your daughter have inherited. The old house is worth little by comparison. Besides, challenging a will as watertight as Frieda Koslowski's rarely ends up in favor of the plaintiff." He looked resolutely into Joachim's eyes, then he turned to Josephine. "I have something else for you," he said, taking a brown envelope out of the thick file before him.

The envelope felt heavy in Josephine's hand. *Please read this only once you are settled in my—or rather your—house,* it said on the outside in Frieda's distinctive handwriting.

"I'm starting to see how Berliners protect their own." Joachim Roth stood up abruptly. "I can see I have no additional business here." He looked darkly at Josephine. "So this is the thanks we get for our hospitality in the Black Forest! I don't even want to know what you did to creep into Frieda's good books." Without another word, he left the notary's office.

"Please don't take that too seriously, young lady. I have experienced far worse in such matters. One last thing: the key to the house has been deposited with one Clara Gropius. A neighbor. Mrs. Koslowski assured me that you know each other well," said the notary.

Josephine nodded.

"Oh, by the way . . ." He cleared his throat. "It is highly unusual, I must say, for a young woman such as yourself to come into such an inheritance. It may well be that you don't wish to live in the house in question. It is rather run-down, if I may be so bold. If that is the case, my office would be happy to assist you, should you wish to sell it. And when it comes to investing the monies realized, we would naturally be prepared—"

Josephine stood up before the notary could continue. "That is very kind of you," she said. "But I will accept Frieda's inheritance as she intended me to."

\*

Dust motes danced in the May sunshine when Josephine unlocked Frieda's house. She had turned down Clara's offer to accompany her. She had to do this alone.

She stood hesitantly in the doorway and breathed in the old familiar smell of the house. The slightly sour smell of the apples stored in the cellar—would they still be any good?—and the moldy odor of old seed potatoes. There was a faint whiff of the violet soap that Frieda had always been so keen on, a thin, pale-purple sliver of which still rested beside the sink. Everything smelled as it always had. Yet everything was different. What was missing was the perfume of Frieda's life: the smell of pancakes and bacon fat, the spicy aroma of the red wine she loved to drink. The smell of the pieces of liver she fried for Mousie. And the acrid bite of Frieda's oil paints.

She was surprised to see a large bouquet of lilacs, which Clara had left out on the kitchen table for her, no doubt with the best intentions. Frieda herself had never been able to bring herself to snip so much as a single cluster of flowers from the old lilac bush. She believed that flowers belonged in the garden, not in the house.

A moment later, Jo saw a shadow flit past her along the floor. It was Frieda's cat, meowing hungrily and arching her back against the old stove. "Well come on, then," her expression seemed to command.

Josephine finally stepped inside the house and began searching for something she could feed the cat. She found a half-full bottle of milk on the floor beside the sink, undoubtedly Clara's doing as well. Jo dribbled a little into the food bowl, then went over to the sofa, with its long-faded wine-red velvet cover. Frieda had tossed a crocheted blanket over it. The blanket consisted of gray, brown, and beige squares, and Jo had watched the blanket grow as Frieda had added new squares whenever she had wool left over from her knitting.

With a melancholy sigh, Josephine pressed her cheek to the blanket. It smelled dusty and old. And a little bit of Frieda . . .

Apart from the sound of the cat greedily lapping up milk, all was quiet. Josephine could not remember ever having experienced such a silence. No droning machines, no gossipy, garrulous women sharing her living space, no beating of hammer on iron. Would she ever grow accustomed to such quiet? Would she ever! She smiled. Then she took out the letter the lawyer had given her. *Please read this only once you are settled in my—or rather your—house.* Josephine nodded. All right, she was here. She carefully opened the envelope. But before she could begin to read, the cat jumped up onto her lap as if it were the most obvious thing in the world to do and began cleaning itself.

*Dear Josephine,*

*I would so love to be with you right now. I would make you a cup of tea and something good to eat. But the dear Lord had other plans for me. Who am I to question that? And nor should you. Rather, you should look ahead. There is a great deal to do! The house, the garden, Robert's old workshop—all of it is waiting to be brought back to life. Feel free to do what you like with them! Throw away whatever you don't like. Or better yet, give it to the needy. Berlin has more than enough of them, after all. Don't worry, you have enough money to buy whatever you need new—and lovelier and better things at that. From now on, you will not want for anything. You are a well-to-do young woman, Josephine! There is money that no one knows anything about—not Langbein, the notary, not my nephew, Joachim. I wanted it that way. You will find your starting capital in the fat vase on the mantelpiece. You know it, the one with the broken handle. When you were a child, it was the one you loved the most, because it is so colorful.*

Josephine gently lifted the cat from her lap and stood up.

The vase left behind a dust-free circle on the mantelpiece when Josephine took it down. She hesitated for a moment, then reached into the dark interior of the vase and pulled out a rolled-up bundle of bills. And another. And another. Hundreds of marks. Jo stared numbly at the money. She looked frantically toward the door, then to the window. What if someone was watching her and tried to rob her? She hurriedly stuffed it all back in the vase and set it back exactly where it had been.

Then she crept back to the sofa and sat down beside the cat, which had curled up into a small ball. For a while, she simply sat, as if paralyzed. Finally, she stood up.

Like a marionette dangling on stiff strings, she went to the heavy wooden door that separated the house from the workshop. She paused, her hand on the door handle. In all these years, she had never once entered the workshop. But why not? Perhaps because she had not particularly liked Frieda's husband, Robert?

Josephine had to try out several of the keys on the key ring Clara had given her before she found the one to the workshop. The door creaked loudly when Jo opened it.

The room was pitch black and cold, much colder than the house. Josephine felt her way over to a window, opened it, then pushed the shutters open. A square of bright-yellow sunlight fell across the room, flooding the old tools, which hung in perfect rows along the walls, in a golden glow. Josephine looked around, mesmerized.

Hammers, wrenches, pliers, files, a few pairs of shears. Boxes of nails, rolls of wire, sandpaper and sanding blocks in different sizes. Several folding rulers. A pair of diagonal pliers. A fretsaw and a fine handsaw. An enormous chisel. Boxes of iron clamps and clips and other bits and pieces. A crate full of rags and bandages and a bottle opener.

In one corner at the back, she even found a black, sooty forge, where one could heat metal for smaller welding work.

Josephine felt her knees grow weak, and she began to tremble all over. She was soon shaking so much that she could no longer stay on her feet. With no consideration given to her clean skirt, she dropped onto the grimy linoleum floor.

She had landed in paradise. It was a dusty, old-fashioned paradise, to be sure. But that didn't matter. What was it Frieda had written? *The house, the garden, Robert's old workshop—all of it is waiting to be brought back to life.*

Josephine took a deep breath. Her lungs expanded, and her heart pounded with delight as it never had before.

Until this moment, her plans had always been vague. She knew what it was she wanted to do, just not how to do it. But here on this cold, wax-yellow linoleum, all the big questions were gone.

Jo saw her future ahead of her, unclouded.

# Chapter Twenty-Two

The next day, Josephine resigned from the shoe factory and collected the last of her wages. Later that evening, she moved into her new house.

She had plenty of dry wood, and she soon had a fire going in the fireplace so she could heat some water. In the pantry, she found various cleaning materials, rags, brooms, brushes, and sponges, and within an hour, had wiped down all the countertops, scrubbed the floor, and cleaned the food cupboard's shelves. She threw Clara's bouquet of lilacs on the compost heap in the garden; after that, the house smelled only of cleanliness and well-being.

Then came the huge task of tidying up. Frieda had been a great collector. The cupboards were crammed full of remnants of fabric, wool, stones, newspapers and magazines, and jars and tins of all sizes. *I can't see myself doing much knitting for a while,* she thought with a smile. She was about to toss the basket of half-used balls of wool into the fire, but she stopped herself—perhaps she could use it for something after all. Besides, burning wool smelled horrible.

She decided to use the fabric remnants as cleaning rags in the workshop. And the newspapers . . . Perhaps she should read a few to find out what she had missed in the last few years? As she heaved a pile of them onto the small table in front of the sofa, one of them slid to the floor. The pages were as full of holes as Swiss cheese. Some pages had a large square cut out of the middle, while others were missing the entire upper third, and yet others all the advertising down the side. Josephine laughed. How could she have forgotten Frieda's habit of reading the newspaper with a pair of scissors in her hand? There really wasn't much left of the papers to read. But they would still make a good fire starter.

After all her work, Josephine took a break and looked around critically. There was no need to change the furnishings, she decided. Frieda's old sofa and her solid bed were good enough. But why then did she feel that something was missing?

Following her instincts, Jo pulled the kitchen table out from the wall. Frieda had stacked her own hand-painted oils against the wall behind the table, almost as if she were ashamed of them. Only the backs of the canvases were visible. One at a time, Josephine freed the paintings from their relegated existence. A vase filled with blue larkspur appeared. Then a single flower painted in colors that ranged from pale pink to deep violet, surrounded by tendrils of dark-green leaves. Jo didn't know the name of the flower but knew they grew in the middle of summer, in a far corner of Frieda's garden. Then came a tendril of a wild grapevine, a silver, shining snail creeping along it. A few landscapes—was that the Spree? And here was the Brandenburg Gate, the sun setting behind it.

Jo pored over the beautiful paintings, wondering why Frieda hadn't hung them up. Then she marched into the workshop, found a hammer and nails, and set to work.

*That's what was missing,* she thought with delight when she stepped back half an hour later and inspected her handiwork. Everything looked so colorful, fresh, and lovely! She had given the house a character all its own, without expelling Frieda's ghost in the process. On the contrary, her spirit filled the rooms more than ever.

Josephine's first night in the house was short and restless, spent battling the cat for rights to the bed, and she was up and about well before dawn.

***

"Josephine? Josephine Schmied?" The baker's wife's eyes were as round as the raisin buns steaming in a basket on the counter. "Is it really you? I thought you . . ."

Josephine smiled, her mouth askew. "Thank God I wasn't put away for life back then . . . Now, I'd like four rolls and a loaf of black bread."

The baker's wife made a dismissive gesture. "It was just one of those stupid boyish pranks! And to think they gave you such a long sentence. Everyone on the street thought it was completely unwarranted. That Herrenhus even went to the police about something like that . . . He should have been keeping a better watch over his things! And such a punishment . . . As if all of us weren't young and foolish once." Her face took on a dreamy aspect. Then she said in a more businesslike tone, "A piece of crumb cake, perhaps? It's still warm . . ."

"Yes, please," said Josephine and added, "I live in Frieda's house now, by the way. She left it to me." Better for people to know about it from the start. Then maybe the gossip could be kept within reasonable bounds.

"Frieda . . . what?" The woman stiffened like a pillar of salt, the bag of bread frozen in her hand. "When the neighbors hear that," she murmured to herself, and it was clear that she could hardly wait to pass it on.

Josephine smiled and laid a few pennies on the counter, then took the bread bag from the woman. At the door, she turned back. "Incidentally, it wasn't a stupid boyish prank."

The baker's wife frowned. "It wasn't?"

"If anything, it was a stupid girlish prank!" With a cheerful farewell, she went on to Ammann the butcher, two doors down. "Josephine? Is that really you?" A mixture of astonishment and joy shone on the face of the aging butcher's wife. "How lovely to see you again."

Josephine smiled and placed her order.

"You want to open your own workshop?" said Mrs. Ammann, when Josephine had told her all her news. "Fixing things . . . Can you do that?"

"I believe so. Do you have anything that needs repairing?" asked Jo excitedly. She would never have guessed that she would get so much sympathy.

The old woman disappeared through the door that led into the back of the butcher shop and returned with a large, heavy machine.

"Our mincer. Something's not working right. We can't affix it to the table anymore. If you can get that sorted out . . ."

"With pleasure!" Josephine said with delight, as she leaned across the counter to take the machine from the woman.

With her shopping and her first commission under her arm, Josephine walked home. She wondered if she should look in on her parents now or later. Shutters were flung open on one house after another all along the street. A few curious heads appeared at the windows.

Josephine greeted all of them pleasantly, and nearly all of them had a few friendly words for her in return. She garnered an occasional envious look when people learned of her inheritance, but most believed that Frieda's house was in the right hands with Josephine.

"We were afraid some rich stranger would come along and tear down the house to build a factory," said Mr. Kleinmann, the cobbler.

As far as her prison term was concerned, the general opinion was that Moritz Herrenhus should have done a better job of looking after his beloved bicycle.

"Opportunity makes the thief. Isn't that what they say?" said Mr. Kleinmann's neighbor, old Mrs. Otto, the widow who ran the hardware store. "Herrenhus and your father could have sorted that out among themselves, as neighbors. God knows the police didn't need to get involved!" She accompanied her remark with a look of disgust toward the smithy.

Mr. Kleinmann shook his head and added—though not in an unfriendly tone—"Riding bicycles . . . You young women today are mad!" When he had disappeared back into his workshop, Mrs. Otto waved Josephine closer.

"Riding a bicycle—how does it feel?" she asked in a whisper.

Josephine smiled broadly. "Just marvelous!"

By the time she arrived back at Frieda's house, she no longer feared that the residents of Luisenstadt would despise her because of her past. Several of them had announced that they would stop by in the next day or two with things in need of repair—a cooking pot whose handle had broken, a butter churn that no longer turned, an iron with a broken latch that kept falling open.

The crumb cake and the rolls smelled wonderful, as did the smoked sausage. Josephine's stomach murmured in anticipation. A hearty breakfast was just what she needed for the day ahead. Now that her first assignments were coming in, she really had to make some headway on the workshop. As for her parents . . . let them find out from the neighbors that she was back in Luisenstadt. It would serve them right!

Jo tackled the workshop until late in the afternoon. The workbench, she decided, was in the wrong place. She wanted to have it directly under the window, where she could take advantage of the light for more detailed work. It took her half a day and moving all kinds of levers just to shunt the heavy piece into place. The tools needed to be resorted and some of them cleaned. A few were simply too old to be of any use to her. At the end of that first day, Jo looked around and felt that she had accomplished absolutely nothing.

On the second day, she got out of bed even earlier. She didn't bother with fresh bread and went straight to work. Around midday, she lost focus working on an empty stomach and clumsily tore her hand open on a saw. It began to bleed badly, so she wrapped the wound in a few old cloths and carried on with her work.

By the end of the second day, she was more or less satisfied with her work. Late that evening, she repaired the butcher's mincer. Between Frieda's husband's tools and what she had learned from Gerd Melchior, it was child's play.

When, on the third day, there was a knock at the door and Gerd Melchior himself was standing there, Josephine thought for a moment that she was seeing a ghost.

"What're you gawkin' at all startled like? You're the one who sent for me," said Melchior, confused.

Jo laughed. She had been so busy that she had completely forgotten about the letter she had written asking him for help.

With her mentor's help, the rest of her work was quickly finished. He suggested a better way of storing her tools, and between them they put together a list of equipment and materials that Josephine would have to buy. At one point, he turned and saw Frieda's handicrafts basket sitting on the workbench, and he was taken aback.

"An old memento, eh? Pity, I'd have liked to have got to know the old lady. Get in touch whenever you need something! I'll be glad to help you out," he said. In parting, he pummeled Jo in a comradely way on the shoulder.

\*\*\*

Saturday was warm, the breeze already carrying the sweet mildness of the coming summer. Jo sat on the garden seat that was against the back wall of the house, a glass of raspberry juice in her hand. The cat jumped up and settled beside her. The wooden boards of the back of the seat had soaked up the warmth of the May sun. Josephine leaned back with a sigh of pleasure, easing her muscles, which were sore from the strain of moving things around. Looking at the weeds growing ever wilder all around her, she realized that she shouldn't be sitting around. But tending the garden would have to wait. She couldn't do everything at once.

She could be pleased with her first week's work, for she had accomplished a good deal. A great deal, in fact. She had even been to visit her parents and paid off her debt in full. The stunned look on her father's face was one she would not soon forget!

Now she was as exhausted—but also as satisfied—as she had ever been in her life.

Jo sipped her drink, savoring it. Tomorrow, Clara and Isabelle were coming to visit. Jo could hardly wait to show her friends all the work she had done. But she wanted even more for Monday to come. Then she could really get to work!


"So? What do you think?" Josephine stood with her arms folded, an expectant look on her face.

"It's turned out beautifully," Clara breathed, her head tilted back.

Isabelle, too, looked up at the large enamel sign that Josephine had mounted over her workshop, big enough to be read from far away.

### REPAIRS OF EVERY SORT—BICYCLES WELCOME

The words were emblazoned in blue letters on a white background. Around the inscription were stylized images of hammers, tongs, and chisels. It was a sign—what was she supposed to say about it?

"That you have the confidence . . ." said Clara softly.

Josephine shrugged. "I've learned my trade. It will work."

Isabelle furrowed her brow, struck by Josephine's faith in herself and the proud note of self-reliance in her voice. "What if the customers don't come? Perhaps *they* don't think you can do it. You're just a woman, after all. What will you do then?" she asked.

But Jo just laughed. "Then I'll go peddling for customers! Besides, I'm hoping to soon be able to count the men and women from the cycling club among my clientele. You could really use a decent mechanic."

"Ah, so *we're* supposed to be your customers. I see. Don't you think you should grace us with your presence just once first? The others find it rather strange that you haven't paid us so much as a single visit since you were accepted into the club. Some of them are asking themselves if they made a mistake by agreeing to let you join," said Isabelle, sounding somewhat put out. The truth, however, was that no one except Irene was asking that. The rest were far too preoccupied with other matters to care. But Josephine didn't need to know that. A little guilt wouldn't do her any harm!

"Oh, Isabelle, you wouldn't believe how much I've been wanting to." Jo sighed longingly. "I'd love to go out and just buy myself a bicycle. I've got the money now. But I've got so many more important things to take care of."

More important things. Uh-huh. Isabelle picked up a hammer and was surprised at how weighty it was. Like everything in Jo's life seemed to be. Her own house, a repair shop. Customers of her own, money of her own. A dream of a lifetime. Compared to that, it was hardly any surprise that the cycling club and their friendship mattered beans. She dropped the hammer again, carelessly. If that was the case, she could have spared herself the trouble of championing her old friend. Although—if she were honest—Josephine's acceptance into the club had had less to do with her intercession and a lot more to do with Adrian's. He'd gone to a lot of trouble, in numerous separate discussions, to convince Irene and the others that it could only benefit the club's reputation if they accepted "common people," too. And to convince them that they wouldn't be able keep them out forever, the times being what they were. Soon, even servants, cooks, and chambermaids would be able to afford a bicycle. No one really believed him, but everyone liked Adrian and they knew that he had once thrown all his weight behind the founding of the club. As a result, little by little, he had been able to erode the resistance to Jo's membership.

Isabelle screwed up her nose, feeling disgruntled. Adrian, the *good* man. The one who wanted to better the world! The one with a heart for the weak, the lame, and the sick. A man who'd love to put every worker in a palace and crown him king. He only lacked heart where she was concerned—otherwise, he would have long ago found a way to get them both out of this miserable engagement mess they were in.

Isabelle took a deep breath. Enough gloom and doom! Everything would work out somehow. She only had to look at Josephine to know that it was possible. Just then, Jo was explaining at great length which tools she needed for a particular job. Isabelle knew she would never want to spend her own days doing such tedious work. But if that was what Jo wanted, then . . .

Nor did Clara seem especially interested. There! She was stifling a yawn behind her hand! Isabelle grinned as their eyes met conspiratorially.

A moment later—just as Jo was pulling yet another file out of her toolbox—Clara clapped her hands like a child. "I'm dying to see your house. Can we go in? Your own little nest. Oh, Josephine, who would ever have thought?" She had already hooked Jo's arm in hers, and together they stepped through the doorway and into the house.

Isabelle trotted behind with a smirk. But her smile vanished the instant she entered the house.

"I don't believe it. It looks just like it used to!" she said, horrified.

Jo nodded proudly. "I'd like to keep Frieda's memory fresh, so I haven't changed anything. All I've done is hung up her paintings. Do you like them?"

"They're very colorful," said Clara, politely.

Isabelle ran the tips of her fingers over the worn—in places downright fraying—material of the old sofa. "If I were you, I'd sell off all this old stuff. You've probably got fleas in there!" She took a quick step away from the sofa. The notion didn't seem all that far-fetched.

"Oh, Isabelle, now you're exaggerating," Jo replied, laughing. "I think everything's lovely the way it is, and, fortunately, there's no one telling me what do about these things. Isn't that wonderful?" She looked at her two friends, seeking their blessing. "For the first time in my life, I can do whatever I want. I am truly independent."

"But . . . it isn't in a woman's nature to be independent," Clara replied with a frown. "A woman needs a strong man at her side. I'm glad that Gerhard takes so many decisions off my shoulders. I wouldn't know up from down if I were on my own. I imagine it's like that for you and your Adrian, isn't it?"

It took Isabelle a moment to realize that Clara had spoken to her.

"No, not at all," she replied curtly. As if she'd ever let Adrian tell her what to do! Where did Clara get such an absurd notion? It was enough to have her father laying down the law; the last thing she needed was a fiancé doing the same.

"Isabelle and Adrian are only engaged, after all. Not married, not yet," said Josephine with such a strange undertone that Isabelle flared up.

"What's that supposed to mean? That it doesn't count? An engagement is still a promise to marry." And that was a promise her father wanted to see honored. A wedding this year—there wasn't a day that went by that he didn't bring it up. She had run out of ways to string him along. They had already used illnesses, business crises in Adrian's father's firms, and Adrian's taking an extended overseas trip.

"All right, all right!" Jo raised her hands defensively, then pointed toward the stove. "How about we cook something nice? I've got vegetables and a good piece of meat. A bracing soup, that's what I'm in the mood for."

"Cooking soup?" Isabelle stared at her friend in surprise. A chilled bottle of sparkling wine, a few elegant snacks, or at least an inaugural cake—that was the least she had been expecting!

But Clara had already grabbed a knife and begun peeling carrots. "Who would have ever thought the three of us would be cooking together one day? This will be fun!"

Isabelle still stood indecisively in the center of the room. Fun? That's the last thing it would be!

"You're welcome to sit and watch," said Josephine, nodding toward the kitchen bench. "Although I'm sure your Adrian would be happy if you could put together a decent meal."

Isabelle was about to snap back, "He is not *my* Adrian." Instead, she said, "I don't get involved with such menial tasks. We have staff for that." She gave the cat, which had just made itself comfortable in the middle of the corner bench, a shove. Instead of making room, the beast hissed at her. Isabelle sat on a chair.

"As soon as the practice is running better and we've paid off our debts, I'm supposed to be getting a maid myself," Clara said. "Gerhard doesn't like to see me having to work so much. A lady should dignify a house and fulfill social obligations. And she should have a good dose of rest every day. Gerhard says that anything else goes against what nature intended. And that is truer than ever in my condition." Clara sighed and stroked the gentle curve of her belly, then dropped the carrots into the boiling broth.

*Strange that Clara hasn't said a word about being pregnant before now,* thought Isabelle. A baby on the way for the first time . . . Wasn't that a special moment in a woman's life? Jo immediately embraced Clara, and Isabelle felt as if she should do the same, but Clara did not seem particularly happy about her condition.

"Your first child . . . Congratulations! You must be beside yourself with joy?"

Clara shrugged. "Gerhard would have preferred that I be available to help him in the practice a little longer."

Josephine laughed. "Then he should have been more careful. As a doctor, he must know how babies are made better than most people."

Isabelle and Clara joined in her laughter, but Clara's somber expression did not fade. She took the herbs that Jo had picked from the garden and chopped them finely with a practiced hand. "I like to work! Even when I was helping out in the pharmacy, hard work never bothered me. And once the baby has arrived and I've recovered from the birth, I'll go right back to it. Regardless of what Gerhard says," she added defiantly.

Jo nodded. "The more work, the better!"

*How nice to see you agree about that,* Isabelle thought. Because Josephine seemed immune to her needling today, she decided to start in on Clara instead. "Your doctor seems to have quite a detailed idea of what goes against a woman's nature. Is he still so adamantly against seeing women on bicycles?"

To Isabelle's satisfaction, Clara visibly flinched. "We haven't talked about it for a very long time," she replied slowly. "You must know how many victims of bicycle accidents come to see us. They arrive with broken bones, broken wrists, scrapes. And women get injured more often. They seem to be particularly clumsy."

"Does that surprise you?" Josephine answered. "Women simply don't get enough practice! The more practice you get, the less risk there is that you'll have an accident."

"Women get too little practice? I know at least one young lady to whom that unfortunately does not apply: Adrian's darling sister, Irene," said Isabelle, her voice laced with sarcasm. "She spends every free minute training. The men are complaining that she uses the track too often for herself."

"Why is that? Why don't the men and women simply use the track together?"

"And why does Irene train so much at all?" Clara asked.

"Why, why?" Isabelle mimicked her friends. "Irene wants to beat me in the next race, whatever it takes, I suspect," she said to Clara.

But it was Jo who replied, "I hope you're not going to let her. Just wait until I've got my own bicycle, then we'll train together. Irene won't stand a chance!"

"Training, phooey!" said Clara dismissively. Her eyes flashed mischievously when she said, "I've got a much better idea. I don't know this Irene at all, but from everything you've said about her, she seems to be a rather unpleasant person."

For the first time that day, Isabelle and Josephine were in agreement about something. They nodded.

"Perhaps a little abrasion would do Adrian's sister good?" She looked at them with such innocence . . .

"Clara!" Isabelle and Jo said simultaneously.

"Explain yourself . . ." Jo added.

Clara laughed. "Itching powder, that's all I'm saying."

"Itching powder?"

"Yes. From powdered rosehip kernels. My father uses the powder in an ointment for treating rheumatic complaints. It itches terribly, for hours. A pinch of the stuff sprinkled on the saddle could really put one off riding a bicycle."

"Itching powder . . ." Isabelle and Josephine looked at each other, then all three young women broke into ringing laughter. For a brief moment, they were once again the three carefree young girls who had practiced riding bicycles in the Herrenhus yard.

\*

Petra Durst-Benning

A short while later they all sat down to eat. The soup tasted outstanding, Isabelle had to admit. *How had they managed that?* She was about to help herself to more when there was a knock at the door.

"Who could that be?" Josephine stood up and went to the door. *"You?"*

"I hope I've not come at an inconvenient time, but . . . may I come in?"

Adrian! Isabelle put the ladle down. What on earth was he doing here?

"We're eating, but there's enough for you, too." Jo held the door open, inviting him in.

Isabelle gave her fiancé a cool greeting, then said, "Hadn't we agreed on six?"

Adrian, who had sat down next to Clara on the bench, nodded apologetically. "I'm early, I know. Your mother wanted me to wait at the house, but when she told me where you were, I thought I . . . I thought . . ."

"It's all right," said Jo, interrupting his stammering and passing him a bowl of soup.

"It's already after five?!" Clara cried, glancing at Frieda's old wall clock. "Oh God, Gerhard must have been waiting for me for ages! I said I'd only be gone a little while." She stood up abruptly. "He doesn't like it if I just disappear."

"You're only two houses away. If he missed you so much, he could easily come by," said Josephine with a laugh.

Once Clara had left—or fled—Isabelle pushed her own chair back with exaggerated irritation. Adrian was just lifting his spoon to his mouth when she looked down at him and said, "Let me make one thing crystal clear. I am not like Clara, and I will never let any man push me around like that. Nor check my every move. So if you're considering sniffing around after me in the future, think again. I'm going home now—alone—and I'm going to pretty myself up. You, my dear Adrian,

266

will pick me up at six o'clock on the dot for the Berlin Ballet premiere, as agreed." She gave Josephine a taut nod, then she, too, left.

Adrian seemed to have lost his appetite after that. Besides, he was far more interested in seeing Jo's workshop, and Jo, of course, was delighted to show it to him.

"You've set it up perfectly," he said once she had shown him everything. "And I've already learned from experience that you know your way around a bicycle."

Josephine grinned. "And? Has the new fork proved its worth?"

Adrian nodded. "Even so, I'm planning to buy a second bicycle. A touring machine for long road trips. The bicycle I have now is designed specifically for speed on a track." Without a thought for the fine fabric of his pants, he sat down on one of the old workshop stools.

"You're really an avid cyclist, aren't you?" said Jo, pulling up the second stool and sitting down beside him. She glanced discreetly at the rusty workshop clock. Half past five. Adrian would have to leave soon . . .

"Avid is almost an understatement—I'm a cycling addict! I'm in the saddle every free minute. It's like an insatiable hunger," said Adrian and gave her a skewed smile.

"Believe it or not, I know exactly what you mean. An unquenchable craving . . . I can't think of a better way to put it. Once you've felt that sense of freedom, there's no turning back." Jo and Adrian smiled, understanding each other completely.

"So how is it that you don't own your own bicycle and refuse to borrow one?"

"Personal reasons," said Jo quickly. "But thanks to Frieda, my greatest dream will now come true sooner than I thought. I can finally buy myself a bicycle," she said, sweeping a few unruly strands of hair from her forehead. If only she'd made more of an effort with her hair! But she had not counted on anyone other than her girlfriends coming by.

"Although I have no idea where to go. Until just recently, I had far more pressing problems than figuring out which bicycle maker made which machines, or thinking about price or quality." She held her breath. Perhaps Adrian would offer to help her?

But to her great disappointment, all he said was, "The bicycle market has certainly become hard to navigate. Although there are more and more manufacturers entering the market all the time, the range of bicycles hasn't grown much. A good bicycle is still extremely expensive—too expensive, if you ask me—a consequence of all the manual work that goes into building them. I'm still convinced that bicycles could be produced more cheaply if anyone wanted to do it. But producers and customers alike would still prefer to think of a bicycle as a luxury." His eyes sparkled with entrepreneurial zeal. He looked as if he had a lot more to say on the subject, but then he waved his hand dismissively. "I'm sorry, I don't want to bore you. You probably think I can't talk about anything else. But that's really not true." He looked bashfully at the floor. "I have another idea, too . . ."

"What is it?" Jo asked eagerly.

But Adrian stood up. "I should go. Isabelle doesn't like to be kept waiting," he said with a tinge of regret. His hand already on the door handle, he turned back. "I wish you all the luck in the world, Josephine Schmied."

"Thank you," said Jo, her voice hoarse, as she struggled with a sudden surge of anguish. She did not know where it came from. She simply knew that she could have spent a long time sitting there in the workshop with Adrian.

He was almost at the garden gate when he abruptly stopped. Then quickly, as if not to give himself the time to reconsider, he turned and said, "What do you think? Could we go and look for bicycles together? Me for my touring machine and you for a woman's bicycle?"

Jo's distress vanished. With a surge of joy, she replied, "What about at the end of the week?"

\*\*\*

"The entire street is talking about it." Sophie Berg shook her head. "She comes back after all these years, just like that, and turns everything topsy-turvy!" She discreetly wiped one finger over Clara's sideboard, as if checking for dust.

Clara, who had just set the table for lunch, decided to ignore her mother's gesture. She had dusted just that morning, and thoroughly.

"First of all, Josephine is not turning anything topsy-turvy. All she's done is open a repair shop. Secondly, the people aren't just talking; they're making use of Josephine's services in droves. When I went down to the pharmacy yesterday, I saw three people going into her shop. And it's only the fourth day."

"Also," said her husband, who was just coming through the door, "I just saw your friend out in front of her workshop with Oskar Reutter. They seemed to be shaking on some sort of deal."

Clara hurried into the kitchen for the lunch terrine. It was Friday, so they were having roast potatoes with herring. Tomorrow would be a vegetable stew, and on Monday sweet pancakes. Gerhard liked to adhere to a set routine.

"We've needed a repair shop in the neighborhood for a long time," Clara said, picking up the thread of the conversation. "It just shows that Josephine has good instincts." She filled Gerhard's plate as she spoke. Everything had to be done quickly during his short midday break. A piece of potato fell onto the clean tablecloth with the second spoonful.

Gerhard raised his eyebrows with disapproval, and her mother did the same.

"Oskar Reutter? Let's hope he knows what he's doing. A handshake with someone like her isn't worth a thing," said Sophie Berg, stroking smooth an imaginary wrinkle in Clara's white tablecloth.

Clara folded her arms and looked crossly at her mother. "Why are you being so spiteful? And why don't you call her by name? *Her* name is Josephine. You've known her since she could walk. She used to be my best friend, and she still is."

"Best friend? That's hardly the case! Clara, my dear, you are simply too kind for your own good. I really must take better care that other people don't go on exploiting you," said Gerhard, in a fond but chiding tone. "You spent weeks looking after Frieda Koslowski's house. You looked after the garden and took care of the cat. And what thanks has Josephine ever shown you? Did she offer you so much as a mark last Sunday for all your work?"

Clara frowned at her husband. "As if I'd accept money for that! I was happy to do it."

"That's fine, Clara. It reflects well on you. But am I supposed to accept that you neglect your own familial obligations in the meantime? Last Sunday, I sat here on my own for hours while you amused yourself with your friends." He waved one hand vaguely toward Frieda's house.

"I already explained to you that I simply lost track of the time. I'm sorry—" Clara began, but her mother cut her off sharply.

"Must you always contradict your husband? You certainly did not learn such unseemly behavior from me, my child. Gerhard works hard day after day. It is your job to entertain him with pleasant conversation at the table, not deliver stubborn speeches all the time. For my part, may I say, I never had much time for Josephine Schmied," she said, her lips pressed together thinly.

Gerhard smiled warmly at his mother-in-law, then reached out and squeezed her right hand. "You needn't take every word your daughter says so earnestly. Most women in Clara's condition don't think clearly. I can't tell you how many times I've heard her speak the purest nonsense in the practice." Then his tone grew cool, his eyes colder. "As far as that Josephine Schmied is concerned, she is not a good person for you to spend time with; that much is now clear to me. It is utterly unnatural for a woman to occupy herself with technical matters. At this rate, the fairer sex will end up challenging the men for work!" He snorted disdainfully. "For an unmarried woman to open a workshop by herself, well, it is an absurdity. As soon as time allows, I will pay a visit to the trade guild and bring this dissolute state of affairs to their attention. I am fairly sure that the activities of this . . . person . . . will soon come to an end after that." He smiled at Clara and her mother, then returned to his lunch.

Clara felt a jolt in her stomach. It was not from the unborn child.

# Chapter Twenty-Three

Adrian directed the carriage driver to Feuerland. He asked the driver to stop not far from the shoe sole factory where Josephine had worked until recently.

"They sell bicycles here?" Jo asked in surprise. Surely she would have noticed if that were the case. There were no signs, not the slightest indication of what went on in the old warehouse in front of them. She felt doubtful as she followed Adrian inside. A moment later, she stopped in her tracks.

"I don't believe it . . ." She looked around in amazement. Dozens of bicycles were lined up in neat rows, all awaiting new owners.

"This ought to be enough of a selection, don't you think?" Adrian asked with a smile. "There's a salesman back there. Let's start with your bicycle. My touring cycle can wait."


"For the young lady, I would recommend the women's bicycle from Opel. Please, take a look. The Opel comes fitted with Michelin tires. It's very exclusive, very luxurious." The salesman—a fat, bald man who looked like he'd never climbed onto a bicycle in his life—looked at Adrian expectantly.

"But I find forty-two pounds rather heavy," Adrian replied. "There must be lighter women's bicycles on the market by now."

Josephine stood beside him without a word. How good this place smelled! Like rubber tires and machine oil. Like saddle leather, freedom, and a wonderful life.

The salesman gestured dismissively. "For a pleasant Sunday outing, it makes no difference whether a bicycle weighs forty pounds or seventy pounds. The young lady will no doubt feel perfectly secure on such a well-made machine." He stepped over to a different bicycle. "Here we have another pretty woman's bicycle—this one has a particularly attractive blue frame. It's most feminine! At two hundred and thirty marks, it is more of a midrange bicycle. A beautiful machine for a most enjoyable outing." The man underscored his words with a fluid gesture.

Outings! Jo rolled her eyes inwardly. The man had no other concept of how a woman might cycle.

"Speaking of which, we also have very pretty cycling outfits in the rear of the store. Perhaps the young lady might like to take a look around back there while the gentleman and I discuss the technical merits of the bicycles?" It was the first time that the man had addressed Josephine directly since they had entered the store a good half hour earlier. His smile was one he might give a well-behaved child.

"Irene always buys her cycling outfits here. They're very fashionable," Adrian said offhandedly.

"Right now, I am not the least bit interested in clothes," Josephine said with chagrin. It was really very kind of Adrian to come with her and give her advice, but she wanted to go into the technical merits of the bicycles herself! "And I would very much appreciate it if you would deign to show me a *modern* bicycle. Machines like these have been around for years!" Ignoring the horrified look on the salesman's face, Jo started walking down the long aisle lined with bicycles up on stands.

German, English, even American manufacturers were represented, and all were similar to Moritz Herrenhus's Rover. These bicycles were undoubtedly all very good, but there had to be something new. The engineers and technicians who designed and built bicycles certainly couldn't have been asleep for the last four years.

In the middle of the aisle, Josephine finally found what she was looking for. The sleek machine was painted deep black, and the saddle was made of black leather. When she picked it up, it felt almost feather light. "Full Roadster, England," she read on the label affixed to the handlebars. Unless she was mistaken, one of the men in the bicycle club rode exactly this machine. She had admired it at length on her first visit to the club. A pleasant feeling came over her. She cleared her throat.

"The Full Roadster here . . . does it only come with these foam-rubber tires? Or could I get it with the more elastic pneumatic tires?" Moritz Herrenhus had told her that pneumatic tires were a revolutionary advance in bicycle technology.

The salesman, busy with Adrian a few bicycles farther down, stopped short. Almost unwillingly, he gestured for Adrian to follow him to where Josephine stood. When he reached her, he said, "An English import, that one. From Liverpool, to be exact. The Full Roadster is a safety bicycle of the first order. The manufacturer claims that this particular machine offers the best performance for the price. The riding characteristics . . ." The salesman rattled off his knowledge skillfully, but he turned to talk directly to Adrian, who listened with interest.

Jo felt as if she would explode with anger. She took a single sharp step toward the salesman, who retreated in surprise. "In case you misunderstood, *I'm* the one considering buying *this* bicycle. You should therefore take me equally seriously as a customer," she said. The salesman took another step back, nearly knocking over a bicycle as he did so.

Jo continued, "Or I can walk out of here and go somewhere else. Bicycle shops in Berlin are like fleas on a dog, after all!" Taking satisfaction in the flabbergasted look on the salesman's face, she added, pointing at the English bicycle, "And now I would like to take this one out for a test ride."

"But . . . that is the best bicycle we have. It is not intended for women," the salesman replied in dismay. "And it's expensive, too. Very expensive . . ."

Jo merely shrugged. "I don't care."

"You'd better do what the young lady says," Adrian said, smiling. "I think she knows more about bicycles than most gentlemen."

The test ride was a true delight. Josephine could have screamed for joy as she rode down Feuerland's main street. How many times had she dreamed of just this moment? And now it was finally here.

When she came back, Adrian was waiting excitedly for her.

"So?"

Jo was grinning from ear to ear.

She counted out two hundred and seventy marks with shaking hands and handed them to the salesman, who maintained an unfriendly distance to the last. He was not used to women being involved in such transactions . . . and then putting so much money on the table at the end.

"When do we go for our first ride?" Adrian asked as soon as they were back outside. Unlike Josephine, he had not been able to find a bicycle that caught his fancy. "We could meet at the club tomorrow. I train every day in the late afternoon." He waved over the carriage, which had been waiting in the shade, and was about to instruct the driver to load the bicycle on board when Josephine stopped him. She laid one hand on his right arm. But she immediately pulled her hand away as if she had received an electric shock. With great effort, she forced herself to say, "Don't take this the wrong way, but . . . I would like to take my first ride by myself. Right now. I still have to find out whether I will even enjoy riding on a track."

"I understand." Adrian held the bicycle out to her, though he looked a little perplexed.

Before Jo could reconsider, she threw her arms around him. "Thank you. If you hadn't shown me this place, I would not now be the proud owner of this marvel!"

He returned her embrace, which they held a beat longer than necessary. Jo felt dizzy.

"But the second ride is mine, all right? I'm more than happy to ride through the streets," said Adrian, when they had separated. It sounded like he was asking her to dance.

Jo bit her bottom lip.

"What about Isabelle?" she asked slowly. She had not mentioned to her friend that Adrian would be accompanying her when she bought her bicycle. Had *he* told his fiancée about it?

"Isabelle." For a moment, Adrian seemed confused, as if he wasn't sure if he knew anyone by that name. "She doesn't like to ride through the streets," he said. "She likes to be out on the track where everyone can admire her."

It occurred to Jo that his remarks about his fiancée didn't sound particularly kind. But the rapid beating of her heart was muddling her thoughts. Should she or shouldn't she? It was just a bicycle ride, nothing more. She pulled herself together and said, "I don't have any time to ride during the day. I work until late every evening at the repair shop," she said, not without a certain pride. She had never believed it possible that the people of Luisenstadt would make such regular use of her workshop. And the best part was that everyone had been happy with her work so far. But no one had brought in a bicycle yet . . .

"So when were you thinking of cycling?" Adrian asked with a frown.

"While the world is still asleep," Jo replied and smiled defiantly at him. "If the good gentleman can get himself out of bed, we could go out tomorrow morning. Five o'clock at the Schlesischer train station!" Without waiting for an answer, she took her new bicycle, swung onto the black leather saddle, and pedaled away.

***

When Josephine left the house the next morning, she was met by a refreshing coolness in the air. The fading lilac bush in Frieda's garden exuded the last of its perfume, while the elderberry bush beside it was waiting for June to open its own flowers. A few early birds were chattering excitedly, and the clattering of hooves could be heard a few streets away—probably the milkman with his old horse.

With a light heart, Josephine fetched the Roadster from the workshop and set off. As she rode through the still-dormant streets, she recalled her early-morning excursions with Isabelle. But the farther she rode, the less she thought of the past and the more anxious she felt.

Would Adrian be waiting for her at the Schlesischer station? She didn't even know where he lived. Perhaps the journey would be too great for him? Or he was a late sleeper? As the scion of a wealthy family, he was at leisure to decide for himself when he got up in the morning.

Did she even want him to be there waiting for her? Adrian was Isabelle's fiancé . . . Was she on the verge of doing something that went against her principles? She never again wanted to touch anything that belonged to someone else. Wouldn't it therefore be smarter to cycle by herself? It was not too late to change her route . . .

Josephine pedaled harder.

She saw him from a distance—and felt a surge of irritation at the way her heart leaped at the sight of him. He looked very handsome, with his gleaming blond hair and athletic body. She wondered whether he did any kinds of sports other than cycling. What did she really know about Isabelle's fiancé . . .

*Isabelle's fiancé . . . and don't forget it!* she heard in her head.

As she approached, Adrian let out an appreciative whistle, raised his eyebrows, and said, "I'm not surprised you didn't want to look at the cycling outfits yesterday." He looked her up and down admiringly, his eyes silvery in the morning light.

"Is there a problem?" Josephine asked with a hint of prickliness, as she pulled to a stop. Suddenly, what he thought of her seemed to matter. But when she had combed through Frieda's clothes the night before in search of something suitable for riding, she had focused only on what would be practical.

On her way back from Feuerland, she had decided that she never wanted to ride in a skirt again. With every turn of the wheels, she had been afraid that the material would get tangled in the spokes. She could not understand how the other women in the cycling club could still expose themselves to that risk.

But she had not managed to find anything useful in Frieda's wardrobe. Frieda's old skirts were even more old-fashioned and voluminous than her own. But then, in the back corner of the wardrobe of Frieda's deceased husband, she had found a treasure: a pair of leather pants as pliable and soft as gloves. She had only ever seen anything like them in the Black Forest. Perhaps they had been a gift from Frieda's nephew at some point? Elated, Jo had worn her find into the parlor and taken up the pants laboriously, by hand, until they came down to her ankles and fitted as if tailor-made. She had then pulled on a snug-fitting dark-blue wool jacket that emphasized her slim physique. The blue set off her hair perfectly—which was once again a silky, shining blond, and which she had tied back into a simple ponytail. Josephine had felt very satisfied with her appearance when she looked in the mirror. But under Adrian's gaze, her self-confidence began to crack.

"I think your outfit is very chic, if a little . . . daring," Adrian replied with a grin. "Luise Karrer from the club also wears pants when she rides on the track. But I very much doubt that she would wear them out on Berlin's streets. And she would never look as pretty as you if she did."

Josephine smiled radiantly. "Let's be honest—this is the only way to ride seriously," she said as soberly as she could. "I used to wear pants when I cycled years ago, but back then I hid my face beneath a man's cap that I pulled down over my face. And sometimes . . ." She laughed, embarrassed at the recollection, "Sometimes I even drew on a mustache with coal to make people on the street think I really was a man."

"Men wear pants and women wear skirts. That's just the way it is," said Adrian in a tone that suggested that, as far as he was concerned, the topic was closed.

"Most people might see it that way," Josephine replied. "But I wear whatever I like. If that bothers you . . ." As attractive as she found Adrian, it was better that he know that about her from the start.

"And you *do* whatever you like. No need to remind me about that," Adrian remarked in a sarcastic tone, and both of them laughed.

Without discussing either their direction or their destination, they rode off.

Their route led them across the city. Adrian, who rode ahead, kept the pace fast and steady, but not too fast. He looked back a few times to assure himself that Josephine was still with him. "Everything OK?"

Jo nodded as she breathed deeply in and out. She had to work quite hard to keep up with Adrian, but she never told him that. Her calves burned and, at first, she tried desperately to think of something interesting to talk about. Adrian would think she was dull as dishwater if she just pedaled along in silence. But she soon realized that talking was not necessary, and she relaxed.

At Humboldt Harbor, Adrian turned north, and they rode alongside the ship canal for a while. The water that morning gleamed as blue as the sky; the shoreline was lined with benches and well maintained. A few times, they had to duck below low-hanging willow branches, but otherwise the riding was easy.

Adrian pointed off to the right. "My family lives back there," he said.

Josephine looked across the canal at the uncrowded rows of white villas behind wrought-iron fences, sprawling estates with garden houses, tea pavilions, and multistory mansions. This was where the wealthiest families in Berlin lived, Isabelle had explained as they rode through the area one morning years ago.

"But I live in a small apartment in the city," said Adrian. "It's very central, just behind the post office, in a building that belongs to my family."

*Why is he telling me all this?* Josephine wondered.

At North Harbor, they stopped. "Hungry? They serve solid breakfasts here," said Adrian, pointing to a rustic-looking inn that appeared to be doing brisk business even at this early hour.

Jo had been so intent on her sewing the night before that she had never gotten around to eating anything. She nodded.

"Would you get a load o' that one!" said one of the harbor workers, pointing at Jo. "See which one o' them wears the pants . . ."

Adrian grinned.

Jo walked into the inn, her head held high. She ignored the looks and lewd comments from the harbor workers. Once they had settled in at a cozy table by the window, Adrian went to the counter. He returned a couple of minutes later with two tin mugs of steaming, milky coffee and a large plate of open sandwiches, including minced pork with onion rings, smoked sprats with onion pieces, and herring rolls with cucumber. Josephine didn't know where to start.

They had cycled together in silence, and they ate together in silence, as well. But it was no embarrassed hush that settled over them, the kind that occurs between strangers who have run out of things to talk about. It was a pleasant, even sensual, silence. Jo could not remember a meal ever tasting as delicious.

"Sparkling wine and French champagne are all well and good, but the simple life has its merits," said Adrian suddenly. His gaze drifted longingly out the window. "The people here—what they do, how they live—for me, that's authentic." He offered Josephine the last half roll.

She declined it with a smile. "One more bite and I won't be able to get back on the bicycle." Then she went on, "You know, loading and unloading boats all day isn't really special. But you—no doubt your father has put you in an extremely powerful position, hasn't he?" She had seen a number of articles in the newspaper about the family's company and knew that it produced all kinds of technical devices. Just a few days earlier, Josephine had come upon a picture of Adrian's father, Gottlieb Neumann. Although the article was about yet another groundbreaking invention the company could claim as its own, the old gentleman in the photograph had looked very stern.

Adrian snorted. "If only that were the case! If you think I'm one of those engineers notching up one technical coup after the other, then I hate to disappoint you. I sit in an office all day long, and my job is to check horribly long rows of numbers that others have put together, checking that no gremlins have crept in! I rarely turn up anything at all. Any semicompetent bookkeeper could do my job, but Father insists that someone from the family do it. And that someone, unfortunately, is me. I sometimes wonder why I studied economics in Munich at all!"

"Economics," Josephine repeated. What exactly would that include?

Adrian nodded. "If only Father could see that I could put my education to much better use. I would start by tackling the production conditions—we're far from exhausting the opportunities there. And if you ask me, that's true of the entire industry."

"You mean looking for opportunities to exploit the workers even more than they already are being exploited?" said Josephine sarcastically. She felt a surge of disappointment rising inside her. She hadn't thought he was in the same breed as Herrenhus. *But why wouldn't he be?* jeered a venomous voice inside her. She barely knew the man, so why did she think only good of him?

Adrian looked at her in confusion. "Who said anything about exploiting the workers? Although it's urgent that something be done about that. Working hours need to be reduced to a maximum of twelve hours a day. And workers need to get two breaks, during which they're allowed to leave the factory to get some fresh air. It's preposterous that there are still factory owners who literally lock their workers inside!"

Josephine nodded, pleasantly surprised. Moritz Herrenhus was just such an owner. He kept his seamstresses slaving away behind locked doors and windows, since he was constantly worried that one of them might steal a bit of his fabric.

"I've been badgering my father for weeks to do something about organizing health insurance for our workers. But to no avail. It is simply unacceptable that a family has to go hungry just because one of the parents has gotten sick and can't work." Adrian banged his fist on the table. The subject seemed very close to his heart.

"But . . ." began Jo, uncertainly, "if a man can't work, he can't earn anything. How many times did I hear my father complain about terrible pain in his back? And still he shod five, six horses a day. If he hadn't we'd have had no money coming in at all."

"That may be the case for an independent tradesman. He alone is responsible for his own well-being. But a factory owner bears the responsibility for all of his workers, even if most businessmen have been reluctant to acknowledge that," Adrian replied. "If everyone paid into a health insurance scheme—workers *and* factory owners—meaning if everyone behaved with mutual solidarity, it would be easy to ensure proper care in case of sickness or an accident."

"What does that have to do with the production conditions you mentioned earlier?" Jo shook her head, a little confused. What a strange conversation! But even stranger was how much she was enjoying it.

"Health insurance is just one brick in a big wall," said Adrian. "My main objective would be to make production more efficient and therefore cheaper, but not at the expense of the workers. I would do it with better machines, more fluid processes, better purchase prices based on higher volumes . . ."

Jo took a sip of her coffee, which had gone cold by then. "That might well mean advantages for the factory owners, but what do the simple workers get out of it?"

Adrian grinned. "A great deal, in fact. Think about it: up until now, so many useful inventions have remained the privilege of a wealthy minority. Sewing machines, washing machines, the bicycle. And for the simple reason that someone proclaims such things to be luxury goods."

Jo laughed. "Like the salesman in the bicycle shop! He emphasized how luxurious and exclusive his bicycles were in every other sentence!"

"But bicycles and many other things could be produced far more economically if only the will to do so were there." Adrian leaned across the table. "Have you ever heard of the so-called invisible hand?"

Jo had not. Nor could she remember ever talking to anybody who was so passionate about anything. The fire that burned in Adrian's eyes as he spoke—she would have given anything to have them burn like that for her . . .

"The famous Scottish economist, Adam Smith, was the first to talk about the invisible hand. In his brilliant book, *The Wealth of Nations*, he describes how, when a businessman improves his productivity—even though he does so out of pure self-interest—he does a great service to society at the same time." Adrian nodded as if to underline the accuracy of the statement.

"Because he produces his goods more cheaply and more people can afford them?" Jo was not certain that she had understood, but Adrian's renewed nodding confirmed that she was on the right track.

"Exactly. When self-interest and the common good meet, the market can be said to be steered by an invisible hand. Imagine the logical conclusion for the masses: machines for cooking, baking, cleaning, and washing wouldn't any longer be considered luxury goods. They would ease the burden on factory workers, maids, and housewives. Instead of spending Saturdays washing clothes or cleaning the house, people would be able to use their limited leisure time for enjoyable pastimes. Cycling, for example! Because bicycles do not have to remain a luxury product forever. Wouldn't that be wonderful?"

Jo swallowed apprehensively. How clever Adrian was and how well-read . . . but she could certainly sympathize with the things he was talking about.

"When I had to work all day punching holes in shoe soles, I almost died of boredom. I would have given a great deal to be able to escape the misery for an hour or two!"

"The things you've experienced," said Adrian, and she heard in his voice the same admiration that she had just felt for him.

"It's nothing special," she murmured. What would Adrian say when he found out that she had spent three years in prison?

"Oh, yes it is! You have experienced firsthand what thousands upon thousands of workers have to endure every single day. For me, their lot is purely theoretical. Of course, I know I can't change everyone's life. Not everyone can live in a villa. But perhaps I can do something to make their lives more bearable," he said. "It *must* be possible to produce bicycles more cheaply. A bicycle for under a hundred marks— that would be the goal! And if we can't do it in Germany, then perhaps a factory in England or America can."

"So why don't you find out?" Josephine asked. As she uttered the words, she had the strange feeling she sounded exactly like Frieda.

\*\*\*

It was Saturday afternoon. Exhausted but satisfied with her second week of work as her own boss, Josephine was about to close up the workshop when she saw Oskar Reutter coming around the corner with a handcart that held something large and square. A new commission? Jo sighed. She had been looking forward to her first official visit to the cycling club . . . and to seeing one person there in particular. But work came first.

Reutter greeted her cheerfully, then heaved a heavy iron chest onto Jo's workbench. She realized at a glance that not only were the bands broken, but the hinges as well. "I can weld the bands at the forge. But I won't be able to use the old rivets again. I'll have to make new ones to reconnect the bands to the chest. It could be expensive . . ."

"The chest is an heirloom, and I'm very fond of it. Money is no object," he said as he lifted a second item from the cart. It was a plain but elegant Gustav Becker wall clock, with the pendulum no longer attached.

"Our new maid is terribly scattered. She banged the clock with her back while she was cleaning. Her back was unharmed, but the clock suffered," Reutter explained with a smirk.

"It looks as if I'll have to fashion a new mount for the pendulum out of brass."

Oskar Reutter smiled. "It's worth it! I love new things, but I have a soft spot for the old ones."

"You're not alone," said Josephine with a laugh, as she gestured toward all the objects lined up on her floor waiting to be repaired.

She tried to sneak a look at the gold-plated watch from Frieda's jewelry box, which she wore as a pendant on a leather band around her neck. Oskar Reutter noticed and said, "That's a lovely piece, and it will become a rare one soon. People are asking about watches that you can wear on an armband these days. Pocket watches and pendant watches are too *old-fashioned*." He said the last word with a hint of sarcasm. "But you know what? Even I couldn't resist the new fad." He pushed up the sleeve of his jacket and showed Jo a gold watch on a brown leather band.

"How practical! That would be perfect for cycling," said Jo. "I'd better leave Frieda's watch here, or I'll end up catching the cord on the handlebars."

"Cycling . . ." said Oskar Reutter slowly. "Sometimes I can't tell anymore whether it's a blessing or a curse."

"Would you like to come into the house for a minute? I've got some fresh lemonade," said Josephine. The club could wait. If Oskar Reutter wanted to chat, she'd be glad for his company. He was not only an important customer but also a neighbor and friend—and there were far worse topics than cycling!

As soon as they were settled at Frieda's old kitchen table, Reutter took up his thread again. "We live in exciting times. Everything is changing. Nobody wants the old stuff anymore. The horse dealer behind Lausitzer Platz paid me a visit yesterday. He's closed his shop and is moving out to the country to manage his sister's farm. But because more and more horse-and-carriage companies are giving up their trade, he had a hard time getting rid of his horses. And that's just the beginning!" The old man paused for breath, then went on, "All of society is in upheaval. Sometimes, our world feels like a carnival carousel, turning faster and faster. And bicycles are partly responsible for that."

"But cycling is something only few can enjoy, so how can it possibly be changing society?"

"Ah, I daresay your impression of things is false. There are considerably more cyclers out and about than there were a few years ago. Perhaps not in our neighborhood, but it's a different story just a few streets away." Oskar Reutter sipped his lemonade. "I know this because they're coming to my store in droves asking for sporting caps instead of elegant hats, and jackets with a lot of pockets instead of fine tailcoats. They're leaving my cigars behind, too—bad for the health, a young man told me just yesterday. My cigars? Bad for the health?" Oskar Reutter looked so indignant that Josephine had to make an effort to suppress a smile.

"Just a year or two ago, young couples used to come to me to buy a piano. Or a handsome cherrywood wall clock. I often had to consent to payment in installments, but I was always happy to do that. But today?

The young groom would rather put his money toward a bicycle. The furnishings get sacrificed, of course, but it appears that's something he and the lady of the house are willing to accept."

Josephine's brow creased. "But bicycles are still so expensive."

Oskar Reutter shrugged. "You don't need to tell me that! But it makes no difference. People find anything to do with bicycles fascinating. More fascinating than the Lord above, I might add. Pastor Hohenheim told me that he loses several pews of his congregation whenever there's an important cycle race in the city."

"They actually choose a race over church?"

Reutter grinned, seeming to downright enjoy Josephine's look of disbelief. "The bookshop owner told me he's suffered a serious drop in sales because people would rather go to the cycle track and watch the riders than pick up a book."

Josephine was speechless. Did Adrian know all this? It sounded as if his vision of the future had already become a reality.

Jo pulled her Roadster out of the workshop and was about to swing onto the saddle when she saw Clara walking down the street on the arm of a tall man. She had not seen Clara since her friends' visit, despite living only a few houses away. *I will finally get to meet the good doctor,* thought Jo. He was very good-looking, and she could see why Clara had fallen head over heels in love with him. But her delight at seeing her friend did not last long.

"Josephine!" Clara shrieked. It was not a greeting. She was pointing at Josephine's legs. "You're wearing pants?" Clara's voice grew even shriller and she seemed to be clinging to her husband's arm.

"I'm on my way to the cycling club, and a skirt is just plain dangerous. What are you looking so horrified about? Don't you remember how we sewed a skirt into pants to ride the bicycles years ago? Oh, of course you don't remember. You were lying in the hospital with a broken leg. At least you got to know each other there . . ." She looked at Clara's husband with an expectant smile. "It's a pleasure to finally get to meet you," she said and held out her hand to the doctor.

Gerhard Gropius looked at her with the kind of disgust usually reserved for vermin. Then he turned to Clara.

"Some women don't have even the vaguest sense of decorum. It's a disgrace! I very much hope that you know to keep your distance." And with that, he pulled Clara onward by the arm.

Josephine lowered her hand. What was that all about?

When she finally arrived at the track, it was already five in the afternoon. She leaned her bicycle against the wall and kept a lookout for Adrian, her heart pounding. She wanted so much to tell him about her talk with Oskar Reutter. But not much was happening at the club that afternoon. A few sweaty young men were just leaving the track, which was immediately commandeered by a small group of women, and two older men in street clothes were just leaving. It was the Pentecost weekend, and many Berliners were taking advantage of the glorious weather to go out to the country, Oskar Reutter had told her. Another new fad!

Had Adrian left the city, too? Perhaps with Isabelle?

Jo entered the women's clubroom, feeling rather glum. She was even more disappointed not to have the opportunity to thank the other members for accepting her into the club—there was no one there. Jo left the clubroom and pushed her bicycle out onto the track. That's what she was really there for, after all.

Her first lap was exciting. The surface was dangerously fast, the tight curves not something she was used to, but after a few minutes, Jo found her rhythm. Soon, all thoughts of the strange encounter with Clara and her husband, of Adrian, Isabelle, and the rest of the world scattered to the wind. Although she did not feel as if she was working especially hard, her heart was hammering in her chest. She tried breathing more deeply, the way she did when she rode up a long incline. But instead of slowing down, her heart soon felt like it was pounding in her throat. She felt slightly dizzy and reluctantly rolled to a stop. Leaning against the fence, she watched the women who had gone out on the track ahead of her. They were still pedaling at high speed and apparently without effort. They were even chatting with one another! Did she really have so little stamina? But she had been able to keep up with Adrian all the way to North Harbor.

"Worn out already?" One of the riders pulled up beside her and smiled. It was Luise Karrer. She extended a gloved hand to Jo. "Welcome to the club. I was thinking you weren't ever going to show up again."

"You've all got so much stamina. How do you do that?" Jo asked once she had officially introduced herself.

"Train often, train long," Luise replied. "Track riding goes by different rules than riding on the street. Or rather, weaknesses come to light faster, because you're always comparing yourself directly to others."

Josephine nodded. She had never considered that before.

"It can't have anything to do with your bicycle," Luise said, running an admiring hand over the shiny black frame of the Roadster. "And your outfit is certainly athletic enough."

Josephine laughed bitterly. "You should have heard the comments from my neighbors when they saw me leaving my house in pants."

"The petit bourgeois mindset! I think you look *très à la mode*," said a second rider, who had just joined them. She herself wore an elegant pair of culottes, tailored to fit quite snugly. "My name is Chloé. I'm Freddy Stich's wife," she said in a French accent. She looked expectantly at Jo.

But when Jo simply introduced herself in return, Luise said, "Freddy Stich is one of our most famous racers, if not *the* most famous."

Jo looked sheepish. "Excuse me. I really know nothing about these things. And nothing about the right way to train, either, apparently. Here I am, sweating and puffing, but you both look positively relaxed after your long stint just now."

"A lady never sweats," Chloé replied, raising her eyebrows.

They all laughed. Once they had stowed their bicycles, they went into the clubhouse together like old friends. Josephine kept a lookout for Adrian—but in vain.

"Your friend Isabelle is a very good cyclist. And very well trained as well. I'm sure she can give you a few tips for training on the track," said Luise, when all three were seated with a cup of coffee.

"Tips!" Chloé dismissed the notion. "One will tell you lots of sleep. The next says it's all about eating plenty of meat and potatoes. Yet another will tell you that you have to swear off alcohol completely. Then there are those like my Freddy, who does all sorts of gymnastics to stretch his muscles before he gets on his bicycle. And before big races, he even uses a laxative to cleanse his body on the inside." She rolled her eyes to show what she thought of such training methods. "I say you have to find out for yourself what's right for you. A glass of champagne in the evening—or even in the morning!—has never done me any harm."

"With all due respect to a glass of champagne, you can't deny that a healthy and regular lifestyle is a prerequisite for a successful cyclist," Luise responded. "I'll tell you what you need to build up the endurance for track riding: ten hours of sleep a night, healthy food and lots of different types of food, a short siesta every day to let your body recuperate, and a short walk to relax the muscles. That's the only way to go around the track for hours on end."

Josephine—who had gone to bed at midnight, gotten up at six, lived on potato soup for days, and had an aching back from bending over her workbench—nodded miserably.

"What is that all about?" she asked, picking up a magazine she had noticed a few minutes earlier.

Her distraction worked, for Luise said, "That's the *Draisena*, the first magazine for women cyclists. That issue came out yesterday, hot off the press in Dresden. I've only flipped through it once, and I'm quite impressed."

"Does it have photographs and illustrations?" Chloé asked, snatching the magazine out of Jo's hand.

Jo looked over Chloé's shoulder while she leafed through the magazine. There were no photographs but quite a few illustrations, many of them very funny.

"The Cycling Woman in the Eyes of Society" was the headline of one article. In its subheading, the writer posed the question: "Will the industrialist's wife and her cook soon be riding side by side?" The text was accompanied by a caricatured illustration in which a finely attired high-society woman was pedaling along beside her fat cook.

Luise laughed. "If Isabelle saw that . . ."

"Or Irene," Chloé added.

A few pages later, they found the article "Fresh Air and Light Exercise Bring Health to Every Cycling Woman." The magazine was filled with countless advertisements trumpeting women's bicycles, cycling capes, dog whips, raincoats, and cyclists' provisions.

"Cyclists' provisions—what is that supposed to mean?" Jo asked with a giggle. Perhaps Oskar Reutter should be carrying those instead of cigars.

Luise raised her eyebrows. "It's a very serious matter, my dear. Anyone who cycles for any length of time has to eat the right food. Nuts, dried fruit, cookies—food that renews your strength."

Josephine nodded, impressed.

Chloé turned the page. "What's this? 'Racing—An Illness Spreading Among Cycling Women.'" she read aloud, glowering. "It looks as if *Draisena* has something against women's races. That's a shame . . ."

"Maybe it's just that one writer," Luise said, sounding hopeful.

Josephine shrugged. "Everyone has the right to an opinion. It's surprising enough that there's a magazine just for us."

*

A little while later, she saw him after all. Dressed in a black suit and gleaming black top hat, with a leather portfolio under one arm, he looked like a stranger to her. Adrian's expression was grim, his eyes distracted. He saw her just as he was walking out.

"Josephine . . ."

"It doesn't look as if you've come here to ride," she said, her voice faltering a little.

"My father is receiving an honorary title at the City Palace soon. The emperor is naming him to the commerce council. My father put me on the list of speakers, and I cleverly left my notes here in my locker. I'm just here to pick them up." He frowned as if he had a toothache.

An honorary title. The commerce council. The emperor. And Isabelle at Adrian's side, surely dressed in layer upon layer of the finest lace.

Josephine took a reluctant step back.

Adrian went over and removed a chestnut leaf from the spokes of her bicycle. "Looks like you've tried the Roadster out on the track. How did it go?"

Josephine suddenly felt like crying, but she pulled herself together. "The Roadster was just fine. But, I . . . I have no stamina!"

"Then we should do what we can to see that you get some. How about going for a ride again next week—while the world is still asleep?"

Jo hesitated.

"Say yes," Adrian whispered, suddenly stroking her cheek. His face was so close to hers that she could feel his breath on her skin. Warm and sweet. "Please say yes. Knowing I'm going to see you again will make this evening easier to bear. You don't know how much I would rather be with you . . ."


An hour later, it began to rain, and it didn't stop all weekend. The days felt long and the nights even longer. Outside was cool, inside chilly, but

Josephine felt no desire to light the fire. She had no interest in doing anything! She paced back and forth like a tiger locked in a cage, unsure what to do with herself. She would have had more than enough work but knew she shouldn't start hammering away in the workshop on a church holiday.

She eventually attempted to distract herself by reading through the pile of old newspapers as she sat bundled on the sofa in the old crocheted blanket with the cat curled beside her. She would have felt a great deal lonelier still if she hadn't had that one sentence to warm her heart.

*"You don't know how much I would rather be with you . . ."*

# Chapter Twenty-Four

"The staircase alone! It was designed by the famous architect Schinkel, and the walls, the floor, and the ceiling are all made of cream-colored marble with a tinge of pink." Isabelle could hardly contain her excitement. Her eyes sparkled, her cheeks were flushed, and she looked prettier than ever. "The salon where the ceremony itself took place was all decked out in a princely red—no, an imperial red!—unlike anything you've ever seen."

Josephine nodded. She was using a foul-smelling but extremely effective paste to give Oskar Reutter's iron chest a final polish. She was eager to finish it up because her first bicycle had just been brought in for repairs! It belonged to one of the women in the club, and she wanted a basket attached and a buckled mudguard straightened. Josephine could hardly wait to get started on it.

"And the evening dresses . . . I have never, ever seen so much silk and lace in one place. The empress . . ."

Isabelle had been talking incessantly since she arrived an hour earlier with a fragrant yeast cake. Josephine had stopped working and made them both a cup of tea. While she sipped her tea and ate cake, everything in her was screaming: *I don't want to hear this!* After half an hour, Jo became so restless that she stood up to get back to work. But instead of leaving, as Jo had hoped she would, Isabelle had followed her into the workshop, where she had blithely continued chattering.

"There was nothing to eat, though, unfortunately. I nearly starved to death! But I don't think the guests could have eaten a bite because they were all in such awe of the emperor. Adrian's father was so puffed up with pride at his new honorary title that he wouldn't have had any room in his paunch anyway."

Just then, the doorbell rang and a man stepped inside. Josephine was just polishing the blackened base of the chest, and her forehead was damp from the exertion. She swept her sticky hair out of her face and made an effort to put on a friendly smile. "Can I help you?"

"Josephine Schmied?" The man wore a gray suit and had a mustache like the emperor's.

"Yes." She watched as the visitor placed his briefcase on her workbench.

"Are you the owner?"

"Yes. Why?" Jo and Isabelle glanced at one another. What did the man want? Who was he?

"Johann Schmolke, from the Chamber of Trades. It has been brought to my attention that you are operating a craftsman's establishment here, without being in possession of the requisite qualifications. Your papers, please!" The man held out his hand to her.

"What papers? What qualifications?"

"Business registration, tax books, trade certification," the man rattled off. "And in your case, I would also like to see papers demonstrating your legal capacity." He looked her over from head to foot. "Are you even of legal age?"

"Of course," said Jo. "But what—"

"Would you be so kind as to show us *your* papers first, Mr. Schmolke?" Isabelle said. "After all, anybody could walk in here and say he was from the Chamber of Trades." Her tone was friendly but firm.

While the man fumbled indignantly in his pockets, Josephine thought frantically. She didn't have any of the things the man had asked for! What could she do? She peered nervously at the identity card the man held under her nose. Damn it! He really was from the Chamber of Trades.

"What kind of operation do you run here, exactly? I see a forge, I see tools . . . Is this a smithy? A metalworking shop? A plumbing business? I have never heard of a . . . woman being involved in any of those professions!" He gestured toward a few metal pipes.

Jo took a deep breath. *Stay friendly and don't lose your nerve now,* she told herself.

"My gosh, I am not doing anything like the work of a skilled tradesman here. All I do is fix a few small things that people have broken. Or that have broken all by themselves, just because they're old."

Isabelle stepped forward. "It's like this: Miss Schmied is a great help to clumsy people like me. Not ten minutes ago, I tore open my skirt on the garden fence, and Miss Schmied has promised to sew it up for me. That's really very kind of her, don't you think? I pay her a few pennies for the service and have one less thing to worry about."

Miss Schmied! Josephine could barely suppress a smile. She had some idea what Isabelle was up to and was certain that she had *not* torn her skirt more than a few seconds ago. Hoping that the man would drop his interrogation when faced with their "women's affairs," she quickly brought out Frieda's old basket of wool from behind the workbench.

"Sometimes I even have to crochet or knit a few rows, just imagine!" She giggled childishly.

The man pushed out his bottom lip doubtfully and his mustache twitched. "I see. Your work consists primarily of handicrafts. But how is it then that this workshop is so well equipped?" He whacked the forge lightly with his walking stick, and the forge rang metallically.

Josephine lowered her eyes and tried to make her voice sound sad. "All of it was left behind by my poor departed . . ." Her poor departed

who? She searched helplessly for the appropriate word. She had neither
known Frieda's husband well nor liked him very much.

"God rest his soul," said Isabelle helpfully.

The man twirled at his mustache. "So, repairs and sewing. It would
seem I have been sent here on the basis of false assumptions. I see no
infringement of the trade regulations." He sounded almost regretful. "If
you would show me your business registration and proof of payment of
taxes—I'm sure it can't be much—then I will leave you in peace." For
the first time since his arrival, he granted her something resembling a
smile.

"Business registration . . ." Josephine writhed like an eel. "Well . . ."

"I can't believe it!" Isabelle nearly shouted, once the man was gone
again. "You open your workshop and forget to register it? And you
don't even pay taxes?"

Josephine could have sunk through the floor, she felt so ashamed.
On the one hand, she was grateful that Isabelle was there. Who knows
whether she would have been able to keep the man at bay on her own?
On the other, it rankled her that Moritz Herrenhus's daughter had seen
her fail so miserably.

"I only opened my doors two weeks ago! And there were so many
other things to take care of that . . . that . . ." Helplessly, she gave it up.
"I would have gotten around to it eventually," she added rather lamely.

"Oh, I'm sure. What now? The man will be back in two weeks, and
you have to produce a guarantor. Where do you think you'll come up
with one of those?"

*What business is it of yours?* Jo felt like screaming. Instead, she said
quietly, "I don't know."

The officer from the Chamber of Trades had been quite upset.
"Considering your immaturity and obvious inexperience in business

matters, I find it appropriate that a man stand as guarantor for you and keep an eye on you," he had said.

Who would do such a thing for her? And why was a guarantor even necessary? She should have asked him that but had felt too intimidated. "I hope this isn't the beginning of the end," she murmured.

"You're not going to throw in the towel that fast, I hope! Should I ask Adrian?" said Isabelle in a more placating tone.

"God, no!" said Josephine, looking sharply at her friend. "Don't you dare say a word to anyone at the club about how stupid I've been."

Isabelle waved it off. "Adrian would certainly help you out. That's his thing, you know. He'd much rather improve the lot of all the world's factory workers, but if I ask him nicely, I'm sure he'd help you, too."

It was suddenly all too much for Jo: Isabelle's stories about the City Palace, which had left Jo with a dull sense of not belonging. The unnerving visit from the official. The question of who had reported her to the Chamber of Trades. Her anger at her own naïveté.

"Why do you speak that way about your fiancé? I may not be as worldly and clever as you, and I'll never be invited to the Imperial Court, but there's one thing I *do* know: if I had a fiancé, I would never talk about him like that!" She took the filthy rag and threw it at her friend, leaving a drab smear on Isabelle's skirt.

Isabelle looked at her in surprise. But then the old, mocking lines reappeared at the corners of her mouth.

"What do you know about love? Nothing, that's what. Not a thing!"

Josephine recoiled as if bitten by a snake. Isabelle was right. Just one more thing that showed how stupid and inexperienced Josephine was. All she "knew" about love had come from the young women in prison. But their boasting and coarse descriptions of what happened between a man and a woman had nothing to do with love. Love . . . Didn't that mean a mutual admiration on some higher plane? That you appreciated each other, listened to each other, understood each other without words? That you had shared interests or could at least be enthusiastic about what the other cared about? That you longed for the one you loved and could not wait to see him again? Just like she and . . .

Josephine placed her hand over her heart as the realization struck her.

Had she already been in love for some time? Oh God, if that were true—

"And you know nothing about me, either," Isabelle snapped, dragging Josephine out of her thoughts. "But instead of asking how I am and what's going on with me, you draw your own conclusions and judge me. Some friend you are!"

Isabelle had never before shed tears in front of Jo. Isabelle could be moody and haughty, but most of the time, she only showed the world her happier side. It had never occurred to Jo that it might all be an act. Isabelle had everything anyone could wish for, didn't she?

At once ashamed and helpless, Jo could only stand and look at Isabelle, who had collapsed sobbing onto the bench, her head buried in her arms. "I'm sorry. I didn't mean it like that," she said. If only she'd kept her mouth shut. But a moment later, Isabelle threw herself into Josephine's arms.

"You don't know how terrible it all is!" she sobbed into Josephine's breast. "I can't take it much longer. If something doesn't happen soon, I'm going to kill myself!"

They went into the house arm in arm. Isabelle let Jo lead her to the sofa and wrap her up in the old woolen blanket. Frieda's cat jumped up onto Isabelle's lap, as if she sensed the young woman's need for warmth. Josephine went into the kitchen and made more tea.

With her hands wrapped securely around her teacup, Isabelle began to speak. Hesitantly at first—as if, looking back, she found it hard to believe the whole story herself—she told Josephine about the deal Moritz Herrenhus had made with Gottlieb Neumann, and about what Adrian and she had decided to do in return.

"Your engagement is a sham? You've spent the last few years only *acting* like you're in love?"

Faced with Jo's surprise, Isabelle managed a small smile. "If you look at it that way, we've done a pretty good job, haven't we? Don't get me wrong. I like Adrian a lot; he's a wonderful man, smart, handsome . . ." She shrugged. "But he's not the man I want to spend the rest of my life with. I don't love him," she said bluntly.

So many questions shot through Jo's head that she didn't know where to begin. "What about him?" she finally said, holding her breath.

"We've probably only succeeded at our game for this long because there are no feelings involved on either side."

No feelings. Adrian wasn't Isabelle's. He didn't love her. Still, they were engaged . . . Josephine shook her head as if to free it from the mess of cobwebs snaring her thoughts. Was it possible for happiness to make you dizzy?

"And no one has ever caught on? In all this time?"

"People only see what they want to see. Father was in seventh heaven. For the first time in my life I felt I was good enough in his eyes, and for the first time in years, he left me in peace! Adrian and I just had to turn up together occasionally at official functions. And we're both at the cycle club a lot. But we pursue our own interests there and rarely actually see each other. From the very start, it was clear that we would have to play our little game to the point of an engagement. Our fathers wanted to see rings." The diamond sparkled when Isabelle held up her hand. "It worked. Father gave Gottlieb Neumann the loan he needed, and the EWB was saved. Adrian was a hero in his father's eyes. And *I* finally had some peace."

"It was all about saving a company? About money?" Jo asked.

"Isn't that what it's usually about?" said Isabelle cynically. "Maybe now you can understand why I'm not always whispering declarations of love in his ear."

Jo nodded. "And you've kept this to yourself all this time?"

"Who was I supposed to tell?" said Isabelle bitterly. "Clara? She would have just looked at me all horrified with her doe eyes and uttered some platitude or another. Someone from school who'd pass it on to Irene in an instant?" Isabelle took Josephine's hand and said, "Not a word to anyone, not even Adrian if you happen to run into him. Is that clear?"

Josephine averted her gaze. She and Adrian had arranged to go cycling the next morning.

"Do you swear you won't breathe a word?" Isabelle repeated insistently. Then she began to sob again. "It's far too late for the truth." The desperation lingered deep in her eyes as she said, "Father wants us to marry this autumn."

Josephine lay awake deep into the night. For years, she had looked up to Isabelle, admired her for her lifestyle, perhaps even envied her a little for it. Their beautiful house, the servants. The elegant parents. The wealth. Her own bicycle even when she was still just a girl. How had Jo not seen that it was just a gilded cage? Poor Isabelle . . .

And what did all of it mean for her? How was she supposed to see Adrian now? She couldn't talk about the situation with him; she had promised Isabelle she wouldn't. She would simply have to wait and see whether he confided in her, too.

In any case, had anything really changed? Adrian's and Isabelle's wedding was still planned for autumn. Even if a miracle happened and their plans collapsed, Adrian was the son of a major industrialist, and she was a silly little goose who didn't even know that one had to register a business. She surely had better things to do than chasing illusions of love!

A guarantor . . . Would Oskar Reutter ever do something like that for her? *I really should put the business first,* she thought before she fell asleep.

***

A few houses away, another young woman could not sleep. *How much longer will Gerhard sit at his desk and work on his treatise?* Clara wondered, as the clock in the living room struck midnight. On an impulse, she swung her legs over the side of the bed and went downstairs to fetch him.

"Listen to this!" he said when he saw her standing in the doorway.

"From 'Women and Cycling: A Medical Perspective.' Just listen: 'Society, it would seem, is content to sit back and watch the immoral goings-on of increasing numbers of viragoes on two wheels, and thus to complacently accept the spread of this most unwomanly of affectations. It is high time that we, as men of medicine, speak out against this state of affairs. For the riding of bicycles has consequences for women so serious that one can only warn against the practice in the strongest of terms. Let us start with the way a cyclist crouches atop a bicycle, in a position so unseemly for a woman. Who, after all—with the wind rushing about one's ears—gives a thought to the danger of serious accumulations of blood forming in the pelvic regions? Menstrual complaints, an absence of bleeding, or excessively painful periods are only a few of the many possible ramifications. Or let us take the hunched posture of a woman on a bicycle, which is not dissimilar to the arched back of a cat. The fear of pitching headlong over the handlebars results in such a frenzy of adrenaline that she imperils not only her own health but also that of her unborn children! Who would be surprised to find that such a neglectful attitude to one's health might well diminish a woman's procreative ability? Forgotten is the very reason for which God created women: to bear children. Most certainly not to ride a bicycle . . .'"

How zealously his eyes shone! Gerhard had read so quickly that small threads of spittle had gathered in the corners of his mouth. As Clara listened to her husband's rant, she found herself fighting a growing nausea. Her knees trembled, and she felt like squatting on the floor. But decency prohibited her from doing so. *Stand up! Stand straight!* a strident voice inside her ordered.

"Very interesting," she said, her voice hoarse, when he had finished. "What . . . what do you have in mind with that?"

A tight smile played on Gerhard's lips as he said, "For some weeks now, I have been exchanging letters with a number of my colleagues. They have also been working on various pamphlets of their own, all denouncing women riding bicycles. We will be submitting our work to different Berlin newspapers. It is high time that the public found out the truth. One thing I will say to you here and now, my dear"—he fixed her with his avid eyes—"the days of that women's cycling club are numbered. I will see to it personally!"

# Chapter Twenty-Five

*Early 1896*

"Look here, all of it handmade! And the frame, too—also handcrafted. Of particular note are the mudguards, wrought one hundred percent by hand." The pride in Carl Marschütz's voice was unmistakable as he presented his firm's best bicycle. The machine, set up on a stand of polished steel, gleamed in the bright light of the salesroom. "As Nuremberg's first bicycle factory, we have an enviable reputation for quality. But as the son of the founder of the EWB, I'm sure you know perfectly well what I'm talking about."

Adrian nodded tensely. He had been on his feet since well before dawn, and he had only reached the Velocipedfabrik Marschütz & Co. in Nuremberg at two in the afternoon after a strenuous train journey. On Adrian's arrival, Carl Marschütz had scurried excitedly across the snowy yard to meet him. Adrian was both amazed and thrilled to discover that Carl was only a few years older than Adrian himself and had already built a successful bicycle manufacturing company.

"Do you know what the people call our machines? *Hercules bicycles.* I love it! What do you think, should I market them officially by that name?"

"Naming a bicycle after one of the heroes of Greek mythology . . . Wouldn't that be a little over the top?" Adrian asked, squinting a little.

"Not at all! After all, a bicycle is something very special."

Adrian took a deep breath to keep his impatience in check. *Something very special*—he couldn't bear to hear that one more time! "But if your bicycles are so popular, you must have some interest in producing far more of them," he said. For him, this was the crux of the matter.

Carl Marschütz looked appreciatively at his guest. "I can see that you have a true entrepreneurial spirit. Yes, in fact, we have plans to do just that. To be honest, I think about practically nothing other than how we can produce economical bicycles for the masses."

Adrian looked at his counterpart with interest. Perhaps his journey had been worthwhile after all . . .

"Come with me. I would be happy to show you our factory." Marschütz led Adrian from the showroom out into a large hall where several dozen men were busy assembling bicycles. The place smelled of rubber and lubricants, beer and sweat, and the men talked loudly as they worked. Adrian smiled—what a change from the sterile production rooms of the EWB!

"We've increased our production from a hundred machines in the first year to four hundred last year," said Marschütz, putting an immediate damper on Adrian's enthusiasm.

"Is there anything to stop you from increasing that to four *thousand*? This place would certainly be big enough . . . and I'm sure that mass production like that would lead to considerable savings in manufacturing costs."

Carl Marschütz furrowed his brow. "I can't say *I'm* sure. Producing a bicycle takes quite a number of specialists. Trained men want to be well paid and that costs money."

"You could buy larger machines and produce many of the parts by machine."

The man shook his head, horrified at the thought. "Building a bicycle with machines? That might work for aprons or pots and pans, but not for something as exclusive as a bicycle. How could I possibly present that to my customers?"

*Another dead end!* thought Adrian as he made his way back to the train station. It was a bleak winter's afternoon, and a cold east wind blew among the bare trees. Adrian buttoned his overcoat all the way up and wrapped his scarf tighter around his neck.

It was not the first such call he had made. Previously, he had paid a visit to the Fahrradfabrik Dürkopp & Co., which promoted itself as having the first "series production" of bicycles in the world, in Bielefeld. The company had previously specialized in sewing machines, and this in itself had struck Adrian as promising; certainly they would be familiar with effective industrial production methods. But when he arrived, Adrian had seen that a great deal of manual labor went into the machines they produced. Too much, in Adrian's opinion. The bicycles, accordingly, were of the highest quality but also extremely expensive. *Was I mistaken, or was one of the bicycles called "Diana"?* he wondered as he waited for his train. What was this new fashion, naming bicycles like that? Wouldn't mythologizing the bicycles that way distance the broader layers of society from bicycles even more?

A light snow had begun to fall. The train station at Nuremberg felt desolate, squalid. Adrian was relieved when the train finally pulled in. He looked for an empty compartment, leaned back into the soft upholstery, and looked out the window at the colorless landscape, the afternoon already moving toward night. Adrian closed his eyes and let his mind wander.

"A bicycle for less than a hundred marks. Why don't you find out if there's a producer who can make that happen? Then your dream of a bicycle business for the common man won't forever remain a dream," Josephine had said to him, a look of challenge in her eyes. That had been in May of the previous year.

He had not felt up to the task at first. Where was he supposed to start? And how? But then, in the fall, he had gathered his courage. The wedding had been postponed yet again—this time Isabelle had had a severe case of flu. Now, whenever his work at the EWB allowed, he went off for a day, sometimes two, to do research. The first thing he discovered was that bicycle factories were shooting up like mushrooms all over the empire. Many factories and workshops already involved in producing hardware and rubber goods had turned to making bicycles on the side. They could smell the profits the field offered. But there were also factories that were dedicated exclusively to making bicycles. Adrian had gathered the addresses of these companies and then he had started to visit them. But he never went anywhere on Wednesdays! Because every Wednesday, well before dawn, he and Josephine went out cycling, and their outings had become sacred to him.

His research had so far proven both heartening and depressing. Bicycle production in Germany was increasing enormously from one year to the next. But prices remained high. Some of the producers simply had no interest in seeing the prices come down. Others bridled at the idea of machine production.

"This isn't America. Machines don't take work away from people here," the manufacturer in Mannheim had told him in a disdainful voice. Adrian had snorted softly—that's why the poor in America could afford a bicycle.

His thoughts turned to Josephine. But did he really want to think about her now? No, too complicated. He forced his thoughts back to his factory visits.

Everywhere he went, he had been met with a friendly reception. "You're the son of Gottlieb Neumann?" the factory owner in Mannheim had asked. The man had then asked whether Adrian's father was thinking about entering the bicycle market, to which Adrian could only, regretfully, say no. "Then why are you here?" the man had asked him.

What was he supposed to say? Adrian sighed. That he was looking for a way to be independent? That he no longer wanted to be ordered around by his father?

Never, not one single time, had Adrian voiced his dream of being able to sell low-cost bicycles. Why should he? The whole world assumed that he would gladly fill the role of his father's successor. No one had any idea that he derived no pleasure from his work at the EWB. No one except Josephine. But that he considered selling bicycles to be his mission in life was something that he had so far kept even from her. He didn't want to rant to her about vague, abstract plans. He wanted to have something to show for himself, something to impress her with. She ought to be able to look up to him and say, "Well done!"

Well done? So far, the entire undertaking had been a failure from start to finish . . . From that perspective, at least, it was good that he had kept his mouth shut.

Adrian gazed out with empty eyes at the forests and farmlands. It was nearly dark. The fir trees seemed grim and threatening, and a swarm of hungry rooks wheeled above a field in the last gleams of day, hoping to discover a starving mouse or something else edible.

What now? Was his dream at an end? And was it the end of a future with the woman he loved and treasured and wanted to spend his life with, and to hell with what the rest of the world thought?

The end of his dream . . . The thought terrified him. He reached up and loosened his tie. But the sense of anxiety, the feeling that he could not breathe, remained.

The fact was, his life was not his own. A few visits to bicycle factories did not change that. He was fooling himself, and his efforts were ridiculous. At twenty-four, he had nothing to show anyone except his degree. Even his apartment was not his.

He had to act, and he had to act soon, or there would be no more chance to escape. After the last postponement, a new wedding date had been set for Maundy Thursday, just before Easter. But he had no intention of standing at the altar with Isabelle, then or on any other day. The thought of being bound forever to a woman he didn't love—and who did not love him!—was unbearable.

Josephine . . . It was to *her* that he wanted to declare his love! He wanted to take her in his arms, kiss her, stroke her hair, and press his lips to the skin at the base of her neck. He wanted her to look up to him. He wanted to be able to say to her, *Here I am and here I'll stay, at your side. If you'll have me.*

Instead, all they had were their secret bicycle outings. Occasional touches as accidental as that of a falling autumn leaf. Hasty glances from beneath lowered eyelids—glances that could be read any number of ways. All of it completely harmless, right? Two cycling acquaintances out training together. Was a life together even possible? Or were they simply too different?

Adrian sighed deeply. He would probably have to give up his plan of doing business with German bicycle manufacturers. But he had another plan in mind as well. One that was just as daring, and just as promising. But whether he possessed the courage to see it through, he did not know.

Instead of walking the twenty minutes from the station to his city apartment, as he normally would have, Adrian took a cab. He had had enough for one day and just wanted to get home and relax.

But that was not to be. When he opened the heavy wood-paneled front door to the building, he saw a figure crouching at the top of the stairs in front of the door to his apartment.

"Isabelle! What are you doing here?"

She was pale, and she'd obviously cried her eyes dry. She followed him silently into his apartment—something she had never done before.

"Let's go into the sitting room. Has something happened? Say something, how can I help you?" Adrian said as he helped her out of her fur coat.

"I can say what I have to say here," Isabelle said brusquely, buttoning her coat instead of unbuttoning it. A moment before she had looked so vulnerable, but now her eyes turned hard.

"All anyone ever talks about at home is the wedding. Guest lists, the wedding dress, the menu, the ceremony in the church. It's driving me mad!"

"Do you think I'm happy about it? Damn it, why didn't we think about how we'd get ourselves out of this mess back then?"

"Back then? I don't care about back then! *You* have to do something *now*. I can't manage this all on my own. I want to have my freedom back, and the sooner the better. If I ever marry, it will be for love! Not because our fathers signed a pawn ticket. And while we're on the subject . . ." Her face was full of hate and her eyes bored into Adrian as she went on. "It was *your* father who profited most from our engagement. That makes it *your* job to put an end to this! And in such a way that I get out of it in one piece, with my reputation intact. I expect a plan from you, and soon. If I don't get it, I'll throw myself under a train, and you'll be to blame. How do you think that will feel, Adrian Neumann?"

As Adrian watched her leave, he wondered whether some whim of fate had sent his fiancée there that day, of all days. On the very day he himself was pondering his future so deeply.

He slipped off his boots, slung them toward the wardrobe. In the kitchen, he poured himself a glass of wine. But instead of going into the sitting room and making himself comfortable in one of the large leather armchairs, he sat down at the kitchen table and drank it all in one large swig.

A bitter laugh escaped his throat.

The question of whether he had enough courage for his second plan was now utterly moot. He had no other choice. He had to act.

***

Josephine smiled as she pulled a yellow cardigan out of Frieda's wardrobe. Her old friend had called it her daffodil cardigan and always had taken it out promptly on the first of March. The first of March was still a week away, but on the spur of the moment, Josephine decided to invoke Frieda's spring ritual early. The sweater perfectly suited the dark-brown skirt and blouse she had recently bought for herself. Oskar Reutter had talked her into buying them when she had dropped in to visit him shortly after the New Year. He had told her that she shouldn't just work all the time, that she ought to treat herself to something nice now and then. After all, she was a young woman with a successful business—and as her guarantor, checking the monthly accounts, he knew exactly *how* well. Did Josephine realize that she was already quite a well-to-do young woman? Jo had laughed and told him no, she hadn't really been aware of that, then added that she was far more afraid that the situation might change. In the end, she had only bought the outfit because Mr. Reutter had offered her a special discount.

Now, though, looking at herself in the mirror, she was pleased. No doubt the other members of the club would dress up today as well.

Josephine moistened her hair with a little water, then kneaded it with both hands until curls began to form. She pinched her cheeks to give them a little blush, then looked herself over one last time with a critical eye. With her shoulder-length curls that she always wore loose, she was certainly no ballroom belle, but her hair suited her face and added something a little daring to her look, and she liked that.

After giving the cat some milk in a bowl, she tucked in her skirt, swung onto her bicycle, and rode off.

Today was a special day. The men and women in the club wanted to ring in the new season with a big party. After the reduced opening times of the winter, the club was going to open daily again starting in March. That mattered little to Josephine, who still preferred to ride on the street, where she had, in the meantime, built up her stamina greatly. The longest stretch that she and Adrian had ridden had taken four hours. Summer, autumn, winter—no one could tell her when to ride! For Josephine, there was no such thing as bad weather, and she enjoyed experiencing the changing seasons from the saddle of her bicycle. Only in recent weeks, when the streets were buried under snow, had she taken a break from cycling. But she had continued to see Adrian. He had come to see her in the workshop several times under various pretexts. Once there was something that needed to be repaired on his bicycle. Another time it was his watchband that had torn.

Adrian . . . Josephine's heart beat faster, and it had nothing to do with the gentle grade she was cycling up just then.

Once she had found out that Adrian and Isabelle's engagement was not genuine, she no longer felt any guilt about taking something that belonged to someone else. Their rides together had become an important part of her life, perhaps the most important. She looked forward to them with a practically feverish excitement. And when she saw him on those early mornings—when a broad smile swept across his serious face at the sight of her—she sensed that he, too, harbored feelings for her, even though he had never openly expressed anything of the sort. But what had never been could still come to pass.

In recent weeks, since the previous autumn, in fact, she had had the growing sense that something was brewing inside Adrian. That he was struggling inwardly, searching for a way out of the mire. Maybe even searching for a solution that would leave the way to her open? Josephine prayed to God daily that her suspicions were not false, and that Adrian would soon open his heart to her. But she doubted anything like that would happen that evening.

She was past the hill now, and the streets of Berlin were flat again. Josephine pedaled harder. Perhaps Adrian would ask her to dance? That would surely be acceptable between members of the same club, wouldn't it?

Even from outside, she heard the angry shouts and voices raised in indignation, and when she pushed open the door to the clubroom, the noise grew louder still.

"It's a scandal!"

"It's outrageous is what it is. It's slander, a smear campaign!"

"Ten pages! Can you believe it?"

"Oh, no. Listen to this . . ."

Instead of lifting their glasses of sparkling wine in toasts as planned, the women and several of the men were gathered around newspapers spread across a table, reading passages aloud to one another.

"Listen: 'Anemia and Neurasthenia: The Latest Trend in Diseases Among Women, Resulting from the Unsavory Practice of Riding Bicycles!' Written by a Dr. Köppke," read Melissa. "He's got an imagination."

Luise Karrer tapped on the paper in front of her. "This one claims that the sport makes you infertile. 'The considerable jolts experienced while cycling damage the female reproductive organs.' I wonder where my four children came from, then."

"The stork brought them. Didn't you know that?" said one of the younger men sitting around the table. Unlike the women, they appeared to find the whole thing more amusing than annoying.

"What's going on?" Jo asked as she sat down next to Isabelle and gestured toward the table, which was set for dinner but also covered in newspapers. She glanced discreetly around the room. Adrian was sitting with Chloé's husband at a table in the rear. He saw her, and they exchanged a nod, then Isabelle claimed all of Josephine's attention when she exclaimed loudly, "Well, I never! This article was penned by a certain Dr. Gerhard Gropius!"

"That's Clara's husband," said Josephine, who snatched the newspaper out of Isabelle's hand and began reading.

## Women and Cycling: A Medical Perspective

Society, it would seem, is content to sit back and watch the immoral goings-on of increasing numbers of viragoes on two wheels and thus complacently accept the spread of this most unwomanly of affectations. It is high time that we, as men of medicine, speak out against this state of affairs.

"Most unwomanly of affectations . . ." Josephine said aloud as she looked up from the newspaper. "I find it sad that there are still men in this world who denigrate our sport like this. But that's no reason to get so upset."

"Then read on," said Luise, who was sitting on the opposite side of the table.

The fear of pitching headlong over the handlebars results in such a frenzy of adrenaline that she imperils not only her own health but also that of her unborn children! Who would be surprised to find that such a neglectful attitude to one's health might well diminish a woman's procreative ability? Forgotten is the very reason for which God created women: to bear children. Most certainly not to ride a bicycle . . .

"What kind of rubbish is this?" Josephine asked.

Luise laughed. "And you haven't read the other articles yet. That's one of the more harmless ones."

"But what . . . How is it that . . ." Jo spread her hands to indicate all of the newspaper pages.

"The newspaper is calling it a special supplement," Luise said. "Ten extra pages in the middle of the newspaper, full of essays from doctors and professors from all over the empire. The good doctors must have been corresponding with each other for months to put together this libelous campaign."

"I know what they're after with all this," said Gertrude. "They want to cut off our freedom! They want us to sit at home and wait on our husbands instead of riding through the city." She tapped on an article in front of her. "Listen to this one: 'It is undisputed that women, too, feel a certain need for exercise. It would, however, be far preferable for them to treadle honorably at the spinning wheel or sewing machine than to pedal ignobly at a bicycle.'"

"A spinning wheel? Does he think we live in the Middle Ages?" Chloé said heatedly, impatiently waving away the waitress who had come up behind her. She and most of the others had lost their appetite.

"Unbelievable!" Josephine shook her head. "What do *you* have to say about it?" she asked, turning to Isabelle, who was sitting beside her with a faint smile on her lips. "What, do you think this is funny?"

Isabelle's smile did not falter. "No, no, I find it just as terrible as you do. But . . ." She pulled Jo toward her and whispered in her ear. "Today is a wonderful day. I just received some very, very good news." Her look was as meaningful as it was mysterious.

"You two will have more to whisper about in a minute," said Fadi Nandou. "The worst article of all is at the end. It's from a doctor in Braunschweig. He writes: 'Based on countless examinations, observations, and scientific inquiries, as well as my own great knowledge of human nature, it is beyond a doubt that many women exploit the riding of bicycles for masturbatory purposes.'"

Shocked and indignant gasps sounded on all sides.

Jo started. "Masturbatory"—what did that even mean? She took the pages from Fadi and read on.

> Have you never asked yourself why so many women spend every free minute aboard a bicycle? While cycling, certain motions on the saddle pommel lead to sexual excitations, stimulations that females of a certain demeanor seem to require in the same way they need air to breathe. In this regard, it is but poor consolation that such "women" are of a species already corrupted long before they took up the "sport" of cycling.

Josephine felt her face flush. No one could believe that she . . . while she was riding . . . or that any other woman . . . How degrading. And how impertinent!

"Enough is enough!" said Luise, and she banged the table so hard with her fist that the wine glasses clinked. "We will not allow ourselves to be vilified in this disgraceful way. Paper and pen, please. We will write a rebuttal, one with teeth!"

The manager who ran the clubhouse stepped up to the table just then and cleared his throat. "Nothin's goin' to be written nowhere now! The soup's finished, and it will be served this minute."

No one paid much attention to the delicious food. The talk at the table revolved around the extraordinary articles in the paper. The fact that a Berlin newspaper would even publish such a thing left the women perplexed. They had all believed that times had changed. That *they* had changed them . . .

While Jo joined in the conversation, Isabelle continued to sit in silence, her blissful smirk fixed in place. What had gotten into Jo's friend?

Dessert was just being served when she noticed Adrian stand up. At the door, he signaled to Jo discreetly to follow him outside.

With shaking hands, Jo set her napkin on the table, murmured an apology, and disappeared.

Outside, Adrian suggested they go for a walk. Josephine was happy to do so; a little fresh air would be most welcome after all the excitement in the club.

In the glow of the gas lamps, the street lay silent and peaceful. As they walked down toward Halensee Lake, Josephine inhaled the faint smell of spring that hung full of promise in the air. As far as she was concerned, they could walk like that to the end of the world. She would have liked nothing more than to take Adrian by the arm. But she could not. Instead they walked so close beside each other that their arms touched repeatedly, as if by accident.

"I'm going away. To America. I'll be leaving before Easter," said Adrian. At first Josephine did not understand what he had said.

"You're doing what?" she asked with a laugh.

"In Boston, that's a city in the state of Massachusetts, there's a manufacturer named Albert Augustus Pope. He makes bicycles by the thousand. All of the German makers are talking about him. Most of them despise him, because he makes most of the parts for his bicycles by machine. But there are also some who admire him, because no one else in the world makes or sells as many bicycles as cheaply as he does. Thirty thousand a year, they say."

"What does that have to do with you?" She could not fake even a trace of enthusiasm or interest in her voice. She knew what was coming.

Adrian stopped beneath a gas lamp. As airily as if he were talking about an excursion out to Wannsee lake, he said, "I'm going to take a look at the factory. And if I like the bicycles and they're really as inexpensive as they say, I would like to import them to Germany. A bicycle for a hundred marks—remember?" He smiled mischievously.

The last thing Josephine could do just then was smile. "But America is at the other end of the world! And crossing the Atlantic is dangerous. You'll be gone for half an eternity . . ." There was so much more she wanted to say. *Don't leave me. Spring is just around the corner, then summer, and who's going to go riding with me? There are people who make bicycles in Germany, too!* But what right did she have to talk to him like that?

As if he could read her mind, Adrian said, "The German producers are too inflexible. They insist on handmade bicycles. I can't do business with them. I *have* to go to America. I've already booked my passage . . . as I said, I'll be leaving before Easter."

"But . . ." Jo protested helplessly, "What do Isabelle and your family have to say about it?"

Adrian sniffed. "I told Isabelle this afternoon. She's over the moon. She hopes this will mean the whole topic of the wedding is off the table once and for all. And my father . . . I'm going to leave a letter for him that explains everything."

"A letter. Isn't that a bit cowardly?" Josephine frowned. "Why don't you simply tell him your plans?"

"You don't know my father," said Adrian bitterly. "He'll sweep aside every word I say like dust. He'd never let me go. I fit too well into his plans." He took her hands in his, looked deep into her eyes, and said, "This is the only way, believe me! If I manage to build up the import business, I'll be free of all constraints. Free for you . . ."

His last words were like a warm breath on her face. *"Free for you . . ."*

They walked on in silence. Halensee Lake came into view. Hand in hand, without a word, as if it were the most ordinary thing in the world, they strolled to one of the benches by the lake. Adrian spread out his woolen scarf on the bench, and when they had sat down, he said, "I love you, Josephine."

"And I love you, too," she said.

It was a simple admission of what both had known for a long time.

"It's *you* I want to marry, not Isabelle!" Adrian went on, his voice heavy with emotion. "But I can only do that when I can provide for you as a man ought to. The moment my father finds out that I'm not willing to marry Isabelle, he'll throw me out of the company. I'll be left without a penny. I'd have nothing to offer you. Nothing. The only reason I'm going to America is for you . . . When I come back in the fall, I want to have something to show for myself."

Josephine frowned. *I love you.* She had been waiting for months to hear these words from him. And yet . . .

"I can provide for myself. You could help me in the workshop, we could expand it together—you would certainly not be penniless," she said proudly. "Why don't you just admit that you want to run away from all of the problems you have with your father? Why don't you admit that an adventure is more important to you than making a fresh start here, with your family?"

Adrian recoiled like a beaten dog, and Josephine immediately regretted her harsh words. "I'm sorry, that was cruel of me. I don't have any right to speak like that. But . . . it's because I don't want you to leave!" she cried desperately. "I'm scared for you. What if something were to happen to you on your travels? Without you . . . without you, I cannot imagine what my life would be like."

Adrian took her in his arms, and for a long moment each took pleasure in the warmth and closeness of the other.

"It's thanks to you that I even have the courage to undertake such a journey," Adrian murmured into her hair. "You were the one who showed me how important it is to follow one's own path, not to always heed what others say, but to follow one's own inner convictions. Maybe, in my place, you would act differently. But I have to follow this path that leads to America. It is my way."

Josephine nodded. What else could she possibly say to keep him there?

"I haven't told you everything yet," Adrian continued. "I'm going to take my bicycle with me and board a ship to New York in Hamburg. From New York, I'm going to cycle up to Boston to visit Pope. Once I've wrapped up negotiations there, I'm going to ride one of his machines down the East Coast to the South, then back up to New York. I'll be covering a good two thousand miles altogether." In his excitement, he shifted forward to the edge of the bench. "I'll be able to show the whole world that the bicycle is the best means of transport there is! Think of what I'll be able to tell my customers. It's an unbeatable sales pitch!" He laughed triumphantly.

"And you think you'll be back by autumn? You'll never manage that!" Josephine pulled free of his embrace. "Have you gone completely mad? Are you, too, giving in to this craze for doing everything bigger, faster, farther? The whole cycling world is being taken over by it! Didn't you read that article about the man who wanted to travel the world by bicycle and was murdered by highwaymen? America is a dangerous place, and . . ." At a loss for words, she waved her hands wildly in the air.

"Don't worry, I'll be careful. When I get to New York, I'll buy a revolver, then anyone who tries something stupid will get a dose of lead," said Adrian with a grin. He tried to pull her close again, but Josephine pushed him away.

"A revolver? Is that supposed to make me feel better?" she asked, her voice trembling. It took everything she had not to burst into tears. Taking a deep breath, she said, "Then I guess all I can do is wish you bon voyage." She smiled sadly.

"I'll think about you every day," he said quietly. "About you and about our future together."

His lips were soft, softer than she had imagined. All thoughts of America vanished as Josephine lost herself in Adrian's embrace.

\*\*\*

At the beginning of April, everyone gathered at the station to make Adrian's send-off a memorable one. The club members were all present, waving a large pennant embroidered with the words "Bon Voyage, Adrian!" Even Adrian's family had come to say good-bye to their son. Conspicuously absent, though, were Moritz Herrenhus and his wife. A brass band played a brisk marching tune, and it seemed everyone wanted to clap Adrian on the shoulder, shake his hand, or give him a piece of good advice. The mood was bright and animated, and a sense of adventure filled the air.

Josephine stood on the platform a little off to one side, watching the scene with mixed feelings. Had it been her words that had caused Adrian to come clean with his father?

The week before, Adrian had gone to his father and revealed to him that he was planning to travel to America, to try his luck over there.

"He took it remarkably calmly," Adrian had reported to Jo later. So, he wanted to prove himself. To build something of his own . . . He was more his father's son than he'd thought, old Neumann had said, then given Adrian an approving clap on the shoulder. When the old man had asked him what the story was with the wedding, Adrian had merely shrugged.

"Postponed or canceled, I don't care either way," his father had declared to his baffled son. Then he explained that he had paid back the loan from Moritz Herrenhus down to the last cent, and they owed the family nothing.

Adrian had been utterly mystified. "Why didn't you tell me that?"

Old Neumann had looked at him in surprise. "I thought you liked the girl!"

Adrian had said nothing about Josephine to his father. "Everything at the proper time," he told her.

Everything at the proper time? Josephine sighed deeply. What if his time ran out in America? Would Adrian return at all? Or would he find a new love over there? *Don't be so pessimistic!* she chided herself silently.

When Isabelle and Adrian embraced in a farewell, his eyes met Josephine's. A moment later, Adrian came over to her. When he held out his hand to her a little stiffly, Jo wanted to wrap her arms around him and never let him go.

"Never doubt my love for you," he whispered. "Don't worry about me, promise me that. I'll come back to you. And that will be the start of the rest of our lives." His voice was more intense than she had ever heard it.

All at once, Josephine's heart felt light. Everything would work out; she was sure of it!

"You're in big trouble if all you think of is the men, and you don't bring back a decent number of women's bicycles! I like to fix those the most," she said. "Now go, or your train will leave without you."

# Chapter Twenty-Six

Adrian arrived in New York after a largely uneventful nine-day crossing. He allowed himself two days to visit the city that the whole world seemed to be talking about. There were plenty of bicycles vying for the roads with the coachmen and horsemen, just as they did in Berlin. When Adrian finally set off for Boston, he drew a great deal of attention on his bicycle. He was often stopped by people who showered him with questions. Once, he was even interviewed by a newspaper reporter who'd been sent to write an article about the German on his bicycle. What a pity that he would probably never get to see the article himself, he thought with regret.

The streets were not as smooth as those back home, but he still made good progress. Because he was riding along the coast, he was frequently rewarded with sweeping views of the ocean. He spent the first two nights in simple hotels and dined on freshly caught fish grilled over an open fire. He arrived at the Pope Manufacturing Co. on the third day, having ridden more than two hundred miles.

Adrian was puzzled as he pushed his bicycle between two stone pillars. On the right, hanging by a loose nail, dangled the factory sign, so burned and blackened that only a few letters on it were still legible.

The gate itself—probably an artistically wrought affair once upon a time—was full of melted, misshapen blobs. Adrian stopped. He gripped the handlebars of his bicycle, feeling a rising panic as he tried to orient himself amid the enormous cloud of dust that hung over the site. Where were the huge warehouses, the offices? All he saw were mountains of rubble strewn with charred metal and scorched rubber. Adrian watched as dozens of men with dust-smeared faces and grim expressions loaded wheelbarrows with rubble one shovelful at a time, pushed them out to the road, and loaded the contents onto countless horse-drawn carts. The work was dirty and hard, and the men looked worn out.

When Adrian had more or less recovered from his shock, he stopped the next man to walk by. The man was wearing a dusty suit and had a notebook in his hand.

"Excuse me, sir, but . . . I wanted to visit the bicycle factory."

The man looked up at him. "Then you must be blind. The factory's gone," he said in a cold voice. "The fire destroyed everything back on March twelfth. Our warehouses, thousands of half-finished and complete bikes, our offices . . ." The man made a sweeping gesture with his hands. "All burned to the ground, down to the last receipt. There's nothing left, not a goddamned thing."

It would not have taken much for Adrian to burst into tears. *This* was what he had crossed the ocean for? But he pulled himself together. "I'm terribly sorry. It's just . . ." He briefly outlined his situation, then asked about other bicycle factories in the area.

"There are none. Nothing anywhere around here. Mr. Pope made quite sure the competition did not survive. Good luck to you, mister," the man said, though it sounded more like a taunt. Then he walked away.

Adrian pushed his bicycle back out between the pillars of the gate. He was about to hop on when someone beside him cleared his throat.

"Excuse me, sir . . ."

Adrian looked up.

"I overheard your conversation just now, as I rolled my wheelbarrow past. You're looking to buy bicycles?"

Adrian nodded. "In Germany, they say that the bicycles here are turned out more or less continuously, instead of being made by hand. And Pope's prices are apparently unbeatable. And now this!"

"It's a disaster! We were truly the fastest, the best, and the cheapest. I am . . . uh, I *was* an engineer here, but Lord knows where we go from here. Though for what you have in mind, would you settle for the second fastest, second best, and second cheapest bike manufacturer in the country?"

"Who . . . who do you mean?" Adrian held his breath. Had the blowhard with the notebook lied to him? Was there a second company somewhere around here?

"I'm a Chicago man. I worked in a bike factory there, too. It's called the Western Wheel Works. Pope poached me away from them, and look what happened. Had I not been swayed by his overtures and money, I'd still have a job to do, instead of . . ." The man sighed. "Anyway, the Crescent Bikes that the Western Wheel Works makes are just as good as Pope's. When I left the company, production was up to fifty thousand a year."

Adrian felt the seedling of hope growing in him again. "Western Wheel Works . . . Do you happen to know how much your old employer sold its Crescent Bikes for?"

"The depends entirely on how many you're willing to order. The more bicycles, the bigger the discount. That's how we do business in America! But on average, I think a Crescent'll set you back . . ." The man grinned and named a sum that was so low that Adrian nearly fainted from surprise.

"Chicago, you say?" He tried to place the city on his mental map of the United States. Wasn't that in Illinois? By a gigantic lake? He would have to ride halfway across the country, east to west . . .

That made no difference! Eager to get started, he looked at the man.

"Can you tell me which road I have to take to get to Chicago?"

The man frowned. "Which road? We've got roads here on the East Coast that connect the main trade centers. I guess they've got the same out west. But there *are* no roads that cross America!"

\*\*\*

**IMPORTANT: TO ALL CLUB MEMBERS**

**NEXT SATURDAY, SUSANNE LINDBERG WILL BE DELIVERING A TALK IN OUR CLUBROOMS. WE WOULD LIKE ALL MEMBERS TO BE PRESENT!**

Josephine turned from the poster to Isabelle. "Do you know this Susanne Lindberg?"

Isabelle shrugged. "Not personally. She's a well-known Danish cyclist."

"So what does she want by coming here? And what kind of talk is it?"

"How should I know?" replied Isabelle. "Ask Irene, she's the one who got in touch with her." Isabelle's mood soured at the thought of her former future sister-in-law. She had thought that their relationship would improve once her engagement to Adrian was off—after all, Irene had been against their relationship from the start—but Irene blamed Isabelle for Adrian's departure, claiming that Isabelle had driven him away with her moodiness—what a lot of rubbish!

"I think I'll go. A talk about cycling is always interesting," Josephine said, pulling Isabelle out of her ruminations.

It was Saturday afternoon. With the glorious summer weather, the racetrack was very busy. Though some of the men still grumbled about it, women and men had begun using the velodrome together, considerably extending the training times and opportunities for the women. But Josephine and Isabelle had spent the morning on a long cycling tour through the outskirts of Berlin. It had been Jo's idea to go out riding together again. Isabelle had only agreed after some hesitation, but she soon found herself greatly enjoying the ride. They had even decided to go out together more often. On their return, Isabelle had suggested that they pay a spontaneous visit to the clubhouse and treat themselves to a glass of lemonade. Jo had agreed, though she replied that she needed to go by her house first to pick something up. After their stop, they rode on to the track, with Josephine holding a long tube tucked under her arm.

"Frieda's world map. I think we'll get a lot more use out of it here," said Josephine, rolling out the map. She pinned it to the clubroom wall, then took the postcards that had been trickling in from Adrian and attached them beside the map.

Satisfied, Josephine stepped back and admired her handiwork. "Now we can plot Adrian's route based on where the postcards are from."

"I really don't know why you find all that so fascinating, but if you want to follow Adrian's route, then be my guest," Isabelle said.

"You could show a little interest. I know he isn't your fiancé anymore, but he's still a member of the club. And a trip like this isn't something that's done every day."

Isabelle waved dismissively. What did she care about Adrian's trip to America? She began leafing through a magazine on the table.

"Clara's charming husband is at it again. Listen to this one," she said and began to read aloud: "'Until just a few years ago, no decent woman left her house without a chaperone or male relative at her side. These days, however, we see viragoes cycling around utterly unescorted, and carrying on far-too-familiar acquaintanceships with the opposite sex. Where are these girls' parents, you ask? They are sitting back and watching as their darling daughters succumb to their sexual perversions. It is my view that such paragons of parenthood are themselves sick and in need of a proper upbringing!'"

"Sexual perversions?" Josephine cried. "The man's mad. The only perverse thing is him." She grabbed the magazine from Isabelle. "When Luise and Gertrude see this . . ."

Isabelle looked indifferently at her friend. While the others got terribly worked up every time such an article appeared, she just thought they were ridiculous. No sensible reader would give any credence to something like that; in fact, the doctors who wrote such diatribes degraded only themselves. Not a single one of them had come up with any proof for their scandalous claims.

As it was, she found it all very tiresome and boring. Much like her life. For a while, things had looked so promising. She had felt nothing but relief when Adrian had sailed away. Finally, she was free again! Isabelle loved once again being the center of attention at balls, receptions, and parties, and she flirted and danced her way through the nights.

Of course, the fact that Adrian had stood her up at the last moment was the subject of gossip wherever she went. But given her high spirits, she quickly took the wind out of the sails of anyone who tried to taunt her. They were forced to see that the jilted bride did not seem to be suffering overly.

Her father, on the other hand, had flown into a rage, screaming as he never had before, to the point where the servants had fled to their rooms and locked the doors. To the outside world, however, Moritz Herrenhus put on a brave face, going so far as to claim that he had always been skeptical of their engagement.

Thinking about her father's performance made Isabelle feel ill. She knew perfectly well that he was silently keeping a lookout for a new marriage candidate. Then the whole miserable game would start again.

"That's strange," Josephine murmured. "Adrian wanted to ride down the East Coast."

"So? Isn't he doing that?" asked Isabelle.

Josephine traced her finger over the world map. "Judging from his postcards, he's riding west. What do you suppose it means?"

The door opened and Isabelle was spared any conjecturing.

In the doorway stood a man whom Isabelle guessed to be in his midtwenties. His hair was dark brown and curly, and it hung rakishly over his shoulders and face. His eyes, too, were brown, and rimmed by thick eyelashes. He was remarkably handsome with an adventurous look to him . . . as if he would shrink from nothing and no one. He was of average height, with broad shoulders and powerful forearms and even more powerful cyclist's calves. The backpack he wore, and was just then removing, gave the impression that he'd just walked in from a long cycling journey. When he looked around inside the near-empty clubhouse, he almost turned around and left.

He was about to close the door behind him when Isabelle straightened up in her chair and asked so hastily that she nearly choked, "Can I help you?"

"I heard that Berlin was good for cycling," said the man in a dialect that she did not recognize. "My name is Leonard Feininger, but everybody calls me Leon. You might have heard of me."

*His voice sounds like warm honey,* thought Isabelle, instantly enraptured.

"Well here's someone who thinks a great deal of himself," Jo whispered in her ear as she joined Isabelle at the table.

Isabelle threw Jo a look that said, *Shouldn't you be doing something with your map?*

Leon Feininger . . . She had, in fact, heard the name before. She swept a lock of red hair out of her face and said, "You're in the right place! Our club is the best in Berlin. Our riders are represented in all the big races, mostly in the front ranks. We even have a very successful women's team." Oh God, what was she doing? She sounded like she was trying to impress him! She felt her cheeks flush. The man must think she was a silly fool.

"Ah, your own women's team. Just the two of you?" Leon Feininger raised his eyebrows and smiled.

Isabelle shook her head sheepishly.

"Of course not! There are a lot more of us," Josephine answered belligerently. "But just as it should be in a good cycling club, they're all out training. Which the two of us already have behind us for today, right, Isabelle?"

Isabelle, who had collected herself somewhat, looked at Leon's backpack. "You look like you've come a long way. Would you like to stay a short while?" She gestured toward the chair opposite her own. "Perhaps you'd like to tell me why I'm supposed to have heard of you over a cup of coffee." She gave him her most charming smile, together with a well-practiced bat of her eyelashes.

Leon Feininger didn't want coffee. He asked for a glass of red wine, which he sniffed at length before draining it in a single gulp. Only when he had a second glass in front of him did he begin to tell them about himself.

He was the son of a winemaker in the Rhineland-Palatinate region. But he had left the region because, as a sportsman, he saw no future for himself there. He had heard that in Berlin he'd find not only a lot of track racers but also many long-distance cyclists. He had come here with the intention of pitting himself against Berlin's best. He wanted to find—or perhaps *invent*—a new challenge there.

Isabelle hung on his every word, mesmerized. How the man could talk . . . Suddenly she saw in her mind's eye the photographs of a cyclist grinning at the camera, his bicycle held victoriously over his head.

"I know who you are!" she cried. "I read about you in a magazine! The writer called you the 'Hero of Road and Mountain.' You're . . ." She waved her hand in the air as if the words she was looking for were hovering there to be caught. "You're the one who rode his bicycle over the Alps to Italy. And . . . weren't you also the man who once rode from Vienna to Berlin in record time?"

"There wasn't just *one* article written about those rides. There were dozens." Leon smiled complacently. "But it's really no surprise. I did the Vienna to Berlin stretch in just under thirty-one hours, after all, which was less than half the time of the previous record holder, an officer on horseback."

"Really?" said Josephine, leaning closer. "That's very interesting. When was that?"

Isabelle felt like jabbing her friend in the ribs. "Didn't you want to go and visit Clara?" she hissed. Actually, they had planned to go visit the young mother together—it was a good time to pay a visit, because her horrible husband was away at a medical conference—but all thought of visiting Clara had vanished from Isabelle's mind. She turned back to her intoxicating guest.

"My last adventure—which was also covered in all the papers—was the race from Paris to Brest. I came in with the leading group."

"Paris to Brest," purred Isabelle breathlessly.

"And here I am. Seeking new adventures." Leon leaned forward across the table. Playfully, he took her hand and turned it so that he could look at the rings she wore. Isabelle returned the challenge in his eyes.

"Who knows? Maybe you've already found the first." She smiled like a cat lapping cream.

***

"You should have seen Isabelle. She was laughing like you wouldn't believe. She practically threw herself at the man. And the looks that flew between them! What was it I read in one of Frieda's novels? 'They sank into each other's gaze.'" Josephine frowned. "I've never seen Isabelle quite like that before."

"Sounds to me like they were falling in love," said Clara airily, covering her son in his bassinet with a pale-blue blanket. They took turns rocking the child.

"He's asleep, thank God," Clara whispered a little while later. They tiptoed out of the child's room into the sitting room next door, where Clara had set out everything for coffee.

"You look tired," said Josephine, pouring the coffee, which was by now completely cold. Clara let her do so without protest. The currant cake was soaked through and had taken on an unappetizing brown shade. Fruit flies swarmed around it. Jo flapped her hands to shoo the insects away. She had no appetite for it at all . . .

"I *am* tired! Matthias sleeps three hours a night, if that. He starts howling the moment he wakes up. I tried ignoring him at first, thinking he would eventually stop on his own. But Gerhard gets all in a huff as soon as Matthias starts crying, and he *does* need to sleep at night. So I have to hurry out and pick him up from his cradle as soon as he makes a peep. And because I'm so afraid of missing that first peep, I hardly get to close my eyes at all. It's not much better during the day, as you've just seen." Clara was unable to suppress a yawn.

Josephine nodded. She had arrived an hour earlier, and all they had done in that time was try to get the bawling child to sleep.

"Is it normal for a baby to cry so much? Your husband's a doctor. He should know what's going on with Matthias. Maybe he gets gassy? Or . . ." Jo shrugged helplessly. Babies weren't exactly her specialty.

Clara let out a bitter laugh. "Gerhard says it's my fault. I've passed my poor, nervous disposition on to Matthias. And he says I don't give Matthias enough motherly care." Fighting tears, she cried out, "I'm with my son day and night! What else can I possibly do?"

"Your poor, nervous disposition?" Jo frowned. "Your husband seems to have some very strange ideas, and not just where cyclists are concerned."

Clara took her hand. "Which makes me all the more grateful that you still come to visit. Believe me, I find Gerhard's newspaper articles to be a terrible embarrassment! But he won't stop writing them. The conference he's gone to in Bonn is all about the negative effects of cycling on women. He's really heading in the wrong direction."

"You could call it that," said Jo drily.

A long silence ensued. Jo looked around inside Clara's home. Everything looked as though it had come out of a doll's house: lace doilies, a silver tray, fresh flowers in a vase on the sideboard. A faint hint of lavender hung in the air, reminding Jo of the smell inside the pharmacy. Everything was clean. At least, far cleaner than her own home, where dust collected in the corners and cat hair covered the sofa. This was the kind of home where the signature of a good housewife could be read with ease. *So why do I feel so uncomfortable?* Josephine wondered. Was it the knowledge that Gerhard Gropius lived there? Or did it have more to do with the fact that Clara appeared to be anything but a happy young wife and mother?

It was Clara who broke the silence, asking in an affectedly cheerful voice, "So what are the other club members saying about your guest from Rhineland-Palatinate?"

"Everyone's thrilled to have him there. And no wonder. The man is a born storyteller. He has a wonderful smile, he's good looking . . . and he's amassed quite an impressive list of bicycle performances. Assuming, of course, that everything he says is true. But I think it probably is."

Clara smiled. "It sounds like you might be a little in love with the man yourself."

"Me? Not on your life!" Jo said, laughing. "Oh, he's perfectly nice. But I also think he's a devil-may-care guy who's mainly out for himself. When Isabelle asked him who was helping his parents with their vineyard in his absence, all he did was shrug. As if he didn't care at all."

"But in a family business like that, every hand is needed," said Clara. "It nearly makes me sick to see how my father has to slave away in the pharmacy on his own. I'd love to help him, but how?"

"Why don't you take on a nursemaid for Matthias? A girl from a big family who knows her way around a young child . . . That couldn't be so hard to find, could it?"

"Oh God, I can't imagine ever suggesting such a thing to Gerhard! He thinks it's a mother's duty to look after her children. Women who don't are bad mothers." Clara suddenly looked very unhappy. "Besides, I have all the housework to do. And the accounts for the practice. All of that comes first."

Josephine did not want to get into a fight with Clara, so she changed the subject. "I'll be very interested to see where things go with Isabelle and Leon."

Placing one hand on Josephine's arm, Clara said, "If it goes anywhere at all, give Isabelle a piece of advice from me. She should think hard about what she's doing. In the end, everyone has to sleep in the bed they've made for themselves."

# Chapter Twenty-Seven

"My dear colleagues, ladies and gentlemen, cyclists all, it is my very great pleasure to introduce the Danish professional cyclist, Susanne Lindberg!" Irene Neumann looked around at the assembled audience excitedly as everyone clapped.

It was good that Irene had insisted on holding Susanne Lindberg's talk in the generous rooms of the men's club, even though she was mainly there to speak to the women. Every seat was filled, and people were standing, crowding in at the edges of the room. Many men had decided to come along as well. Jo watched as Isabelle squeezed closer to Leon. Everyone at the club was gossiping about their dalliance.

"Susanne Lindberg is twenty-five years old and a member of the famed Danish Bicycle Club," said Irene. "She dropped her studies to devote herself entirely to cycling, which she has pursued with great success. She has ridden in practically every race there is, against male competitors. To list all of her successes would take far more time than we have tonight, but she is the true grande dame of women's cycling, and her successes have contributed tremendously to the greater general acceptance of our sport. Dear Susanne . . ." She waved her guest over to her on the improvised stage.

An attractive and petite young woman climbed up onto the podium. Josephine guessed that she weighed no more than a hundred pounds.

"Ladies and gentlemen, it is an honor to be able to speak to you here tonight," the woman began, speaking excellent German. She radiated enthusiasm and strength, and within moments, the entire audience was hanging on her every word.

"Both the First Berlin Cycling Club for Women and the original men's First Berlin Cycling Club enjoy a reputation second to none. The quality of your riders is known far beyond the borders of the German Empire."

The club members thanked her for the praise by rapping their knuckles against the tables.

"I know that no cyclist likes a long detour," said Susanne Lindberg and smiled conspiratorially at her audience, "so I will come straight to the point." She paused momentarily for effect and signaled to a man to come forward.

"I would like to introduce my fiancé, Charles Hansen. Some of you probably know him from cycling. He is currently involved with a study on behalf of the Danish government. The object of this study is the positive effects of sport on the human mind and body.

"As he began work on this study, Charles hit upon an idea that I fully support. More than support, in fact: I will be one hundred percent part of it!" Susanne Lindberg fixed her audience with a gaze that accepted neither objections nor questions. "Charles would like to organize a long-distance race for women, through Denmark, for the spring of 1897. With this race, we want to prove that women can ride bicycles at least as well as men. And we want to show that the female body does *not* suffer from riding a bicycle. On the contrary, our aim is to prove just what women are capable of!"

Now it was the turn of the women to applaud, while the men just frowned.

"That's brilliant!" Josephine cried. "We must do something like that here, too! That would take down all those hacks who rail against our sport a peg or two."

"How long is your long-distance course going to be?" Leon Feininger asked. "For me, long distance means at least in the realm of Paris to Brest and back to Paris, or Bordeaux to Paris. I don't suppose you can match that, can you?"

His remark was sure to draw a few approving laughs, and it did.

But the laughter stopped when Susanne said, "Our race will take us through Zealand, the largest island in Denmark, from one end to the other, twice. In total, we will cover six hundred miles over no more than four days, though I estimate we can complete the distance in three."

"Six hundred miles in three days?"

"Impossible . . ."

"On a bicycle?"

"A *women's* race?"

". . . never manage that . . ."

"That's something for men!"

Tumult broke out. Everyone began speaking at once. Josephine tried to think of the greatest distance she had covered on a bicycle. Sixty, perhaps seventy-five miles, riding at Adrian's side. Six hundred miles? What a challenge!

It was Irene who finally managed to bring the team back to order.

Then the petite Dane cleared her throat and went on in a quiet but determined voice, "We have a number of extremely talented women cyclists in Denmark these days. A handful of them have already assured me of their participation. But Charles and I would like to make this an international affair."

"So you're here to recruit a few good women to take part. Is that right?" said Isabelle.

Susanne Lindberg nodded.

"Six hundred miles. That's a very long way," Isabelle murmured respectfully.

"I'd say your plan is both daring and propitious," said Leon, though he sounded both dubious and confrontational. "But do you really have any idea what kind of willpower and endurance is necessary for such a distance?"

"Yes. As well as cold-bloodedness, foresight, and a huge amount of courage," Susanne Lindberg added. "Do you think we're beginners? I am well aware that many don't think we possess those qualities. We still struggle against many prejudices. Sometimes, it seems to me that cycling has become harder for us rather than easier." For the first time, her smile disappeared. But then she seemed to pull herself together. "It is all the more important, therefore, to show the world how strong women are!"

The applause came tentatively at first, then grew louder, and even some of the men joined in.

"This race will also send a very strong signal to the Association of German Cyclists," said Irene Neumann. "As you already know, that association is considering banning women's races across the entire empire."

Luise Karrer, who had been quiet until then, asked, "What about the press? Getting a few newspaper writers to accompany the race and report on it would make a huge difference. How else will the public ever hear about it?"

"We have excellent contacts in the Danish press," said Charles Hansen. "But it would naturally be good for the foreign riders to bring journalists of their own as well. A decent drawcard is usually enough to get them interested. Our drawcard is Susanne." He looked with immense pride at his fiancée. "A graceful young woman daring to attempt such a distance by bicycle is a worthy story to many writers."

"If *I* decide to join, then we can certainly count on loads of press," said Fadi Nandou, and all eyes turned to the beautiful Persian woman.

Susanne Lindberg raised her eyebrows meaningfully as she looked first into Fadi's kohl-ringed eyes, then at the rest of the assembly. "Allow me a word of warning: fame in itself is not enough to guarantee participation. Anyone who wants to take part in our race has to be able to demonstrate race experience and be willing to undertake the hardest training imaginable during the next six months. You will have to spend more hours on a bicycle than you ever have before. You will have to ride rain or shine, and you will have to get used to riding at night . . ."

A pleasant tingling spread through Josephine, something she hadn't felt for a long time. But many of her clubmates clearly thought differently, practically slumping in their seats as Susanne went through her list. It was obvious that they had not imagined it would be so difficult.

"We will sleep in simple accommodations, sometimes for only one or two hours in a cold barn. From a sanitary perspective, expect the most primitive conditions. A scoop of water from a well by the road will have to do for a quick splash." She looked intently into her audience. "And then there's the question of money. Every woman who takes part will have to bring her own bicycle with her, along with suitable equipment and proper clothes. We will send out a clothing guide well in advance of the race. It is, of course, very important that the public be well-disposed toward us. Every participant will also be required to pay for her own travel expenses. Charles will cover the cost of the first night's accommodation in Copenhagen, as well as all meals during the race."

"How does a race like that work?" asked Isabelle. "I mean, does everyone ride in one group? And what about the route itself? Would we be riding on good roads the whole way, or riding over sticks and stones?"

Susanne raised her voice. "Why don't we let one of the men with long-distance experience tell us what it's like. Leon?"

Leon didn't need to be asked twice. "A long-distance race is fundamentally different from short road or track races," he began. "For one thing, it takes place alongside all the usual traffic on the roads. The stretch is not closed as it would be for other races, which means that each rider is responsible for his own safety. And part of the route will naturally cross rough terrain, as well. Although riders all start together, the field soon drifts apart so that each rider rides alone. Usually, small groups form and ride short sections together. But at the end of the day, each rider has to ride the race for himself. That means that each competitor has to decide how long he will ride at a stretch, as well as when he will take a break to eat, drink, and take care of any other business."

A few laughed, but Leon went on immediately. "Good physical condition is one thing. But dividing the race up intelligently into riding and resting periods, that's the true art. And then there's the question of sleep: When and for how long? What if you're exhausted and sleep for five or even eight hours? Absurd in a race like that. Which is why there are riders—and I do not lie when I say I am one of them—who ride Paris to Brest and back to Paris without sleeping at all!"

"You ride the whole way without a break?" said Isabelle, awestruck.

Irene snorted. Isabelle's adoration of Leon had not escaped her.

"I take breaks, definitely, but I don't sleep," Leon corrected her.

Josephine frowned. "It all sounds very exciting. But I'm still not clear on one thing: If the route isn't marked and each rider rides on her own, how do you find your way? Especially in a foreign country . . ."

"The route is detailed in a small booklet that also contains the names of the towns and checkpoints where you have to report."

"Report? What for?" asked Isabelle.

"Somebody has to check that you've actually ridden the course you're supposed to! Or some wise guy would come up with the idea of taking a shortcut and saving himself a few miles. At every checkpoint, you get a stamp in your booklet. The race is only over when that's complete." He turned to look at Charles Hansen. "Are you planning to set up food stations at the checkpoints?"

Charles nodded. "We'll have hot soup, drinks, and cakes on hand about every hundred and twenty miles."

"A lot can happen to a person and a machine over six hundred miles," said Josephine. "Do you have a doctor and a mechanic on hand?" If she were to take part, she would know what to do if her bicycle broke down. But would the others?

Susanne Lindberg said no, then asked, "Do you know somebody?"

"Perhaps." Josephine shrugged casually, but inside she was suddenly brimming with excitement. Gerd Melchior would be just the man for repairs! She would write him a letter that same evening. No doubt he'd be very happy to see something other than prison bars for a change.

Luise Karrer twisted her mouth and said, "We can ask Dr. Gerhard Gropius if he'd like to come along."

"We could certainly ask his wife," said Isabelle when the laughter had died down. "When Clara used to ride with us, she always had bandages and ointments handy, remember, Jo? As a chemist's daughter, she knows her way around cuts and grazes."

Josephine sighed. "There's just one catch: Gerhard Gropius would *never* allow his wife to go to Denmark with us."

When the talk was over, Jo went over to one of the windows and inhaled the sweet summer air. She closed her eyes for a moment and shut out the excited voices of her clubmates. Her mind grew calm.

Should she? Or not? It was so tempting . . . Since Adrian's departure, her life consisted of nothing but work and cycling. But here was the prospect of something truly exciting!

She had the money to pay for it. And as long as Adrian was away in America, she had enough time to train. If he came back in late autumn, he would even be able to help her with that.

Josephine turned back to the people in the room. She took a deep breath, then said in a loud voice, "Well, if you can use me . . . I would like to come along."

The individual conversations ceased, and all eyes turned to Jo, the first woman to pledge her participation.

"I would probably join you, too," said Isabelle slowly, and she exchanged a look with Leon.

"Do you happen to need a capable male rider, too?" Leon asked.

Lindberg and Hansen both nodded, then said they would need not only *one* man, but several, as protective chaperones for the women. Charles Hansen, in particular, was excited at the prospect of the famous Leon Feininger joining them for the race.

"I'll ride, too," said Irene.

"But not without me!" Luise shouted. Everyone laughed.

Susanne Lindberg smiled. "Charles and I will have to speak with each of you individually, of course. But if those interviews go well—and I'm sure they will—then we've got three, no, four German women coming along, which is excellent!"

"Would you let a fifth rider take part?" said Jo. "I have someone in mind who would be more than suitable for something like this."

"I know exactly who you mean," cried Isabelle brightly. Spontaneously, she threw her arms around Jo's neck and pressed a kiss to her cheek. "What a brilliant idea!"

On a signal from Irene, the club manager began to distribute glasses of sparkling wine. When everyone had a glass, Susanne raised her voice. "Here's to our great adventure!"

"Here's to six hundred miles through Denmark!" Charles Hansen called.

"Here's to us!" said Leon.

Josephine took a sip of sparkling wine, and the tiny bubbles prickled pleasantly on her tongue. Who would have thought that one talk could have such far-reaching effects?

# Chapter Twenty-Eight

Roads made of nothing more than slippery clay that clogged his spokes and brought his wheels to a standstill. Prairies where his bicycle sank so deeply into sand that he had no choice but to dismount and push his bicycle for miles.

Parched landscapes where the only things that grew were thorn bushes. In one day, he had to patch his front tire three times because of the needle-sharp barbs.

Deep gorges where no daylight penetrated and the sound of his wheels on the dry riverbed echoed ominously off the bare rock walls.

Roads littered with human waste and animal bones, rutted stretches dotted with twisted sheets of iron, smashed bricks, and broken glass.

A few miles outside of one town, the street disappeared into nothing. Though the land was crisscrossed with thousands of miles of rails for trains, the road system hobbled along far behind Europe. Often, Adrian had no choice but to ride along the railway embankments and hope that he would be fast enough to dodge approaching trains.

He carried a dog whip, which he had to use zealously to keep stray dogs and packs of coyotes at bay.

Around Pittsburgh, the air was black from coal dust, and breathing made his lungs burn; the fine grit settled in his eyes and filled every pore. Just before Cleveland, he rode into a plague of locusts, the air turning dark with the chirping, prehistoric-looking insects that greedily ate the land around them bare. Adrian had pedaled on quickly, not only to escape the locusts, but also the devastation on the faces of the farmers, who could only stand and watch as a year's work was destroyed in a matter of hours.

Once, he got caught in a wildfire, and he pedaled like never before in his life. He was able to escape the raging flames, but his skin was red and swollen from the heat for days afterward.

The journey from Boston to Chicago took him from May until the start of September. Luckily, he had kept his health and not suffered any serious accidents along the way.

He had met Americans who had outdone each other with their hospitality, had passed through towns where he had drawn a crowd in minutes, everyone wanting to know *everything* about his great journey. People had bought him beer, and they had served him hot chili beans and deliciously spiced steaks that had been grilled over an open fire.

He had also encountered Americans who had set their dogs on him. One farmer had aimed a shotgun at him and growled, "Git off my land." Adrian was only too happy to do so. But that was the gravest threat he had faced.

America. What a huge, crazy country.

Now he had ridden almost twelve hundred miles, and Lake Michigan lay blue and glittering before him in the cold autumn light. On the shores of the lake, Chicago spread its wings, its many-storied buildings looming skyward. An icy wind nearly blew him off his bicycle, and his bicycle lamp swung wildly from left to right as he pedaled along Wells Street, which led him into the very heart of Chicago. He could not stop grinning.

He had done it! He had reached his goal.

*

He dismounted in front of the Hotel Victoria, which was owned by a German man who told Adrian where to go buy some decent clothes and food, and where the best whores in the city were to be found. Adrian thanked him for all his tips, but he waved off the last one with a laugh. He had other things in mind!

The tailor Adrian went to visit was German as well. As he was fitted for a pair of pants, they got to talking, and Adrian explained his goal of visiting Western Wheel Works and importing bicycles to Germany.

"Oh, I know the owner of WWW well. Adolph Schoeninger. We're both in the German-American Society. He's got a reputation as a hard-nosed businessman, and it's true that he runs his factory with a strict hand, but he's a fair man. A handshake means as much as the written word. That's people from Württemberg for you."

"He's from Württemberg?" Adrian stared at the tailor in surprise.

"You didn't know that? You've come all this way just to buy bicycles from a countryman."

Despite his hunger, Adrian denied himself the luxury of a long lunch. He wolfed down a frankfurter from a stand, then climbed aboard one of the city's many trams, eager to pay a visit to Adolph Schoeninger as soon as he could.

He gazed out at the city from his seat as it passed by. There were bicycles everywhere! Young men, older men, elegant women, maids in plain uniforms, children, top-hatted gentlemen, and gentlemen with nothing covering their heads at all—all riding along as though it were the most natural thing in the world.

Chicago was a boomtown in every sense, the tailor had told him. Now Adrian knew what he had meant by that. The energy the city and its inhabitants radiated was so powerful that Adrian caught it like a contagious disease. When the huge sign reading "Western Wheel Works & Crescent Bikes" came into view, he leaped out of his seat.


"How many bicycles did you have in mind?" Adolph Schoeninger waved over a foreman and shouted something in his ear so quickly in English that Adrian didn't understand a word. The man immediately ran over to a gigantic machine and began frantically turning various knobs. An octopus-like arm that had been lowering to a table and rising again stopped in midair.

"I'm not sure," Adrian yelled back as he looked wide-eyed around the factory. Many of the machines were completely new to him and looked to have been specially built for manufacturing bicycles. The noise from the countless sheet-metal presses and stampers was deafening. All around them, at long rows of tables and using smaller machines, men were hard at work bolting, welding, assembling. Adrian estimated there were several hundred of them.

Schoeninger said, "I've currently got about six hundred workers here, in two shifts. But I'm always searching for new hands. Last year we produced sixty thousand bicycles. This year, I want to increase that by another ten thousand. To do that, I need good men."

Adrian was speechless.

"Americans are mad about bicycles. Everyone wants one. Someday, the roads of America will be so full of wheels that no one will be able to get through," said Schoeninger with a grin. "And we export on a large scale, too," he went on. "To France, Denmark, most recently to Sweden. And to Germany, of course. But don't worry, I don't have an importer in Berlin yet," he added, when he saw the panic on Adrian's face. "You should know that we look for only *one* wholesaler for each sales region. That wholesaler then sells our bikes to individual customers and to subdealers."

Adrian relaxed. These were things he understood! In Schoeninger's office, they got down to the details: prices, delivery times, terms of payment. The financing was in place; Adrian had organized a loan with EWB's bank before he left. The bank's senior director had been far from convinced by Adrian's "bicycles for all" concept, but his son, who was also the junior director, had shown a great deal of enthusiasm for the idea.

With financing assured and given the mutual goodwill each man felt for the other, a contract was quickly signed, and Adrian Neumann soon became the licensed wholesaler for Crescent Bikes for Berlin and its environs. They'd start with two thousand bicycles at a converted price of fifty marks per bicycle. The numbers made Adrian a little dizzy. If his vision turned out to be wrong, he'd find himself sitting on a mountain of Crescent Bikes and in debt for the rest of his life.

Adolph Schoeninger swept aside his doubts with a flick of a wrist. "If the Germans are even half as mad about bikes as the Americans, you have nothing to worry about. Do the math!" he challenged Adrian. "At a hundred sales a month, you'll have sold twelve hundred in the first year alone. You sell the rest to subdealers. Believe me, you'd only regret a smaller order."

They agreed to a first delivery in March 1897. That was fine with Adrian, as long as the first bicycles arrived for the start of the following season.

The two men parted like old friends. Schoeninger presented Adrian with a factory-new bicycle, which Adrian gladly accepted. His old machine was so worn out after its long cross-country journey that the only person who'd be pleased to see it now would be a Chicago scrap dealer.

Adrian could hardly wait to try out his new bike. Schoeninger had assured him that the roads from Chicago to Indianapolis were good. And from Indianapolis he could take the train back to New York in style.

That same evening, he marched into the telegraph office. To the man on duty, who turned out *not* to be German, Adrian dictated:

*All well. Assignment completed successfully. Looking forward to getting home and to the future. Adrian.*

The addressee was Miss Josephine Schmied, Görlitzer Strasse 27, Berlin, Germany.


Adrian stood helplessly beside his bicycle. An hour earlier, he had passed a tree on which had been nailed a roughly hewn sign that read "Lafayette, 12 miles." He should have reached the town by now. Had he taken a wrong turn? Tired from riding into a constant headwind, he pedaled on.

He was not, he knew, concentrating as well as he should have been. He had had difficulty focusing on the road ever since leaving Chicago. His mind was spinning with plans for the future.

Soon, he could only vaguely make out the road in front. But there was no trace of a town anywhere. Hadn't he seen that barn before? He sensed he was riding in circles.

Adrian stopped and lit his lamp. His senses were much sharper than they had been during the day. Every sound in the bushes startled him, and he began breathing faster. He squinted to see better. The road widened a little, then curved. Some way ahead he could see a farmhouse, or perhaps just the ruins of a farmhouse, like so many he had passed. He jumped when he heard a rustling noise behind him. But when he turned around, he saw nothing. *Don't start imagining things!* he admonished himself and pedaled faster. Just beyond that little clearing in the woods up ahead, he might—

There were three of them. Evil-looking men with hard faces, ragged clothes, and a demeanor that made it clear they had nothing to lose.

Two of them jumped out of the spiky bushes and onto the road in front of Adrian, blocking his path. The third came out behind him. Adrian was trapped.

"Money, watch—give me everything you have!" one of the men said, waving a rifle in Adrian's face.

Adrian pulled his watch from his wrist and handed it over. He could only stand and look on, his heart hammering in his chest. The men stank of whiskey. Oh God . . .

The leader felt the leather wristband of the watch, which had grown limp with wear. "Not good," he said. "Gold! Give me your gold watch!"

"I don't have a gold watch!" said Adrian. "Here, my money . . ." With shaking hands, he took out his wallet, and in a move that was both courageous and contemptuous, he tossed it at the men's feet. There wasn't much left in it, anyway. He'd have more money wired from Germany when he got to Indianapolis.

As the man who had taken the watch from him bent down to pick up the wallet, the other two laughed and said something in a slang that Adrian didn't understand.

It was now or never! Adrian took advantage of the moment to make his escape. He took off, pedaling madly, heedless of everything except getting away. But he had to get off the street. He swerved into the bushes. Thorny branches whipped him in the face. One scratched his left eye, but he kept going. A moment later, he was riding across an open field. If only he knew where to go next . . . He could hear the heavy steps of the men some distance behind him. Adrian pedaled even harder.

The shot came without warning and hit him in the back of his left knee. His leg was knocked off the pedal, and he fell backward over his rear wheel. He landed on his back on something hard, a rock or a branch.

Then he passed out.

# Chapter Twenty-Nine

"Ow, you stuck me!" Isabelle spun around as if she'd been bitten by a tarantula, not jabbed with a pin.

Josephine sighed as she took one of the pins she was holding between her lips and attached a large pocket to the back of Isabelle's jacket. When she was finished, she pulled over a kitchen chair and asked Isabelle to sit down and lean forward.

"All right, imagine that you're sitting on your bicycle. Put both hands out in front of you. Now reach back with one hand and try to reach the button on the pocket."

"No problem," said Isabelle with a shrug. "Look, I can even close it again with one hand." She jumped up and gave Josephine in quick kiss on the cheek. "You're a treasure! The jacket's just perfect. I can fit a sandwich in the pocket, with a bit of fruit and some chocolate, and then we can eat whenever we want, without having to get off. We'll have the best cycling clothes of them all!"

Jo beamed. "Don't forget the two breast pockets I sewed on. You can stuff a handkerchief and a few caramels in those. A backpack would restrict you a great deal more, so this will give us a real advantage."

Each of the women competing in the race was to wear a discreet riding outfit. Susanne Lindberg had explained that each rider would have to supply a pair of dark-colored bloomers for herself, as well as a jacket in dark blue, black, or gray. A red scarf around their necks would identify them as participants in the six-hundred-mile race. Charles Hansen would hand out the scarves to every participant in Copenhagen. When Josephine asked if they would be allowed to wear pants instead of bloomers, Susanne Lindberg had told her no. They did not want to shock the Danish country people unnecessarily. It was most important that they leave a good impression wherever they went.

Jo could not object to that.

Still, if she had to wear bloomers and a jacket, then she would make them as practical as possible. Because they had been unable to find anything suitable in the catalogs, she had decided to modify standard items of clothing to suit her needs. She bought herself a sewing machine at Reutter's Emporium and went to work, adding pockets, a buttonhole in the cuffs, and a button at the elbow. Now she could easily roll up the sleeve of her jacket, push the button through the buttonhole, and turn it into a short-sleeved jacket. For the bloomers, she had sewn a wide belt of thin but flexible waterproof leather, with a hidden pocket for important documents. That way, neither sweat nor rain could damage them. When Isabelle saw Jo's practical riding outfit, she absolutely had to have the same thing, so Jo set to work on a second set of clothes.

But when Isabelle then said to her, "Look . . . do you think you could also modify Leon's things?" Jo had had enough.

"I am *not* a seamstress! Besides, your Leon is such a vain piece of work that nothing I do would be good enough," she replied, more harshly that she intended.

Instead of getting huffy, Isabelle laughed. "My dear, sweet Leon certainly has a sense of style. The best is only just good enough for him, and he knows exactly what suits him and what doesn't. I have never met a man with such unerringly good taste." Her eyes had taken on a dreamy look, and she let out an adoring sigh. "But why should that surprise us? He comes from a large wine-growing estate, after all. His family's roots go back hundreds of years, and they're deeply connected to their traditions. My God, you can't compare Leon to the pale fellows around here. He's in a class all his own."

Josephine did not even have a chance to protest, because Isabelle went on.

"His family live like the landed gentry in England. I could listen for hours to his stories about the harvest, when everyone pitches in to gather the grapes into the big presses. And then there are the traditional feasts, when all the villagers sit together at long tables and eat and drink and celebrate." She sighed longingly. "Oh, I would love to see it all with my own eyes one day."

Jo furrowed her brow. "A city girl like you out in the country? It wouldn't be fun for long. I admit I don't know much about rural life, but when I was down in the Black Forest, all the farmers I saw worked hard. Slogging away in their fields from dawn till dusk, first afraid that a cold spell in spring would freeze the buds on the fruit trees, then fearing thunderstorms and hail in summer. A farmer's life is no bed of roses, I'm sure of that!"

"Leon's family lives in Rhineland-Palatinate, not in the Black Forest. And everything in Rhineland-Palatinate is much better and nicer. Besides, I can scarcely believe that the family personally slogs away, as you put it, in the vineyard from dawn till dusk. That's what you employ other people to do," Isabelle said haughtily.

Josephine dropped the subject. She went to the oven and took out the baked potatoes she had put in an hour earlier. Jo sprinkled them with a few herbs that she had picked in summer in Frieda's garden and dried in the garden shed. They smelled irresistible.

"My mouth is already watering."

While Jo put the potatoes onto two plates, she said over her shoulder. "Leon this, Leon that . . . Don't you worry that it's all moving too quickly? You hardly even know the man. Your father would never agree to your marrying him, would he?" She thought of what Clara had said about having to sleep in the bed you had made. But she had no desire to sound older than her years just then.

"You're starting to sound like Irene," said Isabelle. "She doesn't like the idea of me seeing Leon, either. Last weekend, she said to me, 'The moment Adrian leaves, you throw yourself at the next one!' Outrageous, isn't it?"

Josephine gave a neutral shrug. Actually, Irene wasn't that far off . . .

"She's just very loyal to her brother. That's a good thing," Jo said. "Maybe she's worried that you're so in love that you'll neglect your training. We've all got a big goal ahead of us, after all."

"Has it ever occurred to you that love can give you wings?" Isabelle asked, beaming at Josephine over the top of her plate. "Oh, Jo, you overthink these things. You know, when you're in love—no, I'll put it another way—when you *love*, the world suddenly looks completely different. It looks fresh and rosy, like it is covered in icing. All will turn out for the best. I'm sure of it. In the spring we'll ride in a grand race and show the entire world what we women can do. And as far as Leon and I are concerned—everything will work out there, too." She patted Jo's hand patronizingly. "Just wait. The first time you feel Cupid's arrow, you'll know where my optimism comes from."

*If you only knew,* thought Josephine. When Adrian's telegram had arrived two days earlier, she could have hugged everyone in Berlin!

*All well. Assignment completed successfully. Looking forward to getting home and to the future. Adrian.*

"You're right," Jo said in a soft voice. "I'm sure everything will be fine. I certainly want it to be."

They had just finished eating when there was a knock at the door. It was the postman with another telegram.

"From Adrian? For *you*? Why doesn't he write to the club? And why a telegram? Why not a postcard?" Isabelle was aflutter with questions.

"I don't know," Jo murmured, embarrassed. "Maybe because I'm always at home and can receive it . . ." She would have liked to put the telegram aside and wait until Isabelle had left to read it. But there was no way to do that. With shaking hands, Josephine tore open the envelope.

Before she knew what happened, Isabelle had snatched the envelope out of her hands.

"Let's see what Mr. Ride-Across-America has to report!" A moment later, she let the thin sheet of paper drop, her face white as chalk.

"Oh God . . ."

\*\*\*

The news spread like wildfire among the club members: a robbery on a lonely back road. A bullet wound. One knee badly injured. And he'd been on his way home! It was a stroke of luck that a family of farmers who'd lost their way found him late that same night. They had loaded him onto their cart and pulled him all the way to a hospital in Chicago, where his wounded knee had finally been seen by a doctor. There was no way that he would be able to travel again for a while.

A knee injury. Exasperating, certainly, but he was lucky nothing worse had happened. That, at least, was the prevailing opinion in the club. Outwardly, Josephine agreed, but that was only one among many feelings swirling inside her just then. How bad was the knee injury? Why didn't Adrian just get them to bandage it and take the next train to New York? Was he in too much pain? And if he was, what were the doctors doing about it? When would he be fit to travel again?

She wanted to write to him but didn't even know what hospital he was in. Long, newsy letters would have helped him pass the time and lifted his spirits. But as it was, she had no choice but to send good thoughts his way and hope that, somehow, they arrived.

She missed him terribly. With every day he was gone, her desire to see him grew stronger. She had so much to tell him. Even just telling him about her training regime would take hours.

Every morning at five o'clock, she set off for a two-hour ride through the waking city in the dull light of the gas lanterns. She used every incline she could find to train for climbing Danish hills, and she practiced high-speed cycling on the wide, flat boulevards. Unfortunately, she would have to wait until spring for it to be light enough to ride out into the country again.

After that first training session, she freshened up at home and ate a bracing breakfast. Susanne had emphasized how important it was to eat a healthy diet. Then she went into her workshop and worked there until at least six in the evening. She had more than enough work to keep her busy: many cyclists who only went out riding in the warmer months took their bicycles to her for routine maintenance and cleaning. She enjoyed the work, but it was also hard and tiring. Instead of falling into a lazy heap after work—which she often felt like doing—her next training session would call. Some days went better than others. According to Susanne, regular endurance training was vital. Six hundred miles by bicycle was no trivial undertaking. You needed to be in outstanding condition just to finish. And that condition only came from a thousand and one hours on a bicycle.

On Saturdays and Sundays, the club members who planned to go to Denmark took longer rides together. Jo used the group rides to discreetly observe the physical condition of the others. When it came to sheer hours spent on the bicycle, Isabelle and Luise had a clear advantage: neither worked, so they could ride for as long as they liked. Irene, however, had been working in her father's company since Adrian had left. Josephine had found her much more likeable since then. And no matter how hard they trained—whether it was raining buckets or so gusty that an icy east wind nearly blew them off the road—Irene almost never complained.

Josephine would have told Adrian all these things and more if she had had an address to write to. But instead she had to make do with putting a candle in the window on Christmas Eve. She leaned the postcard that he had sent her against the candle. On the front, in large, curved letters, were the words "Merry Christmas" with a sprig of mistletoe underneath, decorated with silver glitter. The card was beautiful, but Josephine cared more about the words on the back. "All will be well, even if it takes a little longer." Not exactly a grand declaration of his love, but Adrian knew that various club members came and went from Josephine's house, and the card could end up in a stranger's hands at any time. *All will be well, even if it takes a little longer*—for Josephine, those words sounded more beautiful than any Christmas bells.

\*\*\*

In February, Isabelle came down with a terrible cold after getting caught in a snowstorm. Exhausted and fed up, she was restricted to her room with no chance to see Leon.

After a week of reading magazines and consuming broth, she felt overcome by her desire to see him. Still pale and weak, she pulled on a warm jacket, ordered a cab, and went to the club. When Leon saw her, he rode over to the side of the track and jumped off his bicycle.

How sweet his lips were! Isabelle could have stayed in his embrace forever. But she had something important to tell him.

They walked into the clubhouse hand in hand, where Isabelle announced to the rest of the assembled team, "I've had it with the grind. I'm out. The stupid race can go to hell!"

Of course, Josephine, Luise, and even Irene tried to change her mind, and many others gave her good advice for how to make the training palatable again. But Isabelle simply shook her head to all of it. She didn't give a damn what the others thought of her. She was fed up.

But what she had not counted on was Leon's reaction. The man who otherwise took everything he encountered with enviable nonchalance, the man who had proved unflappable until that point, took her firmly by the arm and dragged her out of the building.

"How can you throw away our great adventure, just like that? You and me, six hundred miles together, on the road . . . Doesn't that mean anything to you? I thought you loved me!"

"My decision has nothing to do with our love. I'm just exhausted by the eternal drills! I feel sick just thinking about getting on a bicycle. Sweetheart, please, you have to understand."

Leon shook his head. "I understand nothing. Especially that you think of training as a drill. Don't you have a friend who's a pharmacist's daughter? Why don't you get a few things from her that will make the riding easier? That's what Veit and I do. And all the others who ride long distances."

"Do you mean coca or kola? Doping stuff?" Isabelle frowned. "Irene says it's dangerous garbage."

"Irene!" Leon made a dismissive gesture. "What does she know? Did I ride seven hundred and fifty miles from Paris to Brest and back, or did she? Who do you believe? Your boring clubmate or me, one of Europe's most experienced and successful long-distance cyclists?" He led her to one of the benches set up beside the track and sat her down.

"Have you ever heard of Otto Ekarius?"

Isabelle shook her head. At least Leon no longer appeared as upset as he had two minutes earlier.

"Ekarius works as a doctor in Alsace. God knows what made him start investigating the effects of exotic plants like kola and coca. Maybe his soldiers needed a little pepping up," he laughed. "In any case, Ekarius created several preparations from the kola nut and coca leaves, and many good pharmacies sell them. A sip of juice, a few small pills, and you'll feel better than you've felt for a long time. You're capable of doing things that you would never have believed you could do. Fatigue all but disappears, and you practically have to force yourself to stop! Take it from me: it's not some witches' brew. It's a gift from heaven. Here, try it now." He held out a hand to her.

Isabelle stared uncertainly at the white tablets in his palm. Was that the solution she was looking for?

"But what's the point? What use is it to me if I take those? There's no way we'll have anything like that in Denmark, and then what?"

"We'll see," replied Leon in an easy tone. "Besides, now is now and later is later. Go ahead. Try it. You're not normally such a chicken!" He laughed mockingly. "Or have I been wrong about you?"

Isabelle took five of the tablets and tossed them all into her mouth. They tasted slightly bitter and were hard to swallow.

"What now?"

Leon grinned. "Now we ride. What else?"

# Chapter Thirty

May 1, 1897, was a very special day. At least for the five young women gathered at the train station who were about to embark on the adventure of their lives: Josephine, Isabelle, Irene, Luise, and Lilo, who had arrived in Berlin at the start of March to train with the others.

Unlike her father, Lilo had never held it against Josephine that she had inherited Frieda's house. She had instead congratulated her friend on her good fortune. Lilo's life had changed a great deal over the last few years. Shortly after starting her apprenticeship to become a nurse in the newly built luxury sanatorium in Schömberg, she had fallen in love with the sanatorium's owner. They married a short time later, and Lilo became a well-to-do wife with enough time to pursue her own interests, which, of course, included cycling. She had taken part in a six-day race in Paris a couple of years before, and a year later, when women's racing was banned in Germany, she participated in the first official world championships for women in Austria. Her husband cheerfully funded Lilo's passion for cycling, going so far as to dedicate an entire wall of the sanatorium's dining hall to her sporting successes. The collection of newspaper articles, entry forms, trophies, and cycling memorabilia had grown year after year. So it was no surprise that Josephine had asked Lilo to take part in the Denmark race.

When Susanne Lindberg heard who the fifth German rider would be, she was thrilled. Lilo Ofterschwang was known throughout Europe as a highly experienced and consistently fair sportswoman.

Family, friends, husbands, and clubmates had all come to send off the women. There were even a few reporters, though that was mainly because Leon Feininger and Veit Merz were riding as well.

The only person missing was Adrian Neumann. It seemed that new complications with his knee injury had prolonged his stay in America.

"Watch out, that's valuable freight you've got there!" Isabelle shouted at one of the porters assigned to load the bicycles onto the train.

She threw her arms companionably around Josephine's and Lilo's shoulders.

"We're off! Finally! Isn't it fantastic?"

Lilo nodded. "Now we'll find out if all our training's been worth it."

"And you nearly missed it," said Josephine, giving Isabelle a friendly shove. "Lucky that Leon was able to persuade you to keep going."

"Actually, we should thank Dr. Ekarius for his help in getting Isabelle to stick with it," said Leon with a grin.

The others looked confused, unfamiliar with the name of the doctor.

Lilo held up a leather satchel. "Just in case anyone gets hungry on the trip . . . I had a delicatessen make us a few nice morsels."

"I hope it's healthy. Otherwise Susanne won't be pleased," said Josephine with a smirk.

Lilo shrugged. "Duck foie gras and a glass of sparkling wine. Can you think of any better sports food?"

Laughter rang out all around her.

*

Clara stood a little apart, rolling the baby carriage back and forth as she listened to the excited banter.

Josephine, Isabelle, and Lilo—the cloverleaf. They got on so well together. She had once been one of them—part of a four-leaf clover. A feeling of fury and sadness crept over her—not for the first time—and she felt a keen sense of loss.

Why was Gerhard so preoccupied with women riding bicycles? Couldn't he find something else to spend his energies on? There were so many social ills: the high mortality rate among children in the workers' districts, for example. Or the catastrophic conditions in some of Berlin's hospitals, where overworked doctors and too few staff members barely kept things from descending into chaos. Why didn't Gerhard throw himself into the fray against such deplorable—but real—problems, instead of his never-ending witch hunt against women cyclists? Clara couldn't listen to his droning sermons anymore. He had absolutely forbidden her from having any sort of contact with Josephine and Isabelle. He called them the "businessman's tramp" and the "workshop slattern." If he had known that she was here to see the cyclists off at the station, all hell would have broken loose!

She felt fortunate that Gerhard had told her he'd be having lunch with a colleague that day. Just minutes after he had left the house, she had grabbed the carriage and hurried off with Matthias.

A brass band struck up a march, and Clara looked anxiously into the carriage, hoping the music would not wake her boy. But Matthias went on sleeping peacefully.

Matthias. Her darling. He was all that mattered. He needed her. And Gerhard needed her, too. How could she forget that even for a moment? Clara took a deep breath, then stepped forward lightheartedly to join the gathered women.

"Here, I brought a few things for all of you! Ointment for grazes and a few bandages, just in case. And some cough drops and peppermints." She handed the package to Josephine with a smile.

"I fear we're going to need all of it. Thank you!" Josephine handed the package to Lilo, then threw her arms around Clara. "Keep your fingers crossed for us, won't you?"

"Of course! You've got to show everyone what we women can do, after all," said Clara, her voice breaking with her tears.

\*\*\*

It was his cologne. A whiff of it mixed with the odor of disinfectant in the hallway. Gerhard was there. For whatever reason, he had not gone to have lunch with his colleague. Clara picked up her son from his carriage and stepped inside.

\*\*\*

The closer he got to Berlin, the more excited Adrian became. Soon! Soon he would have done it!

When he had begun the journey home the previous autumn, he never would have believed that it would take him so long. Now, his first shipment of bicycles had actually arrived in Germany ahead of him. His father and his sister had accepted all two thousand bicycles on his behalf and organized their storage in an enormous, empty warehouse. Adrian had no idea of what his family thought about his highly speculative adventure. But he would soon find out.

Adrian looked eagerly out the window of the compartment. His warehouse was somewhere out there. He could hardly wait to inspect the Crescent Bikes. Buying and selling bicycles . . . that was all that he— the most passionate cyclist of them all—had left. He *had* to succeed . . .

He could still not believe that it had taken him so long to return. When he'd first been injured, experienced surgeons had immediately set to work to fix his damaged knee. Right after the operation, they had predicted that he'd be up and riding a bicycle again in a few weeks.

That's when things had begun to go wrong. No matter what disinfectants or salves the nurses used, the wound simply would not heal. Instead, the ointments they had applied mixed with the pus and other fluids oozing from the wound, and the malignant mixture found its way into his bloodstream. Instead of healing, he'd gotten blood poisoning! The nurses quickly applied leeches, and his leg was cupped several times a day.

Thousands of miles on a bicycle, a bullet wound, and now blood poisoning and a raging fever—it was all too much for Adrian's weakened constitution. He fell into a coma for several weeks. After waking again, which few in the hospital believed would ever actually happen—Adrian wanted to know how he had given death the slip. The doctors hemmed and hawed and tossed medical expressions around, but he still didn't understand how he'd survived.

It was one of the nurses who finally revealed to whom Adrian owed his recovery: an aging Potawatomi—an Indian that the man in the bed next to Adrian's had convinced the hospital to call in. Back when the old man's tribe had lived in the marshlands surrounding Chicago, he had been a medicine man. Now, though, he dwelled in one of the poorest of Chicago's suburbs, where Adrian's neighbor also lived. One evening, when most of the doctors had already gone home, the medicine man had appeared at his bedside and examined his leg as Adrian lay there almost lifeless. The next day, the old man returned and smothered Adrian's knee and leg in a foul-smelling paste concocted from herbs. He came back the following day and the next one after that, removing the old dressing and reapplying fresh paste each time. The doctors and nurses resigned themselves to letting the medicine man work. Their patient had nothing to lose.

After ten days, the wound had healed. All that remained was a clean, pink scar though the knee itself could no longer bend. Adrian woke from his coma. When he found out what had happened, it was too late: the man in the next bed had been discharged days earlier. But he badgered the hospital administration until they gave him the man's address. He took a horse and carriage out to the run-down district, thanked both men with all his heart, and gave each of them a hundred dollars.

Adrian's thoughts were interrupted by a shrill scream of brakes. The train was pulling into the station. He was home.

His apartment was stuffy, and he opened the windows to let in the warm May wind. Then he washed, changed, and took a small leather etui out of his travel bag. Then he left his apartment.


Josephine's house was locked. The cat rubbed against him and meowed.

On the workshop hung a sign: "Closed." Beneath that, it explained that items for repair could be dropped off or picked up again starting in mid-May.

Had Josephine gone away somewhere? And if so, where? And why *now*? he wondered, as he stared helplessly at the closed shutters. He needed answers. The emporium owner, who was standing out on the street nearby, would be sure to know. Josephine did business with him regularly. And if that didn't work, he would go to the clubhouse. He would only visit Isabelle as a last resort.

Adrian had just turned to leave when he heard a low sobbing sound come from the garden. He started, and his heart beat faster. Was Josephine perhaps still there?

"Clara?" Adrian looked in horror at the figure curled up on one of Josephine's garden chairs. Clara's arms were covered in red weals and her right eye was badly swollen. She was weeping.

Suppressing a cry of pain, Adrian lowered himself onto another chair. Gently, he raised Clara's chin and sought eye contact with her. "Who did this?" suspecting the answer even as he asked the question.

Instead of replying, Clara made an almost imperceptible motion with her head. Don't mention it. Act as if nothing had happened.

Adrian sighed and tacitly agreed to do as she wished. He was tired from traveling, crushed that Josephine was away, and not fit to wade into a battle between a warring couple.

Clara did him a favor in return: she did not ask him about his condition. But her eyes told him that she knew. "Don't you want to know where Josephine is?" she asked quietly. Haltingly, she began to explain. About Susanne Lindberg's visit, about Jo's decision to ride in the race, and about the grueling training regime she and the others had endured.

"They cycled in all weather, even if it was snowing!" A hint of a smile crossed Clara's face. Her voice grew stronger as she spoke; the other women's courage seemed to be rubbing off on her.

"Josephine, Isabelle, Luise, and my sister are on their way to a six-hundred-mile race?" Adrian was dumbfounded at the thought. He wanted to know more.

"They've been riding ten or twelve hours at a time the last few weeks. Can you even imagine?"

"I met Charles Hansen years ago at a race meeting. He's a careful man. I don't doubt that he's organized the race as well as it could be done and that he's looking out for the safety of the cyclists." Adrian was still trying to overcome his surprise, but elation was growing inside him. His Jo, off on such a grand adventure!

"A few men are going along, too. As a kind of protective escort. Veit Merz and Leon Feininger are among them."

"I know Veit Merz, of course, but I can't say I've ever heard of Leon Feininger."

"Oh, that will change soon enough. Trust me!" Clara said with a trace of mischief.

Adrian would have liked to find out more about the man who had become a permanent guest at the cycling club, but Clara said nothing more about him.

"I would have loved to go along. Not as a rider, God forbid! But as an observer, as a tourist, as they say these days. But my husband . . ." Clara bit down on her lip. She summarized the campaign that her husband had instigated against the women's cycling club.

"He can denounce women's cycling to hell and back, but that's no reason to hit you," replied Adrian angrily. "Clara, you can't just accept your husband's forbidding your friendship with Jo. She's your friend; you've known each other since you could walk. Besides, however much a couple may disagree, it is beneath the dignity of a gentleman to attack someone weaker. You can tell him that from me."

"Who says I'm weaker?" Clara shot back, and Adrian saw a spark of anger flash in her normally docile eyes.

But instead of responding, Adrian had an idea forming in his head. What would happen if . . .

He took a deep breath and asked, "When did they leave? Did Josephine tell you anything about their plans for the next few days? The race isn't going to start tomorrow morning, is it?"

Clara said they were going to have two days to acclimatize in Copenhagen first. Then the race would start on May 4.

It was May 1. Adrian did some quick calculations in his mind. Then he smiled.

"That throws all my plans out the window, but what the hell! I'd probably regret it forever if I didn't go."

"You want . . . to go to Copenhagen? But you just got home! I don't know if that's a good idea. Isabelle . . ."

Adrian held up one hand. "I'm not interested in Isabelle," he said. "It's Josephine I'll be there to support."

Clara's eyes widened. "You and Josephine?" She laughed softly. "Why doesn't that surprise me? At some level, I've suspected it for a long time."

"Because you're a true friend." Adrian took Clara's hand in his. "Why don't you come along? I'll pay for the trip. If you like, I'll try to talk your husband into giving you his blessing."

But Clara shook her head. Then she stood up and smoothed her skirt. With a steady voice and a steadier gaze, she said, "My place is here, with my son, just as you belong with Josephine. But I'll promise you this: when Josephine and the rest of you get back to Berlin, I'll be standing at the station to welcome you!"

# Chapter Thirty-One

"The most important thing is remembering to drink! You should be refilling your flasks with fresh water at least every two hours." Charles Hansen scanned the assembled group intently. "Every farmstead you pass has a well. The water is of a good quality across Denmark. We've informed every farmer along the route about the race, and you should meet friendly, helpful people wherever you go. If anyone offers you fresh milk, drink it! And if they offer you the schnapps bottle instead, a nip of that won't do you any harm, either."

The men and women all laughed.

All the participants had come together that first evening in the hotel dining room and gotten to know each other over a traditional, solid Danish meal. Susanne Lindberg placed great store in harmony and amity. "What counts here is not a competitive mindset, but the will to finish the race," she had said more than once. The evening might never have come to an end if Charles Hansen had not prompted them to go to bed. Getting enough sleep was an absolute must before such a race!

*

The next morning, Charles Hansen handed out the small booklets that they needed to have stamped at each checkpoint. The first checkpoint was in a village called Kalundborg, about sixty miles outside Copenhagen. The next was fifty miles ahead, and so on.

Kalundborg, Slagelse, Næstved, Vordingborg—Josephine was having trouble just pronouncing the names of the Danish towns, and she had no idea what to expect once she reached them. Her anxiety was growing by the hour. She could hardly wait to finally get going.

After receiving the booklets, the entire squad went out cycling together. It was a leisurely ride, so that everyone could get used to pedaling again after the long train journey. Susanne and Charles set the pace, and most of the riders found it far too slow.

Charles Hansen continued his explanations during their third meeting.

"As you well know, the race is to take place over four days. That's ninety-six hours. How many of those hours you choose to sleep is up to you. We recommend, however, that you take a break after ten or twelve hours of riding. It will do no one any good if you are exhausted and have an accident. Whether you choose to lie down in the grass or ask a farmer to sleep in his shed for the night, or happen to find a small pensione—all of that is entirely up to you."

Ten or twelve hours in the saddle followed by a short break lying on the grass? Josephine and Isabelle turned and looked at each other with raised eyebrows.

"Don't go getting scared now," Isabelle whispered, and Jo nodded vigorously. Both giggled excitedly.

"Ninety-six hours for six hundred miles—that's half an eternity," said Leon with some contempt. "Do you seriously expect us men to ride at such a snail's pace?"

The women grumbled. None of them was planning to ride at a snail's pace!

"Each of you will choose your own tempo," said Charles Hansen, once he had managed to restore order. "That applies to the women as well as the men."

Leon grinned. "What happens if I ride away from our dear Susanne here and steal the show from her at the end? Would that be all right? I mean, you're calling this event a women's race, right?"

Now it was Susanne's turn to answer. "I would be more than happy to have somebody set the pace for the entire route. If you think you're up to it, then by all means go ahead."

Charles Hansen and the Danish women laughed.

But Leon frowned and said nothing. He was supposed to be the pacemaker for another rider? Was Suzanne trying to pull his leg? It appeared they had no idea what an outstanding cyclist he was.

Charles Hansen cleared his throat. "Let's return to the logistics. Each day, we will set up *one* food station for you. After eating, you will have the opportunity to make sandwiches to take with you before you get going again. Dried fruit and nuts will also be provided. However, we advise you in the strongest terms to eat something warm when you reach each food station!"

Josephine nodded. Susanne and her fiancé seemed really to have thought of everything. Oh, if only they could get going . . .

Isabelle rocked restlessly in her chair and rubbed her hands together nervously. She had been feeling an uncomfortable tingling in the hands and feet all day. Could it be from the kola syrup Leon had bought for her at a local pharmacy? They hadn't brought any pep pills or kola with them from Berlin because Leon had claimed they would be available everywhere—apparently Ekarius's wonder drugs had been a favorite among Danish cyclists for ages.

But he had been wrong! They had been unable to find anything of the sort in Copenhagen, and the stuff he'd brought back the previous evening had nearly driven her up the wall. Whether or not it would help her on the long tour remained to be seen.

Charles Hansen was just launching into an explanation of where they could find shelter for the night when there was a knock at the door. Everyone turned around.

It took a moment for Isabelle to realize who it was standing there with a broad grin on his face. That . . . that was impossible!

"Adrian!" Irene's voice nearly choked in disbelief.

"Adrian! I don't believe it!" shouted Veit Merz. "A remarkable fellow," Veit said to Leon, who was sitting beside him.

Josephine rose to her feet as if in a trance. But Isabelle was faster. She shot up from her stool and practically launched herself at her former fiancé. She planted herself in front of him with her arms folded across her chest. "What do you think you're doing, showing up here? You've got no business coming back into my life. You come barging in right in the middle of our meeting, inconsiderate—"

"Hello, Isabelle. Nice to see you." With a tolerant smile, Adrian pushed her gently out of the way. "Please let me by." He shook Charles Hansen's hand. "I'll be leaving again in a moment, then you can carry on with your meeting. I'm sure we'll find time to talk later," he said to Hansen, and also to Irene, who was pushing her way through to him. Adrian looked straight ahead as he limped through the room.

"Your leg!" Irene cried. "What . . ."

Isabelle watched in shock as Adrian walked down the aisle. What was wrong with his leg? And why was Josephine suddenly looking so oddly transfigured? Why was she going up to him?

"Josephine . . ."

"You came . . ."

"I . . . couldn't . . . Your adventure . . . alone."

"I . . . missed you so much . . ."

"And I . . ."

What was all that whispering? That sounded like two lovers purring away! Isabelle gave a hysterical laugh. No, she must be mistaken. Her ears and eyes were playing tricks on her . . . That horrible kola syrup, the tension before the race, her frayed nerves . . .

"Adrian, what's this all about?" asked Irene, her voice frosty.

"I don't believe it!" Veit repeated himself. "Our Jill-of-all-trades and you? I need a schnapps for that. Oh, to hell with it, schnapps for everyone! Waiter!"

Isabelle could only look on in shock as Adrian and Josephine lost themselves in an embrace, utterly forgetting the world around them.

*This is impossible. Not those two. This—is—not—possible!*

Charles Hansen cleared his throat. "Well, by the looks of it, we can welcome another true cycling great to our meeting. What an honor! No doubt Adrian will tell us all about his trip to America later. But for now I'd like to suggest that we get back to our agenda and—"

"You two are together?" shrieked Isabelle, recovering from her initial shock. "You got involved behind my back?" She knocked Adrian's arm off Josephine.

"Isabelle . . . What is it? Come on, sit down." Leon tried to pull her away, but she shook him off like an annoying insect.

"Let me go! This is my battle." Her glare bored into Josephine's flushed face. "How long has this been going on? How long have you been lying to me, *dear friend*? Have you been laughing yourself sick behind my back?" Her voice sounded shrill in her own ears, but she couldn't help herself. The sense of betrayal washed over her like an enormous wave, and she gasped for air, trying to keep her head above water.

"Isabelle, calm down, please," said Adrian. "You just said yourself that you and I have nothing more to do with each other. Why are you so upset?" He placed one hand on her arm in an attempt to placate her, but that only made Isabelle more furious.

"How can anyone stoop so low?" She curled her fingers into fists. Just a nudge, and she—

"Enough!" snapped Irene. "I'm astounded myself and less than pleased at this . . . development. But I think we should all behave like adults and—"

"Adults? You're one to talk!" Isabelle hissed at her. "You're not the one *adults* sold like a head of cattle! You didn't have years of your youth taken away. Ask your darling brother how he and I ended up engaged! Maybe he's finally found the guts to tell you the truth about that." She was shaking so hard that she was having trouble articulating her words properly.

"Isabelle, *chérie* . . ." Leon held a schnapps glass under her nose. "Have a sip. It will calm you down."

She swatted his hand away. "And while we're on the subject of truth . . ." Slowly, like a snake facing a hypnotized rabbit, she turned to Josephine.

Never in her life had she been so disappointed by another human being. She would have trusted Jo with anything. And now this.

"Does your dear paramour happen to know the whole truth about you? Does Adrian Neumann, son of the *great* Gottlieb Neumann, know that you weren't just away somewhere for *those* years, but that you were in prison for being a common thief?"

That was when the real commotion started. Questions were shouted from all sides, and the group cast questioning—and disparaging—looks at Josephine and Adrian. Josephine in prison?

Susanne Lindberg and her fiancé exchanged a look of deep concern. This frenzy was the last thing they needed on the eve of the race. A scandal could endanger the whole undertaking!

Charles Hansen turned to Isabelle, Josephine, Adrian, and Irene and tried to make himself heard over the din. "I think the four of you should leave the room and go try to sort out this . . . matter elsewhere.

Better now than during the race. Once we get started, it will be all about fairness and a spirit of cooperation—"

Isabelle interrupted him harshly. "Thank you for your suggestion, dear Charles. But there's nothing to sort out. A great deal is clear to me now."

"But Isabelle, it isn't what you think at all!" Josephine cried. "Adrian and I, we didn't betray you, we—"

"Shut up!" Two words, like strokes from a whip.

Isabelle stalked toward the door, trembling with fury. "I'll see you on the racecourse." It sounded like a threat.

# Chapter Thirty-Two

Instead of going to bed at a decent hour, as Charles had advised all of the racers to do, Josephine had spent half the night awake. She and Adrian had had so much to talk about, and her years in prison were the least of it.

"Moritz Herrenhus wanted to get you out of the way," Adrian said flatly once she had told him everything. "He let you use his bicycle for months. There's no way he should have been so upset that you borrowed it secretly. But that's just like the man—he probably didn't like the fact that his daughter was spending so much time with a free spirit like you." Josephine's past changed nothing about how he felt about her.

And they had talked about Isabelle, too, of course. And about America. Adrian had raved about the bicycles waiting for him in Berlin. When Josephine tried to raise the subject of his injured leg, he waved it off casually. "Later . . ." was all he said.

When they finally had parted and Jo was lying in bed, so many things were going through her head that she couldn't sleep at all.

\*

By the next morning, Jo felt so wound up that if the race didn't start soon she thought she'd throw some kind of fit.

It was a picture-perfect day, bright and sunny. The starting line had been set up on the outskirts of Copenhagen, on the road that led westward, first to Roskilde, then Kalundborg. The snow-white houses gleamed in the sunlight, and a few seagulls that had found their way into the city flapped and squawked overhead.

Of course, the members of Susanne's and Charles's home club were there, as well as Susanne's own family. But very few of Copenhagen's citizens had turned out, as the race had not been heavily publicized in advance. Charles Hansen planned to sing the praises of the race and the participants afterward, with the motto "See what women can do when no one's looking!"

Josephine had no interest in the press or anyone else. Adrian was there, and that was all that mattered to her. Now there was only one more thing she wanted: to start! When she looked into the faces of her fellow riders, she saw that they all wanted the same thing. She caught Lilo's eye, and they grinned at each other.

All around her, final adjustments were being made to bicycles, hats were being straightened, jackets buttoned, provisions distributed, and final prerace sandwiches eaten. The women's voices were more shrill than usual, their faces flushed with excitement. One or two drank a glass of sparkling wine to calm their nerves, a practice that earned a look of disapproval from Susanne Lindberg. The air was practically vibrating.

Josephine crouched and, for the hundredth time, looked to see that her bicycle was ready. Gerd Melchior had checked each of the bicycles thoroughly the evening before, but better to be safe than sorry.

Out of the corner of her eye, she saw Isabelle arrive, Leon at her side. Her expression was rigid, and she wore an elegant cycling outfit. The jacket with all the pockets that Jo had painstakingly sewn for her was nowhere to be seen. Instead of greeting the others with a handshake, as was the custom, she simply gave the group a nod.

Adrian stood nearby with Gerd Melchior and raised one thumb in the air. "I've got my great cycling adventure behind me. Now it's your turn!" Adrian had said to her the night before, just before he left. "Enjoy every mile, and don't worry about anything or anyone, you hear me? I'll be with you in spirit." He was going to follow in one of the support wagons and meet her later at one of the checkpoints.

Adrian traveling in a carriage. Josephine felt a knot form in her throat. She felt like crying, but would that have changed anything? No doubt the German doctors would be able to get his knee working again. If they couldn't . . .

To take her mind off Adrian, Jo checked her tools. A screwdriver, a pocketknife, patching gear, and a few odds and ends—just what would fit in the bottom pocket on the back of her jacket and wasn't too heavy. If she got a puncture, she would not be forced to wait for Gerd Melchior or one of the other mechanics.

Next, Jo checked her provisions. She had five rolls, a few handfuls of dried fruit, and two pieces of Danish cake packed with almonds and marzipan. That would have to do for the first one or two hundred miles. Her two metal flasks were filled with water. On Adrian's advice, she had dropped a cube of sugar in each one. The sugar would dissolve and give her a burst of energy with every sip.

Jo stretched her legs. They felt good. Strong, supple, with no sign of the cramps she had suffered a few times during her training.

Her bicycle, her equipment, her physical condition—she had never felt more ready. The waiting was unbearable.

\*\*\*

"Ladies, gentlemen, this is a historic day. Because with this race, we will show that women are just as capable of great performances as men, if not greater. From today on, the fairer sex will be known as the stronger sex. Susanne and those riding with her will put to shame all those lies about the weakness of women that have proliferated—without a shred of evidence."

Charles Hansen's cheeks were flushed and his eyes flashed with anticipation as he looked around the group assembled before him.

"A long-distance race like ours deserves to be called by another name. The reason is simple. Unlike other cycling competitions, competitiveness is not what we are all about. We are not haggling over which rider is a few minutes faster than another. We are not *racing*. What binds us, rather, is the will to reach our goal together, with our love of cycling carrying us to the finish line. Which is why I want to impress the following upon all of you: If you see a rider, man or woman, standing by the road in need of help, stop and ask what the matter is. Share your food! Let him or her take a drink from your flask! And if a rider breaks down, see how you can help. It is time for community spirit to prevail. Arguments, jealousy, and childish quarrels have no place in the next six hundred miles." He looked meaningfully at Isabelle, then Josephine.

Jo nodded. She would not be the one to start something.

Charles Hansen stepped over to Susanne, whispered something in her ear, and gave her a quick kiss. Then he turned back to the other riders one last time.

"I wish you all an enjoyable ride through our beautiful Zealand. Bon voyage, or as we say in Danish, *god rejse!*"

***

For the first hour, Susanne and the thirty other participants rode together. The mood was buoyant, as if they were off on a jaunt to the seaside. They laughed and joked, and some swapped stories about other tours they had done. Susanne talked about her wedding plans. "After we get married, I want to have at least a dozen children," she admitted with a laugh.

"If you can still have any after this tour . . . Cycling makes women infertile, or hadn't you heard?" joked Luise, drawing laughter, but with a hint of bitterness.

To Josephine's great relief, the others treated her perfectly normally; some were even friendly. No one seemed to put too much store in Isabelle's talk of prison. Everyone had seen how worked up she was, after all. And no one took her accusation—that Jo had betrayed her and stolen her former fiancé—seriously. Conversation focused on the ride ahead.

As the enormous cathedral in Roskilde came into view, Susanne abruptly increased the tempo—the fun was over. A group of ten, mostly Danish and French women, went with her, as did Isabelle, Veit Merz, and Leon Feininger.

Josephine considered increasing her own speed but decided against it. Her pace felt just right. So why change it?

"Let them go," said Lilo, drawing up beside Jo. "Whoever takes the lead now usually ends up pedaling in behind the rest at the end." Changing the subject, she said, "So, did you get a chance to talk things out with Isabelle?"

Jo told her she hadn't.

"What I don't get is why you didn't come clean to Isabelle long ago," said Lilo. "To be honest, if I were in her shoes, I'd be angry, too."

"What about? Isabelle's and Adrian's engagement was a farce from the start. It wasn't as if she had any real claim to him. You should have heard how disparaging she was every time she talked about him," Jo answered heatedly. "Besides, what was I supposed to come clean about? A few hugs and kisses? We only discovered that we had fallen in love just before he left. Apart from a few postcards and one or two letters, I hadn't heard from him since then. So what exactly was I supposed to confess to her?"

"Well, if that's the case . . ." Lilo frowned. "Then why is Isabelle getting so upset?"

Josephine swerved to dodge a pothole. "I have no idea. I never thought that Isabelle would be offended. I thought she'd be happy for me."

"Maybe it's just the timing. A lot of women riders get pretty overwrought right before a race. Isabelle's been quite prickly over the last few days, don't you think?"

"Does that surprise you?" Jo replied. "With all the pills and stuff that Leon's been giving her . . ." She shook her head. Of course, she had tried a few of the miracle pills herself, but she'd lost all sense for her own body. Unable to feel whether she was close to exhaustion or not, she had pushed herself much too far, and it taken forever for her to regain her strength. It had been a frightening experience.

Lilo raised her eyebrows. "Isabelle is taking a little dope?"

"More than a little," Jo replied and picked up the pace.

They rode into Kalundborg, where the first checkpoint had been set up by the harbor. Jo was rapt as she looked at the first stamp in her booklet. How lovely it would look when all fifteen stamps were in it!

Susanne and her group had passed the checkpoint a good half hour earlier, they discovered. Lilo and Jo exchanged a look. The Dane really seemed to be in a class of her own.

Jo decided to continue on. Lilo opted to stay and find a bathroom and catch up with her later. When Josephine saw Irene pull up alongside her, she sighed. *Oh, here it comes,* she thought. The nagging questions, the arrogant remarks, and—

"Don't worry, I'm *not* going to ask you about my brother," said Irene.

Jo glanced at her sideways in surprise. "Well, you know . . ." she began, without actually knowing what she wanted to say.

Leaning low over the handlebars, Irene grinned back at her. "Forget it. It can't be any worse than the thought of having Isabelle for a sister-in-law. Who knows, maybe you and I will get along famously one day?" There was certainly a dose of sarcasm in her voice, but she did not sound angry.

"Who knows?" Jo said with a smile, enjoying the tailwind that carried them along the coast as if on the wings of angels.

With the wind came an inner lightness. What kind of merciful fate was it that allowed her to take part in this race? Breathing deeply, Jo took in the open countryside and the deep blue of the water beyond.

"Magnificent, isn't it?" said Irene, and her usually arrogant voice sounded almost humble.

Jo nodded but said nothing. She felt an unpleasant dryness in her mouth. When she tried to gather enough spit to swallow, she couldn't do it. A slight dizziness came over her, and her bicycle wobbled and nearly slid off the road. *What's going on? Concentrate!* Jo coached herself. Then she realized she'd forgotten to drink. Frightened by her own carelessness, she dug her flask out of a pocket and drank almost half the water in one gulp. A quarter of an hour later she felt better and decided to eat a roll before her hunger got to her as well.

A good hundred and fifty miles after the start of the race, Josephine, Irene, and an Englishwoman who had joined them reached Vordingborg, the southernmost point on the route. For all three riders, the race so far had gone well. They had managed to keep up a steady, brisk pace without burning up too much energy. Lilo pedaled into town shortly after they arrived.

"What do you think? Want to keep going?" Lilo asked.

Josephine considered what to do. Thanks to the tailwind, she was not feeling especially exhausted, so she set off with Lilo and Irene for Køge, where Charles Hansen had set up a support station and made sleeping arrangements for the riders.

Darkness settled over them, and they had to light their gas lamps to be able to see the road ahead.

Thirty miles on, Jo's legs began to feel heavy. She had eaten all her bread and drained five water bottles. All she could think about was some hot soup. After another twenty-five miles, Josephine rode down toward Køge Bay. It was eleven o'clock at night, and she desperately hoped that the catering station hadn't packed everything away for the night. Her legs were heavy and stiff, and she knew she couldn't ride another mile. If she didn't get something to eat, she would probably have to give up . . .

When the church tower where the checkpoint was set up came into view, Josephine felt both relief and a sense of elation. This only increased when she saw Adrian standing beside the station.

"So? How do you feel? You've got more than a quarter of the course behind you. Isn't that fantastic?" Without waiting for her answers, he went on to tell her which riders had arrived in Køge and when. Susanne Lindberg and her team had gotten there first, of course, followed by Isabelle and Leon. Leon was giving a journalist an interview even as Adrian spoke. All the other riders were grabbing a few hours of sleep.

Josephine's legs were shaking so much that she could hardly hold herself upright. But Adrian's enthusiastic descriptions gave her a little surge of strength. His cheeks glowed with excitement, and in his eyes Jo saw a dozen different emotions: respect for the racers, enthusiasm for the sport, the pleasure of being able to experience the comradeship of the riders, if only from the side of the road. And, of course, a little melancholy.

"We've already changed horses three times, but you're still on the same bicycles, an amazing feat! And your time is great, Jo. If you keep on like this, you'll be one of the first to cross the finish line," he said with genuine pride.

"That's going to change if I don't get something to eat and soon. Because I'll die on the spot like a flogged horse," she replied with a laugh. Wobbling a bit, she joined the short line that had formed at the food table. The soup smelled enticingly of beef and potatoes, and Josephine's stomach growled audibly as the servers filled her soup bowl to the brim. She grabbed a few rolls and added two sweet pastries to the top of the pile.

Adrian had spread a blanket on the grass in the shelter of the church wall. A flaming torch that was stuck in the ground beside the blanket gave off a warm light, and the church wall still radiated the warmth of the day's sun. With a sigh, Jo lay back on the blanket, while Irene and Lilo took their food into a barn that Charles had rented for the riders a short distance away.

Never in Jo's life had any soup tasted that good. Never had a roll been so delicious. Jo ate everything down to the last crumb. Full and content, she leaned against Adrian's shoulder and was suddenly so tired that she dreaded the idea of getting back on the bicycle.

"Sleep a little," said Adrian, spreading his arms out gently. "I'll wake you up in four hours, I promise."

After a long and deep farewell kiss, Jo pedaled on toward Copenhagen.

She didn't mind riding alone. The taste of Adrian's lips rode with her.

Copenhagen. The starting point was not the end of the race, not by a long shot. She wasn't even halfway through the course! After their initial departure from Copenhagen, the riders then had to ride a northern loop of ninety miles that would bring them back to Copenhagen. That would mark the halfway point. Then they would ride the entire route a second time.

*The halfway point . . . If only I were already there,* Jo thought, pedaling away, her legs still feeling stiff.

After half an hour, Jo found her rhythm again. Unlike most of the other women, Jo was used to riding in the dark. And though she had enjoyed riding with Lilo and Irene, it was equally pleasant to ride alone. The air was filled with the scent of the sea and the weeds with yellow flowers that sprouted along the side of the road in thick tussocks. It was a clear night, dry and not too cold—one could not ask for better conditions.

The sky began to grow light again shortly before six. As soon as she could more or less see again, Jo switched off her bicycle lamp to conserve gas—a mistake, as it turned out. It was difficult to detect variations in the road surface in the faint dawn light, and Jo hit a rock as big as her fist. The impact was so hard that she nearly lost her grip on the handlebars. *That was lucky,* she thought as she got over the shock.

A little farther on, the road curved sharply to the left. When Jo squeezed the brakes, nothing happened. The impact with the stone must have knocked off a brake pad. In a panic, she took both feet off the pedals and tried to slow herself down by dragging them on the ground, which was only partly successful. She took the curve dangerously fast, but she made it through safely and then let the bicycle roll to a stop on the straight stretch that followed. She climbed off with a sigh and lit her lamp again—she would need every bit of light she could get for the repair.

The collision with the stone had, in fact, knocked one of rubber brake pads off the front brakes. She had thought of everything except replacement brake pads! First she forgot to drink, then to eat. And now this! How many more mistakes would she make? Jo set about removing the remaining rubber block from its holder. She was in the process of cutting it into two equal halves with the pocketknife when she heard voices behind her. But it was not the hoped-for carriage with Adrian and Gerd Melchior and his mobile workshop.

"Need any help?" asked Leon as he pulled up beside her.

"Thank you, but I'll manage," replied Jo, refitting one half of the brake pad into the holder on the left. The other half would go onto the right.

"Really? I'd be happy to give you a hand," said Leon. He gestured placatingly toward Isabelle, who was waiting impatiently a short distance ahead.

Jo nodded. "I only lost one pad. But you know the old trick: make two out of one! I've already done it. Now I just have to tighten it against the stop, and off we go." She looked around for a stone that she could use as a makeshift hammer to bend the brake holder so that she wouldn't lose the rubber block a second time.

"Well, then . . . safe journey!" said Leon, obviously not entirely convinced that she really knew what she was doing.

"Help yourself," Isabelle called back to Jo scornfully. "You're good at that."

Jo watched sadly as Isabelle rode off. A few minutes later she swung back onto her bicycle and continued on.

# Chapter Thirty-Three

"Did you *have* to stop for that traitor?" Isabelle hissed as soon as Leon had caught up with her. "Helpful as ever, pah! She'll thank you with a knife in your back, just wait."

Leon looked at Isabelle with amusement. "I really don't know why you're getting so upset. Just because Josephine fell in love with one of your former beaus? What would you have done with a cripple anyway?"

Adrian a cripple. Deep in her heart, Isabelle felt a pang of sympathy, but she swatted it away like a fly. "Adrian used to be a first-class rider. It serves them both right that his career's over."

"Spite doesn't suit you, *chérie*," said Leon with a sigh. "Would it bother you if I rode ahead a bit? I won't be able to live with myself if I don't catch up with Susanne and her troop before Helsingør!"

"So you're going to leave me in the lurch now, too? Then take off, go!" said Isabelle, flicking her hand at him uncharitably.

When Leon really did accelerate and ride away, she didn't know whether to be happy or sad about it. She pedaled on, feeling hollow.

Why *was* she taking the news of Josephine and Adrian's relationship so personally? She had embarrassed herself thoroughly with her performance on the eve of the race. And her behavior just now hadn't been exactly sporting, either.

Why did she even care? Was it the feeling that she had been excluded? Betrayed? Was it the ignominy of knowing that Adrian couldn't love her but could love Josephine? Or was it the intimacy, the deep, mutual understanding that the two of them radiated? They obviously just wanted to parade their great love in front of everyone. Well, to hell with that!

The road curved sharply to the left, and Isabelle only leaned into it at the last second. After several miles of straight road, she had not been prepared for a turn like that. Her heart pounding, she pedaled on.

She had to concentrate, damn it. She'd show Jo who the better rider was! Still jittery from the curve, she reached into her saddlebag for her water bottle. But the bottle had slipped all the way to the bottom. In her attempt to get it out, she came within a hair's breadth of crashing, the second time in two minutes. Then she realized that she'd forgotten to fill it back at the checkpoint. Isabelle clapped the bulky saddlebag closed again and instead took a small medicine bottle from a pocket of her jacket. The kola syrup tasted disgustingly sweet, but it at least made her feel as if she'd drunk something. Then her heart started beating uncomfortably quickly. There was not a farm in sight where she might stop and get fresh water. She had to catch up with Leon! He'd surely let her drink some of his water. All she had to do was catch up . . . She pedaled even harder.

Leon . . . He took everything so casually. But she had been finding it harder and harder to do that lately. Too many thoughts were swirling in her head all the time. She couldn't even switch them off at night. Instead of sleeping, she lay awake, her mind churning.

What would happen after the race? Would Leon simply leave again, never to return? What would become of her? Quite apart from the fact that it would break her heart, she would officially have been abandoned by a man for the second time. She could already imagine the gossip. Looks like no man could stand being around her for long!

Leon . . . She was crazy about him. When she was around him, she felt young and carefree. She found his charm more refreshing than any glass of bubbly! Leon . . . She would marry him on the spot.

Isabelle pedaled harder, though the muscles in her thighs already felt as hard as stone.

Did Leon ever think about marriage? They had hardly ever talked about the future.

But Josephine and Adrian—she could practically hear the wedding bells ringing for them already! Did Clara know about them? Had she also betrayed Isabelle?

The road ahead of her was straight as a die again. Had he caught up with Susanne yet? She had to ride faster! Isabelle opened her mouth to get more air. Almost immediately, a fly flew in. She coughed and spat. A moment later, she grew dizzy. *Ignore it.* It wasn't like her to dawdle like this. It was all the fault of that stupid, never-ending whirl of thoughts in her head . . .

Leon. *He loves me. He loves me not. He loves me . . .* As children, she and Josephine and Clara had played that game with daisies. In more innocent times. Friends. She had none anymore. She was alone. But hadn't she always been alone?

Isabelle tasted something salty on her lips. It wasn't the damp sea air. Ride, spin, faster. Maybe the speed would help her escape the grinding in her mind. Faster, faster.

It seemed to work . . .

But then she experienced a flat, empty feeling somewhere down near her belly. Was it hunger? Thirst? She couldn't tell. She didn't want to eat another slice of stale bread.

Maybe Leon had managed to rustle up something better for her? One of those sweet pastries they had in the patisseries in Copenhagen and a cup of hot tea.

Isabelle turned her wrist to check the time on her watch. A surge of panic welled up in her as she stared at the hands on the watch face. What did the position of the hands mean? It was just before eight in the morning. They had started almost twenty-four hours earlier. She saw a sign that read "Slangerup" nailed to a large oak tree. The name sounded familiar. Had she passed this point before? No, that other village was called Jyderup. What strange names. She started to giggle uncontrollably. Did this mean she would be in Copenhagen soon? Copenhagen . . . turning point. A place to turn around. How idiotic of Charles Hansen not to just have the race finish there. Three hundred miles would not set any long-distance records for women, but it was still nothing to sneeze at, right?

Charles Hansen and Susanne Lindberg. Another one of those couples . . . Still no sign of Copenhagen. Was she making any progress at all? Or was she falling farther and farther behind?

Isabelle whimpered as she battled into the wind. She was so alone. And so tired. Where was Leon?

The sun climbed quickly into the sky and grew glaringly bright. Isabelle squinted against it. Her eyes teared up and she could not see clearly. It was all so stupid. The race, the route, the others. But was that any wonder in a women's race? Her laughter sounded strange to her own ears and gave her an eerie feeling. What was wrong with her?

Then all she saw was darkness. Her bicycle began to swerve, then veered across the road and down an embankment. Isabelle tumbled headlong over the handlebars onto the grass. The sun was gone. She felt no thirst. No hunger. Finally.

***

Slangerup. Like so many Danish villages, this one had been founded by a Viking. *But where had all those wild seafarers come from?* Jo wondered as she rode past the sign. She'd do better to focus on the winding road instead of pestering herself with unnecessary questions.

It was only eight thirty in the morning, but the sun was already high above the horizon. It felt much brighter here in the north, so close to the sea. Visibility was difficult in the glaring light, and she longed for her peaked cap. As soon as she reached Copenhagen, she would stop and get the cap out of her bag.

Copenhagen . . . She would soon have half the route behind her. And she would see Adrian there. He and Gerd Melchior were somewhere behind her. If none of the riders had a serious breakdown that held them up, then the two men would arrive in Copenhagen shortly after her. She decided that she would wait half an hour for Adrian, and if he didn't show up by then, she would ride on.

She was doing well, timewise. Almost three hundred miles in twenty-four hours—wasn't that amazing? Of course, she knew she wouldn't be able to keep up that pace. She would have to take another nap around midday. But she still felt good. Better than good, in fact. She felt fantastic!

Josephine's smile vanished when she saw something glittering on the side of the road ahead. Was that broken glass? She squinted in an effort to see better. If it was glass, she'd have to be careful not to slice open a tire. She slowed a little. Then she saw that it was a bicycle lying in the high grass of the embankment. A bicycle she knew only too well.

*Oh, no. Please no!* A shudder ran through her as she came to a stop. Instead of putting her bicycle down carefully, as she normally would, she let it drop in the middle of the road.

"Isabelle? Then she slapped her hand over her mouth in horror.

Isabelle lay fifteen feet below, her head tilted strangely backward, her arms thrown out from her body. Her skirt had blown up around her, half covering her face. Even from where Jo stood, she could see blood on Isabelle's left temple. Her eyes were wide open and not moving.

Josephine looked around frantically. She needed help! Why wasn't there anyone around?

She slid hastily down the steep embankment, grasping at the sharp-edged tufts of grass to avoid falling. Her hands burned as if on fire. When she finally reached Isabelle's seemingly lifeless body, she put a trembling hand to Isabelle's throat. She felt a weak pulse there, like the flapping of butterfly wings. *Thank you, dear God, thank you.*

Her friend was only unconscious. But she might have suffered a concussion or broken something. Jo studied Isabelle's inert body. What should she do? What *could* she do? She didn't want to hurt her by moving her the wrong way. To do *something*, she straightened Isabelle's skirt and put her legs together. Then she lifted her right arm and moved it back and forth very slowly. It didn't appear to be broken. Carefully, she stepped over her friend and did the same with her left arm, which also seemed to be all right. When she had both arms in a more or less natural position, Jo scrabbled along the embankment until she was sitting behind her friend's head. She took her handkerchief out of a pocket, moistened it on her tongue, and dabbed away the blood on Isabelle's temple. Fortunately, it was just a minor cut. Then she stroked Isabelle's mussed hair out of her chalky face and whispered her name softly. Isabelle didn't move. What if she had broken her neck?

Josephine pushed both hands under Isabelle's head.

"Isa . . . don't be afraid . . ." Sweat dripped from Jo's forehead—*she* was the one who was terribly afraid—as she ran her fingers over Isabelle's head and neck. She felt the strong bones where the spine became the neck, the twin strands of muscle to the left and right, the small indentations behind the ears. Everything felt good. But she was no doctor.

She heard a low groan. Startled, Jo stopped her examination.

Isabelle blinked once, twice. "Josephine?"

"Yes, it's me . . ." Jo stroked Isabelle's cheek with relief. "Everything will be all right."

Isabelle groaned again, then closed her eyes.

Jo looked down helplessly at her friend. What now? "Can you lift your head? I'll help you . . . Does that hurt? No?" Inch by inch, she moved Isabelle's head until it was finally resting in her lap.

"What . . . happened? Where am I?" She opened her eyes and looked around uneasily. She tried to get up, but like an injured animal caught in a snare, she only managed to turn left and right in vain.

Jo held her gently but firmly. "You've had an accident. I think you should just lie like this for a while." She leaned forward to give Isabelle's face a little shade. Isabelle's body felt hot. Was it the relentless sun? Or did she have a fever? Jo had no idea.

What now? She would never be able to get Isabelle back up the slope on her own. In her mind, she ran through the positions of the other riders. Susanne and her group had ridden past this point much earlier, as had Leon, apparently. Irene was also ahead, no doubt. Lilo and Luise Karrer! Both of them had left Køge just after her—

"I . . . thirsty . . . water . . ."

"Water. Of course." Jo reached into her jacket. Why hadn't she thought of that? She lifted Isabelle's head a little, then put the flask to her lips.

Isabelle greedily swallowed a few mouthfuls.

"Do you want to eat anything? I've still got an apple." As she spoke, Jo took out the apple, the last of her provisions, and held it out to Isabelle, but Isabelle shook her head.

Jo hoped to bring a little color back to Isabelle's deathly pale cheeks, but a moment later, Isabelle's head sank back onto Josephine's lap and she fell unconscious again.

Jo could have wailed. She adjusted her legs and leaned back against the sandy slope. An exposed root dug painfully into her right shoulder blade, but when she tried to move, Isabelle groaned loudly. With a sigh, Jo stayed where she was.

*Dear God, please send help soon!* Exhausted in both mind and body, Josephine closed her eyes.

She could not have said how long she sat there like that. Although it felt like an eternity, it was only a little past ten when Adrian and Gerd Melchior found them.

"It shook me to my core when I saw your bicycle lying in the middle of the road," said Adrian. "But putting it there was a good idea! I don't know if we'd even have spotted you otherwise."

The two men picked up Isabelle, and with Josephine's help, they got her back up to the road. Gerd pushed aside the tools and spare parts covering the floor of the wagon, and they laid her down on a blanket.

"What about you? Everything all right?" Adrian lifted Jo's chin to look her in the eye.

Jo smiled. "I'm fine. I've just had another hour's sleep, whether I wanted it or not. But Isabelle . . . I'm worried about her. She might have some kind of internal injury." Before she knew it, she started to cry.

Adrian gently wiped away her tears. "That's the tension, sweetheart. But don't worry too much. I think that Isabelle is just totally exhausted. It looks like this race was too much for her. And her wonderful boyfriend didn't exactly help her take it at a reasonable pace. Where is he, by the way?"

"I'd like to know that myself," Jo sighed, pressing one fist into her sore back. "When I got here, she was lying there, God knows for how long." She chewed her lip. *Would it be unsporting of her to . . .* After a short pause, she cleared her throat.

"Would it be possible . . . You and Gerd are here now, and Copenhagen isn't far, and Isabelle will be safe in a hospital there. I mean . . ." Josephine looked longingly at her bicycle, which was still lying on the road.

Without a word, Adrian went over to the wagon and dug out a water bottle and two sandwiches wrapped in paper. He held them out to her with an encouraging smile. "Provisions for the next sixty miles. As you know, the next food station's in Kalundborg." He kissed her. "Now get going! But carefully, please, one accident's enough."

Jo climbed back onto her bicycle and immediately felt her spirits rise. Isabelle was in good hands. What mattered now was the race.

# Chapter Thirty-Four

The cramps began after Ballerup, a small town just west of Copenhagen. At first, it was only her right calf, which started pulling painfully tight every time she straightened her leg. Then her left calf started to cramp, too. Josephine took her feet off the pedals and stretched and twisted her legs every way she could think of, hoping the cramps would disappear on their own. But when she started to pedal again, the cramping in her right calf grew so sharp that she cried out in pain. Her bicycle wobbled dangerously for a second, and she had no choice but to roll to the side of the road and climb off. She massaged her calves, close to tears from the pain. But after the crabbed position she'd just endured while sitting with Isabelle, she wasn't entirely surprised.

She climbed back onto her bicycle, her face contorted with pain. Even light pedaling was hard, but at least she was moving again. After just a few miles, she had to dismount again; the cramps were becoming unbearable. Massage the calves, drink some sugar-water, hope it would help, mount up, ride a short way, dismount again when the cramps returned—the next hour passed in a crippling rhythm. When Roskilde came into view, she was both aggravated and furious. It just wasn't acceptable for cramping calves to ruin her race!

Unless she was mistaken, there was a farm with a large watering trough just beyond the next checkpoint in Roskilde. She'd noticed it the first time she rode past because it appeared to be much better tended than most of the other farmsteads in the region. Maybe it would help to soak her feet in water for a while?

After getting her stamp in Roskilde and a ten-minute ride at a snail's pace, she reached the trough. There was no one in sight. The farmers were undoubtedly all out in their fields. All the better! This way she didn't have to come up with tedious explanations.

Awkwardly, Jo lifted first one leg, then the other, into the trough, then sat on the edge of it. The water was ice cold. Josephine formed her hands into a bowl, held them under the faucet above the trough, and drank greedily. She splashed the refreshing water over her face, cooling her skin, which was hot and burned from the merciless sun. She sighed, feeling suddenly invigorated. She never wanted to leave here!

After a quarter of an hour, though, she swung her chilled legs over the edge of the trough and set them on the sandy ground. She felt fresher and stronger than she had for hours. But when she took a step toward her bicycle, a new cramp struck, this time in her right thigh . . .

What now? She couldn't just sit in the trough for hours as if it was a bathtub! In desperation, Jo rummaged through her pockets for anything that might help her. Suddenly, she heard a loud male voice behind her: "Hey!"

Jo spun around. A big, powerfully built man with a similarly massive dog at his side stood before her. The dog's head reached the man's hip.

The farmer and his watchdog. Just what she needed.

"*Hvad er der i vejen?*" the man snapped. His face was shot through with red veins, which could either be a sign of too much aquavit, or the result of working out in the raw sea air. Jo straightened up clumsily.

"*Hvad med dig her?*"

What she was doing there? All she wanted to do was be on her way again! She took a step back, but the man spread his feet and planted himself between her and her bicycle, blocking her path.

"Stop!" It sounded like the crack of a whip. The man's dog growled.

Jo's heart was hammering in her chest as she tried to move past, first on the left, then on the right, without success.

"I'm sorry, I didn't mean to disturb you. I just wanted . . . water." She pointed to the trough. "*Vand*—do you understand?" she asked, the word that Charles Hansen had used so many times suddenly coming to her. "*En flaske med vand.*" A bottle of water. "Can I please go now?"

The farmer nodded, but he did not move aside. Then he pointed to her shaking legs.

"*Du er syg?*"

"Am I what? Sick? *Ney . . .*" Jo bit on her lip. If she said the wrong thing now, he'd probably think she was easy prey and—

The farmer pointed to the bicycle and uttered something in Danish. Jo understood only two words. *Susanne Lindberg.*

"Yes!" she shouted with relief. "I'm riding in the race! But my . . ." She gestured at her trembling legs.

The man's dour expression transformed into a broad grin. This was followed by an excited but completely incomprehensible speech in which Susanne's name came up several times.

Relieved but still plagued by cramps, Jo went to move past the man to her bicycle. But the farmer was faster. He picked it up and held it out to her. Then he said something that Jo took to mean that she should wait. Gesticulating wildly, he ran back to the farmhouse.

She waited. With the pain in her right thigh, she would only be able ride a few hundred yards, anyway. No longer afraid, she now hoped the man would bring her a glass of milk or something to eat.

But when the farmer returned, all he had in his hands was a small glass jar. He removed the lid and held the jar under Jo's nose.

The smell was so sharp and penetrating that Jo instantly started to cough. She waved her hand frantically in front of her face to clear the stench.

The farmer laughed. Then he handed her the jar and made a motion with his hand as if he were rubbing his right leg.

Jo looked doubtfully at the farmer, then at the dark-brown stinking ointment. She'd heard many times that people in the country had miracle cures for all kinds of ailments. But should she try the stuff? The better question, she realized, was, what did she have to lose? Either the stuff would help with her cramps and she could continue riding, or her race was already over.

Jo dipped a finger into the jar and dug out a little blob of ointment.

The man turned away respectfully so that she could lift the hem of her bloomers and rub the stuff into her leg. She found the entire situation so ludicrous that she had to suppress a laugh.

The ointment, at first quite thick, instantly softened on her skin. Moving her hand in a circle, Jo massaged it into her thigh.

She felt its effects immediately. At first, it was just a light prickling on her skin. Then it began to burn, a sensation that moved from the surface down into the deeper layers of her skin. She felt her hardened muscles grow warm and soft again, and the pain vanished. Jo raised her eyebrows in surprise. What kind of wonder substance was this?

*"God?"* shouted the farmer over his shoulder.

Jo laughed. "Good? I'll say! This is . . . amazing!"

The farmer turned and clapped her on the shoulder so hard that Jo feared she might have a new injury to deal with. Then he signaled to her to keep the jar.

"Really?" Jo grinned broadly.

Jo swung her leg high and mounted her bicycle as if she'd never had a cramp in her life. "Thank you so much! You've saved me, I mean it!"

The farmer, who understood nothing of what she said but could clearly interpret her joy and relief, laughed.

*"God rejse!"*

*

The air smelled deliciously of seaweed, salt, and the smoke from the many fish-smoking operations in the area. The entire coast here made its living off fishing, which was not surprising considering the numerous small fjords, some of which penetrated a long way inland. Dozens of small fishing boats bobbed up and down in these sheltered tendrils leading in from the open sea. Along the shores, men with their hats pulled low hauled in large nets and carried crates of fish from the boats to land, their work accompanied by the constant screeching of seagulls fighting for scraps.

Josephine felt exhilarated as she rode past all of it. There was so much to see!

Still, her encounter with the farmer had left her thoughtful. Until today, she had never been in any serious danger on any of her rides, but how quickly that could change. She wanted to ride in the company of others going forward. But she hadn't seen any of the other racers since the unfortunate incident with Isabelle. And when she rode into the next checkpoint, she was the only one there collecting a stamp for her booklet. *Was anyone else actually still riding?* she wondered, simultaneously worried and annoyed. What if she, too, had an accident? Adrian was a living example that her fears were not unfounded. When she thought about what had happened to *him* . . .

Josephine had kept a tight lid on any thoughts of Adrian's disability since starting the race thirty hours earlier. Now, though, she saw him constantly in her mind's eye, and the way he had to hobble with his damaged leg. They had shot him like a mangy dog. A callous robbery on an open road for a watch and a few dollars had changed his entire life from one moment to the next.

How lightly he had dismissed his inflexible knee! As if he were dealing with a sniffle that would go away in a couple of days. But what if the doctors at the Charité hospital in Berlin could not help him, either? What if he could never ride a bicycle again? What then?

"I've got my great cycling adventure behind me. Now it's your turn!" he'd said to her. She would ride to the ends of the earth for him. But would that be enough? Would he ever give voice to his envy? How would she feel then?

*You think some useless thoughts,* she chided herself and was relieved when she saw the pretty half-timbered houses of Kalundborg appear against the light of the setting sun. Things were what they were. No one could force fate. All they could do was make the best of what they had, and that was exactly what she planned to do. Adrian was the man she wanted to spend the rest of her life with, and no smashed knee or other handicap would change that. Now she just wanted to get her next stamp. Gradually, her booklet was filling up.

The next food station had been set up in Vordingborg. As on the previous day in Køge, Charles Hansen had rented a barn where the riders could sleep for a few hours. As she rode up, Jo was besieged by reporters following the race. How did she feel? Which stretch had been the hardest so far? What did she think of Denmark? Did she think she'd be able to finish the race?

Although Charles Hansen had warned all the riders to be friendly with the reporters, Jo answered their questions as succinctly as she could.

She was just leaning her bicycle against the wall of the barn when she heard a voice behind her, "You've made it this far, too?"

"Lilo!" Josephine turned and embraced her friend. "It's so good to finally see one of you again!"

Lilo grinned. "Did you think we'd given up? No way! I've already been here for two hours. I was just about to head off again, but what the heck. I'll keep you company while you eat. Irene rolled in fifteen minutes ago. I'd love to hear how the race has been going for both of you."

"Irene was just fifteen minutes ahead of me . . ." Jo murmured. That meant that they had been just a few miles apart the whole time. If Jo had known that, she might not have felt so lonely over the last few hours . . .

"So Adrian and Gerd Melchior haven't come in yet?"

Lilo told her no, but Jo had not expected it to be otherwise. It would have taken them quite a while to get Isabelle to the hospital, then change horses and get going again. They may have taken a shortcut or followed the route in the other direction to make themselves available to other cyclists.

Charles Hansen had hired three coaches with helpers, tools, and spare parts as escort vehicles, and one of those was standing at the ready in Vordingborg. Jo asked the man to change her provisional front brake pads, then she went arm in arm with Lilo to the table with the food and drinks.

Josephine discovered that seven of the thirty starters had dropped out. She silently asked herself whether that number included Isabelle. But she didn't want to bring that up before she got something to eat.

Susanne Lindberg and her fellow Danish riders had left Vordingborg long before. Susanne had to be superhuman, because it seemed she took hardly any breaks at all. No one knew exactly how far ahead she and her team were. According to an English rider, Leon Feininger and Veit Merz had joined the lead group now, too. *How nice for Leon,* thought Josephine grimly. All that mattered to him was riding with the leaders, even though his girlfriend was lying half dead in a hospital!

She was just spooning out a generous helping of mashed potatoes when Luise Karrer pedaled in. And with the words, "I can't go on," she threw first her bicycle, then herself, onto the grass.

Lilo, Irene, and Jo looked at her. All of them knew that feeling. They also knew that Luise would pull herself together in a few minutes.

They joked about their disheveled appearance. Their hair was mussed and dusty; their faces were streaked with perspiration, road grime, and tears of pain; and their clothes stank of sweat and toil. But who cared? They were all still healthy and chipper.

Jo, sadly, had to dissent on that last point. Over a cup of tea and sweet pastries, she told the others about Isabelle's accident. They were appalled.

"And Adrian's the one who takes her to hospital . . ." Irene made a face. "Looks like she's still keeping him on his toes!"

Luise told them that she had accidentally rolled over a dead rabbit and crashed north of Copenhagen. "Rotten little beast," she said. "I'm lucky I didn't end up like Isabelle."

Then Irene reported that she had suffered such terrible cramps in her legs at one point that she had thought she would have to give up. Jo laughed and told them about her encounter with the farmer. Then she handed Irene the jar of brown ointment.

"It burns like fire!" Irene cried as she applied a little to one calf. "Are you sure you didn't get this stuff from an Indian?"

Josephine looked at her in confusion.

Irene grinned. "Didn't Adrian tell you? It took an Indian medicine man to heal his leg, and he used some kind of stinking ointment as well."

"My medicine man looked more like a Viking," replied Jo with a laugh.

"Who knows? Maybe Susanne rubs her whole body with that horrible stuff, and that's what makes her so fast," said Luise, standing up with a groan.

Lilo set off again a short while later. She wanted to take the last third of the course slowly but without another nap. She had done it that way on her previous long-distance races and wanted to do the same here in Denmark.

Josephine, however, decided to grant herself a few hours of sleep. Irene and Luise did the same.

Only when Charles Hansen had personally assured them that he would wake them again at midnight did Jo lie down in the barn. The hay smelled wonderful, and it felt softer than the finest feather bed. Neither Luise's snoring nor the rustling of mice around her feet stopped her from falling into a deep sleep in minutes.

Something was different. Jo sensed it almost instantly as she mounted her bicycle again. But what? She pedaled away with a sense of foreboding.

The air was moist and heavy, and Jo's lungs hurt when she breathed. It was a dingy, overcast night, not at all like the night before. There were no stars in the sky, and her gas lamp only dimly lit the road ahead.

"There's rain in the air," said Irene, pulling up on her left.

Jo nodded. That's what it was! The weather had been so glorious up to now that the possibility of rain had never crossed her mind.

To avoid endangering each other on the gloomy road, Jo, Irene, and Luise had decided to keep a distance of several yards between them and to take turns riding in front. Irene was the first to take the lead. Jo pedaled along mechanically behind her clubmates. She felt like screaming with pain every time she made the slightest movement in the saddle. She had rubbed her skin so raw that it stung. Her bones ached like an old woman's, her eyelids were heavy, and her eyes burned with exhaustion. The night—which she otherwise loved so much—stretched ahead of her in terrifying endlessness.

First, she heard a roar from the east, the direction of the sea. Then the wind came up and began lashing Zealand's coast. Josephine soon felt as bent from the wind as the bizarrely formed trees she'd seen throughout the area. At first, she tried to brace herself against it, which cost her a lot of energy and didn't help. She rode on, hunched over, her left leg working harder than her right. Irene, banked crookedly ahead of her, rode and swore. Jo had to smile.

Jo was just passing Luise to take her turn at the front when she felt the first raindrops. Every drop was cold and painful on her chafed skin, and her fingers were soon so ice-cold and stiff that just holding onto the handlebars was agony.

"Shouldn't we get under cover?" she screamed over the wind and rain.

"Yes, but where?" Irene yelled back.

Jo narrowed her eyes. Irene was right. They were riding through a barren dune landscape, and there was not a house, barn, or even large tree in sight.

"Maybe we should ride side by side for a while," Luise shouted, coming up on Josephine's left. Irene joined them. "Now let's be sure we don't have an accident," she said, spitting out a wet strand of hair from between her lips.

They rode on through the rain in silence. Soon they were soaked through to their underwear.

*I can't go on.* Josephine didn't know whether she had just thought the words or spoken them aloud. She looked first to Luise, then to Irene, riding doggedly beside her, stubbornly looking straight ahead.

The words must have been in her head. But even in there, they were dangerous enough . . .

"I can't go on . . ."

Josephine turned her head in surprise.

"Yes you can!" Irene hissed.

Her face twisted in pain, Luise pedaled on.

Jo felt like crying. "My chest . . . Breathing hurts so much . . ." She wanted to throw herself onto the wet sand and never get up again.

"You think I'm doing any better?" Irene snapped at her. "Pull yourself together, damn it!"

Jo nodded, feeling dismal.

*

Dawn began to break around six o'clock. The wind and rain stopped as if someone had thrown a switch. The three exhausted women looked at one another. Was God just fooling with them?

Two hours later, Copenhagen came into view. Copenhagen—the start and the end of the race—but only once they had completed the long loop north of Copenhagen a second time!

*What I wouldn't give to have the race be over now . . .* thought Jo. For the first time in all the years that she had been riding, she had lost her love of cycling. All she wanted was for the pain to stop. And to sleep. She was so tired . . .

"Eight hours to cover less than eighty miles. What a miserable section," said Irene when they stopped to warm up and reenergize themselves with a glass of schnapps in one of the fishermen's shacks on the harbor. "We're not going to win anything by riding like that!"

Jo, who had recovered a little in the warmth of the shack, looked up in surprise from her herring sandwich. "What do you want to win? It's been clear from the start that Susanne Lindberg will come in first."

"Exactly," said Luise, pushing her empty schnapps glass back across the grubby counter. "Besides, it's the principles of the race that matter more. Cooperation. And a common goal."

"Everyone who sticks it out for six hundred miles is a winner," Josephine added.

Irene snorted. "If you don't care about finishing with a decent time, that's up to you. I won't think any less of you for it. And as far as Susanne's concerned, she can win whatever she likes. But speaking for myself, I want to cross the line as soon as possible behind her."

Josephine rolled the last mouthful of schnapps back and forth over her tongue. Perhaps it would take away a little of the bad taste she'd had in her mouth the last couple of hundred miles. If she were honest with herself, she'd been hoping to finish as close behind Susanne as she could, too. But the trials of the previous night had made her question her plan.

"Well . . ." said Luise slowly. "You're right. If we're going to all this trouble in the first place . . ."

"Do you really think we can do it?" Jo asked tentatively, feeling new strength even as she asked the question.

Irene grinned. "Want me to show you how?" She threw a few coins on the counter and jumped up from her chair. A moment later, she was out at the bicycles.

Josephine put down her half-finished sandwich and looked at Luise. "Shall we?"

Luise nodded grimly. "You bet!"


It was as if someone had thrown a switch not only on the weather but inside the women. Suddenly, Josephine found riding fun again. Her legs once again did what they were supposed to do, namely, to pedal on, strong and steady.

As they were given their final stamps, Josephine's heart swelled with pride. Every empty square was now filled—a visual record of her accomplishment.

From there, it was a mere thirty miles to their goal. They were in the home stretch!


It happened ten miles outside Copenhagen. The culprit was a large rock. Irene managed to dodge it with her front wheel, but her back wheel slammed into it. A metallic clang sounded and all three women stopped.

"Damn, it's buckled," said Irene, inspecting her back wheel.

Jo let out a quiet sigh. Then that was that . . .

Irene's eyes sparkled. "Don't think a little thing like this is going to stop me, or even slow me down!" She swung herself back onto her saddle.

"But . . . you can't!" Jo and Luise cried out simultaneously. Both of them had suffered buckled wheels before, and they knew how horribly the bicycle vibrated afterward. Fadi Nandou had once described it as like having a thousand bumblebees in your behind. But Irene didn't care.

"What's taking you so long?" Irene called from a hundred yards ahead, and she even managed to take one hand off the handlebars of her wobbly machine and wave back at them. With her rump swaying back and forth like the rear end of a cow, she looked ridiculous. Josephine and Luise began to giggle uncontrollably.

"Now we know which one of us is *truly* obsessed," said Luise, and she set off in pursuit of her clubmate.


The finish line had been constructed from two freshly cut trees, to whose leafy branches someone had tied many golden bands that fluttered merrily in the wind. *I'll never forget this image,* thought Josephine, and she felt a lump form in her throat.

A loud cheer went up when the three women crossed the line. After sixty hours and six hundred miles, they were at the very limit of their strength but also elated.

Tears of joy rolled down Jo's face as they waved to the crowd. She was laughing and crying at the same time, and had goose bumps all over, from her toes to her scalp. Had they really done it? Yes, they had done it. They had crossed the finish line, undeterred by all manner of obstacles. And in just sixty hours!

Jo dismounted painfully from her bicycle, her entire body so tired and overstrained that her arms and legs were trembling. Then she, Irene, and Luise threw their arms around each other and danced with joy.

It did not dampen their spirits in the slightest to know that Susanne Lindberg and two other women had reached the finish just under six hours ahead of them. Hearing that she had come in three hours ahead of Leon Feininger and the other men was the best news of all. Veit Merz had had to drop out early with a knee problem, and fourteen other men and women had also withdrawn. Others were still pedaling; only half of those who'd begun the race had a chance of making it to the finish.

"Thank you," said Josephine to Irene as they made their way to the improvised changing rooms. "Without you, I probably would have given up."

"Nonsense," Irene replied brusquely. "A Neumann never gives up! And the way I see it, you'll be one of us soon enough. Look, there's Adrian . . ."

Her tired legs were forgotten. Josephine ran to the man she loved.

"I'm so proud of you," Adrian whispered after a fervent embrace. "Six hundred miles on a bicycle . . . You're among the first women to do it, ever! With this race, you've shown that women are just as capable as men."

Jo looked up at him, her eyes shining. "Do you think so?"

Adrian nodded. "We'll have women lining up to be our customers when they hear what you've done. This race is the best free advertising for women's cycling! And you are the best spokeswoman imaginable."

Josephine frowned in mock indignation. "Me? A spokeswoman? And who said anything about my being free? You'll have to offer me at least a little something. After all, I'm a *winner* now!" She said the last words with feigned arrogance.

"How about this?" With an elegant flourish, Adrian took a leather case from his pocket and opened it.

Josephine had to muffle a cry when she saw the gold ring set with a ruby.

"The ruby stands for your fighter's heart," said Adrian, his voice heavy with emotion. "You taught me how important it is not only to dream my dreams but to fight for them. Without you, I'd probably still be sitting in my father's offices, pushing numbers around."

Jo looked at the ground. "That's not—" she began, but Adrian laid one finger gently but firmly to her lips.

"To me, you are the most beautiful, the best, and the most wonderful woman in the world. I can't imagine my life without you anymore, but my life with you becomes clearer every day." Adrian's face was infused with love. "Will you marry me?"

"Oh," said Jo in a small voice. "If that's how it is . . ." She threw her arms around his neck, stood on tiptoes, and kissed him on the lips. "Yes, I will."

# Epilogue

*Berlin, four weeks later*

Josephine ran out of the warehouse for the umpteenth time. It was just before one in the afternoon, and they wanted to open the doors at two. Still no guests in sight. Good. That gave her a chance to check everything one final time. She wanted everything at their opening party to be perfect, down to the last detail.

She and Adrian had been busy with the preparations all week. Working together was so much fun that they regularly lost track of time and worked until late in the night.

The first thing they did was rid the bikes of the dust they had accumulated on their long transatlantic journey and polish them until they gleamed. They were fortunate that all of them had arrived in perfect condition. The warehouse in the industrial area of Feuerland that Irene had rented only as an interim solution turned out to be perfect for their purposes, and Adrian had immediately signed a long-term lease with the owner.

Men's and women's bicycles stood neatly separated into two distinct sections. The sight of all the elegant Crescent Bikes lined up side by side made Josephine's heart beat a little faster every time she looked at them.

When Adrian had first shown her the bicycles, she had immediately taken one of the women's models for a test ride. She fell in love with it right away. The Crescent Bike was elegant, agile, and fast—Josephine felt completely stable and safe. As for the price . . . They would sell the bicycles for one hundred and eleven marks, Adrian decided. It was below anything else on the imported bicycle market, and given their own purchase price of fifty marks, they would still earn a tidy profit, said Adrian, who was hoping for high sales.

*Who knows? Perhaps we'll make our first sale today,* Josephine thought, as she admired the colorful pennants she and Adrian had strung over the entrance. Large vases filled with sunflowers stood on the floor to the left and right of the main door. Their sign—eight feet long and three feet high, emblazoned with "Neumann's Crescent Bikes and Repair Shop"—gleamed yellow and blue in the sun.

Everything was ready . . .

"Jo? Josephine, where are you?" Josephine's heart fluttered when she saw Adrian striding toward her. He already seemed so much nimbler than just a few weeks earlier. The therapy that the doctors in the Charité had prescribed really seemed to be working.

"You haven't changed yet?"

Josephine laughed. "Aren't I pretty enough for you like this?" she said, displaying the oil-smeared dress she had worn to clean the bicycles. Her ruby engagement ring sparkled in the sunlight as she gave a playful twirl in the grimy outfit.

Adrian had officially announced their engagement as soon as they returned from Denmark. He had not allowed himself to get into any discussions with his father. "Either you welcome my bride or you don't say a word," he had said, which had stopped the old man in his tracks. But the magnate had fought enough wars to know when he was beaten.

With a slightly cantankerous air, he had accepted Josephine into his family, but he had grown friendlier when he heard that Josephine had built up her own workshop from scratch. "I started that way myself, way back when. Beginnings are always the best," he had said with a sentimental note in his voice. Then he shook both her and Adrian's hands firmly and wished them the best of luck.

"The wine is cold, and the plates of hors d'oeuvres will be here in half an hour . . ." Adrian looked over the long tables covered with white tablecloths. "You're really sure we shouldn't open your workshop today?" he said and looked at Josephine with his head tilted inquiringly.

She nodded. "That door stays closed. We don't want to give people the impression that the first thing a Crescent Bike needs is a workshop, do we?"

Adrian laughed. "But I'm allowed to mention it, aren't I? It's a service bonus we're offering, after all: 'Free repairs for a year!'" He swept his hands in the air as if displaying a banner. "I doubt any of our competitors can match that."

It had been Adrian's idea to move Josephine's workshop out of Luisenstadt. The move had been a difficult decision, because it meant losing several of her favorite customers, including Oskar Reutter. But from a business perspective, the move was the right one. She consoled herself with the knowledge that Adrian wanted to move into Frieda's house with her after their wedding in December.

"Certainly you can mention it. But our cleverer customers might already know we do repairs from our sign!" Josephine said. She looked toward the entrance. "Do you think Isabelle and Leon will come?" She hadn't seen her old friend since their return from Denmark.

Adrian shrugged. "No idea. Maybe she's calmed down, maybe not. I ran into Leon at the club a few days ago. He told me that Isabelle is back on her feet again and doing fine. The doctors in Copenhagen chastised her for going too far with all the dope. Too much kola syrup can cause not only a circulatory collapse but death from cardiac failure."

For a moment, they stood in troubled silence.

Then Jo, suddenly anxious, said, "What if no one comes at all?"

"That's the last thing I'm worried about," Adrian laughed. "The minute you offer free food, people will be there, believe me. Besides, our friends and clubmates wouldn't let us down!"

"Then maybe I really should go and change," she said. And she hurried off toward the office, where she had stowed her dress.

***

Clara took a deep breath. Then she knocked on the door of her husband's office.

Gerhard was sitting at his desk, as he always did on Saturday afternoon, finishing up the weekly accounts for the practice.

"I've dropped Matthias off with my mother. He can stay there until this evening," said Clara, setting down a cup of tea beside him. Black tea, steeped for three minutes, with a slice of lemon, just the way he liked it.

"Hmm," he said without looking up from the rows and columns of numbers.

"No doubt you saw the big announcement in the paper," Clara went on. "The one about Adrian Neumann's grand opening of his new business. That's where I'm going now." She held her breath as she waited for his reaction. It wasn't long in coming.

"What do you mean? I forbid you—"

"But I won't let you forbid me, never again," Clara broke in. She was shaking so hard on the inside that she had to steady herself on the edge of his desk. It took all her effort to keep her voice calm. "I've been thinking about a great deal over the last few weeks. About you and me and my friends Josephine and Isabelle. You know, they've become real heroines since the race in Denmark! You're such a keen newspaper reader . . . No doubt you've seen the articles praising what they did."

She couldn't do anything about the slightly hateful tone of her voice. "No, I will not let you stop me!" she said sharply as soon as Gerhard opened his mouth to reply. "Fine, be an enemy of women's cycling for the rest of your life. And you don't have to like Jo and Isabelle. They don't like you, either. But they are *my* friends, and they will *stay* my friends. I will not let you deny me those friendships." She pulled on her gloves as if such a scene between them was the most normal thing in the world. But her heart was pounding. She saw his expression growing darker, and she stepped quickly back to the door before he could lay a hand on her. With her fingers already on the handle, she paused. "And there's something else I've been wanting to say to you for a long time." She took a deep breath. "Don't you ever hit me again. Do you hear me? Never again."

She left the room. Unfortunately, she did not turn back, or she would have seen the look of utter dismay on her husband's face.

*** 

"Stop the coach. We have to pick something up," said Isabelle when they were in front of the best flower shop in the city.

"You ordered flowers? Great!" said Leon, jumping out of the carriage to hold the door open for Isabelle. How fortunate that women thought of such things!

"Not flowers," said Isabelle, taking hold of his hand and stepping out. "Something better."

"A laurel wreath?" said Leon, heaving the wagon-wheel-sized arrangement into the carriage. Across the wreath was a silken banner. "'Laurels have a bitter reek, for those who have, and those who seek,'" Leon read aloud. "That's a strange saying . . . What does it mean?"

"It's an old folk adage," Isabelle replied. "Jo will understand what I'm trying to say." As the coach rolled off again, she looked out joylessly at the passing city.

Leon, who had grown accustomed to Isabelle's strange frame of mind in recent weeks, sighed. Whatever he said or did, however charming he might be—he had only rarely managed to make her laugh since their return from Denmark.

"I looked death right in the eye!" she had screamed when he had complained about her bad mood. "Nothing is the same after that. Nothing, don't you see?"

Yes, he saw. And no, he didn't.

She had survived. So why did she have to suddenly start thinking so deeply about everything?

Another thing he didn't understand was his own reaction to her strange behavior. Normally, if he found himself involved with a moody woman, he would simply have packed up and left. But with Isabelle . . . there was something about her that held him back. Was it his guilt over not being with her in her hour of need?

Leon was not the kind of man to think long or hard about his own feelings, but he had known for a long time that a great deal more bound him to Isabelle than to his previous liaisons. Her titian hair, her catlike eyes, and her striking cheekbones. Her full lips and the way the top one could curl so saucily—Leon never tired of looking at Isabelle. He couldn't get enough of her, it was true, and that had nothing to do with guilt.

But there was more to it than that: the fact that she came from a rich family, that she had good morals, a good education—those were all things that Leon secretly admired, though he would never openly admit such a thing. She had the courage to stand up to her father, and the fortitude to not let anyone dictate how she ought to live her life. Weren't they alike in that regard? He, too, had no intention of working himself to death in his parents' vineyard! They were two kindred souls . . . Was that the root of the attraction between them? Or did the fact that Isabelle was a "good match" play a role? *At the very least, a rich wife can't hurt,* he thought with a grin. Cycling was an expensive pastime. If he'd had better equipment, there was no way Susanne Lindberg would have gotten the better of him in Denmark!

Leon searched his mind feverishly for something to cheer Isabelle up. It was rare for him to find himself at a loss for words. But before he could come up with something, Isabelle signaled to the driver to pull over again and stop near the Victory Column.

With her arms folded across her chest, she looked at him sullenly and said, "What do you have in mind for our future? Do you think I'm the kind of girl you can string along forever? I want clarity. Certainty. I want a future. A future worth living for. Look around!" She made a sweeping gesture toward the city around them. "Everyone here has plans! Everyone except me." She sounded desperate, but a little like a sullen child, too.

Leon found her simply enchanting. "Who says so?" he heard himself answering. "You're coming with me, of course. Berlin is a wonderful city, but I miss the forests and mountains of the Rhineland-Palatinate. I'm overdue for some training in the mountains. Besides, in June they start cutting back the foliage in our vineyard, and every hand is needed." *What am I going on about?* he asked himself. He'd always tried to dodge the work in the vineyard. But suddenly he felt a strange urge to hold a pair of pruning shears in his hands again. His nose longed for the smell of the fire they made from the vine cuttings.

Isabelle looked at him wide-eyed. Her future lay in his hands—her eyes told him nothing less.

Leon straightened up. "Now that I've gotten to know your home, it's time you got to know mine. Who knows, maybe you'll like life in Rhineland-Palatinate so much that you'll want to stay longer?" Leon doubted that very much, but he was finding so much pleasure in his speech that he didn't question it anymore.

"Was that a proposal of marriage?" asked Isabelle breathlessly.

Leon screwed up his face as if he had a toothache. How he hated that word! He'd managed to avoid it successfully all these years. But now he merely shrugged and said, "I guess it probably was. Not that I would have lasted much longer as a free man! But you need a fellow as crazy as me beside you. That doesn't leave me with much choice but to marry you, does it?"

A moment later they were in each other's arms. Having Isabelle's body pressed so close to his went straight to his core. With a groan, he tried to slip his right hand under her skirt, but his exertions were interrupted by the clearing of a throat.

"Should we be gettin' along now, or what?" the coachman shouted down to them.

\*\*\*

How quickly the tide could turn . . . Isabelle could have hugged the world! From the depths of despair one moment to a bright and beautiful future the next. She pictured herself as Leon's wife. A winemaker in beautiful Rhineland-Palatinate. She gave a giddy laugh as they walked across the large yard that led to Adrian's bicycle shop.

She had been terribly jealous of him and Josephine and all their plans. But then again, wasn't running a bicycle shop rather average?

"We won't stay long, all right?" she said and smiled meaningfully at Leon. "My parents are away in Potsdam for the weekend."

"And what does that have to do with how long we spend at Adrian's party?"

"Well, it means two things. First, we'll have the house to ourselves," she said, casting him a coquettish look. "And second, no one will be there to stop me when I pack my things."

"Pack your things? You mean . . . you want to fly the coop? Just like that?"

"Yes," said Isabelle plainly. She had rarely managed to really throw Leon, which made this moment even more delicious. "My father would never allow me to marry you. He dug up a new marriage candidate for me long ago."

"But . . . you'd be risking a serious rift! Wouldn't that cause some trouble? I mean, brides get a dowry, don't they? And—"

"As if I care about my father's money," Isabelle scoffed. "Besides, you said yourself that you miss your home. The sooner we go, the better. As far as I'm concerned, we can leave tomorrow!" She grinned. "Oh, there are our young lovers now," she said, pointing to Adrian and Josephine, who were just stepping outside.

After a rather stiff greeting and congratulating them on the opening, Isabelle handed them the laurel wreath. "Here. For you," she said to Josephine. "Thank you for saving my life in Denmark. Whatever else might come between you and me, I will never forget that."

"It was nothing, really," murmured Josephine. She held up the silken band with the saying printed across it. "'Laurels have a bitter reek, for those who have, and those who seek.'"

Isabelle shrugged. "Well, *one* victory isn't enough. The next one has to come sometime. And then the next. It can put you under a lot of pressure. That's not for me!" she said with deep conviction. "From now on, I'm only going to ride a bicycle for pleasure. There are great adventures to be had away from the road. Isn't that true, darling?" She looked fondly at Leon.

"Ahem." The sound made all four of them turn.

"Excuse me, I don't mean to disturb you," said a stout young woman. She had calloused hands and the red cheeks of someone who spent most of her time working outside. "I'm a washerwoman. One of them bicycles would sure come in handy for bringin' the wash back to my customers. Could you help me choose one?"

Josephine and Adrian exchanged a look and smiled. Then Adrian said, "My fiancée will be very happy to take care of you."

Isabelle smiled as Josephine walked off with her very first customer.

# Notes:

*If anything [can] change the German character, it will be the German woman. She herself is changing rapidly—advancing, as we call it. Ten years ago no German woman caring for her reputation, hoping for a husband, would have dared to ride a bicycle: today they spin about the country in their thousands. The old folks shake their heads at them; but the young men, I notice, overtake them and ride beside them.*

Jerome K. Jerome, *Three Men on the Bummel,* 1900

- 1958—The German Cycling Federation (Bund Deutscher Radfahrer) lifts the ban on competitive cycling for women that had been in place since 1896.
- 1984—Women's cycling becomes an Olympic sport.
- 1984—The inaugural Tour de France for women takes place but is discontinued a few years later.
- For those wanting to find out more about the state of long-distance riding today, I would recommend visiting the website of my technical advisor for this book, extreme cyclist Christian Mayer: www.christian-mayer.net (in German). Through his diary entries, one can experience what it is like to take part in races like Paris–Brest–Paris (PBP), the Kelheim twenty-four-hour race, or the biggest

of them all, the Race Across America (RAAM).

- From Christian, I learned that, from a technical standpoint, bicycles have improved tremendously in the last hundred years. Long-distance races, however, are still a long slog; ultimately, they start and end in the cyclist's head.

- Schömberg's role as a location for mountain-air sanatoria really did begin in 1888. It was Hugo Römpler, a businessman from Erfurt, Germany, who recognized the potential of Schömberg's healthy climate. More sanatoriums began to appear starting in 1890. "Germany's Davos" was brought to my attention in a nice letter from one of my readers, M. Vögele from Schömberg, and I would like to thank her here and now for the information she sent!

- The two cycling clubs mentioned by name in my book are fictional. It is true, however, that Berlin was a mecca for competitive cycling at that time.

- Women's cycling also had its beginnings in Berlin, and it found a very popular spokeswoman in journalist Amelie Rother.

- The Marschütz & Co. bicycle factory in Nuremberg really did exist, producing bicycles in large numbers from 1896 onward. Their Hercules bicycle soon became a well-known brand.

- The idea of sending Adrian Neumann to America was suggested by the book *Meine Radreise um die Erde—Der Bericht des ersten deutschen Fahrrad-Weltreisenden anno 1895* (*My Bicycle Journey Around the World—The Report of the First German to Travel the World by Bicycle, 1895*) by Heinrich Horstmann. A reprint of Horstmann's book was published by Maxi Kutschera Verlag, Leipzig.

- The Western Wheel Works in Chicago and the Crescent

Bike both really existed. The founder of the Western Wheel Works, Adolph Schoeninger, who originally came from Württemberg in Germany, introduced a form of assembly line ten years before Henry Ford did.

- The Pope Manufacturing Company of Boston, founded by Albert Augustus Pope, was likewise real. Thanks to aggressive tactics, the company grew to become the largest manufacturer of bicycles in America. However, the company's fortunes waned following a fire in 1896 that destroyed the offices and a large number of bicycles.

- Susanne Lindberg and her fiancé really did organize a one-thousand-kilometer (approximately 621-mile) race in Denmark in 1897. Josephine's participation is fictional. The actual route they followed is unknown; at least, I was unable to find any unequivocal source. I have described what I imagine to be the most probable route.

- The Barnim Road Women's Prison was officially called the Königlich-Preußisches Weibergefängnis (Royal Prussian Women's Prison). It had maternity and mother-and-child wards, but I was not able to discover whether it really had a juvenile division. Such institutions for young offenders were first established during the German Empire.

- My cycling hero, Leon Feininger, is based on the real racing cyclist Josef Fischer, who first rode from Vienna to Berlin in 1893.

The fortunes of Jo, Clara, and Isabelle continue in volume two of the trilogy, to be published in 2016.

# About the Author

*Photo © Privat*

Petra Durst-Benning is one of Germany's most successful and prominent authors. For more than fifteen years, her historical novels have been inviting readers to go adventuring with courageous female characters and experience their exciting lives for themselves. Her books have enjoyed great success overseas as well, and several have been adapted for television. Petra Durst-Benning lives with her husband in Stuttgart.

# About the Translator

*Photo © 2012 Ronald Biallas*

Born in Australia but widely traveled, Edwin Miles has been working as a translator for more than ten years, primarily in film and television.

After studying in his hometown of Perth, Western Australia, Edwin completed an MFA in fiction writing at the University of Oregon in 1995. While there, he spent a year working as fiction editor on the literary magazine the *Northwest Review*. In 1996, he was shortlisted for the prestigious Australian/Vogel Literary Award for young writers for a collection of short stories.

After many years living and working in Australia, Japan, and the United States, he currently resides in his "second home" in Cologne, Germany, with his wife, Dagmar, and two very clever children.